THE WORLD'S CLASSICS

THE TWO DROVERS
AND OTHER STORIES

WALTER SCOTT (1771–1832) was born in Edinburgh
of a Border family. After attending the High School and
University of Edinburgh he followed his father into the
profession of the law, becoming an advocate (barrister) in
1792. In 1799 he was appointed Sheriff-Depute for the
county of Selkirk, and in 1806 a Clerk of the Court of
Session—appointments which he retained until the end of
his life. His first major publication was a collection of
ballads entitled *The Minstrelsy of the Scottish Border*
(1802–3). He became famous as a poet with *The Lay of the
Last Minstrel* (1805), *Marmion* (1808), and *The Lady of the
Lake* (1810). In 1814 he published his first novel, *Waverley*,
set during the Jacobite rising of 1745. Its success encouraged him to produce more historical novels, set in
different countries and periods. Those set in Scotland,
like *Redgauntlet*, have usually been regarded as his best.
Scott's work was widely acclaimed in Europe and
America. He spent the income from his writings on
establishing a house and estate at Abbotsford, near
Melrose. He was awarded a baronetcy by the Prince
Regent in 1818. Partnership in the printing firm of James
Ballantyne and Co. involved him in a financial crash in
1826. His last years were darkened by illness and the need
to continue his output of writing to pay off the debts incurred. His *Journal* of those years is the most moving of
his works. He died at Abbotsford in 1832; his biography
was written by his son-in-law, John Gibson Lockhart.

GRAHAM TULLOCH is a Senior Lecturer in English at
the Flinders University of South Australia. He is the author
of *The Language of Walter Scott* (1980) and is currently working on a history of the Scots language since 1700.

LORD DAVID CECIL (1902–1986) was the author of a
number of works of criticism and biography including
books on Jane Austen, Thomas Hardy, Charles Lamb,
and Lord Melbourne His study *Sir Walter Scott* was
published in 1933

THE WORLD'S CLASSICS

SIR WALTER SCOTT
The Two Drovers
and Other Stories

Edited by
GRAHAM TULLOCH

With an Introduction by
LORD DAVID CECIL

Oxford   New York
OXFORD UNIVERSITY PRESS
1987

Oxford University Press, Walton Street, Oxford OX2 6DP

Oxford New York Toronto
Delhi Bombay Calcutta Madras Karachi
Petaling Jaya Singapore Hong Kong Tokyo
Nairobi Dar es Salaam Cape Town
Melbourne Auckland

and associated companies in
Beirut Berlin Ibadan Nicosia

Oxford is a trade mark of Oxford University Press

Introduction © David Cecil 1934, revised 1987

Preface, Note on the Text, Select Bibliography,
Explanatory Notes © Graham Tulloch 1987

Chronology © Claire Lamont 1982

First published in the World's Classics 1934
First published as a World's Classics paperback 1987

British Library Cataloguing in Publication Data

Scott, Sir Walter, 1771–1832
The two drovers and other stories. —
(The World's classics)
I. Title   II. Tulloch, Graham
823'.7[F]   PR5303

ISBN 0–19–281718–3

Library of Congress Cataloging in Publication Data

Scott, Walter, Sir, 1771–1832.
The two drovers, and other stories.
(The World's classics)
Bibliography: p.
Contents: Wandering Willie's tale—Chronicles of
the Canongate—The highland widow—[etc.]
1. Scotland—Fiction. I. Tulloch, Graham, 1947–
II. Title.
PR5303.T85 1987   823'.7   86–18202

ISBN 0–19–281718–3 (pbk.)

Printed in Great Britain by
Hazell Watson & Viney Ltd.
Aylesbury, Bucks

CONTENTS

CONTENTS

INTRODUCTION
by DAVID CECIL

SIR WALTER SCOTT is not usually thought of as a short-story writer. Indeed, many people refrain from reading him on the ground that he is the author of stories discouragingly long. But they make a mistake. Lurking amid the battalions of his giant novels are a handful of short stories; and they are the most satisfactory things he ever wrote.

Not that his specific merits are the specific merits of the classic masters of the short story. Scott's vision is not swift or microscopic; neither is his mode of expression terse. His imagination was a simple, massive, slow-moving affair, oblivious of the detailed and evanescent. It was stirred exclusively by large themes, it concerned itself solely with their salient features; and even over these it took its time. All the same, the short-story form was the best for him; because it gave least scope to his faults.

This sounds a negative virtue. Yet it is a supremely important one. For Scott is such an extraordinary mixture of faults and virtues. His creative power is of the highest intensity. He is master of character, incident, and setting; he is successful alike in the comic and the pathetic; he can describe with equal vividness a crowd or a man, a wild battle-scene of covenanter and cavalier, or old Mr Oldbuck too early for the coach; he never repeats himself. Above all, he combines the substance of the realist with the intensity of the romantic. He can evoke the homely and every-day as convincingly as he can the passionate and the fantastic. No other English novelist is both so variously and so powerfully gifted.

Yet many others have written more perfect books; for Scott's strength as a creator is only equalled by his weakness as a craftsman. He can tell the story well enough; makes us see each scene, keeps us always interested to know what is going to happen next. But of the craftsman's central virtue, the sense of form, he had much less. Though his imagination was incessantly fired to conceive individual incident and character, it was never fired to conceive a complete book. So that in order to organize his scattered inspirations into any sort of whole, he had to fit them uncomfortably into a makeshift framework of plot, copied from the conventional novel of his day, complete with standardized hero and heroine and intrigue. The consequences of this are that the book lacks balance. The life-like figure of Bailie Nicol Jarvie is forced to take a part and a subsidiary part in the artificial adventures of Frank Osbaldistone; the pathos of the Mucklebackit family is an irrelevant episode in the tedious career of Lovell. And secondly, his books are filled up with a lot of dead matter, that, as often as not, eclipses their living inspiration. We can hardly see the jewels of Scott's imagination for the ponderous pinchbeck setting with which he has seen fit to surround them.

Now, in a short story he was less liable to fall into these errors. A short story is the record of an isolated incident. Scott had no need to construct a framework for his inspirations, for they are not designed to form part of a larger unity. In consequence there are no barren tracts in his short stories. Mrs Bethune Baliol is as solidly real a figure as Bailie Jarvie; but unlike Bailie Jarvie she is not forced to take an incongruous part in a stagy plot: Robin Oig's trial is as dramatic a scene as that of Evan Maccombich, and our interest in it is not weakened by the fact that it is sandwiched between pages of dreary padding. Moreover, the form is appropriate to the imaginative conception it is there to embody. Mrs Baliol does not play second fiddle to a waxwork heroine; she is a principal character in the tale in which she appears; Robin Oig's trial is the climax of the story of which it forms part, not a subsidiary episode. In his short stories, and in his short stories alone, do we see Scott's jewels with their splendour undiminished by their setting: in them alone his inspiration shows unqualified by his technical incapacity.

And the whole of his inspiration, too. Like that of other great writers his imaginative range has its limitations. As Hardy's imagination is stirred only when he is depicting human nature in relation to nature, so Scott's is only stirred when he is depicting it in relation to its historic past. He sees man exclusively in terms of his nation, his family, his church, the ancient traditions of his race, the wild or civilized landscape of soul and body in which he has grown up. And this means that important parts of human life are outside his range. He says little of that private life which is the same in any environment; the relation of the individual to other individuals, to the opposite sex, to his own career, the life of the individual soul. All the same his range is a very wide one, embracing some of the most fundamental facts, some of the intensest feelings of human experience. It covers all that variety of character, comic and serious, whose distinguishing features arise from local conditions and historic circumstances; it covers all the situations, tragic and thrilling, which come from the clash of traditions, devotion to clan, or creed, or country, revenge for an ancient wrong; it involves all the violent and romantic emotions which are born from such situations and characters, patriotism, family feeling, regret for the past, the glamour of remote civilization, ancient places, historic associations, the chill of fear embodied in spectre and supernatural premonition that come from a sense of the presence of the past still active in after days. It includes, in fact, some of the essential material of the ghost story, the historic novel, the novel of national character, romantic poetry, and heroic tragedy. All these are represented in these short stories. 'My Aunt Margaret's Mirror' and 'The Tapestried Chamber' are ghost stories: 'Mr Croftangry's Memoirs' is a collection of Scottish character studies: 'Wandering Willie's Tale' is a ghost story, a study of Scottish character, and has a touch of the historical romance as well: 'The Death of the Laird's Jock' and 'The Highland Widow' are historical romances, studies of Scottish character, and also heroic tragedies: 'The Two Drovers' is a heroic tragedy, a study of national character, and at one moment it strikes the supernatural note. There is no aspect of Scott's range, no field in which his imagination is fired to exhibit his tremendous talents, unrepresented in these six stories.

Not that they are all equally good stories. 'The Death of the Laird's Jock', indeed, is not a story at all, only a note for one. In a few words it retails an anecdote of Scottish Border history that had struck Scott's fancy. And it does so with sufficient force to indicate what a magnificent thing he could have made of it, if he had treated it at length. But he has not. His imagination has been fertilized; but he has not given it time to mature into a fully realized artistic conception. 'The Death of the Laird's Jock' remains an embryo; and as such, save to the specialist student of Scott's artistic method, uninteresting.

'My Aunt Margaret's Mirror' and 'The Tapestried Chamber' are also not completely successful; for a different reason. No writer can give a convincing picture of a world that he has not had a personal acquaintance with. Scott's great characters are all creatures of that eighteenth- and late seventeenth-century Scotland whose child he was. Moreover, he is most at home with peasants and men: he draws aristocratics with a less certain hand. The people in 'The Tapestried Chamber' are English aristo-crats; those in 'My Aunt Margaret's Mirror' are aristocratic women in a period two hundred years before his own. The result is that none of them have much individuality; they are merely conventional pegs on which he hangs his plots. This is not a fatal defect; for the effect of a ghost story does not depend on its characters. But it does diminish its force; the supernatural strikes a far less eerie chill to our veins if we do not feel that it is happening to real human beings. Further, the plot of 'The Tapestried Chamber' takes Scott outside his true emotional range. His supernatural is the historico-supernatural: he can communicate, none better, a sense of the spirit of another age still active in its surviving creations; can make us hear the ghostly footsteps echoing through the ruined manor house, see the smile flickering on the lips of a time-blackened portrait, the spectral hand twitching the faded folds of the arras. But his imagination was too robust, too unintrospective, successfully to stir the darker, more intimate, hauntings of the inner soul. He is no Henry James to summon up the demons of guilt and madness, to oppress us with a sense of ultimate evil. The atmosphere, picturesque and antiquarian, with which he clothed the super-natural, is pleasant rather than otherwise. And, in consequence, the demoniac old lady of Wood-ville Castle does not fill us with that terror and loathing which we are told she inspired. Beside the masterpieces in her kind: Peter Quint, roaming malevolent and restless round the scene of his unspeakable sin, Thrawn Janet shuffling in deathly distortion down the stairs of Balweary Manse, she seems no more than a quaint gargoyle. Still 'The Tapestried Chamber' is a good story; it has an excellent plot admirably told. If it is not in the highest degree frightening it is continuously exciting.

'My Aunt Margaret's Mirror' has a more conventional theme. But it, too, is well told; and it makes no demand on Scott's imagination that it is not able to fulfil. Its spectres are there less to terrify the reader than to stir his romantic fancy. This they do splendidly. Scott makes the most of every possibility for picturesque effect that his plot affords him. Damiotti's mysterious room in the murky Edinburgh street, with the swords crossed naked on the altar, its fitful candle light, its mirror troubled with shifting, gleaming visions of pageantry and bloodshed, and, over all, the figure of the sorcerer himself, white-stoled, scarlet-shod, and with burning eyes, all these combine to compose a magnificent costume piece in the high romantic manner.

Of the other four stories, 'The Highland Widow' also falls short of perfection, as a result of a failure completely to realize its characters. But it is another sort of failure. Its chief characters, Elspeth and Hamish MacTavish, are the Scottish peasants whom Scott understood best; and there is nothing unreal in his general conception of them. But in order to give the effect of the Gaelic tongue they would have spoken to one another, he endows them with a form of speech which, in the mouths of English-speaking characters, sounds highly artificial. It is not only that it lacks the ease and spontaneity essentially characteristic of the spoken as opposed to the written word. It is of its nature unnatural, a dreadful Ossianesque jargon, turgid with apostrophe, ejaculation, and lengthy simile. And the characters that speak it seem a trifle imper-sonal and stagy.

All the same, 'The Highland Widow' is a story that only a very great writer could have written. Its theme is on the grand scale; a proud, pas-sionate character forced, by the pressure of national tradition, ignorantly to drive the son, whom she loves more than anything else in the world, to an ignoble and violent death. And Scott

rises superbly to the height of his great argument.
If he fails to realize the characters completely, he
realizes every implication of their situation. He
makes us feel all the immediate drama of the
story: as it unfolds itself before us in a series of
pictures, we respond, breathless with tension, to
the romance of its setting, the suspense of its
crisis, the horror of its catastrophe. He also gives
us a sense of its wider significance as a representative incident of a historic process, the gradual
extinction of the old Highland society beneath the
encroaching strength of England. And finally, as
the plot reaches its awful climax, it looms before
us in the light of a yet more tremendous
background, the cosmic landscape of human
destiny. We are stirred by the tragic emotions;
pity, terror, and awe at the intensity of man's
feelings, the inescapable sadness of his lot, his
helplessness to resist the decrees of indifferent
Fate. Here that robust, daylit quality of Scott's
imagination, which tends to weaken the effect of
his ghost stories, is a positive advantage to him.
For it makes us feel that this appalling story is no
fantasy of a morbid fancy but a solemn, substantial fact of normal human experience.

Mr Croftangry's Memoirs attain no such
dramatic heights. Indeed, designed as they are,
not as a complete story, but as an introduction to
a collection of stories, they are not dramatic at
all. They have no plot; they are a series of portraits in Scott's humorous-realistic vein, the vein
that gave us Dandie Dinmont and Nicol Jarvie.
Moreover, space prevents Scott from penetrating
at all deeply into their characters. Yet, within
their limits they are admirably vigorous and

solid. They are drawn in that direct, unanalytic eighteenth-century manner which he inherited from Fielding. They are all 'character parts'. But Scott's peculiar range of imagination enables him to describe them in a wider aspect than Fielding could. Christie Dean and Mrs Bethune Baliol are presented to us, not just as isolated individuals like Tom Jones, but against the historical and social backgrounds which produced them. And in addition to their individual significance they have the significance that comes from the fact that they are representative of these backgrounds. Christie Dean, unforgiving, trustworthy Presbyterian; that enthusiastic Celt, Janet McEvoy, so loyal to the king, so scornful of the Law; the orderly, sardonic Edinburgh lawyer, Mr Fairscribe; above all, Mrs Baliol, with her formal, old-fashioned French manners, her homely northern common sense, her Scottish reverence for her ancestors; in these, as in some gallery of brilliant Raeburns, the characteristic elements that went to make up Scottish society of the early nineteenth century rise before us embodied in living human beings.

There remain 'Wandering Willie's Tale' and 'The Two Drovers'. And these we can praise without reservation. They are the only two perfect things Scott ever wrote, they are among the glories of English literature. Considered in any of its three aspects, 'Wandering Willie's Tale' is equally a masterpiece. It is a masterpiece of character-drawing. Steenie, the hero, reckless and rascally, yet with a characteristic Scottish prudence, the savage old Redgauntlet and his sly son, and the narrator himself, at once so romantic and so sardonic, a few brief strokes are enough to establish these before us as vividly as though we had seen them. It is a masterpiece of historical evocation: the fierce, moss-troopers' Scotland of 1700, rollicking, blood-stained, superstitious, is set before us as convincingly real as the world of our own time; yet in no smallest detail untrue to its period. It is, with Burns's 'Tam o' Shanter', the leading example in literature of Scottish popular diablerie; that curious species, at once homely and Gothic, at times grotesquely comic but shot through with an authentic thrill of supernatural terror. 'Wandering Willie's Tale' has a further distinction of its own, its style. Scott's ordinary English narrative-writing is as forcible and easy as everything else about him. But it is nothing more. His vernacular dialogue is style in a higher sense; it combines the naturalness and life of spoken speech with the verbal felicity, the rhythm, musical in itself, yet always appropriate to the thought that it expresses, which marks great prose. In 'Wandering Willie's Tale', Scott for once tells a story wholly in this vernacular. So that it is the only one of his works which is a sustained masterpiece of writing.

But even 'Wandering Willie's Tale' is not such an achievement as 'The Two Drovers'. Not that 'The Two Drovers' is more perfect. But it triumphs on a higher plane. Like 'The Highland Widow', it is a heroic tragedy: and it has all its merits, its dramatic force, its capacity to convey historic significance, to stir the tragic emotions. But it is unmarred by 'The Highland Widow's' touch of artificiality. In it Scott shows his realistic power as much as his romantic. Robin Oig and

Harry Wakefield, the protagonists in the story, are no stage types, but solid flesh and blood individuals. So that their story is as substantially real as 'Mr Croftangry's Memoirs', and as imaginatively exciting as 'Wandering Willie's Tale'. Its form is as good as its substance. The story is ushered in by a note of the supernatural —the premonition which compels his grandmother to urge Robin not to set out for England —perfectly adjusted to establish that atmosphere of fatality which is its appropriate element: then, relaxing the tension, Scott proceeds soberly and firmly, without procrastination or digression, to build up the situation and characters: finally, as the climax approaches, he deepens the tone, quickens the speed to sweep the reader into a sustained mood of tragic excitement. At the actual culmination he rises above himself to achieve a stroke of constructive genius. Some comment on the action is needed beyond that implicit in its facts, if we are to realize the deeper significance of that brawl between two farmers, which is the ostensible subject of the story. But if the writer makes it himself, if the puppet-master appears in person behind his puppets at the crisis of their fortunes, he will weaken the dramatic illusion, at the moment at which it is most important that it should be preserved. To meet this difficulty Scott hits upon the bold and original course of putting the comment in the mouth of the Judge presiding at Robin's trial; the last four pages of the story consist of a verbally reported judicial summing up. He is amply justified. The comment comes to the reader enforced by all the added gravity that adheres to a considered pronouncement of official justice; while the objective reality of the drama is not diminished for us by the introduction of an external commentator.

But the outstanding merit of the story lies neither in its substance nor its structure, but in its style. It is not a sustained masterpiece of writing like 'Wandering Willie's Tale', for it is not written in Scottish dialect. But it gives Scott's style the chance, as 'Wandering Willie's Tale' does not, to show its rarest capacity, its capacity for expressing dramatic emotion. In life, people are not able to express intense emotions adequately. And the majority of novelists faced with a dramatic situation either make their characters inarticulate and life-like or articulate and unreal. The dual power of Scott's imagination enables him to achieve the merits and avoid the defects of both these courses. At his best he can make characters express their strongest feelings both fully and realistically. There are two examples of this in 'The Two Drovers'. Robin Oig, compelled by what he feels to be an irresistible obligation of honour and with no personal feeling of rancour, has killed his best friend.

He threw the fatal weapon into the blazing turf-fire. 'There,' he said, 'take me who likes—and let fire cleanse blood if it can.'

The second follows a few sentences later:

While the escort was preparing, the prisoner neither expressed the least interest nor attempted the slightest reply. Only, before he was carried from the fatal apartment, he desired to look at the dead body, which, raised from the floor, had been deposited upon the large table (at the head of which Harry Wakefield had presided but a few minutes before, full of life, vigour, and animation) until the surgeons should examine the mortal wound. The face of the corpse was decently covered with a napkin. To the surprise and horror of the bystanders, which displayed itself in a general *Ah*! drawn through clenched teeth and half-shut lips, Robin Oig removed the cloth, and gazed with a mournful but steady eye on the lifeless visage, which had been so lately animated that the smile of good-humoured confidence in his own strength, of conciliation at once and contempt towards his enemy, still curled his lip. While those present expected that the wound, which had so lately flooded the apartment with gore, would send forth fresh streams at the touch of the homicide, Robin Oig replaced the covering, with the brief exclamation—'He was a pretty man!'

Robin Oig's words are wholly convincing regarded from the realist's point of view. Indeed, they have an unpredictable inevitability that makes the reader feel that Scott is not inventing, but reporting an actual fact. But they are fraught with a deeper truth, a more essential significance. For in them is concentrated all that stormy complex of thought and emotion which seethed in Robin Oig at this, the crisis of his life; his unchanged love for his friend, his passionate sorrow at his act, his unaltered conviction that he had to do it, his open-eyed acceptance of his punishment, his sense of the tragic irony of human destiny.

This power of realistic eloquence is Scott's supreme title to fame. It is dramatic literature in the highest sense; and dramatic literature of the rarest kind. There is nothing like it elsewhere in our fiction. To find a parallel we must go to poetic tragedy: to Macbeth's reception of his wife's death, 'She should have died hereafter'; to Lear's awakening from madness, 'You do me wrong to take me out o' th' grave'. Scott may be among the most imperfect of English novelists; he is the only one whose great moments can be compared to Shakespeare's.

DAVID CECIL

PREFACE

FOR a long time Scott's short stories, with the possible exception of 'Wandering Willie's Tale', were largely ignored and tended to be overshadowed by the great series of the Waverley Novels. Initial response was unenthusiastic, which is perhaps not surprising if we accept Walter Allen's view that 'The Two Drovers' is the 'first modern short story in English';[1] examples of new genres always take some time to gain acceptance. So, despite the approval of writers like Tennyson who considered 'My Aunt Margaret's Mirror' as 'the finest of all ghost or magical stories' and greatly admired 'The Tapestried Chamber'[2] and Robert Louis Stevenson who called 'The Highland Widow' 'Scott's masterpiece',[3] and even though there was a flicker of interest aroused by the centenary of the publication of *Chronicles of the Canongate* in 1927,[4] the first serious attempt to give the stories the attention they deserve came with the original publication of the present collection with its introduction by Lord David Cecil. This introduction, which is reprinted here with slight revisions made by Lord David before his death, has been described by Teut Andreas Riese as 'the most

[1] *The Short Story in English*, Oxford, 1981, p. 9.

[2] Hallam, Lord Tennyson, *Alfred, Lord Tennyson: A Memoir*, London, 1899, p. 847.

[3] *Letters*, ed. Sidney Colvin, London, 1902, ii. 209.

[4] See, for example, George Gordon, '"The Chronicles of the Canongate"', in *Scott Centenary articles*, by Thomas Seccombe et al., Oxford, 1932, pp. 174–84.

perceptive appreciation of Scott's short narr-atives'[5] and it remains a powerful plea for the value of the short stories both in themselves and as a starting point in reading Scott. Nevertheless, in the half century since it was first written a number of changes have taken place in the general critical estimation of Scott and this seems a good opportunity to outline some of them.

One general criticism made by Lord David is that the novels are formless and are provided with unsuitable and conventional plots and heroes while the real vitality lies in minor characters. Many readers will probably still agree that the very best things in the novels are often the minor characters. However, more recent criticism has somewhat redressed the balance. The work of writers like Daiches, Hart, and Welsh has drawn our attention to some of the symbolic significance of Scott's plots and heroes. Part of Scott's skill lies in the use of existing conventions of story and character to dramatize new ideas about the nature of historical change and the predicament of humans in a changing world. Major and minor characters both play their parts in this process.

Scott himself has been an impediment to a just appreciation of his work. In describing the way he wrote his novels he tends to present himself as a rather artless kind of writer using a 'mode of composition' he calls 'Hab nab at a venture'. By this he means that he follows the inspiration of the moment and he further explains that 'I never could lay down a plan—or having laid it down I

[5] Teut Andreas Riese, 'Sir Walter Scott as a Master of the Short Tale', in *Festschrift Professor Dr Herbert Koziol*, ed. Gero Bauer et al., Vienna, 1973, p. 255.

never could adhere to it' (*Journal*, 12 February 1826). Whether or not Scott stuck to his original plans for his novels, recent criticism has made it clear that they are more artfully constructed than he would have us believe. It seems that in the course of writing Scott generally, though perhaps not always, found a suitable form for what he wanted to say. Viewed in this way the contrast between formless novels and well-formed short stories, drawn by Lord David, is greatly lessened.

As well as revision of attitudes to Scott's work in general, there has been some revision of attitudes to individual stories. Most critics still tend, like Lord David, to regard 'Wandering Willie's Tale' and 'The Two Drovers' with particular esteem. Likewise 'The Tapestried Chamber' and 'The Death of the Laird's Jock' are the least regarded of the works included here. (As an aid to a possible reappraisal of those two works we have here, in an Appendix, reprinted, probably for the first time, Scott's earlier version of 'The Tapestried Chamber' and 'A Highland Anecdote', a piece written, like 'The Death of the Laird's Jock', to suggest the subject for a picture.) The most important critical revaluation has been with the introductory chapters to *Chronicles of the Canongate*. This in part arises from a renewed interest in the various personae adopted by Scott in writing his novels. That of Chrystal Croftangry in these introductory chapters has been described by Frank Jordan as 'Scott's Last and Best Mask'. Riese has argued that the first five of these chapters, as well as being 'a series of portraits', as Lord David describes them, 'gain a thematic unity of their own and grow into one autonomous tale' having as their theme 'the futility of the attempt to call back a life which has been swallowed up by time'. He sees the last three chapters as telling of 'Croftangry's resignation to this loss and his resolution to win back the past only in imagination, in the tales of old times which he collects and writes down'.[6] These chapters not only have a unifying theme but also an intimate connection with what follows them. In Chapter 6 we are introduced to Mrs Bethune Baliol, whose greatest talent is the narration of stories and whose memory stretches far back into the past. She represents that ability to recall the past through the imagination to which, as we learn in the final chapter of this introduction, Croftangry has now dedicated himself. From her Croftangry hears the story of 'The Highland Widow'. Having come to terms with his own past, he is in a good position to interpret the past for others and his introduction prepares us for stories dealing with characters coming to terms with their past, both personal and national.

These introductory chapters have another, quite different interest for the reader. Like the early chapters of *Redgauntlet*, they have a strongly autobiographical tinge. Scott began the *Chronicles* soon after both the death of his wife and the financial collapse which threatened, amongst other things, to deprive him of his beloved home and estate, Abbotsford. Both these events would inevitably make him look backwards over his life as Croftangry does. Scott gives Croftangry many of his own characteristics. Like Scott he is approaching sixty, he has accommodated himself

[6] Riese, p. 258.

to financial loss, he sees himself as a preserver of
old traditions, he is happy to live in 1826 but
prefers to write about the last fifty to one hundred
years and, though he has not been a professional
soldier, he likes to watch the cavalry at drill on
Portobello sands, having seen something in his
youth of 'the tramp of horses and the flash of
weapons' (p. 90). (Scott was prevented from
enlisting by his lameness but was an enthusiastic
quartermaster of a volunteer group of cavalry
and, according to one of his friends, he composed
parts of *Marmion* on Portobello sands in the intervals of drilling at Musselburgh.)[7] When Croftangry goes to look at the ancestral estate he lost
through his profligacy he finds the old house has
been replaced by a Gothic monstrosity called
Castle Treddles which we might well see as
Scott's parody of Abbotsford. Finally Mrs
Bethune Baliol is a portrait of Scott's long-
standing friend, Mrs Murray Keith, and the sad
picture of Mr Sommerville gives us a view of the
last days of Scott's own father. Even Croftangry's
speculations at the end of Chapter 5 on whether
or not his *Chronicles* would sell may have an
autobiographical basis. Despite his success in the
past it may well be that Scott felt some anxiety
about the reception of the first of his works of fiction to be published after he had publicly
acknowledged his authorship of the Waverley
Novels and lost his prized anonymity. The whole
atmosphere of these chapters, seen, as John
Buchan puts it, 'in a cold autumnal light which

---

[7] J. G. Lockhart, *Memoirs of the Life of Sir Walter Scott,
Bart.,* Edinburgh, 1837–8, ii. 117.

has lost the riotous colours of summer',[8] seems to reflect Scott's own mood at the time.

The autobiographical element continues in the introductory section to 'My Aunt Margaret's Mirror' which was originally intended to form part of the second series of the *Chronicles*. Here the narrator is unnamed, although, like his aunt Margaret, he would appear to be a Bothwell. His age is exactly that of Scott at the time of writing, and like Scott he has lost those dear to his affections. As a child he suffered from an infirmity and tells a story of a maid's impatience with him at a stile which is almost certainly drawn from Scott's own childhood memories of his lameness. Furthermore, the aunt Margaret whose story he tells is Scott's own aunt Margaret Swinton from whom he originally heard the story. Finally we may note that both Croftangry and Bothwell are men who have come down in the world, and thus provide a channel for expressing some of the feelings Scott himself had after his financial disaster which had for a while threatened him with total ruin.

The description of Mrs Bethune Baliol prepares us for the first chapter of 'The Highland Widow' in which she explains the circumstances through which she became acquainted with the story. While at first sight this section may seem extraneous to the central concerns of the story, it actually serves the important purpose of drawing the reader's attention to the fact that the story is set in a world that is now completely passed away. The tragedy of the story derives from

[8] *Sir Walter Scott*, London, 1932, p. 314.

Elspat MacTavish's unwillingness to accept that the world of her youth is dead. The introductory chapter calls on Scott's readers to look at the world now around them and thus to see how hopeless Elspat's attempt to revive the past is. The modern world, that same modern world that the readers see around them, is against her.

The major objection that many of Scott's readers have to 'The Highland Widow' is Scott's use of a special style of speech for the Gaelic-speaking central characters which is partly based on the supposed translations of the poems of Ossian by James Macpherson.[9] It has been a commonplace of Scott criticism that Scott writes best when he writes in Scots. This may well be true, but it does not mean that Scott could not write effectively in other styles of language. Alexander Welsh has examined the function of contrasting styles in Scott's work[10] but the diversity of styles in Scott is very great and calls for further study. In 'The Two Drovers', for instance, Scott gives another Highlander, Robin Oig, a quite different kind of speech. In the Highlands he speaks Gaelic, rendered as English as with Elspat and Hamish, but in England, where Robin is obliged to give up his native language and to speak English, Scott gives him the conventional literary representation of the speech of Highlanders, where *she* replaces *I*, *be* becomes *pe* and so on. It is a highly artificial language with comic potential but Scott does not use it for comedy. Rather it serves to highlight Robin's dissociation from the

[9] See note to p. 142.

[10] 'Contrast of Styles in the Waverley Novels', *Novel*, 6 (1973), 218–28.

culture around him, a dissociation which is to have tragic consequences. At the end Robin's speech changes again, to a simple biblical style of English which lends him a tragic dignity. In the case of 'The Highland Widow' it should be remembered that the style used by Macpherson in the poems of Ossian was intended to be an epic one and the use of a somewhat similar style by Elspat and Hamish reinforces Scott's view of them as belonging to a heroic but now dead past. They are, of course, real people with realistic motivations for their actions but they are also symbolic figures.

'The Highland Widow' is in fact one of the clearest statements of the classic theme of Scott's work, the need to set the past, however alluring, behind one and to accept the present, however uninteresting it may seem. In his first novel Scott showed how Waverley must set his family's Jacobite past behind him and come to terms with the much less romantic Hanoverian present. Scott had returned to the theme of the sad but necessary death of Jacobitism in *Redgauntlet* only a few years before writing the *Chronicles* and he now returned to it in 'The Highland Widow': Elspat is not only a representative of the old marauding Highland world but also a Jacobite who cannot bear to see her son serving those whom she sees as the Hanoverian usurpers. The Jacobite theme was one of deep personal significance to Scott who grew up surrounded by stories of the Jacobite rebellions[11]

[11] In a letter of 1806 he explains the reasons for his early interest in Jacobitism and writes 'I became a valiant Jacobite at the age of ten years old'; see *The Letters of Sir Walter Scott*, ed. H. J. C. Grierson, London, 1932–7, i. 343.

and it is not surprising that he returned to it in such an autobiographical work as the Chronicles.

Of all Scott's Jacobite stories 'The Highland Widow' has the unhappiest ending. Moreover, unlike both *Waverley* and *Redgauntlet*, it is primarily concerned with the adjustment to change, not by the middle and upper classes, but by the lower classes. In this respect it parallels 'Wandering Willie's Tale'. *Redgauntlet* as a whole is concerned with how people like lairds and lawyers have adapted and will adapt to the decline and death of Jacobitism. By contrast the 'Tale', inserted in Letter 11 of the novel, deals with the adaptation of Steenie Steenson, a small farmer, to an earlier historical change. Steenie has to find a way of throwing off the holds of a fanatical Redgauntlet laird who claims his allegiance even in Hell, just as Darsie in the novel as a whole has to defy a later fanatic Redgauntlet laird who wishes to bind him to the loyalties of the past.

'Wandering Willie's Tale' is the only one of Scott's stories written wholly in Scots. By Scott's time Scots, which had been in the fifteenth and sixteenth centuries a language used for all kinds of written and spoken communication in Scotland, had become severely limited as a literary medium. In particular, though it was used quite widely in verse, it was not used very much in prose. Scott used Scots extensively in the dialogue of his novels and, since 'Wandering Willie's Tale' forms part of the dialogue of *Redgauntlet*, being related by one character to another, Scott was able to write the whole tale in Scots. He thus revived for Scots a role as a language for narrative; it was a model which was

to influence a number of later writers, most
notably Stevenson with 'Thrawn Janet'. Scott
was therefore not only an innovator in the writing
of short stories but also in the use of Scots in
narrative.

'Wandering Willie's Tale' is here presented
out of its original context in *Redgauntlet*. It stands
well alone and benefits from being compared with
Scott's other short stories. At the same time it
also gains significantly when read as part of
Redgauntlet. Since this selection of stories is intended partly for readers who have been
discouraged from reading Scott by the length of
his novels, 'Wandering Willie's Tale' may serve
as a natural bridge to further reading of his work.

ACKNOWLEDGEMENTS

I WOULD like to acknowledge help from various people in preparing this edition. Noel Geeson, Claire Lamont and Finella Topping have kindly answered various queries. Sue Hosking and Paul Sharrad have helped with collecting material for the notes. The Inter-Library Loans staff in Flinders University Library have searched out a number of works not easily found in Australia, and I have also been helped by the staff of the National Library of Scotland where I was able to examine the manuscript of *Chronicles of the Canongate*. Above all, my greatest thanks go to my wife, Sue, who has helped me in numerous ways and especially with the collection of material for the notes and glossary, the collation of texts and the typing. Without her this work could not have been done.

G.J.T.

NOTE ON THE TEXT

'WANDERING WILLIE'S TALE'

'Wandering Willie's Tale' takes up almost the whole of Letter 11 of *Redgauntlet*. Scott had started writing the novel by about March of 1824 (*Letters*, viii. 203) and the last part of the manuscript was received by the printer on 2 June of the same year (*Letters*, viii. 310). It was published anonymously (the title page read 'By the Author of "Waverley"') in three volumes on 15 June 1824 by Constable in Edinburgh and Hurst, Robinson in London. The 'Tale' appears on pp. 225–63. The manuscript is in the National Library of Scotland (Adv MS 19.2.29) and there is a set of proof-sheets, corrected by Scott, in the Pierpont Morgan Library.

INTRODUCTORY CHAPTERS TO *CHRONICLES OF THE CANONGATE*, 'THE HIGHLAND WIDOW', 'THE TWO DROVERS'

These formed the first volume of the first series of *Chronicles of the Canongate* with *The Surgeon's Daughter* occupying the second volume. Scott's first mention of work on the *Chronicles* in his journal is on 28 May 1826, very soon after the death of his wife. He wrote that 'I intend the work as an *olla podrida* into which any species of narrative or discussion may be thrown'. He was pleased with 'The Highland Widow', writing on 8 July 'I may be mistaken but I do think the Tale of Elspat McTavish in my bettermost manner'. However,

his printer and literary adviser, James Ballantyne, was not happy with Scott's new direction:
as Scott put it in the same entry, 'J.B. roars for
chivalry'. On 15 July, he recorded that he had
finished the first volume. At one stage he proposed to call the new work *Conversations of the
Canongate*, but was worried that *Conversations*
might suggest 'Criminal Conversations which
rather abound in the district' (*Letters*, x. 72). He
also thought of publishing it without any indica-
tion of the authorship, hoping 'to escape under
the disguize of one of my own imitators' (*Letters*,
x. 52), but later changed his mind (*Journal*,
17 October 1826). The *Chronicles* appeared in
October as 'By the Author of "Waverley"' but
Scott signed the introduction, thus acknowledg-
ing his authorship of the Waverley Novels in
print for the first time. It was published by Cadell
in Edinburgh and Simpkin and Marshall in London. The manuscript has recently been bought
by the National Library of Scotland (MS 23048).
For some reason it does not include 'The Two
Drovers'.

'MY AUNT MARGARET'S MIRROR', 'THE TAPESTRIED CHAMBER', 'THE DEATH OF THE LAIRD'S JOCK'

In a letter of 27 August 1827 Scott mentions the
idea of a second series of *Chronicles of the Canongate*.
He intended it to include short stories and began
writing 'My Aunt Margaret's Mirror' on 7
November and completed it on 3 December, as
he recorded in his *Journal*. When he had completed at least two stories his publisher, Cadell,
and Ballantyne expressed their disapproval of

them and Scott was persuaded to lay them aside (*Journal*, 11 December 1827). As a result the second series of the *Chronicles of the Canongate* consisted entirely of the novel *The Fair Maid of Perth*. However, on 30 December Scott was offered the editorship of an illustrated annual volume called *The Keepsake* by its proprietor, Charles Heath. He declined the offer but agreed to write something for it and decided that 'these rejected parts of the *Chronicles* which Cadell and Ballantyne criticized so severely . . . might well enough make up a trifle of this kind' (*Journal*, 12 January 1828). Lockhart identifies 'The Death of the Laird's Jock' as one of the stories rejected by Cadell and Ballantyne (*Life*, vii. 108) but, if this was the case, Scott certainly remodelled it considerably, as the form it took in *The Keepsake* was very much one designed for that work. On 11 March 1828 Scott noted in his journal 'I sent Reynolds a sketch of two Scottish stories for subjects of art for his *Keepsake*. The death of the Laird's jock the one, the other the adventure of Duncan Stuart with the stag'. The latter appeared in *The Keepsake for 1832* under the title 'A Highland Anecdote' and is reprinted here in Appendix II. 'The Tapestried Chamber' was presumably one of the rejected stories, but the only one that Scott mentions by name as being reworked for *The Keepsake* is 'My Aunt Margaret's Mirror' (*Journal*, 13 and 24 April 1828). An earlier version of 'The Tapestried Chamber' appeared in 1818 in *Blackwood's Edinburgh Magazine* (iii. 705–7); it is included in this selection as Appendix I. 'My Aunt Margaret's Mirror', 'The Tapestried Chamber', and 'The Death of the Laird's Jock' appeared in *The Keepsake for 1829* (pp. 1–44, 123–42, 186–92). As Scott's Introduction to 'My Aunt Margaret's Mirror' suggests, *The Keepsake* was intended for the Christmas market and was actually published late in 1828. The manuscript of 'The Tapestried Chamber' is in the British Library (Add MS 33,267).

THE 'MAGNUM' EDITION

From 1828 onwards Scott was at work on a new uniform edition of his novels and stories for which he revised the text and provided extensive notes. This was nicknamed the 'Magnum Opus' or 'Magnum'. It appeared in forty-eight volumes between 1829 and 1833 with the last volumes appearing after Scott's death. 'Wandering Willie's Tale' appeared in Volume 35 and the other stories in Volume 41. In preparing the text and notes for the magnum Scott used a copy of his novels with interleaved blank pages on which he could write his notes and corrections. This later became the property of the publishers Adam and Charles Black. They used it in preparing their Centenary Edition of the novels of 1871 and their Dryburgh Edition of 1892–4 which corrected many textual errors in the Centenary Edition. The whereabouts of the interleaved copy with Scott's notes and textual corrections was not publicly known between the late 1930s, when it was offered for sale in New York, and 1984 when parts of it were again offered for sale in the same city. It has now been acquired by the National Library of Scotland. In the absence of the inter-leaved copy the textual authority of the

Centenary and Dryburgh editions could not be verified. Until the newly rediscovered copy has been thoroughly examined the magnum as printed remains the only readily available authority for Scott's final revisions of his novels.

TEXT OF THIS EDITION

The present edition is a corrected reprint of the original World's Classics edition of 1934. That edition was based on the 1912 Oxford Scott and ultimately derived from the Centenary Edition. It thus incorporated a number of incorrect readings from the Centenary and Oxford editions as well as some mistakes of its own. In this reprint the text has been checked against the magnum edition and revised so as to conform with it in all substantive readings and in the spelling of all Scots words. However, the modernized punctuation and spelling of certain words (apart from Scots words) of the original World's Classics edition have been retained. This has the advantage of removing the excessively heavy punctuation of the magnum. The present text is therefore a reprint of the magnum text with modernized spelling of certain non-Scots words and modernized punctuation. The footnotes are all taken from the magnum and are treated in the same way as the rest of the text. Some of Scott's longer notes were omitted from the earlier World's Classics volume. They are included here amongst the editor's notes, prefixed with the words 'Scott's note'. They are reprinted unchanged from the magnum. The two appendices are also

printed as in the original texts. The following
errors in the magnum text have been corrected:

p. 30, l. 2	sewer/same (as in MS; see Notes)
p. 89, l. 1	maybe/may be
p. 124, l. 3	wound/moaned (see Notes)
p. 160, ll. 25–6	his own in it/his own good in it (cf. l. 29)
p. 199, l. 4	her or theirs/her or hers (as in MS and 1st edition)
p. 243, l. 12	gentleman/gentlemen
p. 311, l. 27	localities of the detail/details of the locality (see Notes)
p. 357, l. 40	name/nave

SELECT BIBLIOGRAPHY

BIOGRAPHIES, LETTERS, ETC.

John Buchan, *Sir Walter Scott*, London, 1932

David Daiches, *Sir Walter Scott and His World*, London, 1971

Sir Herbert J. C. Grierson, *Sir Walter Scott, Bart.*, London, 1938

Edgar Johnson, *Sir Walter Scott: The Great Unknown*, London, 1970

J. G. Lockhart, *Memoirs of the Life of Sir Walter Scott, Bart.*, Edinburgh, 1837–8

The Journal of Sir Walter Scott, ed. W. E. K. Anderson, Oxford, 1972

The Letters of Sir Walter Scott, ed. H. J. C. Grierson, London, 1932–7 (with *Notes and Index to Sir Herbert Grierson's Edition of the Letters of Sir Walter Scott*, by James C. Corson, Oxford, 1979)

Scott on Himself, ed. David Hewitt, Edinburgh, 1981

BIBLIOGRAPHIES

James C. Corson, *A Bibliography of Sir Walter Scott 1797–1940*, Edinburgh, 1943

James C. Corson, 'Sir Walter Scott', in *The New Cambridge Bibliography of English Literature*, Volume III, Cambridge, 1969, 670–92

Jill A. Rubenstein, *Sir Walter Scott: A Reference Guide*, London, 1978

Greville Worthington, *A Bibliography of the Waverley Novels*, London, 1931

CRITICAL STUDIES OF SCOTT

James Anderson, *Sir Walter Scott and History*, Edinburgh, 1981

A. O. J. Cockshut, *The Achievement of Walter Scott*, London, 1969

Arthur Melville Clark, *Sir Walter Scott: The Formative Years*, Edinburgh, 1969

David Daiches, 'Scott's Achievement as a Novelist', in *Literary Essays*, Edinburgh, 1956, pp. 88–121 (reprinted in *Walter Scott*, ed. D. D. Devlin, and *Scott's Mind and Art*, ed. A. Norman Jeffares)

D. D. Devlin, *The Author of Waverley: A Critical Study of Walter Scott*, London, 1971

Robert C. Gordon, 'Scott and the Highlanders: The Non-Fictional Evidence', *Yearbook of English Studies*, 6 (1976), 120–40

Robert C. Gordon, *Under Which King? A Study of the Scottish Waverley Novels*, Edinburgh, 1969

Francis R. Hart, *Scott's Novels: The Plotting of Historic Survival*, Charlottesville, 1966

Mary Lascelles, *The Story-Teller Retrieves the Past: Historical Fiction and Fictitious History in the Art of Scott, Stevenson, Kipling, and Some Others*, Oxford, 1980

Georg Lukács, *The Historical Novel*, trans. H. and S. Mitchell, London, 1962

Graham McMaster, *Scott and Society*, Cambridge, 1981

Jane Millgate, *Walter Scott: The Making of the Novelist*, Toronto, 1984

Coleman O. Parsons, *Witchcraft and Demonology in Scott's Fiction*, Edinburgh, 1964

Paul Henderson Scott, *Walter Scott and Scotland*, Edinburgh, 1981

Graham Tulloch, *The Language of Walter Scott: A Study of His Scottish and Period Language*, London, 1980

Eric G. Walker, *Scott's Fiction and the Picturesque*, Salzburg, 1982

Alexander Welsh, *The Hero of the Waverley Novels*, New Haven, 1963

A. N. Wilson, *The Laird of Abbotsford: A View of Sir Walter Scott*, Oxford, 1980

CRITICAL STUDIES OF THE SHORT STORIES

J. T. Christie, 'Scott's *Chronicles of the Canongate*', *Essays and Studies*, N.S. 20 (1967), 64–75

Seamus Cooney, 'Scott and Cultural Relativism: *The Two Drovers*', *Studies in Short Fiction*, 15 (1978), 1–9

Seamus Cooney, 'Scott and Progress: The Tragedy of "The Highland Widow"', *Studies in Short Fiction*, 11 (1974), 11–16

David Daiches, 'Scott's *Redgauntlet*', in *From Jane Austen to Joseph Conrad*, ed. Robert C. Rathburn and Martin Steinmann, Minneapolis, 1958, pp. 46–59 (reprinted in *Walter Scott*, ed. D. D. Devlin)

Neal Frank Doubleday, 'Wandering Willie's Tale', in *Variety of Attempt: British and American Fiction in the Early Nineteenth Century*, Lincoln, 1976, pp. 49–60

Frank Jordan, 'Chrystal Croftangry, Scott's Last and Best Mask', *Scottish Literary Journal*, 7:1 (1980), 73–84

Coleman Oscar Parsons, 'Demonological Background of "Donnerhugel's Narrative" and "Wandering Willie's Tale"', *Studies in Philology*, 30 (1933), 604–17

Teut Andreas Riese, 'Sir Walter Scott as Master of the Short Tale', in *Festschrift Prof. Dr Herbert Koziol zum Siebzigsten Geburtstag*, ed. Gero Bauer et al., Vienna, 1973, pp. 255–65

Kenneth A. Robb, 'Scott's *The Two Drovers*: The Judge's Charge', *Studies in Scottish Literature*, 7 (1969–70), 155–64

Patricia H. Sosnoski, 'Reading *Redgauntlet*', *Scottish Literary Journal*, 7:1 (1980), 145–54

Graham Tulloch, 'Imagery in *The Highland Widow*', *Studies in Scottish Literature* (forthcoming)

Graham Tulloch, 'Scott and the Creation of Dialogue in Scots', in *Sir Walter Scott: the Long-Forgotten Melody*, ed. Alan Bold, London, 1973, pp. 143–66

TEXTUAL STUDIES

Mary Lascelles, 'Scott and the Art of Revision', in *Imagined Worlds*, ed. M. Mack and Ian Gregor, London, 1968, pp. 139–56 (reprinted in her *Notions and Facts*)

G. A. M. Wood, 'Scott's Continuing Revision: The Printed Texts of "Redgauntlet"', *The Bibliotheck*, 6 (1971–3), 121–98

G. A. M. Wood, 'The Great Reviser; or the Unknown Scott', *Ariel*, 2:3 (1971), 27–44

G. A. M. Wood, 'The Manuscripts and Proof-Sheets of *Redgauntlet*', in *Scott Bicentenary Essays*, ed. Alan Bell, Edinburgh, 1973, pp. 160–75

A CHRONOLOGY OF
SIR WALTER SCOTT

1771   Born in Edinburgh, son of Walter Scott, W. S., and Anne Rutherford.

1772–3   suffered from poliomyelitis which left him lame.

1779–83   attended the High School, Edinburgh.

1783–86, 1789–92   attended classes at Edinburgh University; 1786, apprenticed to his father.

1792   admitted to Faculty of Advocates.

1796   *The Chase*, and *William and Helen*, translated from Burger, issued anonymously.

1797   married Charlotte Charpentier.

1799   *Goetz of Berlichingen*, translated from Goethe; *Tales of Terror*; appointed Sheriff-Depute of Selkirkshire.

1801   contributed to M. G. Lewis's *Tales of Wonder*.

1802–3   *The Minstrelsy of the Scottish Border*.

1804   moved to Ashestiel.

1805   *The Lay of the Last Minstrel*; entered into partnership with James Ballantyne & Co., printers; started *Waverley*.

1806   appointed a Principal Clerk of Session.

1808   *Marmion*; edition of *The Works of John Dryden*; completed Joseph Strutt's *Queen-Hoo Hall*.

1810   *The Lady of the Lake*; resumed *Waverley*, but laid it aside again.

1812   moved to Abbotsford.

1813   *Rokeby*; declined offer of Poet Laureateship.

1814   *Waverley*; edition of *The Works of Jonathan Swift*.

1815   *The Lord of the Isles; Guy Mannering.*

1816   *The Antiquary; The Black Dwarf* and *Old Mortality*
       (*Tales of My Landlord*, 1st series).

1817   *Rob Roy.*

1818   *The Heart of Midlothian* (*Tales of My Landlord*,
       2nd series); accepted Baronetcy (gazetted
       1820).

1819   *The Bride of Lammermoor* and *A Legend of Mon-*
       trose (*Tales of My Landlord*, 3rd series); *Ivanhoe.*

1820   *The Monastery; The Abbot*; his daughter, Sophia,
       married J. G. Lockhart.

1821   *Kenilworth.*

1822   *The Pirate; The Fortunes of Nigel; Peveril of the*
       Peak.

1823   *Quentin Durward.*

1824   *St. Ronan's Well; Redgauntlet.*

1825   *The Betrothed* and *The Talisman* (*Tales of the*
       Crusaders); began *Journal.*

1826   financial collapse, caused by the bankruptcy of
       Archibald Constable & Co., and James
       Ballantyne & Co.; *Woodstock.*

1827   acknowledged authorship of Waverley novels;
       Life of Napoleon.

1827–8 *Chronicles of the Canongate* (two series).

1828–31 *Tales of a Grandfather* (four series).

1829   *Anne of Geierstein*; 'Magnum' series of Waverley
       Novels starts to appear.

1830   *Letters on Demonology and Witchcraft.*

1831   voyage to Mediterranean in search of health.

1832   *Count Robert of Paris* and *Castle Dangerous* (*Tales*
       of My Landlord, 4th series).
       Died at Abbotsford, 21 September.

The Two Drovers
and Other Stories

WANDERING WILLIE'S TALE*

YE maun have heard of Sir Robert Redgauntlet
of that Ilk, who lived in these parts before the
dear years. The country will lang mind him;
and our fathers used to draw breath thick if ever
they heard him named. He was out wi' the
Hielandmen in Montrose's time;* and again he
was in the hills wi' Glencairn in the saxteen
hundred and fifty-twa;* and sae when King
Charles the Second came in* wha was in sic
favour as the Laird of Redgauntlet?* He was
knighted at Lonon court, wi' the king's ain
sword; and being a redhot prelatist* he came
down here, rampauging like a lion, with commissions of lieutenancy (and of lunacy* for what
I ken) to put down a' the Whigs*and Covenanters*
in the country. Wild wark they made of it; for
the Whigs were as dour as the Cavaliers* were
fierce, and it was which should first tire the other.
Redgauntlet was aye for the strong hand; and his
name is kend as wide in the country as Claverhouse's or Tam Dalyell's.* Glen, nor dargle* nor
mountain, nor cave, could hide the puir hill-folk*
when Redgauntlet was out with bugle and blood-
hound after them, as if they had been sae mony
deer. And troth when they fand them, they
didna mak muckle mair ceremony than a Hielandman wi' a roebuck—it was just, 'Will ye tak
the test?'—if not, 'Make ready—present--fire!'
—and there lay the recusant.*

Far and wide was Sir Robert hated and feared.
Men thought he had a direct compact with
Satan—that he was proof against steel—and that

bullets happed aff his buff-coat like hailstanes
from a hearth—that he had a mear*that would
turn a hare on the side of Carrifra-gawns[1]—and
muckle to the same purpose, of whilk mair anon.
The best blessing they wared on him was, 'Deil
scowp wi' Redgauntlet!' He wasna a bad maister
to his ain folk, though, and was weel aneugh
liked by his tenants; and as for the lackies and
troopers that raid out wi' him to the persecutions, as the Whigs caa'd those killing times,* they
wad hae drunken themsells blind to his health
at ony time.

Now you are to ken that my gudesire lived on
Redgauntlet's·grund—they ca' the place Primrose Knowe. We had lived on the grund, and
under the Redgauntlets, since the riding days,
and lang before. It was a pleasant bit; and I
think the air is callerer and fresher there than
onywhere else in the country. It's a' deserted
now; and I sat on the broken door-cheek three
days since, and was glad I couldna see the plight
the place was in; but that's a' wide o' the mark.
There dwelt my gudesire, Steenie Steenson, a
rambling, rattling chiel he had been in his young
days, and could play weel on the pipes; he was
famous at 'Hoopers and Girders'—a' Cumberland couldna touch him at 'Jockie Lattin'*—and
he had the finest finger for the back-lilt*between
Berwick and Carlisle. The like o' Steenie wasna
the sort that they made Whigs o'. And so he
became a Tory,* as they ca' it, which we now ca'
Jacobites,* just out of a kind of needcessity, that
he might belang to some side or other. He had
nae ill will to the Whig bodies, and liked little to

[1] A precipitous side of a mountain in Moffatdale.

see the blude rin, though, being obliged to follow
Sir Robert in hunting and hosting, watching
and warding, he saw muckle mischief, and maybe
did some, that he couldna avoid.

Now Steenie was a kind of favourite with his
master, and kend a' the folks about the castle,
and was often sent for to play the pipes when they
were at their merriment. Auld Dougal Mac-
Callum, the butler, that had followed Sir Robert
through gude and ill, thick and thin, pool and
stream, was specially fónd of the pipes, and aye
gae my gudesire his gude word wi' the laird; for
Dougal could turn his master round his finger.

Weel, round came the Revolution, and it had
like to have broken the hearts baith of Dougal
and his master. But the change was not a'thegether sae great as they feared, and other folk
thought for. The Whigs made an unco crawing
what they wad do with their auld enemies, and
in special wi' Sir Robert Redgauntlet. But there
were ower mony great folks dipped in the same
doings, to mak a spick and span new warld. So
Parliament passed it a' ower easy; and Sir Robert,
bating that he was held to hunting foxes instead
of Covenanters, remained just the man he was.[1]
His revel was as loud, and his hall as weel lighted,
as ever it had been, though maybe he lacked the

---

[1] The caution and moderation of King William III,
and his principles of unlimited toleration, deprived the
Cameronians of the opportunity they ardently desired,
to retaliate the injuries which they had received during the
reign of prelacy, and purify the land, as they called it,
from the pollution of blood. They esteemed the Revolution, therefore, only a half measure, which neither comprehended the rebuilding the Kirk in its full splendour, nor
the revenge of the death of the Saints on their persecutors.

fines of the nonconformists, that used to come to stock his larder and cellar; for it is certain he began to be keener about the rents than his tenants used to find him before, and they behoved to be prompt to the rent-day, or else the laird wasna pleased. And he was sic an awsome body, that naebody cared to anger him; for the oaths he swore, and the rage that he used to get into, and the looks that he put on, made men sometimes think him a devil incarnate.

Weel, my gudesire was nae manager—no that he was a very great misguider—but he hadna the saving gift, and he got twa terms' rent in arrear. He got the first brash at Whitsunday put ower wi' fair word and piping; but when Martinmas came, there was a summons from the grund-officer to come wi' the rent on a day preceese, or else Steenie behoved to flit. Sair wark he had to get the siller; but he was weel-freended, and at last he got the haill scraped thegither—a thousand merks—the maist of it was from a neighbour they caa'd Laurie Lapraik—a sly tod. Laurie had walth o' gear—could hunt wi' the hound and rin wi' the hare—and be Whig or Tory, saunt or sinner, as the wind stood. He was a professor in this Revolution warld, but he liked an orra sough of this warld, and a tune on the pipes weel aneugh at a bytime; and abune a', he thought he had gude security for the siller he lent my gudesire ower the stocking at Primrose Knowe.

Away trots my gudesire to Redgauntlet Castle wi' a heavy purse and a light heart, glad to be out of the laird's danger. Weel, the first thing he learned at the castle was, that Sir Robert had fretted himsell into a fit of the gout, because he did not appear before twelve o'clock. It wasna a'thegether for sake of the money, Dougal thought; but because he didna like to part wi' my gudesire aff the grund. Dougal was glad to see Steenie, and brought him into the great oak parlour, and there sat the laird his leesome lane, excepting that he had beside him a great, ill-favoured jackanape, that was a special pet of his; a cankered beast it was, and mony an ill-natured trick it played—ill to please it was, and easily angered—ran about the haill castle, chattering and yowling, and pinching, and biting folk, specially before ill weather, or disturbances in the state. Sir Robert caa'd it Major Weir, after the warlock that was burnt;[1] and few folk liked either the name or the conditions of the creature —they thought there was something in it by ordinar—and my gudesire was not just easy in mind when the door shut on him, and he saw himself in the room wi' naebody but the laird, Dougal MacCallum, and the Major, a thing that hadna chanced to him before.

Sir Robert sat, or, I should say, lay, in a great armed chair, wi' his grand velvet gown, and his feet on a cradle; for he had baith gout and gravel, and his face looked as gash and ghastly as Satan's. Major Weir sat opposite to him, in a red laced coat, and the laird's wig on his head; and aye as Sir Robert girned wi' pain, the jackanape girned too, like a sheep's-head between a pair of tangs— an ill-faured, fearsome couple they were. The laird's buff-coat was hung on a pin behind him, and his broadsword and his pistols within reach;

[1] A celebrated wizard, executed at Edinburgh for sorcery and other crimes.

for he keepit up the auld fashion of having the
weapons ready, and a horse saddled day and
night, just as he used to do when he was able to
loup on horseback, and away after ony of the hill-
folk he could get speerings of. Some said it was
for fear of the Whigs taking vengeance, but I
judge it was just his auld custom—he wasna gien
to fear onything. The rental-book, wi' its black
cover and brass clasps, was lying beside him; and
a book of sculduddry sangs was put betwixt the
leaves, to keep it open at the place where it bore
evidence against the Goodman of Primrose
Knowe, as behind the hand with his mails and
duties. Sir Robert gave my gudesire a look, as if
he would have withered his heart in his bosom.
Ye maun ken he had a way of bending his brows,
that men saw the visible mark of a horseshoe in
his forehead, deep dinted, as if it had been
stamped there.

'Are ye come light-handed, ye son of a toom
whistle?' said Sir Robert. 'Zounds! if you
are——'

My gudesire, with as gude a countenance as
he could put on, made a leg, and placed the bag
of money on the table wi' a dash, like a man that
does something clever. The laird drew it to him
hastily—'Is it all here, Steenie, man?'

'Your honour will find it right,' said my
gudesire.

'Here, Dougal,' said the laird, 'gie Steenie a
tass of brandy downstairs, till I count the siller
and write the receipt.'

But they werena weel out of the room, when
Sir Robert gied a yelloch that garr'd the castle
rock. Back ran Dougal—in flew the livery-men

—yell on yell gied the laird, ilk ane mair awfu' than the ither. My gudesire knew not whether to stand or flee, but he ventured back into the parlour, where a' was gaun hirdy-girdie—naebody to say 'come in', or 'gae out'. Terribly the laird roared for cauld water to his feet, and wine to cool his throat; and Hell, hell, hell, and its flames, was aye the word in his mouth. They brought him water, and when they plunged his swollen feet into the tub, he cried out it was burning; and folk say that it *did* bubble and sparkle like a seething cauldron.* He flung the cup at Dougal's head, and said he had given him blood instead of burgundy;* and, sure aneugh, the lass washed clotted blood aff the carpet the neist day. The jackanape they caa'd Major Weir, it jibbered and cried as if it was mocking its master; my gudesire's head was like to turn—he forgot baith siller and receipt, and downstairs he banged; but as he ran, the shrieks came faint and fainter; there was a deep-drawn shivering groan, and word gaed through the castle that the laird was dead.

Weel, away came my gudesire, wi' his finger in his mouth, and his best hope was that Dougal had seen the money-bag, and heard the laird speak of writing the receipt. The young laird, now Sir John, came from Edinburgh, to see things put to rights. Sir John and his father never gree'd weel. Sir John had been bred an advocate, and afterwards sat in the last Scots Parliament and voted for the Union, having gotten, it was thought, a rug of the compensations*—if his father could have come out of his grave, he would have brained him for it on his awn hearthstane. Some thought it was easier counting with the auld rough knight than the fair-spoken young ane—but mair of that anon.

Dougal MacCallum, poor body, neither grat nor graned, but gaed about the house looking like a corpse, but directing, as was his duty, a' the order of the grand funeral. Now, Dougal looked aye waur and waur when night was coming, and was aye the last to gang to his bed, whilk was in a little round just opposite the chamber of dais, whilk his master occupied while he was living, and where he now lay in state, as they caa'd it, weel-a-day! The night before the funeral, Dougal could keep his awn counsel nae langer; he came doun with his proud spirit, and fairly asked auld Hutcheon to sit in his room with him for an hour. When they were in the round, Dougal took ae tass of brandy to himsell, and gave another to Hutcheon, and wished him all health and lang life, and said that, for himsell, he wasna lang for this world; for that, every night since Sir Robert's death, his silver call had sounded from the state chamber, just as it used to do at nights in his lifetime, to call Dougal to help to turn him in his bed. Dougal said that being alone with the dead on that floor of the tower (for naebody cared to wake Sir Robert Redgauntlet like another corpse) he had never daured to answer the call, but that now his conscience checked him for neglecting his duty; for, 'though death breaks service,' said MacCallum, 'it shall never break my service to Sir Robert; and I will answer his next whistle, so be you will stand by me, Hutcheon.'

Hutcheon had nae will to the wark, but he had stood by Dougal in battle and broil, and he wad not fail him at this pinch; so down the carles sat ower a stoup of brandy, and Hutcheon, who was something of a clerk, would have read a chapter of the Bible; but Dougal would hear naething but a blaud of Davie Lindsay,* whilk was the waur preparation.

When midnight came, and the house was quiet as the grave, sure aneugh the silver whistle sounded as sharp and shrill as if Sir Robert was blowing it, and up gat the twa auld serving-men, and tottered into the room where the dead man lay. Hutcheon saw aneugh at the first glance; for there were torches in the room, which showed him the foul fiend, in his ain shape, sitting on the laird's coffin! Over he cowped as if he had been dead. He could not tell how lang he lay in a trance at the door, but when he gathered himself, he cried on his neighbour, and getting nae answer, raised the house, when Dougal was found lying dead within twa steps of the bed where his master's coffin was placed. As for the whistle, it was gaen anes and aye; but mony a time was it heard at the top of the house on the barti-zan, and amang the auld chimneys and turrets where the howlets have their nests. Sir John hushed the matter up, and the funeral passed over without mair bogle-wark.

But when a' was ower, and the laird was begin-ning to settle his affairs, every tenant was called up for his arrears, and my gudesire for the full sum that stood against him in the rental-book. Weel, away he trots to the castle, to tell his story, and there he is introduced to Sir John, sitting in his father's chair, in deep mourning, with weepers and hanging cravat, and a small walking rapier

by his side, instead of the auld broadsword that
had a hundredweight of steel about it, what with
blade, chape, and basket-hilt. I have heard their
communing so often tauld ower, that I almost
think I was there mysell, though I couldna be
born at the time. (In fact, Alan, my companion
mimicked, with a good deal of humour, the
flattering, conciliating tone of the tenant's address, and the hypocritical melancholy of the
laird's reply. His grandfather, he said, had,
while he spoke, his eye fixed on the rental-book,
as if it were a mastiff-dog that he was afraid
would spring up and bite him.)

'I wuss ye joy, sir, of the head seat, and the
white loaf, and the braid lairdship. Your father
was a kind man to friends and followers; muckle
grace to you, Sir John, to fill his shoon—his
boots, I suld say, for he seldom wore shoon, unless
it were muils when he had the gout.'

'Ay, Steenie,' quoth the laird, sighing deeply,
and putting his napkin to his een, 'his was a
sudden call, and he will be missed in the country;
no time to set his house in order—weel prepared
Godward, no doubt, which is the root of the
matter—but left us behind a tangled hesp to
wind, Steenie.—Hem! hem! We maun go to
business, Steenie; much to do, and little time
to do it in.'

Here he opened the fatal volume. I have
heard of a thing they call Doomsday Book—I am
clear it has been a rental of back-ganging tenants.

'Stephen,' said Sir John, still in the same soft
sleekit tone of voice—'Stephen Stevenson, or
Steenson, ye are down here for a year's rent
behind the hand—due at last term.'

Stephen. 'Please your honour, Sir John, I paid it to your father.'

Sir John. 'Ye took a receipt, then, doubtless, Stephen; and can produce it?'

Stephen. 'Indeed I hadna time, an it like your honour; for nae sooner had I set doun the siller, and just as his honour, Sir Robert, that's gaen, drew it till him to count it, and write out the receipt, he was ta'en wi' the pains that removed him.'

'That was unlucky,' said Sir John, after a pause. 'But ye maybe paid it in the presence of somebody. I want but a *talis qualis* evidence, Stephen. I would go ower strictly to work with no poor man.'

Stephen. 'Troth, Sir John, there was naebody in the room but Dougal MacCallum the butler. But, as your honour kens, he has e'en followed his auld master.'

'Very unlucky again, Stephen,' said Sir John, without altering his voice a single note. 'The man to whom ye paid the money is dead—and the man who witnessed the payment is dead too—and the siller, which should have been to the fore, is neither seen nor heard tell of in the repositories. How am I to believe a' this?'

Stephen. 'I dinna ken, your honour; but there is a bit memorandum note of the very coins; for, God help me! I had to borrow out of twenty purses; and I am sure that ilka man there set down will take his grit oath for what purpose I borrowed the money.'

Sir John. 'I have little doubt ye *borrowed* the money, Steenie. It is the *payment* to my father that I want to have some proof of.'

Stephen. 'The siller maun be about the house, Sir John. And since your honour never got it, and his honour that was canna have ta'en it wi' him, maybe some of the family may have seen it.'

Sir John. 'We will examine the servants, Stephen; that is but reasonable.'

But lackey and lass, and page and groom, all denied stoutly that they had ever seen such a bag of money as my gudesire described. What was waur, he had unluckily not mentioned to any living soul of them his purpose of paying his rent. Ae quean had noticed something under his arm, but she took it for the pipes.

Sir John Redgauntlet ordered the servants out of the room, and then said to my gudesire, 'Now, Steenie, ye see you have fair play; and, as I have little doubt ye ken better where to find the siller than ony other body, I beg, in fair terms, and for your own sake, that you will end this fasherie; for, Stephen, ye maun pay or flit.'

'The Lord forgie your opinion,' said Stephen, driven almost to his wit's end—'I am an honest man.'

'So am I, Stephen,' said his honour; 'and so are all the folks in the house, I hope. But if there be a knave amongst us, it must be he that tells the story he cannot prove.' He paused, and then added, mair sternly, 'If I understand your trick, sir, you want to take advantage of some malicious reports concerning things in this family, and particularly respecting my father's sudden death, thereby to cheat me out of the money, and perhaps take away my character, by insinuating that I have received the rent I am demanding.

Where do you suppose this money to be? I insist upon knowing.'

My gudesire saw everything look sae muckle against him, that he grew nearly desperate—however, he shifted from one foot to another, looked to every corner of the room, and made no answer.

'Speak out, sirrah,' said the laird, assuming a look of his father's, a very particular ane, which he had when he was angry—it seemed as if the wrinkles of his frown made that selfsame fearful shape of a horse's shoe in the middle of his brow; —'Speak out, sir! I *will* know your thoughts;—do you suppose that I have this money?'

'Far be it frae me to say so,' said Stephen.

'Do you charge any of my people with having taken it?'

'I wad be laith to charge them that may be innocent,' said my gudesire; 'and if there be any one that is guilty, I have nae proof.'

'Somewhere the money must be, if there is a word of truth in your story,' said Sir John; 'I ask where you think it is—and demand a correct answer?'

'In hell, if you *will* have my thoughts of it,' said my gudesire, driven to extremity, 'in hell! with your father, his jackanape, and his silver whistle.'

Down the stairs he ran (for the parlour was nae place for him after such a word) and he heard the laird swearing blood and wounds behind him, as fast as ever did Sir Robert, and roaring for the bailie and the baron-officer.

Away rode my gudesire to his chief creditor (him they caa'd Laurie Lapraik) to try if he could

make ony thing out of him; but when he tauld his
story, he got but the warst word in his wame—
thief, beggar, and dyvour, were the saftest terms;
and to the boot of these hard terms, Laurie
brought up the auld story of his dipping his hand
in the blood of God's saunts, just as if a tenant
could have helped riding with the laird, and that
a laird like Sir Robert Redgauntlet. My gudesire
was, by this time, far beyond the bounds of
patience, and, while he and Laurie were at deil
speed the liars, he was wanchancie aneugh to
abuse Lapraik's doctrine as weel as the man, and
said things that garr'd folks' flesh grue that heard
them;—he wasna just himsell, and he had lived
wi' a wild set in his day.

At last they parted, and my gudesire was to
ride hame through the wood of Pitmurkie, that
is a' fou of black firs, as they say.—I ken the wood,
but the firs may be black or white for what I can
tell.—At the entry of the wood there is a wild
common, and on the edge of the common, a little
lonely change-house, that was keepit then by an
ostler-wife, they suld hae caa'd her Tibbie Faw,
and there puir Steenie cried for a mutchkin of
brandy, for he had had no refreshment the haill
day. Tibbie was earnest wi' him to take a bite of
meat, but he couldna think o't, nor would he
take his foot out of the stirrup, and took off the
brandy wholely at twa draughts, and named a
toast at each:—the first was the memory of Sir
Robert Redgauntlet, and might he never lie
quiet in his grave till he had righted his poor
bondtenant; and the second was a health to
Man's Enemy, if he would but get him back the
pock of siller or tell him what came o't, for he

saw the haill world was like to regard him as a thief and a cheat, and he took that waur than even the ruin of his house and hauld.

On he rode, little caring where. It was a dark night turned, and the trees made it yet darker, and he let the beast take its ain road through the wood; when all of a sudden, from tired and wearied that it was before, the nag began to spring and flee, and stend, that my gudesire could hardly keep the saddle. Upon the whilk, a horseman, suddenly riding up beside him, said, 'That's a mettle beast of yours, freend; will you sell him?' So saying, he touched the horse's neck with his riding-wand, and it fell into its auld heigh-ho of a stumbling trot. 'But his spunk's soon out of him, I think,' continued the stranger, 'and that is like mony a man's courage, that thinks he wad do great things till he come to the proof.'

My gudesire scarce listened to this, but spurred his horse, with 'Gude e'en to you, freend.'

But it's like the stranger was ane that doesna lightly yield his point; for, ride as Steenie liked, he was aye beside him at the selfsame pace. At last my gudesire, Steenie Steenson, grew half angry, and, to say the truth, half feared.

'What is it that ye want with me, freend?' he said. 'If ye be a robber, I have nae money; if ye be a leal man, wanting company, I have nae heart to mirth or speaking; and if ye want to ken the road, I scarce ken it mysell.'

'If you will tell me your grief,' said the stranger, 'I am one that, though I have been sair miscaa'd in the world, am the only hand for helping my freends.'

So my gudesire, to ease his ain heart, mair than from any hope of help, told him the story from beginning to end.

'It's a hard pinch,' said the stranger; 'but I think I can help you.'

'If you could lend the money, sir, and take a lang day—I ken nae other help on earth,' said my gudesire.

'But there may be some under the earth,' said the stranger. 'Come, I'll be frank wi' you; I could lend you the money on bond, but you would maybe scruple my terms. Now, I can tell you, that your auld laird is disturbed in his grave by your curses, and the wailing of your family, and if ye daur venture to go to see him, he will give you the receipt.'

My gudesire's hair stood on end at this proposal, but he thought his companion might be some humorsome chield that was trying to frighten him, and might end with lending him the money. Besides, he was bauld wi' brandy, and desperate wi' distress; and he said he had courage to go to the gate of hell, and a step farther, for that receipt. The stranger laughed.

Weel, they rode on through the thickest of the wood, when, all of a sudden, the horse stopped at the door of a great house; and, but that he knew the place was ten miles off, my father would have thought* he was at Redgauntlet Castle. They rode into the outer courtyard, through the muckle faulding yetts and aneath the auld portcullis; and the whole front of the house was lighted, and there were pipes and fiddles, and as much dancing and deray*within as used to be in Sir Robert's house at Pace and

Yule, and such high seasons. They lap off, and my gudesire, as seemed to him, fastened his horse to the very ring he had tied him to that morning, when he gaed to wait on the young Sir John.

'God!' said my gudesire, 'if Sir Robert's death be but a dream!'

He knocked at the ha' door just as he was wont, and his auld acquaintance, Dougal MacCallum —just after his wont, too,—came to open the door, and said, 'Piper Steenie, are ye there, lad? Sir Robert has been crying for you.'

My gudesire was like a man in a dream—he looked for the stranger, but he was gane for the time. At last he just tried to say, 'Ha! Dougal Driveower, are ye living? I thought ye had been dead.'

'Never fash yoursell wi' me,' said Dougal, 'but look to yoursell; and see ye tak naething frae ony-body here, neither meat, drink, or siller, except just the receipt that is your ain.'

So saying, he led the way out through halls and trances that were weel kend to my gudesire, and into the auld oak parlour; and there was as much singing of profane sangs, and birling of red wine, and speaking blasphemy and sculduddry, as had ever been in Redgauntlet Castle when it was at the blithest.

But, Lord take us in keeping, what a set of ghastly revellers they were that sat round that table! My gudesire kend mony that had long before gane to their place, for often had he piped to the most part in the hall of Redgauntlet. There was the fierce Middleton, and the dissolute Rothes, and the crafty Lauderdale; and Dalyell, with his bald head and a beard to his girdle; and

Earlshall, with Cameron's blude on his hand;
and wild Bonshaw, that tied blessed Mr. Cargill's
limbs till the blude sprung; and Dumbarton
Douglas, the twice-turned traitor baith to country
and king. There was the Bluidy Advocate
MacKenyie, who, for his worldly wit and wisdom
had been to the rest as a god. And there was
Claverhouse,* as beautiful as when he lived, with
his long, dark, curled locks streaming down over
his laced buff-coat, and his left hand always on
his right spule-blade, to hide the wound that the
silver bullet had made.* He sat apart from them
all, and looked at them with a melancholy,
haughty countenance; while the rest hallooed,
and sung, and laughed, that the room rang. But
their smiles were fearfully contorted from time
to time; and their laughter passed into such wild
sounds as made my gudesire's very nails grow
blue, and chilled the marrow in his banes.

They that waited at the table were just the
wicked serving-men and troopers, that had done
their work and cruel bidding on earth. There
was the Lang Lad of the Nethertown, that helped
to take Argyle; and the bishop's summoner, that
they called the Deil's Rattle-bag; and the wicked
guardsmen in their laced coats; and the savage
Highland Amorites,* that shed blood like water;
and many a proud serving-man, haughty of
heart and bloody of hand, cringing to the rich,
and making them wickeder than they would be;
grinding the poor to powder, when the rich had
broken them to fragments. And mony, mony
mair were coming and ganging, a' as busy in their
vocation as if they had been alive.

Sir Robert Redgauntlet, in the midst of a' this

fearful riot, cried, wi' a voice like thunder, on
Steenie Piper to come to the board-head where
he was sitting, his legs stretched out before him,
and swathed up with flannel, with his holster
pistols aside him, while the great broadsword
rested against his chair, just as my gudesire had
seen him the last time upon earth—the very
cushion for the jackanape was close to him, but
the creature itsell was not there—it wasna its
hour, it's likely; for he heard them say as he came
forward, 'Is not the Major come yet?' And
another answered, 'The jackanape will be here
betimes the morn.' And when my gudesire came
forward, Sir Robert, or his ghaist, or the deevil
in his likeness, said, 'Weel, piper, hae ye settled
wi' my son for the year's rent?'

With much ado my father gat breath to say
that Sir John would not settle without his honour's
receipt.

'Ye shall hae that for a tune of the pipes,
Steenie,' said the appearance of Sir Robert—
'Play us up "Weel hoddled, Luckie".'

Now this was a tune my gudesire learned frae
a warlock, that heard it when they were worship-
ping Satan at their meetings, and my gudesire
had sometimes played it at the ranting suppers
in Redgauntlet Castle, but never very willingly;
and now he grew cauld at the very name of it,
and said, for excuse, he hadna his pipes wi' him.

'MacCallum, ye limb of Beelzebub,' said the
fearfu' Sir Robert, 'bring Steenie the pipes that
I am keeping for him!'

MacCallum brought a pair of pipes might have
served the piper of Donald of the Isles.* But he
gave my gudesire a nudge as he offered them;

and looking secretly and closely, Steenie saw that the chanter was of steel, and heated to a white heat; so he had fair warning not to trust his fingers with it. So he excused himself again, and said he was faint and frightened, and had not wind aneugh to fill the bag.

'Then ye maun eat and drink, Steenie,' said the figure; 'for we do little else here; and it's ill speaking between a fou man and a fasting.'

Now these were the very words that the bloody Earl of Douglas*said to keep the king's messenger in hand while he cut the head off MacLellan of Bombie, at the Threave Castle,[1] and that put Steenie mair and mair on his guard. So he spoke up like a man, and said he came neither to eat, or drink, or make minstrelsy; but simply for his ain—to ken what was come o' the money he had paid, and to get a discharge for it; and he was so stout-hearted by this time that he charged Sir Robert for conscience-sake (he had no power to say the holy name) and as he hoped for peace and rest, to spread no snares for him, but just to give him his ain.

The appearance gnashed its teeth and laughed, but it took from a large pocket-book the receipt, and handed it to Steenie. 'There is your receipt, ye pitiful cur; and for the money, my dog-whelp of a son may go look for it in the Cat's Cradle.'

My gudesire uttered mony thanks, and was about to retire when Sir Robert roared aloud, 'Stop, though, thou sack-doudling son of a whore! I am not done with thee. HERE we do nothing for nothing; and you must return on

[1] The reader is referred for particulars to Pitscottie's *History of Scotland.*

this very day twelvemonth, to pay your master the homage that you owe me for my protection.'

My father's tongue was loosed of a suddenty, and he said aloud, 'I refer mysell to God's pleasure, and not to yours.'

He had no sooner uttered the word than all was dark around him; and he sunk on the earth with such a sudden shock, that he lost both breath and sense.

How lang Steenie lay there, he could not tell; but when he came to himsell, he was lying in the auld kirkyard of Redgauntlet parochine just at the door of the family aisle, and the scutcheon of the auld knight, Sir Robert, hanging over his head. There was a deep morning fog on grass and gravestane around him, and his horse was feeding quietly beside the minister's twa cows. Steenie would have thought the whole was a dream, but he had the receipt in his hand, fairly written and signed by the auld laird; only the last letters of his name were a little disorderly, written like one seized with sudden pain.

Sorely troubled in his mind, he left that dreary place, rode through the mist to Redgauntlet Castle, and with much ado he got speech of the laird.

'Well, you dyvour bankrupt,' was the first word, 'have you brought me my rent?'

'No,' answered my gudesire, 'I have not; but I have brought your honour Sir Robert's receipt for it.'

'How, sirrah? Sir Robert's receipt! You told me he had not given you one.'

'Will your honour please to see if that bit line is right?'

Sir John looked at every line, and at every
letter, with much attention; and at last, at the
date, which my gudesire had not observed,—
'*From my appointed place*,' he read, '*this twenty-fifth
of November*.'—'What!—That is yesterday!—
Villain, thou must have gone to hell for this!'

'I got it from your honour's father—whether he
be in heaven or hell, I know not,' said Steenie.

'I will delate you for a warlock to the Privy
Council!' said Sir John. 'I will send you to your
master, the devil, with the help of a tar-barrel
and a torch!'*

'I intend to delate mysell to the Presbytery,'
said Steenie, 'and tell them all I have seen last
night, whilk are things fitter for them to judge of
than a borrel man like me.'

Sir John paused, composed himsell, and desired to hear the full history; and my gudesire
told it him from point to point, as I have told it
you—word for word, neither more nor less.

Sir John was silent again for a long time, and
at last he said, very composedly, 'Steenie, this
story of yours concerns the honour of many a
noble family besides mine; and if it be a leasing-
making, to keep yourself out of my danger, the
least you can expect is to have a redhot iron
driven through your tongue, and that will be as
bad as scauding your fingers with a redhot chanter.
But yet it may be true, Steenie; and if the money
cast up, I shall not know what to think of it. But
where shall we find the Cat's Cradle? There are
cats enough about the old house, but I think they
kitten without the ceremony of bed or cradle.'

'We were best ask Hutcheon,' said my gudesire;
'he kens a' the odd corners about as weel as—

another serving-man that is now gane, and that I wad not like to name.'

Aweel, Hutcheon, when he was asked, told them, that a ruinous turret, lang disused, next to the clock-house, only accessible by a ladder, for the opening was on the outside, and far above the battlements, was called of old the Cat's Cradle.

'There will I go immediately,' said Sir John; and he took (with what purpose, Heaven kens) one of his father's pistols from the hall-table, where they had lain since the night he died, and hastened to the battlements.

It was a dangerous place to climb, for the ladder was auld and frail, and wanted ane or twa rounds. However, up got Sir John, and entered at the turret-door, where his body stopped the only little light that was in the bit turret. Something flees at him wi' a vengeance, maist dang him back ower—bang gaed the knight's pistol, and Hutcheon, that held the ladder, and my gudesire that stood beside him, hears a loud skelloch. A minute after, Sir John flings the body of the jackanape down to them, and cries that the siller is fund, and that they should come up and help him. And there was the bag of siller sure aneugh, and mony orra things besides, that had been missing for mony a day. And Sir John, when he had riped the turret weel, led my gudesire into the dining-parlour, and took him by the hand and spoke kindly to him, and said he was sorry he should have doubted his word and that he would hereafter be a good master to him to make amends.

'And now, Steenie,' said Sir John, 'although

this vision of yours tends, on the whole, to my
father's credit, as an honest man, that he should,
even after his death, desire to see justice done to
a poor man like you, yet you are sensible that ill-
dispositioned men might make bad constructions
upon it, concerning his soul's health. So, I think,
we had better lay the haill dirdum on that ill-
deedie creature, Major Weir, and say naething
about your dream in the wood of Pitmurkie.
You had taken ower muckle brandy to be very
certain about onything; and, Steenie, this receipt'
(his hand shook while he held it out),—'it's but
a queer kind of document, and we will do best,
I think, to put it quietly in the fire.'

'Od, but for as queer as it is, it's a' the voucher
I have for my rent,' said my gudesire, who was
afraid, it may be, of losing the benefit of Sir
Robert's discharge.

'I will bear the contents to your credit in the
rental-book, and give you a discharge under my
own hand,' said Sir John, 'and that on the spot.
And, Steenie, if you can hold your tongue about
this matter, you shall sit, from this term downward, at an easier rent.'

'Mony thanks to your honour,' said Steenie,
who saw easily in what corner the wind was;
'doubtless I will be comfortable to all your
honour's commands; only I would willingly
speak wi' some powerful minister on the subject,
for I do not like the sort of soumons of appointment whilk your honour's father——'

'Do not call the phantom my father!' said
Sir John, interrupting him.

'Weel, then, the thing that was so like him,'
said my gudesire; 'he spoke of my coming back

to him this time twelvemonth, and it's a weight
on my conscience.'

'Aweel, then,' said Sir John, 'if you be so much
distressed in mind, you may speak to our minister
of the parish; he is a douce man, regards the
honour of our family, and the mair that he may
look for some patronage from me.'

Wi' that, my gudesire readily agreed*that the
receipt should be burnt, and the laird threw it
into the chimney with his ain hand. Burn it
would not for them, though; but away it flew up
the lum, wi' a lang train of sparks at its tail, and
a hissing noise like a squib.*

My gudesire gaed down to the Manse, and the
minister, when he had heard the story, said it
was his real opinion that though my gudesire
had gaen very far in tampering with dangerous
matters, yet, as he had refused the devil's arles
(for such was the offer of meat and drink) and
had refused to do homage by piping at his bidding, he hoped, that if he held a circumspect
walk hereafter, Satan could take little advantage
by what was come and gane. And, indeed, my
gudesire, of his ain accord, lang foreswore baith
the pipes and the brandy—it was not even till the
year was out, and the fatal day past, that he
would so much as take the fiddle, or drink usquebaugh or tippeny.

Sir John made up his story about the jackanape
as he liked himsell; and some believe till this day
there was no more in the matter than the filching
nature of the brute. Indeed, ye'll no hinder
some to threap that it was nane o' the Auld
Enemy that Dougal and my gudesire*saw in the
laird's room, but only that wanchancy creature,

the major, capering on the coffin; and that, as to
the blawing on the laird's whistle that was heard
after he was dead, the filthy brute could do that
as weel as the laird himsell, if no better. But
Heaven kens the truth, whilk first came out by
the minister's wife, after Sir John and her ain
gudeman were baith in the moulds. And then
my gudesire, wha was failed in his limbs, but not
in his judgement or memory—at least nothing to
speak of—was obliged to tell the real narrative
to his freends, for the credit of his good name. He
might else have been charged for a warlock.

CHRONICLES OF THE CANONGATE

CHAPTER I

MR. CHRYSTAL CROFTANGRY'S ACCOUNT OF HIMSELF

SIC ITUR AD ASTRA. 'This is the path to heaven.'* Such is the ancient motto attached to the armorial bearings of the Canongate;* and which is inscribed, with greater or less propriety, upon all the public buildings from the church to the pillory in the ancient quarter of Edinburgh, which bears, or rather once bore, the same relation to the Good Town that Westminster does to London, being still possessed of the palace of the sovereign, as it formerly was dignified by the residence of the principal nobility and gentry. I may, therefore, with some propriety put the same motto at the head of the literary undertaking by which I hope to illustrate the hitherto undistinguished name of Chrystal Croftangry.

The public may desire to know something of an author who pitches at such height his ambitious expectations. The gentle reader, therefore—for I am much of Captain Bobadil's humour;* and could to no other extend myself so far—the *gentle* reader then, will be pleased to understand that I am a Scottish gentleman of the old school, with a fortune, temper, and person, rather the worse for wear. I have known the world for these forty years, having written myself man nearly since that period—and I do not think it is much mended. But this is an opinion which

I keep to myself when I am among younger folk, for I recollect in my youth quizzing the sexagenarians who carried back their ideas of a perfect state of society to the days of laced coats and triple ruffles, and some of them to the blood and blows of the Forty-five;* therefore I am cautious in exercising the right of censorship which is supposed to be acquired by men arrived at, or approaching, the mysterious period of life, when the numbers of seven and nine multiplied into each other, form what sages have termed the Grand Climacteric.*

Of the earlier part of my life it is only necessary to say that I swept the boards of the Parliament House* with the skirts of my gown for the usual number of years during which young lairds were in my time expected to keep term—got no fees—laughed, and made others laugh—drank claret at Bayle's, Fortune's, and Walker's,*—and eat oysters in the Covenant Close.*

Becoming my own master, I flung my gown at the bar-keeper, and commenced gay man on my own account. In Edinburgh, I ran into all the expensive society which the place then afforded. When I went to my house in the shire of Lanark, I emulated to the utmost the expenses of men of large fortune, and had my hunters, my first-rate pointers, my game-cocks, and feeders. I can more easily forgive myself for these follies, than for others of a still more blameable kind, so indifferently cloaked over that my poor mother thought herself obliged to leave my habitation, and betake herself to a small inconvenient jointure-house which she occupied till her death. I think, however, I was not exclusively to blame in this separation, and I believe my mother afterwards condemned herself for being too hasty. Thank God, the adversity which destroyed the means of continuing my dissipation, restored me to the affections of my surviving parent.

My course of life could not last. I ran too fast to run long; and when I would have checked my career, I was perhaps too near the brink of the precipice. Some mishaps I prepared by my own folly, others came upon me unawares. I put my estate out to nurse to a fat man of business, who smothered the babe he should have brought back to me in health and strength, and, in dispute with this honest gentleman, I found, like a skilful general, that my position would be most judiciously assumed by taking it up near the Abbey of Holyrood.* It was then I first became acquainted with the quarter which my little work will, I hope, render immortal, and grew familiar with those magnificent wilds, through which the Kings of Scotland once chased the dark-brown deer, but which were chiefly recommended to me in those days, by their being inaccessible to those metaphysical persons whom the law of the neighbouring country terms John Doe and Richard Roe.* In short, the precincts of the palace are now best known as being a place of refuge at any time from all pursuit for civil debt.*

Dire was the strife betwixt my quondam doer and myself; during which my motions were circumscribed, like those of some conjured demon, within a circle which, 'beginning at the northern gate of the King's Park, thence running northways, is bounded on the left by the King's garden wall, and the gutter or kennel, in a line wherewith it crosses the High Street to the Water Gate, and passing through the same, is bounded by the walls of the Tennis Court and Physic Garden, &c. It then follows the wall of the churchyard, joins the north-west wall of St. Ann's Yards, and going east to the clack mill-house, turns southward to the turnstile in the King's Park wall, and includes the whole King's Park within the Sanctuary."*

These limits, which I abridge from the accurate Maitland,* once marked the Girth or Asylum, belonging to the Abbey of Holyrood, and which, being still an appendage to the royal palace, has retained the privilege of an asylum for civil debt. One would think the space sufficiently extensive for a man to stretch his limbs in, as, besides a reasonable proportion of level ground (considering that the scene lies in Scotland), it includes within its precincts the mountain of Arthur's Seat, and the rocks and pasture land called Salisbury Crags. But yet it is inexpressible how, after a certain time had elapsed, I used to long for Sunday, which permitted me to extend my walk without limitation. During the other six days of the week I felt a sickness of heart which, but for the speedy approach of the hebdomadal day of liberty, I could hardly have endured. I experienced the impatience of a mastiff, who tugs in vain to extend the limits which his chain permits.

Day after day I walked by the side of the kennel which divides the Sanctuary from the unprivileged part of the Canongate; and though the month was July, and the scene the old town of Edinburgh, I preferred it to the fresh air and verdant turf which I might have enjoyed in the King's Park, or to the cool and solemn gloom of the portico which surrounds the palace. To an indifferent person either side of the gutter would have seemed much the same—the houses equally mean, the children as ragged and dirty, the carmen as brutal, the whole forming the same picture of low life in a deserted and impoverished quarter of a large city. But to me, the gutter, or kennel, was what the brook Kedron was to Shimei; death was denounced against him should he cross it, doubtless because it was known to his wisdom who pronounced the doom that from the time the crossing the stream was debarred, the devoted man's desire to transgress the precept would become irresistible, and he would be sure to draw down on his head the penalty which he had already justly incurred by cursing the anointed of God. For my part, all Elysium* seemed opening on the other side of the kennel, and I envied the little blackguards, who, stopping the current with their little damdikes of mud, had a right to stand on either side of the nasty puddle which best pleased them. I was so childish as even to make an occasional excursion across, were it only for a few yards, and felt the triumph of a schoolboy, who, trespassing in an orchard, hurries back again with a fluttering sensation of joy and terror, betwixt the pleasure of having executed his purpose and the fear of being taken or discovered.

I have sometimes asked myself what I should have done in case of actual imprisonment, since I could not bear without impatience a restriction which is comparatively a mere trifle; but I really could never answer the question to my own satisfaction. I have all my life hated those treacherous expedients called *mezzo-termini*, and it is possible with this disposition I might have endured more patiently an absolute privation of liberty than the more modified restrictions to which my residence in the Sanctuary at this period subjected me. If, however, the feelings I then experienced were to increase in intensity according to the difference between a jail and my actual condition, I must have hanged myself or pined to death; there could have been no other alternative.

Amongst many companions who forgot and neglected me of course when my difficulties seemed to be inextricable, I had one true friend; and that friend was a barrister, who knew the laws of his country well and, tracing them up to the spirit of equity and justice in which they originate, had repeatedly prevented, by his benevolent and manly exertions, the triumphs of selfish cunning over simplicity and folly. He undertook my cause, with the assistance of a solicitor of a character similar to his own. My quondam doer had ensconced himself chin-deep among legal trenches, hornworks and covered ways; but my two protectors shelled him out of his defences, and I was at length a free man, at liberty to go or stay wheresoever my mind listed.

I left my lodgings as hastily as if it had been a pest-house; I did not even stop to receive some change that was due to me on settling with my landlady, and I saw the poor woman stand at her door looking after my precipitate flight, and shaking her head as she wrapped the silver which

she was counting for me in a separate piece of
paper, apart from the store in her own moleskin
purse. An honest Highland woman was Janet
MacEvoy, and deserved a greater remuneration
had I possessed the power of bestowing it. But
my eagerness of delight was too extreme to pause
for explanation with Janet. On I pushed through
the groups of children, of whose sports I had been
so often a lazy lounging spectator. I sprung over
the gutter as if it had been the fatal Styx, and I
a ghost which, eluding Pluto's authority, was
making its escape from Limbo lake.* My friend
had difficulty to restrain me from running like
a madman up the street; and in spite of his kindness and hospitality, which soothed me for a day
or two, I was not quite happy until I found
myself aboard of a Leith smack, and, standing
down the Frith with a fair wind, might snap my
fingers at the retreating outline of Arthur's Seat,
to the vicinity of which I had been so long
confined.

It is not my purpose to trace my future progress through life. I had extricated myself, or
rather had been freed by my friends, from the
brambles and thickets of the law, but, as befell
the sheep in the fable, a great part of my fleece
was left behind me. Something remained, however; I was in the season for exertion, and, as my
good mother used to say, there was always life
for living folk. Stern necessity gave my manhood
that prudence which my youth was a stranger to.
I faced danger, I endured fatigue, I sought
foreign climates, and proved that I belonged to
the nation which is proverbially patient of labour
and prodigal of life. Independence, like liberty

to Virgil's shepherd,* came late, but came at last,
with no great affluence in its train, but bringing
enough to support a decent appearance for the
rest of my life, and to induce cousins to be civil
and gossips to say, 'I wonder who old Croft will
make his heir? he must have picked up something, and I should not be surprised if it prove
more than folk think of.'

My first impulse when I returned home was to
rush to the house of my benefactor, the only man
who had in my distress interested himself in my
behalf. He was a snuff-taker, and it had been
the pride of my heart to save the *ipsa corpora* of
the first score of guineas I could hoard, and to
have them converted into as tasteful a snuff-box
as Rundell and Bridge* could devise. This I had
thrust for security into the breast of my waistcoat,
while, impatient to transfer it to the person for
whom it was destined, I hastened to his house in
Brown's Square.* When the front of the house
became visible, a feeling of alarm checked me.
I had been long absent from Scotland, my friend
was some years older than I; he might have been
called to the congregation of the just. I paused,
and gazed on the house, as if I had hoped to form
some conjecture from the outward appearance
concerning the state of the family within. I
know not how it was, but the lower windows
being all closed and no one stirring, my sinister
forebodings were rather strengthened. I regretted now that I had not made inquiry before
I left the inn where I alighted from the mail-
coach. But it was too late; so I hurried on, eager
to know the best or the worst which I could
learn.

The brass-plate bearing my friend's name and designation was still on the door, and when it was opened, the old domestic appeared a good deal older, I thought, than he ought naturally to have looked, considering the period of my absence. 'Is Mr. Sommerville* at home?' said I, pressing forward.

'Yes, sir,' said John, placing himself in opposition to my entrance, 'he is at home, but——'

'But he is not in,' said I. 'I remember your phrase of old, John. Come, I will step into his room and leave a line for him.'

John was obviously embarrassed by my familiarity. I was some one, he saw, whom he ought to recollect; at the same time it was evident he remembered nothing about me.

'Ay, sir, my master is in, and in his own room, but——'

I would not hear him out, but passed before him, towards the well-known apartment. A young lady came out of the room a little disturbed, as it seemed, and said, 'John, what is the matter?'

'A gentleman, Miss Nelly, that insists on seeing my master.'

'A very old and deeply indebted friend,' said I, 'that ventures to press myself on my much-respected benefactor on my return from abroad.'

'Alas, sir,' replied she, 'my uncle would be happy to see you, but——'

At this moment, something was heard within the apartment like the falling of a plate or glass, and immediately after my friend's voice called angrily and eagerly for his niece. She entered the room hastily, and so did I. But it was to see a spectacle, compared with which that of my benefactor stretched on his bier would have been a happy one.

The easy-chair filled with cushions, the extended limbs swathed in flannel, the wide wrapping gown and night-cap, showed illness; but the dimmed eye, once so replete with living fire, the blabber lip, whose dilation and compression used to give such character to his animated countenance,—the stammering tongue, that once poured forth such floods of masculine eloquence and had often swayed the opinion of the sages whom he addressed,—all these sad symptoms evinced that my friend was in the melancholy condition of those in whom the principle of animal life has unfortunately survived that of mental intelligence. He gazed a moment at me, but then seemed insensible of my presence, and went on—he, once the most courteous and well-bred!—to babble unintelligible but violent reproaches against his niece and servant, because he himself had dropped a teacup in attempting to place it on a table at his elbow. His eyes caught a momentary fire from his irritation; but he struggled in vain for words to express himself adequately, as looking from his servant to his niece and then to the table, he laboured to explain that they had placed it (though it touched his chair) at too great a distance from him.

The young person, who had naturally a resigned Madonna-like expression of countenance, listened to his impatient chiding with the most humble submission, checked the servant, whose less delicate feelings would have entered on his justification, and gradually, by the sweet and soft tone of her voice, soothed to rest the spirit of causeless irritation.

She then cast a look towards me, which expressed, 'You see all that remains of him whom you call friend.' It seemed also to say, 'Your longer presence here can only be distressing to us all.'

'Forgive me, young lady,' I said, as well as tears would permit; 'I am a person deeply obliged to your uncle. My name is Croftangry.'

'Lord! and that I should not hae minded ye, Maister Croftangry,' said the servant. 'Ay, I mind my master had muckle fash about your job. I hae heard him order in fresh candles as midnight chappit, and till 't again. Indeed, ye had ay his gude word, Mr. Croftangry, for a' that folks said about you.'

'Hold your tongue, John,' said the lady, somewhat angrily; and then continued, addressing herself to me, 'I am sure, sir, you must be sorry to see my uncle in this state. I know you are his friend. I have heard him mention your name, and wonder he never heard from you.' A new cut this, and it went to my heart. But she continued, 'I really do not know if it is right that any should—If my uncle should know you, which I scarce think possible, he would be much affected, and the doctor says that any agitation——But here comes Dr. —— to give his own opinion.'

Dr. —— entered. I had left him a middle-aged man; he was now an elderly one; but still the same benevolent Samaritan, who went about doing good and thought the blessings of the poor as good a recompense of his professional skill as the gold of the rich.

He looked at me with surprise, but the young lady said a word of introduction, and I, who was known to the doctor formerly, hastened to complete it. He recollected me perfectly, and intimated that he was well acquainted with the reasons I had for being deeply interested in the fate of his patient. He gave me a very melancholy account of my poor friend, drawing me for that purpose a little apart from the lady. 'The light of life', he said, 'was trembling in the socket; he scarcely expected it would ever leap up even into a momentary flash, but more was impossible.' He then stepped towards his patient, and put some questions, to which the poor invalid, though he seemed to recognize the friendly and familiar voice, answered only in a faltering and uncertain manner.

The young lady, in her turn, had drawn back when the doctor approached his patient. 'You see how it is with him,' said the doctor, addressing me; 'I have heard our poor friend, in one of the most eloquent of his pleadings, give a description of this very disease, which he compared to the tortures inflicted by Mezentius*when he chained the dead to the living. The soul, he said, is imprisoned in its dungeon of flesh, and though retaining its natural and unalienable properties, can no more exert them than the captive enclosed within a prison house can act as a free agent. Alas! to see *him*, who could so well describe what this malady was in others, a prey himself to its infirmities! I shall never forget the solemn tone of expression with which he summed up the

incapacities of the paralytic,—the deafened ear,
the dimmed eye, the crippled limbs,—in the
noble words of Juvenal—

> . . . omni
> Membrorum damno, major, dementia, quae nec
> Nomina servorum, nec vultum agnoscit amici.'*

As the physician repeated these lines, a flash of
intelligence seemed to revive in the invalid's eye
—sunk again—again struggled, and he spoke
more intelligibly than before, and in the tone of
one eager to say something which he felt would
escape him unless said instantly. 'A question of
deathbed, a question of deathbed, doctor—a
reduction *ex capite lecti*—Withering against Wili-
bus—about the *morbus sonticus*. I pleaded the
cause for the pursuer—I and—and—Why, I shall
forget my own name—I and—he that was the
wittiest and the best-humoured man living——'

The description enabled the doctor to fill up
the blank, and the patient joyfully repeated the
name suggested. 'Ay, ay,' he said, 'just he—
Harry—poor Harry'——The light in his eye
died away, and he sunk back in his easy-chair.

'You have now seen more of our poor friend,
Mr. Croftangry,' said the physician, 'than I
dared venture to promise you; and now I must
take my professional authority on me, and ask
you to retire. Miss Sommerville will, I am sure,
let you know if a moment should by any chance
occur when her uncle can see you.'

What could I do? I gave my card to the young
lady, and, taking my offering from my bosom—
'If my poor friend', I said, with accents as broken
almost as his own, 'should ask where this came
from, name me; and say from the most obliged

and most grateful man alive. Say, the gold of which it is composed was saved by grains at a time, and was hoarded with as much avarice as ever was a miser's:—to bring it here I have come a thousand miles, and now, alas, I find him thus!'

I laid the box on the table, and was retiring with a lingering step. The eye of the invalid was caught by it, as that of a child by a glittering toy, and with infantine impatience he faltered out inquiries of his niece. With gentle mildness she repeated again and again who I was, and why I came, &c. I was about to turn, and hasten from a scene so painful, when the physician laid his hand on my sleeve—'Stop,' he said, 'there is a change.'

There was indeed, and a marked one. A faint glow spread over his pallid features—they seemed to gain the look of intelligence which belongs to vitality—his eye once more kindled—his lip coloured—and drawing himself up out of the listless posture he had hitherto maintained, he rose without assistance. The doctor and the servant ran to give him their support. He waved them aside, and they were contented to place themselves in such a position behind as might ensure against accident, should his newly ac-quired strength decay as suddenly as it had revived.

'My dear Croftangry,' he said, in the tone of kindness of other days, 'I am glad to see you returned—You find me but poorly—but my little niece here and Dr. —— are very kind— God bless you, my dear friend! we shall not meet again till we meet in a better world.'

I pressed his extended hand to my lips—I pressed it to my bosom—I would fain have flung myself on my knees; but the doctor, leaving the patient to the young lady and the servant, who wheeled forward his chair, and were replacing him in it, hurried me out of the room. 'My dear sir,' he said, 'you ought to be satisfied; you have seen our poor invalid more like his former self than he has been for months, or than he may be perhaps again until all is over. The whole Faculty could not have assured such an interval—I must see whether anything can be derived from it to improve the general health—Pray, begone.' The last argument hurried me from the spot, agitated by a crowd of feelings, all of them painful.

When I had overcome the shock of this great disappointment, I renewed gradually my acquaintance with one or two old companions, who, though of infinitely less interest to my feelings than my unfortunate friend, served to relieve the pressure of actual solitude, and who were not perhaps the less open to my advances, that I was a bachelor somewhat stricken in years, newly arrived from foreign parts, and certainly independent if not wealthy.

I was considered as a tolerable subject of speculation by some, and I could not be burdensome to any; I was therefore, according to the ordinary rule of Edinburgh hospitality, a welcome guest in several respectable families: but I found no one who could replace the loss I had sustained in my best friend and benefactor. I wanted something more than mere companionship could give me, and where was I to took for it?—among the scattered remnants of those that had been my gay friends of yore?—alas!

> Many a lad I loved was dead,
> And many a lass grown old.*

Besides, all community of ties between us had ceased to exist, and such of former friends as were still in the world held their life in a different tenor from what I did.

Some had become misers, and were as eager in saving sixpence as ever they had been in spending a guinea. Some had turned agriculturists—their talk was of oxen, and they were only fit companions for graziers. Some stuck to cards, and though no longer deep gamblers, rather played small game than sat out. This I particularly despised. The strong impulse of gaming, alas! I had felt in my time—it is as intense as it is criminal; but it produces excitation and interest, and I can conceive how it should become a passion with strong and powerful minds. But to dribble away life in exchanging bits of painted pasteboard round a green table, for the piddling concern of a few shillings, can only be excused in folly or superannuation. It is like riding on a rocking-horse, where your utmost exertion never carries you a foot forward; it is a kind of mental tread-mill, where you are perpetually climbing, but can never rise an inch. From these hints, my readers will perceive I am incapacitated for one of the pleasures of old age, which, though not mentioned by Cicero,* is not the least frequent resource in the present day,— the club room and the snug hand at whist.

To return to my old companions. Some frequented public assemblies, like the ghost of Beau

Nash* or any other beau of half a century back, thrust aside by tittering youth and pitied by those of their own age. In fine, some went into devotion, as the French term it, and others, I fear, went to the devil; a few found resources in science and letters; one or two turned philosophers in a small way, peeped into microscopes, and became familiar with the fashionable experiments of the day. Some took to reading, and I was one of them.

Some grains of repulsion towards the society around me—some painful recollections of early faults and follies—some touch of displeasure with living mankind, inclined me rather to a study of antiquities, and particularly those of my own country. The reader, if I can prevail on myself to continue the present work, will probably be able to judge in the course of it, whether I have made any useful progress in the study of the olden times.

I owed this turn of study, in part, to the conversation of my kind man of business, Mr. Fairscribe, whom I mentioned as having seconded the efforts of my invaluable friend, in bringing the cause on which my liberty and the remnant of my property depended, to a favourable decision. He had given me a most kind reception on my return. He was too much engaged in his profession for me to intrude on him often, and perhaps his mind was too much trammelled with its details to permit his being willingly withdrawn from them. In short, he was not a person of my poor friend Sommerville's expanded spirit, and rather a lawyer of the ordinary class of formalists; but a most able and excellent man.

When my estate was sold, he retained some of the older title-deeds, arguing, from his own feelings, that they would be of more consequence to the heir of the old family than to the new purchaser. And when I returned to Edinburgh, and found him still in the exercise of the profession to which he was an honour, he sent to my lodgings the old family Bible, which lay always on my father's table, two or three other mouldy volumes, and a couple of sheepskin bags, full of parchment and papers whose appearance was by no means inviting.

The next time I shared Mr. Fairscribe's hospitable dinner, I failed not to return him due thanks for his kindness, which acknowledgement, indeed, I proportioned rather to the idea which I knew he entertained of the value of such things than to the interest with which I myself regarded them. But the conversation turning on my family, who were old proprietors in the Upper Ward of Clydesdale, gradually excited some interest in my mind; and when I retired to my solitary parlour, the first thing I did was to look for a pedigree, or sort of history of the family or House of Croftangry, once of that Ilk, latterly of Glentanner. The discoveries which I made shall enrich the next chapter.

CHAPTER II

IN WHICH MR. CROFTANGRY CONTINUES HIS STORY

> What 's property, dear Swift? I see it alter
> From you to me, from me to Peter Walter.
>   POPE.*

'CROFTANGRY — Croftandrew — Croftandridge — Croftandgrey—for sa mony wise hath the name been spellit—is weel known to be ane house of grit antiquity; and it is said that King Milcolumb, or Malcolm, being the first of our Scottish princes quha removit across the Firth of Forth, did reside and occupy ane palace at Edinburgh, and had there ane valziant man, who did him man-service by keeping the croft, or corn land, which was tilled for the convenience of the king's household, and was thence callit Croft-an-ri, that is to say, the king his croft;* quhilk place, though now coverit with biggings, is to this day called Croft-angry,* and lyeth near to the royal palace. And whereas that some of those who bear this auld and honourable name may take scorn that it ariseth from the tilling of the ground, quhilk men account a slavish occupation, yet we ought to honour the pleugh and spade, seeing we all derive our being from our father Adam, whose lot it became to cultivate the earth, in respect of his fall and transgression.

'Also we have witness, as weel in holy writt as in profane history, of the honour in quhilk husbandrie was held of old, and how prophets have been taken from the pleugh,* and great captains raised up to defend their ain countries, sic as Cincinnatus* and the like, who fought not the common enemy with the less valiancy that their arms had been exercised in halding the stilts of the pleugh, and their bellicose skill in driving of yauds and owsen.

'Likewise there are sindry honourable families, quhilk are now of our native Scottish nobility, and have clombe higher up the brae of preferment than what this house of Croftangry hath done, quhilk shame not to carry in their warlike shield and insignia of dignity, the tools and implements the quhilk their first forefathers exercised in labouring the croft-rig, or, as the poet Virgilius calleth it eloquently, in subduing the soil.* And no doubt this ancient house of Croftangry, while it continued to be called of that Ilk, produced many worshipful and famous patriots, of quhom I now praetermit the names; it being my purpose if God shall spare me life for sic ane pious officium, or duty, to resume the first part of my narrative touching the house of Croftangry, when I can set down at length the evidents, and historical witness anent the facts which I shall allege, seeing that words when they are unsupported by proofs are like seed sown on the naked rocks, or like an house biggit on the flitting and faithless sands.'*

Here I stopped to draw breath; for the style of my grandsire, the inditer of this goodly matter, was rather lengthy, as our American friends say.* Indeed, I reserve the rest of the piece until I can obtain admission to the Bannatyne Club,[1] when I propose to throw off an edition, limited according to the rules of that erudite society, with a facsimile of the manuscript, emblazonry of the family arms, surrounded by their quartering, and a handsome disclamation of family pride, with *Haec nos novimus esse nihil*,* or *Vix ea nostra voco*.*

In the meantime, to speak truth, I cannot but suspect that though my worthy ancestor puffed vigorously to swell up the dignity of his family,

[1] This Club, of which the Author of *Waverley* has the honour to be president, was instituted in February, 1823, for the purpose of printing and publishing works illustrative of the history, literature, and antiquities of Scotland. It continues to prosper, and has already rescued from oblivion many curious materials of Scottish History.

we had never, in fact, risen above the rank of middling proprietors. The estate of Glentanner came to us by the intermarriage of my ancestor with Tib Sommeril, termed by the Southrons Sommerville,[1] a daughter of that noble house, but I fear on what my great-grandsire calls 'the wrong side of the blanket'.* Her husband, Gilbert, was killed fighting, as the *Inquisitio post mortem* has it, '*sub vexillo regis, apud proelium juxta Branxton*, LIE *Floddenfield*.'*

We had our share in other national misfortunes —were forfeited, like Sir John Colville of the Dale,* for following our betters to the field of Langside;* and, in the contentious times of the last Stewarts, we were severely fined for harbouring and resetting intercommuned ministers; and narrowly escaped giving a martyr to the Calendar of the Covenant,* in the person of the father of our family historian. He 'took the sheaf from the mare', however, as the MS. expresses it, and agreed to accept of the terms of pardon offered by government, and sign the bond in evidence he would give no farther ground of offence. My grandsire glosses over his father's backsliding as smoothly as he can, and comforts himself with ascribing his want of resolution to his unwillingness to wreck the ancient name and family and to permit his lands and lineage to fall under a doom of forfeiture.

[1] The ancient Norman family of the Sommervilles came into this island with William the Conqueror, and established one branch in Gloucestershire, another in Scotland. After the lapse of 700 years, the remaining possessions of these two branches were united in the person of the late Lord Sommerville, on the death of his English kinsman the well-known Author of *The Chase*.

'And indeed,' said the venerable compiler, 'as, praised be God, we seldom meet in Scotland with these belly-gods and voluptuariès, whilk are unnatural enough to devour their patrimony bequeathed to them by their forbears in chambering and wantonness, so that they come, with the prodigal son, to the husks and the swine-trough; and as I have the less to dreid the existence of such unnatural Neroes in mine own family to devour the substance of their own house* like brute beasts out of mere gluttonie and Epicurishnesse, so I need only warn mine descendants against over hastily meddling with the mutations in state and in religion, which have been nearhand to the bringing this poor house of Croftangry to perdition as we have shown more than once. And albeit I would not that my successors sat still altogether when called on by their duty to Kirk and King; yet I would have them wait till stronger and walthier men than themselves were up, so that either they may have the better chance of getting through the day; or, failing of that, the conquering party having some fatter quarry to live upon, may, like gorged hawks, spare the smaller game.'

There was something in this conclusion which at first reading piqued me extremely, and I was so unnatural as to curse the whole concern, as poor, bald, pitiful trash, in which a silly old man was saying a great deal about nothing at all. Nay, my first impression was to thrust it into the fire, the rather that it reminded me, in no very flattering manner, of the loss of the family property, to which the compiler of the history was so much attached, in the very manner which he most severely reprobated. It even seemed to my aggrieved feelings that his unprescient gaze on futurity, in which he could not anticipate the folly of one of his descendants, who should throw away the whole inheritance in a few years of idle expense and folly, was meant as a personal incivility to myself, though written fifty or sixty years before I was born.

A little reflection made me ashamed of this feeling of impatience, and as I looked at the even, concise, yet tremulous hand in which the manuscript was written, I could not help thinking, according to an opinion I have heard seriously maintained, that something of a man's character may be conjectured from his handwriting. That neat, but crowded and constrained small hand, argued a man of a good conscience, well-regulated passions, and, to use his own phrase, an upright walk in life; but it also indicated narrowness of spirit, inveterate prejudice, and hinted at some degree of intolerance which, though not natural to the disposition, had arisen out of a limited education. The passages from Scripture and the classics, rather profusely than happily introduced, and written in a half-text character to mark their importance, illustrated that peculiar sort of pedantry which always considers the argument as gained if secured by a quotation. Then the flourished capital letters which ornamented the commencement of each paragraph, and the name of his family and of his ancestors whenever these occurred in the page, do they not express forcibly the pride and sense of importance with which the author undertook and accomplished his task? I persuaded myself, the whole was so complete a portrait of the man that it would not have been a more undutiful act to have defaced his picture, or even to have disturbed his bones in his coffin, than to destroy his manuscript. I thought for a moment of presenting it to Mr. Fairscribe; but that confounded passage about the prodigal and swine-trough— I settled at last it was as well to lock it up in my own bureau with the intention to look at it no more.

But I do not know how it was that the subject began to sit nearer my heart than I was aware of, and I found myself repeatedly engaged in reading descriptions of farms which were no longer mine, and boundaries which marked the property of others. A love of the *natale solum*, if Swift be right in translating these words, 'family estate', began to awaken in my bosom; the recollections of my own youth adding little to it, save what was connected with field-sports. A career of pleasure is unfavourable for acquiring a taste for natural beauty, and still more so for forming associations of a sentimental kind connecting us with the inanimate objects around us.

I had thought little about my estate while I possessed and was wasting it, unless as affording the rude materials out of which a certain inferior race of creatures, called tenants, were bound to produce (in a greater quantity than they actually did) a certain return called rent, which was destined to supply my expenses. This was my general view of the matter. Of particular places, I recollected that Garval Hill was a famous piece of rough upland pasture for rearing young colts and teaching them to throw their feet,—that

Minion Burn had the finest yellow trout in the country,—that Seggycleugh was unequalled for woodcocks,—that Bengibbert Moors afforded excellent moorfowl-shooting, and that the clear bubbling fountain called the Harper's Well was the best recipe in the world on a morning after a *hard-go* with my neighbour fox-hunters. Still these ideas recalled, by degrees, pictures of which I had since learned to appreciate the merit— scenes of silent loneliness, where extensive moors, undulating into wild hills, were only disturbed by the whistle of the plover or the crow of the heath-cock; wild ravines creeping up into mountains, filled with natural wood, and which, when traced downwards along the path formed by shepherds and nutters, were found gradually to enlarge and deepen, as each formed a channel to its own brook, sometimes bordered by steep banks of earth, often with the more romantic boundary of naked rocks or cliffs, crested with oak, mountain-ash, and hazel,—all gratifying the eye the more that the scenery was, from the bare nature of the country around, totally unexpected.

I had recollections, too, of fair and fertile holms, or level plains, extending between the wooded banks and the bold stream of the Clyde, which, coloured like pure amber, or rather having the hue of the pebbles called cairngorm, rushes over sheets of rock and beds of gravel, inspiring a species of awe from the few and faithless fords which it presents, and the frequency of fatal accidents now diminished by the number of bridges. These alluvial holms were frequently bordered by triple and quadruple rows of large trees, which gracefully marked their boundary, and dipped their long arms into the foaming stream of the river. Other places I remembered which had been described by the old huntsman as the lodge of tremendous wild-cats, or the spot where tradition stated the mighty stag to have been brought to bay, or where heroes, whose might was now as much forgotten, were said to have been slain by surprise or in battle.

It is not to be supposed that these finished landscapes became visible before the eyes of my imagination, as the scenery of the stage is disclosed by the rising of the curtain. I have said that I had looked upon the country around me, during the hurried and dissipated period of my life, with the eyes indeed of my body but without those of my understanding. It was piece by piece, as a child picks out its lesson, that I began to recollect the beauties of nature which had once surrounded me in the home of my forefathers. A natural taste for them must have lurked at the bottom of my heart, which awakened when I was in foreign countries, and, becoming by degrees a favourite passion, gradually turned its eyes inwards and ransacked the neglected stores which my memory had involuntarily recorded, and when excited, exerted herself to collect and to complete.

I began now to regret more bitterly than ever the having fooled away my family property, the care and improvement of which, I saw, might have afforded an agreeable employment for my leisure, which only went to brood on past misfortunes, and increase useless repining. 'Had but a single farm been reserved, however small,' said

I, one day to Mr. Fairscribe, 'I should have had a place I could call my home, and something that I could call business.'

'It might have been managed,' answered Fairscribe, 'and for my part I inclined to keep the mansion-house, mains, and some of the old family acres together; but both Mr. —— and you were of opinion that the money would be more useful.'

'True, true, my good friend,' said I, 'I was a fool then, and did not think I could incline to be Glentanner with £200 or £300 a year, instead of Glentanner with as many thousands. I was then a haughty, pettish, ignorant, dissipated, broken-down Scottish laird; and, thinking my imaginary consequence altogether ruined, I cared not how soon, or how absolutely, I was rid of everything that recalled it to my own memory, or that of others.'

'And now it is like you have changed your mind?' said Fairscribe. 'Well, fortune is apt to circumduce the term upon us; but I think she may allow you to revise your condescendence.'

'How do you mean, my good friend?'

'Nay,' said Fairscribe, 'there is ill luck in averring till one is sure of his facts. I will look back on a file of newspapers, and to-morrow you shall hear from me; come, help yourself—I have seen you fill your glass higher.'

'And shall see it again,' said I, pouring out what remained of our bottle of claret; 'the wine is capital, and so shall our toast be—To your fireside, my good friend. And now we shall go beg a Scots song without foreign graces, from my little siren Miss Katie.'

The next day accordingly I received a parcel from Mr. Fairscribe with a newspaper enclosed, among the advertisements of which one was marked with a cross as requiring my attention. I read to my surprise—

'DESIRABLE ESTATE FOR SALE.

'By order of the Lords of Council and Session, will be exposed to sale in the New Sessions House of Edinburgh, on Wednesday, the 25th November, 18—, all and whole the lands and barony of Glentanner, now called Castle Treddles, lying in the Middle Ward of Clydesdale and shire of Lanark, with the teinds, parsonage and vicarage, fishings in the Clyde, woods, mosses, moors, and pasturages,' &c. &c.

The advertisement went on to set forth the advantages of the soil, situation, natural beauties and capabilities of improvement, not forgetting its being a freehold estate, with the particular polypus capacity of being sliced up into two, three, or, with a little assistance, four freehold qualifications, and a hint that the county was likely to be eagerly contested between two great families.* The upset price at which 'the said lands and barony and others' were to be exposed, was thirty years' purchase of the proven rental, which was about a fourth more than the property had fetched at the last sale. This, which was mentioned, I suppose, to show the improvable character of the land, would have given another some pain; but let me speak truth of myself in good as in evil—it pained not me. I was only angry that Fairscribe, who knew something generally of the extent of my funds, should have tantalized me by sending me information that my family property was in the market, since he must have known that the price was far out of my reach.

But a letter dropped from the parcel on the floor, which attracted my eye, and explained the riddle. A client of Mr. Fairscribe's, a moneyed man, thought of buying Glentanner, merely as an investment of money—it was even unlikely he would ever see it; and so the price of the whole being some thousand pounds beyond what cash he had on hand, this accommodating Dives would gladly take a partner in the sale for any detached farm, and would make no objection to its including the most desirable part of the estate in point of beauty, provided the price was made adequate. Mr. Fairscribe would take care I was not imposed on in the matter, and said in his card he believed, if I really wished to make such a purchase, I had better go out and look at the premises, advising me, at the same time, to keep a strict incognito; an advice somewhat superfluous, since I am naturally of a reserved disposition.

CHAPTER III

MR. CROFTANGRY, INTER ALIA, REVISITS GLENTANNER

Then sing of stage-coaches,
And fear no reproaches
    For riding in one;
But daily be jogging,
Whilst, whistling and flogging,
Whilst, whistling and flogging,
    The coachman drives on.   FARQUHAR.*

DISGUISED in a grey surtout which had seen service, a white castor on my head and a stout Indian cane in my hand, the next week saw me on the top of a mail-coach driving to the westward.

I like mail-coaches, and I hate them. I like them for my convenience, but I detest them for setting the whole world a-gadding, instead of sitting quietly still minding their own business and preserving the stamp of originality of character which nature or education may have impressed on them. Off they go, jingling against each other in the rattling vehicle till they have no more variety of stamp in them than so many smooth shillings—the same even in their Welsh wigs and great coats, each without more individuality than belongs to a partner of the company, as the waiter calls them, of the North coach.

Worthy Mr. Piper, best of contractors* who ever furnished four frampal jades*for public use, I bless you when I set out on a journey myself; the neat coaches under your contract render the intercourse, from Johnie Groat's House to Ladykirk and Cornhill Bridge*, safe, pleasant, and cheap. But, Mr. Piper, you who are a shrewd arithmetician, did it never occur to you to calculate how many fool's heads, which might have produced an idea or two in the year if suffered to remain in quiet, get effectually addled by jolting to and fro in these flying chariots of yours; how many decent countrymen become conceited bumpkins after a cattle-show dinner in the capital which they could not have attended save for your means; how many decent country parsons return critics and spouters by way of importing the newest taste from Edinburgh? And how will your conscience answer one day for carrying so many bonny lasses to barter modesty for conceit and levity at the metropolitan Vanity Fair?

Consider, too, the low rate to which you reduce human intellect. I do not believe your habitual customers have their ideas more enlarged than one of your coach-horses. They *knows* the road, like the English postillion, and they know nothing beside. They date, like the carriers at Gadshill, from the death of John Ostler,[1] the succession of guards forms a dynasty in their eyes; coachmen are their ministers of state, and an upset is to them a greater incident than a change of administration. Their only point of interest on the road is to save the time, and see whether the coach keeps the hour. This is surely a miserable degradation of human intellect. Take my advice, my good sir, and disinterestedly contrive that once or twice a quarter, your most dexterous whip shall overturn a coachful of these superfluous travellers, *in terrorem* to those who, as Horace says, 'delight in the dust raised by your chariots'.*

Your current and customary mail-coach passenger, too, gets abominably selfish, schemes successfully for the best seat, the freshest egg, the right cut of the sirloin. The mode of travelling is death to all the courtesies and kindnesses of life, and goes a great way to demoralize the character and cause it to retrograde to barbarism. You allow us excellent dinners, but only twenty minutes to eat them; and what is the consequence? Bashful beauty sits on the one side of us, timid childhood on the other; respectable, yet somewhat feeble old age is placed on our front;

[1] See the opening scene of the first part of Shakespeare's *Henry IV* [Act ii].

and all require those acts of politeness which ought to put every degree upon a level at the convivial board. But have we time—we the strong and active of the party—to perform the duties of the table to the more retired and bashful, to whom these little attentions are due? The lady should be pressed to her chicken—the old man helped to his favourite and tender slice—the child to his tart. But not a fraction of a minute have we to bestow on any other person than ourselves; and the *prut-prut—tut-tut* of the guard's discordant note, summons us to the coach, the weaker party having gone without their dinner, and the able-bodied and active threatened with indigestion from having swallowed victuals like a Lei'stershire clown bolting bacon.

On the memorable occasion I am speaking of I lost my breakfast, sheerly from obeying the commands of a respectable-looking old lady, who once required me to ring the bell, and another time to help the tea-kettle. I have some reason to think, she was literally an *old Stager*, who laughed in her sleeve at my complaisance; so that I have sworn in my secret soul revenge upon her sex, and all such errant damsels of whatever age and degree whom I may encounter in my travels. I mean all this without the least ill-will to my friend the contractor who, I think, has approached as near as any one is like to do towards accomplishing the modest wish of the Amatus and Amata of the Peri Bathous,

> Ye gods, annihilate but time and space,
> And make two lovers happy.*

I intend to give Mr. P. his full revenge when

I come to discuss the more recent enormity of steamboats; meanwhile, I shall only say of both these modes of conveyance, that

There is no living with them or without them.*

I am perhaps more critical on the —— mail-coach on this particular occasion, that I did not meet all the respect from the worshipful company in his Majesty's carriage that I think I was entitled to. I must say it for myself that I bear, in my own opinion at least, not a vulgar point about me. My face has seen service, but there is still a good set of teeth, an aquiline nose, and a quick grey eye set a little too deep under the eyebrow; and a cue of the kind once called military, may serve to show that my civil occupations have been sometimes mixed with those of war. Nevertheless, two idle young fellows in the vehicle, or rather on the top of it, were so much amused with the deliberation which I used in ascending to the same place of eminence, that I thought I should have been obliged to pull them up a little. And I was in no good-humour at an unsuppressed laugh following my descent when set down at the angle where a cross road, striking off from the main one, led me towards Glentanner, from which I was still nearly five miles distant.

It was an old-fashioned road which, preferring ascents to sloughs, was led in a straight line over height and hollow, through moor and dale. Every object around me as I passed them in succession, reminded me of old days, and at the same time formed the strongest contrast with them possible. Unattended, on foot, with a small bundle in my hand, deemed scarce sufficient good company for the two shabby genteels with whom I had been lately perched on the top of a mail-coach, I did not seem to be the same person with the young prodigal who lived with the noblest and gayest in the land, and who, thirty years before, would in the same country have been on the back of a horse that had been victor for a plate, or smoking along in his travelling chaise-and-four. My sentiments were not less changed than my condition. I could quite well remember that my ruling sensation in the days of heady youth, was a mere schoolboy's eagerness to get farthest forward in the race in which I had engaged; to drink as many bottles as ——; to be thought as good a judge of a horse as ——; to have the knowing cut of ——'s jacket. These were thy gods, O Israel!*

Now I was a mere looker-on; seldom an unmoved, and sometimes an angry spectator, but still a spectator only, of the pursuits of mankind. I felt how little my opinion was valued by those engaged in the busy turmoil, yet I exercised it with the profusion of an old lawyer retired from his profession, who thrusts himself into his neighbour's affairs, and gives advice where it is not wanted, merely under pretence of loving the crack of the whip.

I came amid these reflections to the brow of a hill, from which I expected to see Glentanner; a modest-looking yet comfortable house, its walls covered with the most productive fruit-trees in that part of the country, and screened from the most stormy quarters of the horizon by a deep and ancient wood, which overhung the neighbouring hill. The house was gone; a great part of the wood was felled; and instead of the gentle-man-like mansion, shrouded and embosomed among its old hereditary trees, stood Castle Treddles, a huge lumping four-square pile of freestone, as bare as my nail, except for a paltry edging of decayed and lingering exotics, with an impoverished lawn stretched before it which, instead of boasting deep green tapestry, enamelled with daisies, and with crowsfoot and cowslips, showed an extent of nakedness, raked, indeed, and levelled, but where the sown grasses had failed with drought, and the earth, retaining its natural complexion, seemed nearly as brown and bare as when it was newly dug up.

The house was a large fabric, which pretended to its name of Castle only from the front windows being finished in acute Gothic arches (being, by the way, the very reverse of the castellated style) and each angle graced with a turret about the size of a pepper-box. In every other respect it resembled a large town-house which, like a fat burgess, had taken a walk to the country on a holiday, and climbed to the top of an eminence to look around it. The bright red colour of the freestone, the size of the building, the formality of its shape and awkwardness of its position, harmonized as ill with the sweeping Clyde in front, and the bubbling brook which danced down on the right, as the fat civic form, with bushy wig, gold-headed cane, maroon-coloured coat, and mottled silk stockings, would have accorded with the wild and magnificent scenery of Corehouse Linn.*

I went up to the house. It was in that state of desertion which is perhaps the most unpleasant to look on, for the place was going to decay, without having been inhabited. There were about the mansion, though deserted, none of the slow mouldering touches of time, which communicate to buildings, as to the human frame, a sort of reverence, while depriving them of beauty and of strength. The disconcerted schemes of the Laird of Castle Treddles had resembled fruit that becomes decayed without ever having ripened. Some windows broken, others patched, others blocked up with deals, gave a disconsolate air to all around, and seemed to say, 'There Vanity had purposed to fix her seat, but was anticipated by Poverty'.

To the inside, after many a vain summons, I was at length admitted by an old labourer. The house contained every contrivance for luxury and accommodation;—the kitchens were a model, and there were hot closets on the office staircase that the dishes might not cool, as our Scottish phrase goes, between the kitchen and the hall. But instead of the genial smell of good cheer, these temples of Comus*emitted the damp odour of sepulchral vaults, and the large cabinets of cast-iron looked like the cages of some feudal Bastile.* The eating-room and drawing-room, with an interior boudoir, were magnificent apartments, the ceilings fretted and adorned with stucco-work, which already was broken in many places, and looked in others damp and mouldering; the wood panelling was shrunk and warped, and cracked; the doors, which had not been hung for more than two years, were, nevertheless, already swinging loose from their hinges. Desolation, in short, was where enjoyment had never been; and the want of all the usual means to preserve, was fast performing the work of decay.

The story was a common one, and told in a few words. Mr. Treddles, senior, who bought the estate, was a cautious money-making person; his son, still embarked in commercial speculations, desired at the same time to enjoy his opulence and to increase it. He incurred great expenses, amongst which this edifice was to be numbered. To support this he speculated boldly, and unfortunately; and thus the whole history is told, which may serve for more places than Glentanner.

Strange and various feelings ran through my bosom as I loitered in these deserted apartments, scarce hearing what my guide said to me about the size and destination of each room. The first sentiment, I am ashamed to say, was one of gratified spite. My patrician pride was pleased that the mechanic, who had not thought the house of the Croftangrys sufficiently good for him, had now experienced a fall in his turn. My next thought was as mean though not so malicious. 'I have had the better of this fellow,' thought I; 'if I lost the estate, I at least spent the price; and Mr. Treddles has lost his among paltry commercial engagements.'

'Wretch!' said the secret voice within, 'darest thou exult in thy shame? Recollect how thy youth and fortune were wasted in those years, and triumph not in the enjoyment of an existence which levelled thee with the beasts that perish. Bethink thee, how this poor man's vanity gave at least bread to the labourer, peasant, and citizen; and his profuse expenditure, like water spilt on the ground, refreshed the lowly herbs and plants where it fell. But thou! whom hast thou enriched, during thy career of extravagance, save those brokers of the devil, vintners, panders, gamblers, and horse-jockeys?' The anguish produced by this self-reproof was so strong that I put my hand suddenly to my forehead, and was obliged to allege a sudden megrim to my attendant, in apology for the action and a slight groan with which it was accompanied.

I then made an effort to turn my thoughts into a more philosophical current, and muttered half aloud, as a charm to lull any more painful thoughts to rest—

> '*Nunc ager Umbreni sub nomine, nuper Ofelli*
> *Dictus, erit nulli proprius; sed cedit in usum*
> *Nunc mihi, nunc alii. Quocirca vivite fortes,*
> *Fortiaque adversis opponite pectora rebus.*'[1]*

In my anxiety to fix the philosophical precept in my mind, I recited the last line aloud, which, joined to my previous agitation, I afterwards found became the cause of a report, that a mad schoolmaster had come from Edinburgh, with the idea in his head of buying Castle Treddles.

As I saw my companion was desirous of getting

[1] *Horace*, Sat. II, lib. 2. The meaning will be best conveyed to the English reader in Pope's imitation:—

> What's property, dear Swift? you see it alter
> From you to me, from me to Peter Walter;
> Or in a mortgage prove a lawyer's share;
> Or in a jointure vanish from the heir.
>
> .   .   .   .
>
> Shades, that to Bacon could retreat afford,
> Become the portion of a booby lord;
> And Helmsley, once proud Buckingham's delight,
> Slides to a scrivener and city knight.
> Let lands and houses have what lords they will,
> Let us be fix'd, and our own masters still.

rid of me, I asked where I was to find the person in whose hands were left the map of the estate and other particulars connected with the sale. The agent who had this in possession, I was told, lived at the town of ——; which I was informed, and indeed knew well, was distant five miles and a bittock, which may pass in a country where they are less lavish of their land, for two or three more. Being somewhat afraid of the fatigue of walking so far, I inquired if a horse or any sort of a carriage was to be had, and was answered in the negative.

'But', said my cicerone, 'you may halt a blink till next morning at the "Treddles Arms", a very decent house, scarce a mile off.'

'A new house, I suppose?' replied I.

'Na, it's a new public, but it's an auld house; it was aye the Leddy's jointure-house in the Croft-angry folk's time; but Mr. Treddles has fitted it up for the convenience of the country. Poor man, he was a public-spirited man when he had the means.'

'Duntarkin a public-house!' I exclaimed.

'Ay,' said the fellow, surprised at my naming the place by its former title, 'ye'll hae been in this country before, I'm thinking?'

'Long since,' I replied—'and there is good accommodation at the what-d'ye-call-'em arms, and a civil landlord?' This I said by way of saying something, for the man stared very hard at me.

'Very decent accommodation. Ye'll no be for fashing wi' wine, I'm thinking, and there's walth o' porter, ale, and a drap gude whisky'—(in an under tone)—'Fairntosh, if you can get on the

lee-side of the gudewife—for there is nae gudeman
—They ca' her Christie Steele.'

I almost started at the sound. Christie Steele!
Christie Steele was my mother's body-servant,
her very right hand, and, between ourselves,
something like a viceroy over her. I recollected
her perfectly; and though she had, in former
times, been no favourite of mine, her name now
sounded in my ear like that of a friend, and was
the first word I had heard somewhat in unison
with the associations around me. I sallied from
Castle Treddles, determined to make the best of
my way to Duntarkin, and my cicerone hung by
me for a little way, giving loose to his love of
talking; an opportunity which, situated as he
was, the seneschal of a deserted castle, was not
likely to occur frequently.

'Some folk think', said my companion, 'that
Mr. Treddles might as weel have put my wife as
Christie Steele into the "Treddles Arms", for
Christie had been aye in service and never in the
public line, and so it's like she is ganging back in
the world, as I hear—now, my wife had keepit
a victualling office.'

'That would have been an advantage, certainly,' I replied.

'But I am no sure that I wad ha' looten Eppie
take it if they had put it in her offer.'

'That's a different consideration.'

'Ony way, I wadna ha' liked to have offended
Mr. Treddles; he was a wee toustie when you
rubbed him again the hair—but a kind, weel-
meaning man.'

I wanted to get rid of this species of chat, and
finding myself near the entrance of a footpath

which made a short cut to Duntarkin, I put half-a-crown into my guide's hand, bade him good-evening, and plunged into the woods.

'Hout, sir—fie, sir—no from the like of you—stay, sir, ye wunna find the way that gate—Odd's mercy, he maun ken the gate as weel as I do mysell—weel, I wad like to ken wha the chield is.'

Such were the last words of my guide's drowsy, uninteresting tone of voice; and glad to be rid of him, I strode out stoutly, in despite of large stones, briers, and *bad steps*, which abounded in the road I had chosen. In the interim, I tried as much as I could, with verses from Horace and Prior* and all who have lauded the mixture of literary with rural life, to call back the visions of last night and this morning, imagining myself settled in some detached farm of the estate of Glentanner,

> Which sloping hills around enclose—
> Where many a birch and brown oak grows;*

when I should have a cottage with a small library, a small cellar, a spare bed for a friend, and live more happy and more honoured than when I had the whole barony. But the sight of Castle Treddles had disturbed all my own castles in the air. The realities of the matter, like a stone plashed into a limpid fountain, had destroyed the reflection of the objects around, which, till this act of violence, lay slumbering on the crystal surface, and I tried in vain to re-establish the picture which had been so rudely broken. Well, then, I would try it another way; I would try to get Christie Steele out of her *public*, since she was not thriving in it, and she who had been my mother's governante should be mine. I knew all her faults, and I told her history over to myself.

She was a granddaughter, I believe, at least some relative, of the famous Covenanter* of the name, whom Dean Swift's friend, Captain Creichton,* shot on his own staircase in the times of the persecutions, and had perhaps derived from her native stock much both of its good and evil properties. No one could say of her that she was the life and spirit of the family, though, in my mother's time, she directed all family affairs; her look was austere and gloomy, and when she was not displeased with you, you could only find it out by her silence. If there was cause for complaint, real or imaginary, Christie was loud enough. She loved my mother with the devoted attachment of a younger sister, but she was as jealous of her favour to any one else as if she had been the aged husband of a coquettish wife, and as severe in her reprehensions as an abbess over her nuns. The command which she exercised over her, was that, I fear, of a strong and determined over a feeble and more nervous disposition; and though it was used with rigour, yet, to the best of Christie Steele's belief, she was urging her mistress to her best and most becoming course, and would have died rather than have recommended any other. The attachment of this woman was limited to the family of Croftangry, for she had few relations; and a dissolute cousin, whom late in life she had taken as a husband, had long left her a widow.

To me she had ever a strong dislike. Even from my early childhood she was jealous, strange as it may seem, of my interest in my mother's affections; she saw my foibles and vices with abhorrence, and without a grain of allowance; nor did she pardon the weakness of maternal affection, even when, by the death of two brothers, I came to be the only child of a widowed parent. At the time my disorderly conduct induced my mother to leave Glentanner and retreat to her jointure house, I always blamed Christie Steele for having influenced her resentment, and prevented her from listening to my vows of amendment, which at times were real and serious, and might, perhaps, have accelerated that change of disposition which has since, I trust, taken place. But Christie regarded me as altogether a doomed and predestinated child of perdition, who was sure to hold on my course, and drag downwards whosoever might attempt to afford me support.

Still, though I knew such had been Christie's prejudices against me in other days, yet I thought enough of time had since passed away to destroy all of them. I knew that when, through the disorder of my affairs, my mother underwent some temporary inconvenience about money matters, Christie, as a thing of course, stood in the gap, and having sold a small inheritance which had descended to her, brought the purchase-money to her mistress, with a sense of devotion as deep as that which inspired the Christians of the first age, when they sold all they had and followed the apostles of the Church. I therefore thought that we might, in old Scottish phrase, 'let byganes be byganes', and begin upon a new account. Yet I resolved, like a skilful general, to reconnoitre a little before laying down any precise scheme of proceeding, and in the interim I determined to preserve my incognito.

CHAPTER IV

MR. CROFTANGRY BIDS ADIEU TO CLYDESDALE

Alas, how changed from what it once had been!
'Twas now degraded to a common inn.

GAY.*

AN hour's brisk walking or thereabouts, placed me in front of Duntarkin, which had also, I found, undergone considerable alterations though it had not been altogether demolished like the principal mansion. An inn-yard extended before the door of the decent little jointure-house, even amidst the remnants of the holly hedges which had screened the lady's garden. Then a broad, raw-looking, new-made road intruded itself up the little glen, instead of the old horseway so seldom used that it was almost entirely covered with grass. It is a great enormity of which gentlemen trustees on the highways are sometimes guilty, in adopting the breadth necessary for an avenue to the metropolis, where all that is required is an access to some sequestered and unpopulous district. I do not say anything of the expense; that the trustees and their constituents may settle as they please. But the destruction of sylvan beauty is great, when the breadth of the road is more than proportioned to the vale through which it runs, and lowers of course the consequence of any objects of wood or water, or broken and varied ground, which might otherwise attract notice and give pleasure. A bubbling

runnel by the side of one of those modern Appian
or Flaminian highways,* is but like a kennel,—
the little hill is diminished to a hillock,—the
romantic hillock to a molehill, almost too small
for sight.

Such an enormity, however, had destroyed the
quiet loneliness of Duntarkin, and intruded its
breadth of dust and gravel, and its associations
of pochays and mail-coaches, upon one of the
most sequestered spots in the Middle Ward of
Clydesdale. The house was old and dilapidated,
and looked sorry for itself as if sensible of a deroga-
tion; but the sign was strong and new and brightly
painted, displaying a heraldic shield, three
shuttles in a field diapré,* a web partly unfolded
for crest, and two stout giants for supporters,
each one holding a weaver's beam proper. To
have displayed this monstrous emblem on the
front of the house might have hazarded bringing
down the wall, but for certain would have blocked
up one or two windows. It was therefore established independent of the mansion, being displayed in an iron framework, and suspended
upon two posts, with as much wood and iron
about it as would have builded a brig; and there
it hung, creaking, groaning, and screaming in
every blast of wind, and frightening for five
miles' distance, for aught I know, the nests of
thrushes and linnets, the ancient denizens of the
little glen.

When I entered the place, I was received by
Christie Steele herself, who seemed uncertain
whether to drop me in the kitchen or usher me
into a separate apartment. As I called for tea,
with something rather more substantial than

bread and butter, and spoke of supping and
sleeping, Christie at last inducted me into the
room where she herself had been sitting, probably
the only one which had a fire, though the month
was October. This answered my plan; and, as
she was about to remove her spinning-wheel,
I begged she would have the goodness to remain
and make my tea, adding that I liked the sound
of the wheel and desired not to disturb her house-
wife-thrift in the least.

'I dinna ken, sir,'—she replied in a dry *revêche*
tone, which carried me back twenty years, 'I am
nane of thae heartsome landleddies that can tell
country cracks and make themsells agreeable;
and I was ganging to pit on a fire for you in the
Red Room; but if it is your will to stay here, he
that pays the lawing maun choose the lodging.'

I endeavoured to engage her in conversation;
but, though she answered with a kind of stiff
civility, I could get her into no freedom of discourse, and she began to look at her wheel and
at the door more than once as if she meditated
a retreat. I was obliged, therefore, to proceed to
some special questions that might have interest
for a person whose ideas were probably of a very
bounded description.

I looked round the apartment, being the same
in which I had last seen my poor mother. The
author of the family history, formerly mentioned,
had taken great credit to himself for the improvements he had made in this same jointure-house
of Duntarkin, and how, upon his marriage, when
his mother took possession of the same as her
jointure-house, 'to his great charges and expenses
he caused box the walls of the great parlour' (in

which I was now sitting), 'empanel the same, and plaster the roof, finishing the apartment with ane concave chimney, and decorating the same with pictures, and a barometer and thermometer.' And in particular, which his good mother used to say she prized above all the rest, he had caused his own portraiture be limned over the mantelpiece by a skilful hand. And, in good faith, there he remained still—having much the visage which I was disposed to ascribe to him on the evidence of his handwriting—grim and austere, yet not without a cast of shrewdness and determination; in armour, though he never wore it, I fancy; one hand on an open book, and one resting on the hilt of his sword, though, I dare say, his head never ached with reading nor his limbs with fencing.

'That picture is painted on the wood, madam?' said I.

'Ay, sir, or it's like it would not have been left there. They took a' they could.'

'Mr. Treddle's creditors, you mean?' said I.

'Na,' replied she, dryly, 'the creditors of another family that sweepit cleaner than this poor man's, because, I fancy, there was less to gather.'

'An older family, perhaps, and probably more remembered and regretted than later possessors?'

Christie here settled herself in her seat, and pulled her wheel towards her. I had given her something interesting for her thoughts to dwell upon, and her wheel was a mechanical accompaniment on such occasions, the revolutions of which assisted her in the explanation of her ideas.

'Mair regretted—mair missed?—I liked ane of the auld family very weel, but I winna say that for them a'. How should they be mair missed than the Treddleses? The cotton mill was such a thing for the country! The mair bairns a cottar body had the better; they would make their awn keep frae the time they were five years auld; and a widow, wi' three or four bairns, was a wealthy woman in the time of the Treddleses.'

'But the health of these poor children, my good friend—their education and religious instruction——'

'For health,' said Christie, looking gloomily at me, 'ye maun ken little of the warld, sir, if ye dinna ken that the health of the poor man's body, as weel as his youth and his strength, are all at the command of the rich man's purse. There never was a trade so unhealthy yet, but men would fight to get wark at it for twa pennies a-day aboon the common wage. But the bairns were reasonably weel cared for, in the way of air and exercise, and a very responsible youth heard them their carritch, and gied them lessons in Reediemadeasy.[1] Now, what did they ever get before? Maybe on a winter day they wad be called out to beat the wood for cocks or sicklike, and then the starving weans would maybe get a bite of broken bread and maybe no, just as the butler was in humour—that was a' they got.'

'They were not, then, a very kind family to the poor, these old possessors?' said I, somewhat bitterly; for I had expected to hear my ancestors' praises recorded, though I certainly despaired of being regaled with my own.

'They werena ill to them, sir, and that is aye something. They were just decent bien bodies;—

[1] *Reading made Easy*, usually so pronounced in Scotland.

ony poor creature that had face to beg, got an awmous and welcome; they that were shame-faced gaed by, and twice as welcome. But they keepit an honest walk before God and man, the Croftangrys, and as I said before, if they did little good they did as little ill. They lifted their rents and spent them, called in their kain and eat them; gaed to the kirk of a Sunday, bowed civilly if folk took aff their bannets as they gaed by, and lookit as black as sin at them that keepit them on.'

'These are their arms that you have on the sign?'

'What! on the painted board that is skirling and groaning at the door?—Na, these are Mr. Treddles's arms—though they look as like legs as arms—ill pleased I was at the fule thing, that cost as muckle as would hae repaired the house from the wa' stane to the rigging-tree. But if I am to bide here, I'll hae a decent board wi' a punch bowl on it.'

'Is there a doubt of your staying here, Mrs. Steele?'

'Dinna Mistress me,' said the cross old woman, whose fingers were now plying their thrift in a manner which indicated nervous irritation—'there was nae luck in the land since Luckie turned Mistress, and Mistress my Leddy; and as for staying here, if it concerns you to ken, I may stay if I can pay a hundred pund sterling for the lease, and I may flit if I canna; and so gude-e'en to you, Christie,'—and round went the wheel with much activity.

'And you like the trade of keeping a public-house?'

'I can scarce say that,' she replied. 'But worthy

Mr. Prendergast is clear of its lawfulness, and I hae gotten used to it and made a decent living, though I never make out a fause reckoning or give ony ane the means to disorder reason in my house.'

'Indeed?' said I; 'in that case, there is no wonder you have not made up the hundred pounds to purchase the lease.'

'How do you ken,' said she sharply, 'that I might not have had a hundred punds of my ain fée? If I have it not, I am sure it is my ain faut; and I wunna ca' it faut neither, for it gaed to her wha was weel entitled to a' my service.' Again she pulled stoutly at the flax, and the wheel went smartly round.

'This old gentleman', said I, fixing my eye on the painted panel, 'seems to have had *his* arms painted as well as Mr. Treddles—that is, if that painting in the corner be a scutcheon.'

'Ay, ay—cushion just sae, they maun a' hae their cushions; there's sma' gentry without that; and so the arms, as they ca' them, of the house of Glentanner, may be seen on an auld stane in the west end of the house. But to do them justice, they didna propale sae muckle about them as poor Mr. Treddles did;—it's like they were better used to them.'

'Very likely.—Are there any of the old family in life, goodwife?'

'No,' she replied; then added, after a moment's hesitation—'not that I know of,'—and the wheel, which had intermitted, began again to revolve.

'Gone abroad, perhaps?' I suggested.

She now looked up, and faced me—'No, sir. There were three sons of the last Laird of Glentanner, as he was then called; John and William were hopeful young gentlemen, but they died early—one of a decline brought on by the mizzles, the other lost his life in a fever. It would hae been lucky for mony ane that Chrystal had gane the same gate.'

'Oh—he must have been the young spendthrift that sold the property? Well, but you should not have such an illwill against him: remember necessity has no law; and then, goodwife, he was not more culpable than Mr. Treddles whom you are so sorry for.'

'I wish I could think sae, sir, for his mother's sake; but Mr. Treddles was in trade, and though he had no preceese right to do so, yet there was some warrant for a man being expensive that imagined he was making a mint of money. But this unhappy lad devoured his patrimony when he kenned that he was living like a ratten in a Dunlap cheese, and diminishing his means at a' hands—I canna bide to think on't.' With this she broke out into a snatch of a ballad; but little of mirth was there either in the tone or the expression:—

'For he did spend, and make an end
    Of gear that his forefathers wan;
Of land and ware he made him bare,
    So speak nae mair of the auld gudeman.'*

'Come, dame,' said I, 'it is a long lane that has no turning. I will not keep from you that I have heard something of this poor fellow, Chrystal Croftangry. He has sown his wild oats, as they say, and has settled into a steady respectable man.'

'And wha tell'd ye that tidings?' said she, looking sharply at me.

'Not perhaps the best judge in the world of his character, for it was himself, dame.'

'And if he tell'd you truth, it was a virtue he did not aye use to practise,' said Christie.

'The devil!' said I, considerably nettled; 'all the world held him to be a man of honour.'

'Ay, ay, he would hae shot ony body wi' his pistols and his guns that had evened him to be a liar. But if he promised to pay an honest tradesman the next term day, did he keep his word then? And if he promised a puir silly lass to make gude her shame, did he speak truth then? And what is that but being a liar, and a black-hearted deceitful liar to boot?'

My indignation was rising, but I strove to suppress it; indeed, I should only have afforded my tormentor a triumph by an angry reply. I partly suspected she began to recognize me; yet she testified so little emotion that I could not think my suspicion well founded. I went on, therefore, to say, in a tone as indifferent as I could command, 'Well, goodwife, I see you will believe no good of this Chrystal of yours, till he comes back and buys a good farm on the estate and makes you his housekeeper.'

The old woman dropped her thread, folded her hands, as she looked up to heaven with a face of apprehension. 'The Lord', she exclaimed, 'forbid! The Lord in his mercy forbid! Oh, sir, if you really know this unlucky man, persuade him to settle where folk ken the good that you say he has come to, and dinna ken the evil of his former days. He used to be proud enough—Oh, dinna let him come here, even for his own sake.— He used ance to have some pride.'

Here she once more drew the wheel close to her, and began to pull at the flax with both hands—'Dinna let him come here to be looked down upon by ony that may be left of his auld reiving companions, and to see the decent folk that he looked over his nose at look over their noses at him, baith at kirk and market. Dinna let him come to his ain country to be made a tale about when ony neighbour points him out to another, and tells what he is, and what he was, and how he wrecked a dainty estate, and brought harlots to the door-cheek of his father's house till he made it nae residence for his mother; and how it had been foretauld by a servant of his ain house that he was a ne'er-do-weel, and a child of perdition, and how her words were made good, and——'

'Stop there, goodwife, if you please,' said I; 'you have said as much as I can well remember, and more than it may be safe to repeat. I can use a great deal of freedom with the gentleman we speak of; but I think were any other person to carry him half of your message, I would scarce ensure his personal safety. And now, as I see the night is settled to be a fine one, I will walk on to ——, where I must meet a coach to-morrow, as it passes to Edinburgh.'

So saying, I paid my moderate reckoning and took my leave without being able to discover whether the prejudiced and hard-hearted old woman did, or did not, suspect the identity of her guest with the Chrystal Croftangry against whom she harboured so much dislike.

The night was fine and frosty, though, when I pretended to see what its character was, it might have rained like the deluge. I only made the excuse to escape from old Christie Steele. The horses which run races in the Corso at Rome without any riders, in order to stimulate their exertion, carry each his own spurs, namely, small balls of steel with sharp projecting spikes, which are attached to loose straps of leather, and, flying about in the violence of the agitation, keep the horse to his speed by pricking him as they strike against his flanks. The old woman's reproaches had the same effect on me, and urged me to a rapid pace as if it had been possible to escape from my own recollections. In the best days of my life when I won one or two hard walking matches, I doubt if I ever walked so fast as I did betwixt the 'Treddles Arms' and the borough town for which I was bound. Though the night was cold, I was warm enough by the time I got to my inn; and it required a refreshing draught of porter, with half an hour's repose, ere I could determine to give no farther thought to Christie and her opinions than those of any other vulgar prejudiced old woman. I resolved at last to treat the thing *en bagatelle*, and, calling for writing materials, I folded up a cheque for £100, with these lines on the envelope:

> 'Chrystal, the ne'er-do-weel,
> Child destined to the deil,
> Sends this to Christie Steele.'

And I was so much pleased with this new mode of viewing the subject that I regretted the lateness of the hour prevented my finding a person to carry the letter express to its destination.

But with the morning cool reflection came.*

I considered that the money, and probably more, was actually due by me on my mother's account to Christie, who had lent it in a moment of great necessity, and that the returning it in a light or ludicrous manner was not unlikely to prevent so touchy and punctilious a person from accepting a debt which was most justly her due, and which it became me particularly to see satisfied. Sacrificing then my triad with little regret (for it looked better by candle-light and through the medium of a pot of porter, than it did by daylight and with bohea for a menstruum), I determined to employ Mr. Fairscribe's mediation in buying up the lease of the little inn, and conferring it upon Christie in the way which should make it most acceptable to her feelings. It is only necessary to add that my plan succeeded, and that Widow Steele even yet keeps the 'Treddles Arms'. Do not say, therefore, that I have been disingenuous with you, reader; since, if I have not told all the ill of myself I might have done, I have indicated to you a person able and willing to supply the blank, by relating all my delinquencies, as well as my misfortunes.

In the meantime, I totally abandoned the idea of redeeming any part of my paternal property, and resolved to take Christie Steele's advice, as young Norval does Glenalvon's, 'although it sounded harshly.'

CHAPTER V

MR. CROFTANGRY SETTLES IN THE CANONGATE

——If you will know my house,
'Tis at the tuft of olives here hard by.
As You Like It.

By a revolution of humour which I am unable to account for, I changed my mind entirely on my

plans of life, in consequence of the disappointment, the history of which fills the last chapter.
I began to discover that the country would not
at all suit me; for I had relinquished field-sports,
and felt no inclination whatever to farming, the
ordinary vocation of country gentlemen; besides
that, I had no talent for assisting either candidate,
in case of an expected election, and saw no amusement in the duties of a road trustee, a com-
missioner of supply, or even in the magisterial
functions of the bench. I had begun to take some
taste for reading; and a domiciliation in the
country must remove me from the use of books,
excepting the small subscription library in which
the very book which you want is uniformly sure
to be engaged.

I resolved therefore to make the Scottish
metropolis my regular resting-place, reserving to
myself to take occasionally those excursions,
which, spite of all I have said against mail-
coaches, Mr. Piper has rendered so easy. Friend
of our life and of our leisure, he secures by dis-
patch against loss of time, and by the best of
coaches, cattle, and steadiest of drivers, against
hazard of limb, and wafts us, as well as our letters,
from Edinburgh to Cape Wrath,* in the penning of a
paragraph.

When my mind was quite made up to make
Auld Reekie* my head-quarters, reserving the
privilege of *exploring* in all directions, I began to
explore in good earnest for the purpose of dis-
covering a suitable habitation. 'And whare trew
ye I gaed?' as Sir Pertinax says.* Not to George's
Square—nor to Charlotte Square—nor to the
old New Town—nor to the new New Town—nor

to the Calton Hill; I went to the Canongate; and
to the very portion of the Canongate in which
I had formerly been immured, like the errant
knight, prisoner in some enchanted castle, where
spells have made the ambient air impervious to
the unhappy captive, although the organs of
sight encountered no obstacle to his free passage.

Why I should have thought of pitching my
tent here I cannot tell. Perhaps it was to enjoy
the pleasures of freedom, where I had so long
endured the bitterness of restraint; on the principle of the officer, who, after he had retired from
the army, ordered his servant to continue to call
him at the hour of parade, simply that he might
have the pleasure of saying—'D—n the parade!'
and turning to the other side to enjoy his slum-
bers. Or perhaps I expected to find in the vicinity
some little old-fashioned house, having somewhat
of the *rus in urbe*, which I was ambitious of enjoying. Enough, I went, as aforesaid, to the Canongate.

I stood by the kennel, of which I have formerly
spoken, and, my mind being at ease, my bodily
organs were more delicate. I was more sensible
than heretofore that, like the trade of Pompey in
Measure for Measure—it did in some sort——pah—
an ounce of civet, good apothecary!—Turning
from thence, my steps naturally directed themselves to my own humble apartment, where my
little Highland landlady, as dapper and as tight
as ever (for old women wear a hundred times
better than the hard-wrought seniors of the
masculine sex), stood at the door *teedling* to herself a Highland song as she shook a table napkin

over the forestair, and then proceeded to fold it up neatly for future service.

'How do you, Janet?'

'Thank ye, good sir,' answered my old friend, without looking at me; 'but ye might as weel say Mrs. MacEvoy, for she is na a'body's Shanet—umph.'

'You must be *my* Janet, though, for all that—have you forgot me?—Do you not remember Chrystal Croftangry?'

The light, kind-hearted creature threw her napkin into the open door, skipped down the stair like a fairy, three steps at once, seized me by the hands,—both hands,—jumped up, and actually kissed me. I was a little ashamed; but what swain of somewhere inclining to sixty, could resist the advances of a fair contemporary? So we allowed the full degree of kindness to the meeting,—*honi soit qui mal y pense*,—and then Janet entered instantly upon business. 'An' ye'll gae in, man, and see your auld lodgings, nae doubt, and Shanet will pay ye the fifteen shillings of change that ye ran away without, and without bidding Shanet good-day.—But never mind' (nodding good-humouredly), 'Shanet saw you were carried for the time.'

By this time we were in my old quarters, and Janet, with her bottle of cordial in one hand and the glass in the other, had forced on me a dram of usquebaugh, distilled with saffron and other herbs after some old-fashioned Highland receipt. Then was unfolded, out of many a little scrap of paper, the reserved sum of fifteen shillings which Janet had treasured for twenty years and upwards.

'Here they are,' she said, in honest triumph, 'just the same I was holding out to ye when ye ran as if ye had been fey. Shanet has had siller, and Shanet has wanted siller, mony a time since that—and the gauger has come, and the factor has come, and the butcher and baker—Cot bless us—just like to tear poor auld Shanet to pieces; but she took good care of Mr. Croftangry's fifteen shillings.'

'But what if I had never come back, Janet?'

'Och, if Shanet had heard you were dead, she would hae gien it to the poor of the chapel, to pray for Mr. Croftangry,' said Janet, crossing herself, for she was a Catholic;—'you maybe do not think it would do you cood, but the blessing of the poor can never do no harm.'

I heartily agreed in Janet's conclusion; and, as to have desired her to consider the hoard as her own property, would have been an indelicate return to her for the uprightness of her conduct, I requested her to dispose of it as she had proposed to do in the event of my death, that is, if she knew any poor people of merit to whom it might be useful.

'Ower mony of them,' raising the corner of her checked apron to her eyes, 'e'en ower mony of them, Mr. Croftangry—Och, aye—there is the puir Highland creatures frae Glenshee, that cam down for the harvest and are lying wi' the fever— five shillings to them, and half a crown to Bessie MacEvoy whose coodman, puir creature, died of the frost, being a shairman, for a' the whisky he could drink to keep it out o' his stamoch— and——'

But she suddenly interrupted the bead-roll of

her proposed charities, and assuming a very sage look, and primming up her little chattering mouth, she went on in a different tone—'But, och, Mr. Croftangry, bethink ye whether ye will not need a' this siller yoursell, and maybe look back and think lang for ha'en kiven it away, whilk is a creat sin to forthink a wark o' charity, and also is unlucky, and, moreover, is not the thought of a shentleman's son like yoursell, dear. And I say this, that ye may think a bit; for your mother's son kens that ye are no so careful as you should be of the gear, and I hae tauld ye of it before, jewel.'

I assured her I could easily spare the money without risk of future repentance; and she went on to infer that, in such a case, 'Mr. Croftangry had grown a rich man in foreign parts, and was free of his troubles with messengers and sheriff-officers and siclike scum of the earth, and Shanet MacEvoy's mother's daughter be a blithe woman to hear it. But if Mr. Croftangry was in trouble, there was his room, and his ped,* and Shanet to wait on him, and tak payment when it was quite convenient.'

I explained to Janet my situation, in which she expressed unqualified delight. I then proceeded to inquire into her own circumstances, and, though she spoke cheerfully and contentedly, I could see they were precarious. I had paid more than was due; other lodgers fell into an opposite error and forgot to pay Janet at all. Then, Janet being ignorant of all indirect modes of screwing money out of her lodgers, others in the same line of life who were sharper than the poor simple Highland woman, were enabled to let their apartments cheaper in appearance, though the inmates usually found them twice as dear in the long-run.

As I had already destined my old landlady to be my housekeeper and governante, knowing her honesty, good-nature, and, although a Scotch-woman, her cleanliness and excellent temper (saving the short and hasty expressions of anger which Highlanders call a *fuff*), I now proposed the plan to her in such a way as was likely to make it most acceptable. Very acceptable as the proposal was, as I could plainly see, Janet, how-ever, took a day to consider upon it; and her re-flections against our next meeting had suggested only one objection which was singular enough.

'My honour,' so she now termed me, 'would pe for biding in some fine street apout the town; now Shanet wad ill like to live in a place where polish, and sheriffs, and bailiffs, and sic thieves and trash of the world, could tak puir shentlemen by the throat, just because they wanted a wheen dollars in the sporran. She had lived in the bonny glen of Tomanthoulick—Cot, an ony of the vermint had come there, her father wad hae wared a shot on them, and he could hit a buck within as mony measured yards as e'er a man of his clan. And the place here was so quiet frae them, they durst na put their nose ower the gutter. Shanet owed nobody a bodle, put she couldna pide to see honest folk and pretty shentle-men forced away to prison whether they would or no; and then if Shanet was to lay her tangs ower ane of the ragamuffin's heads, it would be, maybe, that the law would gi'ed* a hard name.'

One thing I have learned in life—never to speak sense when nonsense will answer the purpose as well. I should have had great difficulty to convince this practical and disinterested admirer and vindicator of liberty that arrests seldom or never were to be seen in the streets of Edinburgh, and to satisfy her of their justice and necessity would have been as difficult as to convert her to the Protestant faith. I therefore assured her my intention, if I could get a suitable habitation, was to remain in the quarter where she at present dwelt. Janet gave three skips on the floor, and uttered as many short shrill yells of joy; yet doubt almost instantly returned, and she insisted on knowing what possible reason I could have for making my residence where few lived, save those whose misfortunes drove them thither. It occurred to me to answer her by recounting the legend of the rise of my family, and of our deriving our name from a particular place near Holyrood Palace. This, which would have appeared to most people a very absurd reason for choosing a residence, was entirely satisfactory to Janet MacEvoy.

'Och, nae doubt! if it was the land of her fathers, there was nae mair to be said. Put it was queer that her family estate should just lie at the town tail, and covered with houses, where the King's cows, Cot bless them hide and horn, used to craze upon. It was strange changes.' She mused a little, and then added, 'Put it is something better wi' Croftangry when the changes is frae the field to the habited place, and not from the place of habitation to the desert; for Shanet, her nainsell,* kent a glen where there were men

as weel as there may be in Croftangry, and if
there werena altogether sae mony of them, they
were as good men in their tartan as the others in
their broadcloth. And there were houses too;
and if they were not biggit with stane and lime,
and lofted like the houses at Croftangry, yet they
served the purpose of them that lived there; and
mony a braw bonnet, and mony a silk snood
and comely white curch, would come out to
gang to kirk or chapel on the Lord's day, and
little bairns toddling after; and now—Och,
Och, Ohellany, Ohonari! the glen is desolate, and
the braw snoods and bonnets are gane, and the
Saxon's house stands dull and lonely, like the
single bare-breasted rock that the falcon builds
on—the falcon that drives the heathbird frae
the glen.'

Janet, like many Highlanders, was full of
imagination; and, when melancholy themes
came upon her, expressed herself almost poeti-
cally, owing to the genius of the Celtic language
in which she thought, and in which, doubtless,
she would have spoken had I understood Gaelic.
In two minutes the shade of gloom and regret
had passed from her good-humoured features,
and she was again the little, busy, prating, important old woman, undisputed owner of one flat of
a small tenement in the Abbey-yard, and about
to be promoted to be housekeeper to an elderly
bachelor gentleman, Chrystal Croftangry, Esq.

It was not long before Janet's local researches
found out exactly the sort of place I wanted, and
there we settled. Janet was afraid I would not be
satisfied because it is not exactly part of Croftangry; but I stopped her doubts, by assuring her

it had been part and pendicle thereof in my
forefather's time, which passed very well.

I do not intend to possess any one with an
exact knowledge of my lodging; though, as
Bobadil says, 'I care not who knows it, since the
cabin is convenient.'* But I may state in general,
that it is a house 'within itself', or, according to
a newer phraseology in advertisements, *self-
contained*, has a garden of near half an acre, and
a patch of ground with trees in front. It boasts
five rooms, and servants' apartments—looks in
front upon the Palace, and from behind towards
the hill and crags of the King's Park. Fortunately
the place had a name which, with a little improvement, served to countenance the legend
which I had imposed on Janet, and would not
perhaps have been sorry if I had been able to
impose on myself. It was called Littlecroft; we
have dubbed it Little Croftangry, and the men
of letters belonging to the Post Office have sanc-
tioned the change, and deliver letters so addressed.
Thus I am to all intents and purposes Chrystal
Croftangry of that Ilk.

My establishment consists of Janet, an under
maidservant, and a Highland wench for Janet
to exercise her Gaelic upon, with a handy lad
who can lay the cloth and take care besides of
a pony on which I find my way to Portobello
sands, especially when the cavalry have a drill;
for, like an old fool as I am, I have not altogether
become indifferent to the tramp of horses and
the flash of weapons, of which, though no professional soldier, it has been my fate to see something in my youth. For wet mornings I have my
book—is it fine weather, I visit, or I wander on

the crags, as the humour dictates. My dinner is indeed solitary, yet not quite so neither; for though Andrews waits, Janet, or—as she is to all the world but her master and certain old Highland gossips—Mrs. MacEvoy, attends, bustles about, and desires to see everything is in first-rate order, and to tell me, Cot pless us, the wonderful news of the Palace for the day: When the cloth is removed, and I light my cigar and begin to husband a pint of port, or a glass of old whisky and water, it is the rule of the house that Janet takes a chair at some distance, and nods or works her stocking as she may be disposed; ready to speak, if I am in the talking humour, and sitting quiet as a mouse if I am rather inclined to study a book or the newspaper. At six precisely she makes my tea and leaves me to drink it; and then occurs an interval of time which most old bachelors find heavy on their hands. The theatre is a good occasional resource, especially if Wil Murray*acts, or a bright star of eminence shines forth; but it is distant, and so are one or two public societies to which I belong; besides, these evening walks are all incompatible with the elbow-chair feeling, which desires some employment that may divert the mind without fatiguing the body.

Under the influence of these impressions, I have sometimes thought of this literary undertaking. I must have been the Bonassus* himself to have mistaken myself for a genius, yet I have leisure and reflections like my neighbours. I am a borderer also between two generations, and can point out more perhaps than others of those fading traces of antiquity which are daily vanish-

ing; and I know many a modern instance and
many an old tradition, and therefore I ask—

> What ails me, I may not, as well as they,
> Rake up some threadbare tales, that mouldering lay
> In chimney corners, wont by Christmas fires
> To read and rock to sleep our ancient sires?
> No man his threshold better knows than I
> Brute's first arrival and first victory,
> Saint George's sorrel and his cross of blood,
> Arthur's round board and Caledonian wood.*

No shop is so easily set up as an antiquary's.
Like those of the lowest order of pawnbrokers,
a commodity of rusty iron, a bag or two of hob-
nails, a few odd shoebuckles, cashiered kail-pots,
and fire-irons declared incapable of service, are
quite sufficient to set him up. If he add a sheaf
or two of penny ballads and broadsides, he is a
great man—an extensive trader. And then, like
the pawnbrokers aforesaid, if the author under-
stands a little legerdemain, he may, by dint of
a little picking and stealing, make the inside of
his shop a great deal richer than the out, and be
able to show you things which cause those who
do not understand the antiquarian trick of clean
conveyance, to wonder how the devil he came
by them.

It may be said that antiquarian articles interest
but few customers, and that we may bawl ourselves as rusty as the wares we deal in without
any one asking the price of our merchandise.
But I do not rest my hopes upon this department
of my labours only. I propose also to have a
corresponding shop for Sentiment, and Dialogues,
and Disquisition, which may captivate the fancy
of those who have no relish, as the established

phrase goes, for pure antiquity;—a sort of green-grocer's stall erected in front of my ironmongery wares, garlanding the rusty memorials of ancient times, with cresses, cabbages, leeks, and water purpy.

As I have some idea that I am writing too well to be understood, I humble myself to ordinary language, and aver, with becoming modesty, that I do think myself capable of sustaining a publication of a miscellaneous nature, as like to the *Spectator* or the *Guardian*,* the *Mirror* or the *Lounger*,* as my poor abilities may be able to accomplish. Not that I have any purpose of imitating Johnson, whose general power of learning and expression I do not deny, but many of whose Ramblers* are little better than a sort of pageant, where trite and obvious maxims are made to swagger in lofty and mystic language, and get some credit only because they are not easily understood. There are some of the great moralist's papers which I cannot peruse without thinking on a second-rate masquerade, where the best-known and least esteemed characters in town march in as heroes, and sultans, and so forth, and by dint of tawdry dresses get some consideration until they are found out. It is not, however, prudent to commence with throwing stones just when I am striking out windows of my own.

I think even the local situation of Little Croft-angry may be considered as favourable to my undertaking. A nobler contrast there can hardly exist than that of the huge city, dark with the smoke of ages and groaning with the various sounds of active industry or idle revel, and the lofty and craggy hill, silent and solitary as the grave; one exhibiting the full tide of existence, pressing and precipitating itself forward with the force of an inundation; the other resembling some time-worn anchorite, whose life passes as silent and unobserved as the slender rill which escapes unheard and scarce seen from the fountain of his patron saint. The city resembles the busy temple where the modern Comus* and Mammon*hold their court, and thousands sacrifice ease, independence, and virtue itself, at their shrine; the misty and lonely mountain seems as a throne to the majestic but terrible Genius of feudal times, when the same divinities dispensed coronets and domains to those who had heads to devise, and arms to execute, bold enterprises.

I have, as it were, the two extremities of the moral world at my threshold. From the front door, a few minutes' walk brings me into the heart of a wealthy and populous city; as many paces from my opposite entrance, places me in a solitude as complete as Zimmerman*could have desired. Surely with such aids to my imagination, I may write better than if I were in a lodging in the New Town, or a garret in the old. As the Spaniard says, '*Viamos—Caracco!*'*

I have not chosen to publish periodically, my reason for which was twofold. In the first place, I don't like to be hurried, and have had enough of duns in an early part of my life to make me reluctant to hear of, or see one, even in the less awful shape of a printer's devil. But, secondly, a periodical paper is not easily extended in circulation beyond the quarter in which it is published. This work, if published in fugitive numbers,

would scarce, without a high pressure on the part
of the bookseller, be raised above the Netherbow,*
and never could be expected to ascend to the
level of Prince's Street.* Now, I am ambitious
that my compositions, though having their origin
in this Valley of Holyrood, should not only be
extended into those exalted regions I have mentioned, but also that they should cross the Forth,
astonish the long town of Kirkaldy, enchant the
skippers and colliers of the East of Fife, venture
even into the classic arcades of St. Andrews, and
travel as much farther to the north as the breath
of applause will carry their sails. As for a southward direction, it is not to be hoped for in my
fondest dreams. I am informed that Scottish
literature, like Scottish whisky, will be presently
laid under a prohibitory duty. But enough of
this. If any reader is dull enough not to comprehend the advantages which, in point of circulation, a compact book has over a collection of
fugitive numbers, let him try the range of a gun
loaded with hail-shot, against that of the same
piece charged with an equal weight of lead con-
solidated in a single bullet.

Besides, it was of less consequence that I should
have published periodically, since I did not mean
to solicit or accept of the contributions of friends,
or the criticisms of those who may be less kindly
disposed. Notwithstanding the excellent examples which might be quoted, I will establish
no begging-box, either under the name of a lion's
head or an ass's.* What is good or ill shall be
mine own, or the contribution of friends to whom
I may have private access. Many of my voluntary
assistants might be cleverer than myself, and then

I should have a brilliant article appear among my chiller effusions, like a patch of lace on a Scottish cloak of Galashiels grey. Some might be worse, and then I must reject them, to the injury of the feelings of the writer, or else insert them, to make my own darkness yet more opaque and palpable. 'Let every herring', says our old-fashioned proverb, 'hang by his own head.'*

One person, however, I may distinguish, as she is now no more, who, living to the utmost term of human life, honoured me with a great share of her friendship, as indeed we were blood-relatives in the Scottish sense*—heaven knows how many degrees removed—and friends in the sense of Old England. I mean the late excellent and regretted Mrs. Bethune Baliol.* But as I design this admirable picture of the olden time for a principal character in my work, I will only say here, that she knew and approved of my present purpose; and though she declined to contribute to it while she lived, from a sense of dignified retirement which she thought became her age, sex, and condition in life, she left me some materials for carrying on my proposed work, which I coveted when I heard her detail them in conversation, and which now, when I have their substance in her own handwriting, I account far-more valuable than anything I have myself to offer. I hope the mentioning her name in conjunction with my own will give no offence to any of her numerous friends, as it was her own express pleasure that I should employ the manuscripts, which she did me the honour to bequeath me, in the manner in which I have now used them. It must be added, however, that in most cases I have disguised names, and in some have added shading and colouring to bring out the narrative.

Much of my materials, besides these, are derived from friends, living or dead. The accuracy of some of these may be doubtful, in which case I shall be happy to receive, from sufficient authority, the correction of the errors which must creep into traditional documents. The object of the whole publication is to throw some light on the manners of Scotland as they were, and to contrast them occasionally with those of the present day. My own opinions are in favour of our own times in many respects, but not in so far as affords means for exercising the imagination or exciting the interest which attaches to other times. I am glad to be a writer or a reader in 1826, but I would be most interested in reading or relating what happened from half a century to a century before. We have the best of it. Scenes in which our ancestors thought deeply, acted fiercely, and died desperately, are to us tales to divert the tedium of a winter's evening when we are engaged to no party, or beguile a summer's morning when it is too scorching to ride or walk.

Yet I do not mean that my essays and narratives should be limited to Scotland. I pledge myself to no particular line of subjects; but, on the contrary, say with Burns,

> Perhaps it may turn out a sang,
> Perhaps turn out a sermon.*

I have only to add, by way of postscript to these preliminary chapters, that I have had recourse

to Molière's recipe*, and read my manuscript over
to my old woman, Janet MacEvoy.

The dignity of being consulted delighted
Janet; and Wilkie or Allan* would have made a
capital sketch of her, as she sat upright in her
chair instead of her ordinary lounging posture,
knitting her stocking systematically, as if she
meant every twist of her thread and inclination
of the wires to bear burden to the cadence of my
voice. I am afraid, too, that I myself felt more
delight than I ought to have done in my own
composition, and read a little more oratorically
than I should have ventured to do before an
auditor of whose applause I was not so secure.
And the result did not entirely encourage my
plan of censorship. Janet did indeed seriously
incline to the account of my previous life, and
bestowed some Highland maledictions more
emphatic than courteous on Christie Steele's
reception of a 'shentlemans in distress', and of
her own mistress's house too. I omitted, for
certain reasons, or greatly abridged, what related
to herself. But when I came to treat of my general
views in publication, I saw poor Janet was entirely
thrown out, though, like a jaded hunter, panting,
puffing, and short of wind, she endeavoured at
least to keep up with the chase. Or rather her
perplexity made her look all the while like a deaf
person ashamed of his infirmity, who does not
understand a word you are saying, yet desires
you to believe that he does understand you, and
who is extremely jealous that you suspect his
incapacity. When she saw that some remark was
necessary, she resembled exactly in her criticism
the devotee who pitched on the 'sweet word

Mesopotamia'* as the most edifying note which she could bring away from a sermon. She indeed hastened to bestow general praise on what she said was all 'very fine'; but chiefly dwelt on what I had said about Mr. Timmerman,* as she was pleased to call the German philosopher, and supposed he must be of the same descent with the Highland clan of M'Intyre, which signifies Son of the Carpenter. 'And a fery honourable name too—Shanet's own mither was a M'Intyre.'

In short, it was plain the latter part of my introduction was altogether lost on poor Janet, and so, to have acted up to Molière's system, I should have cancelled the whole and written it anew. But I do not know how it is; I retained, I suppose, some tolerable opinion of my own composition though Janet did not comprehend it, and felt loath to retrench those Delilahs of the imagination, as Dryden calls them,* the tropes and figures of which are caviare to the multitude. Besides, I hate re-writing, as much as Falstaff did paying back*—it is a double labour. So I determined with myself to consult Janet in future only on such things as were within the limits of her comprehension, and hazard my arguments and my rhetoric on the public without her imprimatur. I am pretty sure she will 'applaud it done'.* And in such narratives as come within her range of thought and feeling, I shall, as I first intended, take the benefit of her unsophisticated judgement, and attend to it deferentially—that is, when it happens not to be in peculiar opposition to my own; for, after all, I say, with Almanzor—*

Know that I alone am king of me.

The reader has now my who and my where-about, the purpose of the work, and the circumstances under which it is undertaken. He has also a specimen of the author's talents, and may judge for himself, and proceed or send back the volume to the bookseller as his own taste shall determine.

CHAPTER VI

MR. CROFTANGRY'S ACCOUNT OF
MRS. BETHUNE BALIOL

The moon, were she earthly, no nobler.
*Coriolanus.**

WHEN we set out on the jolly voyage of life, what a brave fleet there is around us, as stretching our fresh canvas to the breeze, all 'shipshape and Bristol fashion', pennons flying, music playing, cheering each other as we pass, we are rather amused than alarmed when some awkward comrade goes right ashore for want of pilotage!—Alas! when the voyage is well spent, and we look about us, toil-worn mariners, how few of our ancient consorts still remain in sight, and they, how torn and wasted, and like ourselves struggling to keep as long as possible off the fatal shore against which we are all finally drifting!

I felt this very trite but melancholy truth in all its force the other day, when a packet with a black seal arrived containing a letter addressed to me by my late excellent friend Mrs. Martha Bethune Baliol, and marked with the fatal indorsation, 'To be delivered according to address, after I shall be no more.' A letter from her executors accompanied the packet, mentioning that they had found in her will a bequest to me of a painting of some value, which she stated would just fit the space above my cupboard, and fifty guineas to buy a ring. And thus I separated, with all the kindness which we had maintained for many years from a friend, who, though old enough to have been the companion of my mother, was yet, in gaiety of spirits and admirable sweetness of temper, capable of being agreeable, and even animating society, for those who write themselves in the vaward of youth; an advantage which I have lost for these five-and-thirty years. The contents of the packet I had no difficulty in guessing, and have partly hinted at them in the last chapter. But to instruct the reader in the particulars, and at the same time to indulge myself with recalling the virtues and agreeable qualities of my late friend, I will give a short sketch of her manners and habits.

Mrs. Martha Bethune Baliol was a person of quality and fortune, as these are esteemed in Scotland. Her family was ancient, and her connexions honourable. She was not fond of specially indicating her exact age, but her juvenile recollections stretched backwards till before the eventful year 1745; and she remembered the Highland clans being in possession of the Scottish capital,* though probably only as an indistinct vision. Her fortune, independent by her father's bequest, was rendered opulent by the death of more than one brave brother, who fell successively in the service of their country; so that the family estates became vested in the only surviving child of the ancient house of Bethune Baliol. My intimacy was formed with the excellent lady after this event, and when she was already something advanced in age.

She inhabited, when in Edinburgh, where she regularly spent the winter season, one of those old hotels which, till of late, were to be found in the neighbourhood of the Canongate, and of the Palace of Holyrood House, and which, separated from the street, now dirty and vulgar, by paved courts and gardens of some extent, made amends for an indifferent access by showing something of aristocratic state and seclusion when you were once admitted within their precincts. They have pulled her house down; for, indeed, betwixt building and burning, every ancient monument of the Scottish capital is now likely to be utterly demolished. I pause on the recollections of the place, however; and since nature has denied a pencil when she placed a pen in my hand, I will endeavour to make words answer the purpose of delineation.

Baliol's Lodging, so was the mansion named, reared its high stack of chimneys, among which were seen a turret or two and one of those small projecting platforms called bartizans, above the mean and modern buildings which line the south side of the Canongate, towards the lower end of that street, and not distant from the Palace. A *porte cochère*, having a wicket for foot passengers, was, upon due occasion, unfolded by a lame old man, tall, grave, and thin, who tenanted a hovel beside the gate and acted as porter. To this office he had been promoted by my friend's charitable feelings for an old soldier, and partly by an idea that his head, which was a very fine one, bore some resemblance to that of Garrick* in the character of Lusignan*. He was a man saturnine, silent, and slow in his proceedings, and would never open the *porte cochère* to a hackney coach; indicating the wicket with his finger, as the proper passage for all who came in that obscure vehicle, which was not permitted to degrade with its ticketed presence the dignity of Baliol's Lodging. I do not think this peculiarity would have met with his lady's approbation, any more than the occasional partiality of Lusignan, or, as mortals called him, Archy Macready, to a dram. But Mrs. Martha Bethune Baliol, conscious that, in case of conviction, she could never have prevailed upon herself to dethrone the King of Palestine* from the stone bench on which he sat for hours knitting his stocking, refused, by accrediting the intelligence, even to put him upon his trial; well judging that he would observe more wholesome caution if he conceived his character unsuspected, than if he were detected and suffered to pass unpunished. For after all, she said, it would be cruel to dismiss an old Highland soldier for a peccadillo so appropriate to his country and profession.

The stately gate for carriages, or the humble accommodation for foot-passengers, admitted into a narrow and short passage, running between two rows of lime-trees, whose green foliage during the spring contrasted strangely with the swart complexion of the two walls by the side of which they grew. This access led to the front of the house, which was formed by two gable ends, notched, and having their windows adorned with

heavy architectural ornaments; they joined each
other at right angles; and a half circular tower,
which contained the entrance and the staircase,
occupied the point of junction, and rounded the
acute angle. One of other two sides of the little
court, in which there was just sufficient room to
turn a carriage, was occupied by some low
buildings answering the purpose of offices; the
other, by a parapet surrounded by a highly-
ornamented iron railing, twined round with
honeysuckle and other parasitical shrubs, which
permitted the eye to peep into a pretty suburban
garden, extending down to the road called the
South Back of the Canongate, and boasting a
number of old trees, many flowers, and even
some fruit. We must not forget to state that the
extreme cleanliness of the courtyard was such as
intimated that mop and pail had done their
utmost in that favoured spot, to atone for the
general dirt and dinginess of the quarter where
the premises were situated.

Over the doorway were the arms of Bethune
and Baliol with various other devices carved in
stone; the door itself was studded with iron nails
and formed of black oak; an iron rasp,* as it was
called, was placed on it instead of a knocker for
the purpose of summoning the attendants. He
who usually appeared at the summons was a
smart lad, in a handsome livery, the son of Mrs.
Martha's gardener at Mount Baliol. Now and
then a servant girl, nicely but plainly dressed
and fully accoutred with stockings and shoes,
would perform this duty; and twice or thrice I
remember being admitted by Beauffet* himself,
whose exterior looked as much like that of a

clergyman of rank as the butler of a gentleman's family. He had been valet-de-chambre to the last Sir Richard Bethune Baliol, and was a person highly trusted by the present lady. A full stand, as it is called in Scotland, of garments of a dark colour, gold buckles in his shoes, and at the knees of his breeches, with his hair regularly dressed and powdered, announced him to be a domestic of trust and importance. His mistress used to say of him,

> He's sad and civil,
> And suits well for a servant with my fortunes.*

As no one can escape scandal, some said that Beauffet made a rather better thing of the place than the modesty of his old-fashioned wages would, unassisted, have amounted to. But the man was always very civil to me. He had been long in the family; had enjoyed legacies, and laid by a something of his own upon which he now enjoys ease with dignity, in as far as his newly-married wife, Tibbie Shortacres, will permit him.

The Lodging—Dearest reader, if you are tired, pray pass over the next four or five pages—was not by any means so large as its external appearance led people to conjecture. The interior accommodation was much cut up by cross walls and long passages, and that neglect of economizing space which characterizes old Scottish architecture. But there was far more room than my old friend required, even when she had, as was often the case, four or five young cousins under her protection; and I believe much of the house was unoccupied. Mrs. Bethune Baliol never, in my presence, showed herself so much offended, as once with a meddling person who advised her to have the windows of these supernumerary apartments built up, to save the tax. She said in ire that, while she lived, the light of God should visit the house of her fathers; and while she had a penny king and country should have their due. Indeed she was punctiliously loyal, even in that most staggering test of loyalty, the payment of imposts. Mr. Beauffet told me he was ordered to offer a glass of wine to the person who collected the income tax, and that the poor man was so overcome by a reception so unwontedly generous that he had wellnigh fainted on the spot.

You entered by a matted ante-room into the eating parlour, filled with old-fashioned furniture, and hung with family portraits which, excepting one of Sir Bernard Bethune, in James the Sixth's time, said to be by Jameson, were exceedingly frightful. A saloon, as it was called, a long narrow chamber, led out of the dining-parlour and served for a drawing-room. It was a pleasant apartment, looking out upon the south flank of Holyrood House, the gigantic slope of Arthur's Seat, and the girdle of lofty rocks called Salisbury Crags;[1] objects so rudely wild, that the mind can hardly conceive them to exist in the vicinage of a populous metropolis. The paintings of the saloon came from abroad, and had some of them much merit. To see the best

[1] The Rev. Mr. Bowles derives the name of these crags, as of the Episcopal city in the west of England, from the same root; both, in his opinion, which he very ably defends and illustrates, having been the sites of druidical temples.

of them, however, you must be admitted into the very penetralia of the temple, and allowed to draw the tapestry at the upper end of the saloon, and enter Mrs. Martha's own special dressing-room. This was a charming apartment, of which it would be difficult to describe the form, it had so many recesses, which were filled up with shelves of ebony, and cabinets of japan and *or molu*; some for holding books, of which Mrs. Martha had an admirable collection, some for a display of ornamental china, others for shells and similar curiosities. In a little niche, half screened by a curtain of crimson silk, was disposed a suit of tilting armour of bright steel, inlaid with silver, which had been worn on some memorable occasion by Sir Bernard Bethune, already mentioned; while over the canopy of the niche hung the broadsword with which her father had attempted to change the fortunes of Britain in 1715, and the spontoon which her elder brother bore when he was leading on a company of the Black Watch[1] at Fontenoy.

There were some Italian and Flemish pictures of admitted authenticity, a few genuine bronzes and other objects of curiosity which her brothers or herself had picked up while abroad. In short, it was a place where the idle were tempted to become studious, the studious to grow idle—where the grave might find matter to make them gay, and the gay subjects for gravity.

[1] The well-known original designation of the gallant 42nd Regiment. Being the first corps raised for the royal service in the Highlands, and allowed to retain their national garb, they were thus named from the contrast which their dark tartans furnished to the scarlet and white of the other regiments.

That it might maintain some title to its name, I must not forget to say that the lady's dressing-room exhibited a superb mirror, framed in silver filigree work; a beautiful toilet, the cover of which was of Flanders lace; and a set of boxes corresponding in materials and work to the frame of the mirror.

This dressing apparatus, however, was mere matter of parade: Mrs. Martha Bethune Baliol always went through the actual duties of the toilet in an inner apartment which corresponded with her sleeping-room by a small detached staircase. There were, I believe, more than one of those *turnpike stairs*, as they were called, about the house, by which the public rooms, all of which entered through each other, were accommodated with separate and independent modes of access. In the little boudoir we have described Mrs. Martha Baliol had her choicest meetings. She kept early hours; and if you went in the morning, you must not reckon that space of day as extending beyond three o'clock, or four at the utmost. These vigilant habits were attended with some restraint on her visitors, but they were indemnified by your always finding the best society, and the best information, which was to be had for the day in the Scottish capital. Without at all affecting the blue stocking, she liked books—they amused her—and if the authors were persons of character, she thought she owed them a debt of civility which she loved to discharge by personal kindness. When she gave a dinner to a small party, which she did now and then, she had the good nature to look for, and the good luck to discover, what sort of people

suited each other best, and chose her company
as Duke Theseus did his hounds,

> ——matched in mouth like bells,
> Each under each,[1]

so that every guest could take his part in the cry;
instead of one mighty Tom of a fellow, like Dr.
Johnson, silencing all besides by the tremendous
depth of his diapason. On such occasions she
afforded *chère exquise*; and every now and then
there was some dish of French, or even Scottish
derivation, which, as well as the numerous assort-
ment of *vins extraordinaires* produced by Mr.
Beauffet, gave a sort of antique and foreign air
to the entertainment, which rendered it more
interesting.

It was a great thing to be asked to such parties;
and not less so to be invited to the early con-
versazione, which, in spite of fashion, by dint of
the best coffee, the finest tea, and *chasse café* that
would have called the dead to life, she contrived
now and then to assemble in her saloon already
mentioned, at the unnatural hour of eight in the
evening. At such times, the cheerful old lady
seemed to enjoy herself so much in the happiness
of her guests that they exerted themselves, in
turn, to prolong her amusement and their own;
and a certain charm was excited around, seldom
to be met with in parties of pleasure, and which
was founded on the general desire of every one
present to contribute something to the common
amusement.

But although it was a great privilege to be
admitted to wait on my excellent friend in the

[1] Shakespeare's *Midsummer Night's Dream*, Act IV, sc. i.

morning, or be invited to her dinner or evening parties, I prized still higher the right which I had acquired, by old acquaintance, of visiting Baliol's Lodging upon the chance of finding its venerable inhabitant preparing for tea, just about six o'clock in the evening. It was only to two or three old friends that she permitted this freedom, nor was this sort of chance-party ever allowed to extend itself beyond five in number. The answer to those who came later announced that the company was filled up for the evening; which had the double effect of making those who waited on Mrs. Bethune Baliol in this unceremonious manner punctual in observing her hour, and of adding the zest of a little difficulty to the enjoyment of the party.

It more frequently happened that only one or two persons partook of this refreshment on the same evening; or, supposing the case of a single gentleman, Mrs. Martha, though she did not hesitate to admit him to her boudoir after the privilege of the French and the old Scottish school, took care, as she used to say, to preserve all possible propriety by commanding the attendance of her principal female attendant, Mrs. Alice Lambskin, who might, from the gravity and dignity of her appearance, have sufficed to matronize a whole boarding school, instead of one maiden lady of eighty and upwards. As the weather permitted, Mrs. Alice sat duly remote from the company in a fauteuil behind the projecting chimney-piece or in the embrazure of a window, and prosecuted in Carthusian silence, with indefatigable zeal, a piece of embroidery which seemed no bad emblem of eternity.

But I have neglected all this while to introduce my friend herself to the reader, at least so far as words can convey the peculiarities by which her appearance and conversation were distinguished.

A little woman, with ordinary features and an ordinary form, and hair which in youth had no decided colour, we may believe Mrs. Martha when she said of herself that she was never remarkable for personal charms; a modest admission which was readily confirmed by certain old ladies, her contemporaries, who, whatever might have been the youthful advantages which they more than hinted had been formerly their own share, were now, in personal appearance, as well as in everything else, far inferior to my accomplished friend. Mrs. Martha's features had been of a kind which might be said to wear well; their irregularity was now of little consequence, animated as they were by the vivacity of her conversation; her teeth were excellent, and her eyes, although inclining to grey, were lively, laughing, and undimmed by time. A slight shade of complexion, more brilliant than her years promised, subjected my friend amongst strangers to the suspicion of having stretched her foreign habits as far as the prudent touch of the rouge. But it was a calumny; for when telling or listening to an interesting and affecting story, I have seen her colour come and go as if it played on the cheek of eighteen.

Her hair, whatever its former deficiencies, was now the most beautiful white that time could bleach, and was disposed with some degree of pretension, though in the simplest manner possible, so as to appear neatly smoothed under a cap of Flanders lace, of an old-fashioned, but, as I thought, of a very handsome form which undoubtedly has a name, and I would endeavour to recur to it, if I thought it would make my description a bit more intelligible. I think I have heard her say these favourite caps had been her mother's, and had come in fashion with a peculiar kind of wig used by the gentlemen about the time of the battle of Ramillies* The rest of her dress was always rather costly and distinguished, especially in the evening. A silk or satin gown of some colour becoming her age, and of a form which, though complying to a certain degree with the present fashion, had always a reference to some more distant period, was garnished with triple ruffles; her shoes had diamond buckles, and were raised a little at heel, an advantage which, possessed in her youth, she alleged her size would not permit her to forgo in her old age. She always wore rings, bracelets, and other ornaments of value either for the materials or the workmanship; nay, perhaps she was a little profuse in this species of display. But she wore them as subordinate matters, to which the habits of being constantly in high life rendered her indifferent. She wore them because her rank required it; and thought no more of them as articles of finery, than a gentleman dressed for dinner thinks of his clean linen and well-brushed coat, the consciousness of which embarrasses the rustic beau on a Sunday.

Now and then, however, if a gem or ornament chanced to be noticed for its beauty or singularity, the observation usually led the way to an entertaining account of the manner in which it had been acquired, or the person from whom it had descended to its present possessor. On such and similar occasions my old friend spoke willingly, which is not uncommon; but she also, which is more rare, spoke remarkably well, and had in her little narratives concerning foreign parts or former days, which formed an interesting part of her conversation, the singular art of dismissing all the usual protracted tautology respecting time, place, and circumstances, which is apt to settle like a mist upon the cold and languid tales of age, and at the same time of bringing forward, dwelling upon, and illustrating, those incidents and characters which give point and interest to the story.

She had, as we have hinted, travelled a good deal in foreign countries: for a brother, to whom she was much attached, had been sent upon various missions of national importance to the Continent, and she had more than once embraced the opportunity of accompanying him. This furnished a great addition to the information which she could supply, especially during the last war when the Continent was for so many years hermetically sealed against the English nation. But, besides, Mrs. Bethune Baliol visited distant countries, not in the modern fashion, when English travel in caravans together and see in France and Italy little besides the same society which they might have enjoyed at home. On the contrary she mingled, when abroad, with the natives of those countries she visited, and enjoyed at once the advantage of their society and the pleasure of comparing it with that of Britain.

In the course of her becoming habituated with

foreign manners, Mrs. Bethune Baliol had, perhaps, acquired some slight tincture of them herself. Yet I was always persuaded that the peculiar
vivacity of look and manner, the pointed and
appropriate action with which she accompanied
what she said, the use of the gold and gemmed
tabatière, or rather I should say *bonbonnière* (for she
took no snuff, and the little box contained only
a few pieces of candied angelica, or some such
lady-like sweetmeat), were of real old-fashioned
Scottish growth, and such as might have graced
the tea-table of Susannah, Countess of Eglinton,*
the patroness of Allan Ramsay,* or of the Hon.
Mrs. Colonel Ogilvy,* who was another mirror by
whom the maidens of Auld Reekie were required
to dress themselves. Although well acquainted
with the customs of other countries, her manners
had been chiefly formed in her own, at a time
when great folk lived within little space and
when the distinguished names of the highest
society gave to Edinburgh the éclat which we
now endeavour to derive from the unbounded
expense and extended circle of our pleasures.

I was more confirmed in this opinion by the
peculiarity of the dialect which Mrs. Baliol used.
It was Scottish, decidedly Scottish, often containing phrases and words little used in the
present day. But then her tone and mode of
pronunciation were as different from the usual
accent of the ordinary Scotch patois, as the accent
of St. James's is from that of Billingsgate.* The
vowels were not pronounced much broader than
in the Italian language, and there was none of
the disagreeable drawl which is so offensive to
southern ears. In short, it seemed to be the

Scottish as spoken by the ancient court of Scotland, to which no idea of vulgarity could be attached; and the lively manner and gestures with which it was accompanied were so completely in accord with the sound of the voice and the style of talking that I cannot assign them a different origin. In long derivation, perhaps, the manner of the Scottish court might have been originally formed on that of France, to which it had certainly some affinity; but I will live and die in the belief that those of Mrs. Baliol, as pleasing as they were peculiar, came to her by direct descent from the high dames who anciently adorned with their presence the royal halls of Holyrood.

CHAPTER VII

MRS. BALIOL ASSISTS MR. CROFTANGRY IN HIS LITERARY SPECULATIONS

SUCH as I have described Mrs. Bethune Baliol, the reader will easily believe that when I thought of the miscellaneous nature of my work, I rested upon the information she possessed and her communicative disposition as one of the principal supports of my enterprise. Indeed, she by no means disapproved of my proposed publication, though expressing herself very doubtful how far she could personally assist it—a doubt which might be perhaps set down to a little lady-like coquetry, which required to be sued for the boon she was not unwilling to grant. Or, perhaps, the good old lady, conscious that her unusual term of years must soon draw to a close, preferred bequeathing the materials in the shape of a legacy to subjecting them to the judgement of a critical public during her lifetime.

Many a time I used, in our conversations of the Canongate, to resume my request of assistance, from a sense that my friend was the most valuable depositary of Scottish traditions that was probably now to be found. This was a subject on which my mind was so much made up, that when I heard her carry her description of manners so far back beyond her own time, and describe how Fletcher of Salton* spoke, how Graham of Claverhouse* danced, what were the jewels worn by the famous Duchess of Lauderdale,* and how she came by them, I could not help telling her I thought her some fairy, who cheated us by retaining the appearance of a mortal of our own day, when, in fact, she had witnessed the revolutions of centuries. She was much diverted when I required her to take some solemn oath that she had not danced at the balls given by Mary of Este, when her unhappy husband[1] occupied Holyrood in a species of honourable banishment;—or asked, whether she could not recollect Charles the Second when he came to Scotland in 1650, and did not possess some slight recollections of the bold usurper who drove him beyond the Forth.

'*Beau cousin*,' she said laughing, 'none of these do I remember personally; but you must know there has been wonderfully little change on my natural temper from youth to age. From which it follows, cousin, that being even now something

[1] The Duke of York, afterwards James II, frequently resided in Holyrood House, when his religion rendered him an object of suspicion to the English Parliament.

too young in spirit for the years which Time has
marked me in his calendar, I was, when a girl,
a little too old for those of my own standing, and
as much inclined at that period to keep the
society of elder persons, as I am now disposed to
admit the company of gay young fellows of fifty
or sixty like yourself, rather than collect about
me all the octogenarians. Now, although I do
not actually come from Elfland,* and therefore
cannot boast any personal knowledge of the
great personages you inquire about, yet I have
seen and heard those who knew them well, and
who have given me as distinct an account of
them as I could give you myself of the Empress
Queen, or Frederick of Prussia;*and I will frankly
add,' said she, laughing and offering her *bonbonnière*, 'that *I have* heard so much of the years
which immediately succeeded the Revolution,
that I sometimes am apt to confuse the vivid
descriptions fixed on my memory by the frequent
and animated recitation of others for things
which I myself have actually witnessed. I caught
myself but yesterday describing to Lord M——
the riding of the last Scottish Parliament,* with
as much minuteness as if I had seen it, as my
mother did, from the balcony in front of Lord
Moray's Lodging in the Canongate.'*

'I am sure you must have given Lord M——
a high treat.'

'I treated him to a hearty laugh, I believe,'
she replied; 'but it is you, you vile seducer of
youth, who lead me into such follies. But I will
be on my guard against my own weakness. I do
not well know if the Wandering Jew*is supposed
to have a wife, but I should be sorry a decent

middle-aged Scottish gentlewoman should be suspected of identity with such a supernatural person.'

'For all that, I must torture you a little more, *ma belle cousine*, with my interrogatories; for how shall I ever turn author unless on the strength of the information which you have so often procured me on the ancient state of manners?'

'Stay, I cannot allow you to give your points of inquiry a name so very venerable, if I am expected to answer them. Ancient is a term for antediluvians. You may catechise me about the battle of Flodden,* or ask particulars about Bruce and Wallace,* under pretext of curiosity after ancient manners; and that last subject would wake my Baliol blood,* you know.'

'Well, but, Mrs. Baliol, suppose we settle our era:—you do not call the accession of James the Sixth* to the kingdom of Britain very ancient?'

'Umph! no, cousin—I think I could tell you more of that than folk now-a-days remember,—for instance, that as James was trooping towards England, bag and baggage, his journey was stopped near Cockenzie by meeting the funeral of the Earl of Winton, the old and faithful servant and follower of his ill-fated mother, poor Mary! It was an ill omen for the *infare*, and so was seen of it, cousin.'*

I did not choose to prosecute this subject, well knowing Mrs. Bethune Baliol did not like to be much pressed on the subject of the Stuarts, whose misfortunes she pitied the rather that her father had espoused their cause. And yet her attachment to the present dynasty being very sincere, and even ardent, more especially as her family had served his late Majesty both in peace and war, she experienced a little embarrassment in reconciling her opinions respecting the exiled family with those she entertained for the present. In fact, like many an old Jacobite,* she was contented to be somewhat inconsistent on the subject, comforting herself that *now* everything stood as it ought to do, and that there was no use in looking back narrowly on the right or wrong of the matter half a century ago.

'The Highlands', I suggested, 'should furnish you with ample subjects of recollection. You have witnessed the complete change of that primaeval country, and have seen a race not far removed from the earliest period of society melted down into the great mass of civilization; and that could not happen without incidents striking in themselves, and curious as chapters in the history of the human race.'

'It is very true,' said Mrs. Baliol; 'one would think it should have struck the observers greatly, and yet it scarcely did so. For me, I was no Highlander myself, and the Highland chiefs of old, of whom I certainly knew several, had little in their manners to distinguish them from the Lowland gentry when they mixed in society in Edinburgh and assumed the Lowland dress. Their peculiar character was for the clansmen at home; and you must not imagine that they swaggered about in plaids and broad-swords at the Cross,* or came to the Assembly Rooms* in bonnets and kilts.'

'I remember', said I, 'that Swift, in his journal, tells Stella he had dined in the house of a Scots nobleman, with two Highland chiefs, whom he had found as well bred men as he had ever met with.'[1]

'Very likely,' said my friend. 'The extremes of society approach much more closely to each other than perhaps the Dean of Saint Patrick's* expected. The savage is always to a certain degree polite. Besides, going always armed, and having a very punctilious idea of their own gentility and consequence, they usually behaved to each other and to the Lowlanders with a good deal of formal politeness, which sometimes even procured them the character of insincerity.'

'Falsehood belongs to an early period of society, as well as the deferential forms which we style politeness,' I replied. 'A child does not see the least moral beauty in truth, until he has been flogged half a dozen times. It is so easy, and apparently so natural, to deny what you cannot be easily convicted of, that a savage as well as a child lies to excuse himself almost as instinctively as he raises his hand to protect his head. The old saying, "confess and be hanged", carries much argument in it. I observed a remark the other day in old Birrel.* He mentions that M'Gregor of Glenstrae and some of his people had surrendered themselves to one of the Earls of Argyle, upon the express condition that they should be conveyed safe into England. The Maccallan Mhor*of the day kept the word of promise, but it was only to the ear. He indeed sent his captives to Berwick,* where they had an airing on the

---

[1] Extract of *Journal to Stella.*—'I dined to-day (March 12, 1712) with Lord Treasurer and two gentlemen of the Highlands of Scotland, yet very polite men.'—Swift's *Works*, vol. iii, p. 7, Edin. 1824.

other side of the Tweed, but it was under the custody of a strong guard, by whom they were brought back to Edinburgh and delivered to the executioner. This Birrel calls keeping a Highlandman's promise.'*

'Well,' replied Mrs. Baliol, 'I might add that many of the Highland chiefs whom I knew in former days had been brought up in France, which might improve their politeness, though perhaps it did not amend their sincerity. But considering that, belonging to the depressed and defeated faction in the state, they were compelled sometimes to use dissimulation, you must set their uniform fidelity to their friends against their occasional falsehood to their enemies, and then you will not judge poor John Highlandman too severely. They were in a state of society where bright lights are strongly contrasted with deep shadows.'

'It is to that point I would bring you, *ma belle cousine*,—and therefore they are most proper subjects for composition.'

'And you want to turn composer, my good friend, and set my old tales to some popular tune? But there have been too many composers, if that be the word, in the field before. The Highlands *were* indeed a rich mine; but they have, I think, been fairly wrought out, as a good tune is grinded into vulgarity when it descends to the hurdy-gurdy and the barrel-organ.'

'If it be really tune,' I replied, 'it will recover its better qualities when it gets into the hands of better artists.'

'Umph!' said Mrs. Baliol, tapping her box, 'we are happy in our own good opinion this evening, Mr. Croftangry. And so you think you can restore the gloss to the tartan, which it has lost by being dragged through so many fingers?'

'With your assistance to procure materials, my dear lady, much, I think, may be done.'

'Well—I must do my best, I suppose; though all I know about the Gael is but of little consequence—indeed, I gathered it chiefly from Donald MacLeish.'

'And who might Donald MacLeish be?'

'Neither bard nor sennachie, I assure you; nor monk, nor hermit, the approved authorities for old traditions. Donald was as good a postilion as ever drove a chaise and pair between Glencroe and Inverary. I assure you, when I give you my Highland anecdotes, you will hear much of Donald MacLeish. He was Alice Lambskin's beau and mine through a long Highland tour.'

'But when am I to possess these anecdotes?— You answer me as Harley did poor Prior—

Let that be done which Mat doth say.
"Yea," quoth the Earl, "but not to-day".'

'Well, *mon beau cousin*, if you begin to remind me of my cruelty, I must remind you it has struck nine on the abbey clock, and it is time you were going home to Little Croftangry.—For my promise to assist your antiquarian researches, be assured, I will one day keep it to the utmost extent. It shall not be a Highlandman's promise, as your old citizen calls it.'

I by this time suspected the purpose of my friend's procrastination; and it saddened my heart to reflect that I was not to get the information which I desired, excepting in the shape of a legacy. I found accordingly, in the packet transmitted to me after the excellent lady's death, several anecdotes respecting the Highlands, from which I have selected that which follows chiefly on account of its possessing great power over the feelings of my critical housekeeper, Janet MacEvoy, who wept most bitterly when I read it to her.

It is, however, but a very simple tale, and may have no interest for persons beyond Janet's rank of life or understanding.

THE HIGHLAND WIDOW*

CHAPTER I

It wound as near as near could be,
But what it is she cannot tell;
On the other side it seem'd to be,
Of the huge broad-breasted old oak tree.

COLERIDGE*

MRS. BETHUNE BALIOL'S memorandum begins thus:—

It is five and thirty, or perhaps nearer forty years ago, since, to relieve the dejection of spirits occasioned by a great family loss sustained two or three months before, I undertook what was called the short Highland tour. This had become in some degree fashionable; but though the military roads* were excellent, yet the accommodation was so indifferent that it was reckoned a little adventure to accomplish it. Besides, the Highlands, though now as peaceable as any part of King George's dominions, was a sound which still carried terror while so many survived who had witnessed the insurrection of 1745; and a vague idea of fear was impressed on many, as they looked from the towers of Stirling northward to the huge chain of mountains which rises like a dusky rampart to conceal in its recesses a people, whose dress, manners, and language differed still very much from those of their Lowland countrymen. For my part, I come of a race not greatly subject to apprehensions arising from imagination only. I had some Highland relatives, knew several of their families of distinction; and, though only having the company of my bower-maiden, Mrs. Alice Lambskin, I went on my journey fearless.

But then I had a guide and cicerone, almost equal to Greatheart* in the *Pilgrim's Progress*, in no less a person than Donald MacLeish, the postilion whom I hired at Stirling, with a pair of able-bodied horses as steady as Donald himself, to drag my carriage, my duenna, and myself, wheresoever it was my pleasure to go.

Donald MacLeish was one of a race of post-boys whom, I suppose, mail-coaches and steamboats have put out of fashion. They were to be found chiefly at Perth, Stirling, or Glasgow, where they and their horses were usually hired by travellers, or tourists, to accomplish such journeys of business or pleasure as they might have to perform in the land of the Gael. This class of persons approached to the character of what is called abroad a *conducteur*; or might be compared to the sailing-master on board a British ship of war, who follows out after his own manner the course which the captain commands him to observe. You explained to your postilion the length of your tour and the objects you were desirous it should embrace; and you found him perfectly competent to fix the places of rest or refreshment, with due attention that those should be chosen with reference to your convenience and to any points of interest which you might desire to visit.

The qualifications of such a person were necessarily much superior to those of the 'first ready', who gallops thrice a day over the same ten miles. Donald MacLeish, besides being quite alert at repairing all ordinary accidents to his horses and carriage, and in making shift to support them where forage was scarce with such substitutes as bannocks and cakes, was likewise a man of intellectual resources. He had acquired a general knowledge of the traditional stories of the country which he had traversed so often; and, if encouraged (for Donald was a man of the most decorous reserve), he would willingly point out to you the site of the principal clan-battles, and recount the most remarkable legends by which the road and the objects which occurred in travelling it had been distinguished. There was some originality in the man's habits of thinking and expressing himself, his turn for legendary lore strangely contrasting with a portion of the knowing shrewdness belonging to his actual occupation, which made his conversation amuse the way well enough.

Add to this, Donald knew all his peculiar duties in the country which he traversed so frequently. He could tell, to a day, when they would 'be killing' lamb*at Tyndrum or Glenuilt; so that the stranger would have some chance of being fed like a Christian; and knew to a mile the last village where it was possible to procure a wheaten loaf, for the guidance of those who were little familiar with the Land of Cakes.* He was acquainted with the road every mile, and could tell to an inch which side of a Highland bridge was passable, which decidedly dangerous.[1] In short, Donald MacLeish was not only our faithful attendant and steady servant, but our

---

[1] This is, or was at least, a necessary accomplishment. In one of the most beautiful districts of the Highlands was, not many years since, a bridge bearing this startling caution, 'Keep to the right side, the left being dangerous.'

humble and obliging friend; and though I
have known the half-classical cicerone of Italy,
the talkative French *valet-de-place*, and even the
muleteer of Spain, who piques himself on being
a maize-eater, and whose honour is not to be
questioned without danger, I do not think I have
ever had so sensible and intelligent a guide.

Our motions were of course under Donald's
direction; and it frequently happened, when the
weather was serene, that we preferred halting to
rest his horses even where there was no established stage, and taking our refreshment under
a crag, from which leaped a waterfall, or beside
the verge of a fountain enamelled with verdant
turf and wild flowers. Donald had an eye for
such spots, and though he had, I dare say, never
read *Gil Blas* or *Don Quixote*, yet he chose such
halting-places as Le Sage or Cervantes would
have described. Very often, as he observed the
pleasure I took in conversing with the country
people, he would manage to fix our place of rest
near a cottage where there was some old Gael,
whose broadsword had blazed at Falkirk or
Preston* and who seemed the frail yet faithful
record of times which had passed away. Or he
would contrive to quarter us, as far as a cup of
tea went, upon the hospitality of some parish
minister of worth and intelligence, or some
country family of the better class, who mingled
with the wild simplicity of their original manners
and their ready and hospitable welcome, a sort
of courtesy belonging to a people the lowest of
whom are accustomed to consider themselves as
being, according to the Spanish phrase, 'as good
gentlemen as the king, only not quite so rich.'

To all such persons Donald MacLeish was well known, and his introduction passed as current as if we had brought letters from some high chief of the country.

Sometimes it happened that the Highland hospitality which welcomed us with all the variety of mountain fare, preparations of milk and eggs, and girdle-cakes of various kinds, as well as more substantial dainties, according to the inhabitant's means of regaling the passenger, descended rather too exuberantly on Donald MacLeish in the shape of mountain dew. Poor Donald! he was on such occasions like Gideon's fleece* moist with the noble element, which, of course, fell not on us. But it was his only fault, and when pressed to drink *doch-an-dorroch* to my ladyship's good health, it would have been ill taken to have refused the pledge, nor was he willing to do such discourtesy. It was, I repeat, his only fault, nor had we any great right to complain; for if it rendered him a little more talkative, it augmented his ordinary share of punctilious civility, and he only drove slower, and talked longer and more pompously than when he had not come by a drop of usquebaugh. It was, we remarked, only on such occasions that Donald talked with an air of importance of the family of MacLeish; and we had no title to be scrupulous in censuring a foible, the consequences of which were confined within such innocent limits.

We became so much accustomed to Donald's mode of managing us, that we observed with some interest the art which he used to produce a little agreeable surprise, by concealing from us the spot where he proposed our halt to be made when it was of an unusual and interesting character. This was so much his wont that when he made apologies at setting off for being obliged to stop in some strange solitary place till the horses should eat the corn which he brought on with them for that purpose, our imagination used to be on the stretch to guess what romantic retreat he had secretly fixed upon for our noontide baiting-place.

We had spent the greater part of the morning at the delightful village of Dalmally, and had gone upon the lake under the guidance of the excellent clergyman who was then incumbent at Glenorquhy,[1] and had heard an hundred legends of the stern chiefs of Loch Awe, Duncan with the thrum bonnet, and the other lords of the now mouldering towers of Kilchurn.* Thus it was later than usual when we set out on our journey, after a hint or two from Donald concerning the length of the way to the next stage, as there was no good halting-place between Dalmally and Oban.

Having bid adieu to our venerable and kind cicerone, we proceeded on our tour, winding round the tremendous mountain called Cruachan Ben, which rushes down in all its majesty of rocks and wilderness on the lake, leaving only a pass, in which, notwithstanding its extreme strength, the warlike clan of MacDougal of Lorn were almost destroyed by the sagacious Robert Bruce. That king, the Wellington* of his day, had accomplished, by a forced march, the unexpected manœuvre of forcing a body of troops round the

[1] This venerable and hospitable gentleman's name was MacIntyre.

other side of the mountain, and thus placed them in the flank and in the rear of the men of Lorn, whom at the same time he attacked in front. The great number of cairns yet visible as you descend the pass on the westward side, shows the extent of the vengeance which Bruce exhausted on his inveterate and personal enemies. I am, you know, the sister of soldiers, and it has since struck me forcibly that the manœuvre which Donald described resembled those of Wellington or of Bonaparte. He was a great man Robert Bruce, even a Baliol*must admit that; although it begins now to be allowed that his title to the crown was scarce so good as that of the unfortunate family with whom he contended—But let that pass.—The slaughter had been the greater, as the deep and rapid river Awe is disgorged from the lake, just in the rear of the fugitives, and encircles the base of the tremendous mountain; so that the retreat of the unfortunate flyers was intercepted on all sides by the inaccessible character of the country, which had seemed to promise them defence and protection.

Musing, like the Irish lady in the song, 'upon things which are long enough a-gone,'[1] we felt no impatience at the slow and almost creeping pace with which our conductor proceeded along General Wade's military road, which never or rarely condescends to turn aside from the steepest ascent, but proceeds right up and down hill, with the indifference to height and hollow, steep or level, indicated by the old Roman engineers.

[1] This is a line from a very pathetic ballad which I heard sung by one of the young ladies of Edgeworthstown in 1825. I do not know that it has been printed.

Still, however, the substantial excellence of these great works—for such are the military highways in the Highlands—deserved the compliment of the poet, who, whether he came from our sister kingdom and spoke in his own dialect, or whether he supposed those whom he addressed might have some national pretension to the second sight, produced the celebrated couplet—

Had you but seen these roads *before* they were made,
You would hold up your hands, and bless General Wade.*

Nothing indeed can be more wonderful than to see these wildernesses penetrated and pervious in every quarter by broad accesses of the best possible construction, and so superior to what the country could have demanded for many centuries for any pacific purpose of commercial intercourse. Thus the traces of war are sometimes happily accommodated to the purposes of peace. The victories of Bonaparte have been without results; but his road over the Simplon* will long be the communication betwixt peaceful countries, who will apply to the ends of commerce and friendly intercourse that gigantic work which was formed for the ambitious purpose of warlike invasion.

While we were thus stealing along, we gradually turned round the shoulder of Ben Cruachan, and, descending the course of the foaming and rapid Awe, left behind us the expanse of the majestic lake which gives birth to that impetuous river. The rocks and precipices which stooped down perpendicularly on our path on the right hand exhibited a few remains of the wood which once clothed them, but which had in latter times been felled to supply, Donald MacLeish informed us, the iron-foundries at the Bunawe. This made us fix our eyes with interest on one large oak which grew on the left hand towards the river. It seemed a tree of extraordinary magnitude and picturesque beauty, and stood just where there appeared to be a few roods of open ground lying among huge stones, which had rolled down from the mountain. To add to the romance of the situation, the spot of clear ground extended round the foot of a proud-browed rock, from the summit of which leaped a mountain stream in a fall of sixty feet, in which it was dissolved into foam and dew. At the bottom of the fall the rivulet with difficulty collected, like a routed general, its dispersed forces, and, as if tamed by its descent, found a noiseless passage through the heath to join the Awe.

I was much struck with the tree and waterfall, and wished myself nearer them; not that I thought of sketch-book or portfolio—for in my younger days misses were not accustomed to black-lead pencils unless they could use them to some good purpose—but merely to indulge myself with a closer view. Donald immediately opened the chaise door, but observed it was rough walking down the brae, and that I would see the tree better by keeping the road for a hundred yards farther, when it passed closer to the spot, for which he seemed, however, to have no predilection. 'He knew', he said, 'a far bigger tree than that nearer Bunawe, and it was a place where there was flat ground for the carriage to stand, which it could jimply do on these braes;—but just as my leddyship liked.'

My ladyship did choose rather to look at the fine tree before me, than to pass it by in hopes of a finer; so we walked beside the carriage till we should come to a point from which, Donald assured us, we might without scrambling go as near the tree as we chose, 'though he wadna advise us to go nearer than the highroad.'

There was something grave and mysterious in Donald's sun-browned countenance when he gave us this intimation, and his manner was so different from his usual frankness that my female curiosity was set in motion. We walked on the whilst, and I found the tree, of which we had now lost sight by the intervention of some rising ground, was really more distant than I had at first supposed. 'I could have sworn now,' said I to my cicerone, 'that yon tree and waterfall was the very place where you intended to make a stop to-day.'

'The Lord forbid!' said Donald, hastily.

'And for what, Donald? why should you be willing to pass so pleasant a spot?'

'It's ower near Dalmally, my leddy, to corn the beasts—it would bring their dinner ower near their breakfast, poor things:—an', besides, the place is not canny.'

'Oh! then the mystery is out. There is a bogle or a brownie, a witch or a gyrecarlin, a bodach or a fairy, in the case?'

'The ne'er a bit, my leddy—ye are clean aff the road, as I may say. But if your leddyship will just hae patience, and wait till we are by the place and out of the glen, I'll tell ye all about it. There is no much luck in speaking of such things in the place they chanced in.'

I was obliged to suspend my curiosity, observing that if I persisted in twisting the discourse one way while Donald was twining it another, I should make his objection, like a hempen-cord, just so much the tougher. At length the promised turn of the road brought us within fifty paces of the tree which I desired to admire, and I now saw to my surprise that there was a human habitation among the cliffs which surrounded it. It was a hut of the least dimensions, and most miserable description that I ever saw even in the Highlands. The walls of sod, or *divot* as the Scotch call it, were not four feet high—the roof was of turf, repaired with reeds and sedges—the chimney was composed of clay, bound round by straw ropes—and the whole walls, roof, and chimney were alike covered with the vegetation of house-leek, rye-grass, and moss, common to decayed cottages formed of such materials. There was not the slightest vestige of a kale-yard, the usual accompaniment of the very worst huts; and of living things we saw nothing, save a kid which was browsing on the roof of the hut, and a goat, its mother, at some distance, feeding betwixt the oak and the river Awe.

'What man', I could not help exclaiming, 'can have committed sin deep enough to deserve such a miserable dwelling!'

'Sin enough,' said Donald MacLeish, with a half-suppressed groan; 'and God He knoweth, misery enough too;—and it is no man's dwelling neither, but a woman's.'

'A woman's!' I repeated, 'and in so lonely a place. What sort of a woman can she be?'

'Come this way, my leddy, and you may judge

'that for yourself,' said Donald. And by advancing a few steps, and making a sharp turn to the left, we gained a sight of the side of the great broad-breasted oak, in the direction opposed to that in which we had hitherto seen it.

'If she keeps her old wont, she will be there at this hour of the day,' said Donald; but immediately became silent, and pointed with his finger as one afraid of being overheard. I looked and beheld, not without some sense of awe, a female form seated by the stem of the oak, with her head drooping, her hands clasped, and a dark-coloured mantle drawn over her head, exactly as Judah is represented in the Syrian medals as seated under her palm-tree. I was infected with the fear and reverence which my guide seemed to entertain towards this solitary being, nor did I think of advancing towards her to obtain a nearer view until I had cast an inquiring look on Donald; to which he replied in a half whisper—'She has been a fearfu' bad woman, my leddy.'

'Mad woman, said you,' replied I, hearing him imperfectly; 'then she is perhaps dangerous?'

'No—she is not mad,' replied Donald; 'for then it may be she would be happier than she is; though when she thinks on what she has done, and caused to be done, rather than yield up a hair-breadth of her ain wicked will, it is not likely she can be very well settled. But she neither is mad nor mischievous; and yet, my leddy, I think you had best not go nearer to her.' And then, in a few hurried words, he made me acquainted with the story which I am now to tell more in detail. I heard the narrative with a mixture of horror and sympathy, which at once impelled me to approach the sufferer and speak to her the words of comfort, or rather of pity, and at the same time made me afraid to do so.

This indeed was the feeling with which she was regarded by the Highlanders in the neighbour-hood, who looked upon Elspat MacTavish, or the Woman of the Tree as they called her, as the Greeks considered those who were pursued by the Furies*and endured the mental torment consequent on great criminal actions. They regarded such unhappy beings as Orestes and Œdipus* as being less the voluntary perpetrators of their crimes, than as the passive instruments by which the terrible decrees of Destiny had been accomplished; and the fear with which they beheld them was not unmingled with veneration.

I also learned farther from Donald MacLeish, that there was some apprehension of ill luck attending those who had the boldness to approach too near, or disturb the awful solitude of a being so unutterably miserable; that it was supposed that whosoever approached her must experience in some respect the contagion of her wretchedness.

It was therefore with some reluctance that Donald saw me prepare to obtain a nearer view of the sufferer, and that he himself followed to assist me in the descent down a very rough path. I believe his regard for me conquered some ominous feelings in his own breast, which connected his duty on this occasion with the presaging fear of lame horses, lost linch-pins, overturns, and other perilous chances of the postilion's life.

I am not sure if my own courage would have carried me so close to Elspat, had he not followed.

There was in her countenance the stern abstraction of hopeless and overpowering sorrow, mixed with the contending feelings of remorse, and of the pride which struggled to conceal it. She guessed, perhaps, that it was curiosity, arising out of her uncommon story, which induced me to intrude on her solitude—and she could not be pleased that a fate like hers had been the theme of a traveller's amusement. Yet the look with which she regarded me was one of scorn instead of embarrassment. The opinion of the world and all its children could not add or take an iota from her load of misery; and, save from the half smile that seemed to intimate the contempt of a being rapt by the very intensity of her affliction above the sphere of ordinary humanities, she seemed as indifferent to my gaze as if she had been a dead corpse or a marble statue.

Elspat was above the middle stature; her hair, now grizzled, was still profuse, and it had been of the most decided black. So were her eyes, in which, contradicting the stern and rigid features of her countenance, there shone the wild and troubled light that indicates an unsettled mind. Her hair was wrapt round a silver bodkin with some attention to neatness, and her dark mantle was disposed around her with a degree of taste, though the materials were of the most ordinary sort.

After gazing on this victim of guilt and calamity till I was ashamed to remain silent, though uncertain how I ought to address her, I began to express my surprise at her choosing such a desert and deplorable dwelling. She cut short these expressions of sympathy by answering in a stern voice, without the least change of countenance or posture—'Daughter of the stranger, he has told you my story.' I was silenced at once, and felt how little all earthly accommodation must seem to the mind which had such subjects as hers for rumination. Without again attempting to open the conversation, I took a piece of gold from my purse (for Donald had intimated she lived on alms), expecting she would at least stretch her hand to receive it. But she neither accepted nor rejected the gift—she did not even seem to notice it, though twenty times as valuable, probably, as was usually offered. I was obliged to place it on her knee, saying involuntarily, as I did so, 'May God pardon you, and relieve you!' I shall never forget the look which she cast up to Heaven, nor the tone in which she exclaimed, in the very words of my old friend, John Home—

'My beautiful—my brave!'*

It was the language of nature, and arose from the heart of the deprived mother, as it did from that gifted imaginative poet while furnishing with appropriate expressions the ideal grief of Lady Randolph.

CHAPTER II

Oh, I'm come to the Low Country,
  Och, och, ohonochie,
Without a penny in my pouch
  To buy a meal for me.
I was the proudest of my clan,
  Long, long may I repine;
And Donald was the bravest man,
  And Donald he was mine.   *Old Song.*

ELSPAT had enjoyed happy days, though her age had sunk into hopeless and inconsolable sorrow and distress. She was once the beautiful and happy wife of Hamish MacTavish, for whom his strength and feats of prowess had gained the title of MacTavish Mhor.* His life was turbulent and dangerous, his habits being of the old Highland stamp which esteemed it shame to want anything that could be had for the taking. Those in the Lowland line who lay near him and desired to enjoy their lives and property in quiet, were contented to pay him a small composition in name of protection money, and comforted themselves with the old proverb, that it was better to 'fleech the deil than fight him'. Others, who accounted such composition dishonourable, were often surprised by MacTavish Mhor and his associates and followers, who usually inflicted an adequate penalty, either in person or property, or both. The creagh is yet remembered in which he swept one hundred and fifty cows from Monteith in one drove; and how he placed the Laird of Ballybught naked in a slough, for having threatened to send for a party of the Highland Watch to protect his property.

Whatever were occasionally the triumphs of this daring cateran, they were often exchanged for reverses; and his narrow escapes, rapid flights, and the ingenious stratagems with which he extricated himself from imminent danger, were no less remembered and admired than the exploits in which he had been successful. In weal or woe, through every species of fatigue, difficulty, and danger, Elspat was his faithful companion. She enjoyed with him the fits of occasional prosperity; and when adversity pressed them hard, her strength of mind, readiness of wit, and coura-

geous endurance of danger and toil, are said often
to have stimulated the exertions of her husband.

Their morality was of the old Highland cast,
faithful friends and fierce enemies; the Lowland
herds and harvests they accounted their own,
whenever they had the means of driving off
the one or of seizing upon the other; nor did the
least scruple on the right of property interfere on
such occasions. Hamish Mhor argued like the
old Cretan warrior:

> My sword, my spear, my shaggy shield,
>   They make me lord of all below;
> For he who dreads the lance to wield,
>   Before my shaggy shield must bow;
> His lands, his vineyards, must resign,
> And all that cowards have is mine.*

But those days of perilous, though frequently
successful depredation, began to be abridged
after the failure of the expedition of Prince
Charles Edward.* MacTavish Mhor had not sat
still on that occasion, and he was outlawed, both
as a traitor to the state and as a robber and
cateran. Garrisons were now settled in many
places where a red-coat had never before been
seen, and the Saxon war-drum resounded among
the most hidden recesses of the Highland mountains. The fate of MacTavish became every day
more inevitable; and it was the more difficult for
him to make his exertions for defence or escape,
that Elspat, amid his evil days, had increased
his family with an infant child, which was a
considerable encumbrance upon the necessary
rapidity of their motions.

At length the fatal day arrived. In a strong
pass on the skirts of Ben Cruachan, the celebrated

MacTavish Mhor was surprised by a detachment of the Sidier Roy.[1] His wife assisted him heroically, charging his piece from time to time; and as they were in possession of a post that was nearly unassailable, he might have perhaps escaped if his ammunition had lasted. But at length his balls were expended, although it was not until he had fired off most of the silver buttons from his waistcoat, and the soldiers, no longer deterred by fear of the unerring marksman, who had slain three and wounded more of their number, approached his stronghold, and, unable to take him alive, slew him, after a most desperate resistance.

All this Elspat witnessed and survived, for she had, in the child which relied on her for support, a motive for strength and exertion. In what manner she maintained herself it is not easy to say. Her only ostensible means of support were a flock of three or four goats, which she fed wherever she pleased on the mountain pastures, no one challenging the intrusion. In the general distress of the country, her ancient acquaintances had little to bestow; but what they could part with from their own necessities, they willingly devoted to the relief of others. From Lowlanders she sometimes demanded tribute, rather than requested alms. She had not forgotten she was the widow of MacTavish Mhor or that the child who trotted by her knee might, such were her imaginations, emulate one day the fame of his father, and command the same influence which he had once exerted without control. She associated so little with others, went so seldom and so

[1] The Red Soldier.

unwillingly from the wildest recesses of the mountains where she usually dwelt with her goats, that she was quite unconscious of the great change which had taken place in the country around her, the substitution of civil order for military violence, and the strength gained by the law and its adherents over those who were called in Gaelic song, 'the stormy sons of the sword.'* Her own diminished consequence and straitened circumstances she indeed felt, but for this the death of MacTavish Mhor was, in her apprehension, a sufficing reason; and she doubted not that she should rise to her former state of importance, when Hamish Bean*(or Fair-haired James) should be able to wield the arms of his father. If, then, Elspat was repelled rudely when she demanded anything necessary for her wants, or the accommodation of her little flock, by a churlish farmer, her threats of vengeance, obscurely expressed, yet terrible in their tenor, used frequently to extort, through fear of her maledictions, the relief which was denied to her necessities; and the trembling goodwife, who gave meal or money to the widow of MacTavish Mhor, wished in her heart that the stern old carlin had been burnt on the day her husband had his due.

Years thus ran on, and Hamish Bean grew up, not indeed to be of his father's size or strength, but to become an active, high-spirited, fair-haired youth, with a ruddy cheek, an eye like an eagle, and all the agility, if not all the strength, of his formidable father, upon whose history and achievements his mother dwelt in order to form her son's mind to a similar course of adventures. But the young see the present state of this changeful world more keenly than the old. Much attached to his mother and disposed to do all in his power for her support, Hamish yet perceived, when he mixed with the world, that the trade of the cateran was now alike dangerous and discreditable, and that, if he were to emulate his father's prowess, it must be in some other line of warfare more consonant to the opinions of the present day.

As the faculties of mind and body began to expand, he became more sensible of the precarious nature of his situation, of the erroneous views of his mother, and her ignorance respecting the changes of the society with which she mingled so little. In visiting friends and neighbours, he became aware of the extremely reduced scale to which his parent was limited, and learned that she possessed little or nothing more than the absolute necessaries of life, and that these were sometimes on the point of failing. At times his success in fishing and the chase was able to add something to her subsistence; but he saw no regular means of contributing to her support, unless by stooping to servile labour, which, if he himself could have endured it, would, he knew, have been like a death's-wound to the pride of his mother.

Elspat, meanwhile, saw with surprise that Hamish Bean, although now tall and fit for the field, showed no disposition to enter on his father's scene of action. There was something of the mother at her heart, which prevented her from urging him in plain terms to take the field as a cateran, for the fear occurred of the perils into which the trade must conduct him; and when she would have spoken to him on the subject, it seemed to her heated imagination as if the ghost of her husband arose between them in his bloody tartans, and laying his finger on his lips, appeared to prohibit the topic. Yet she wondered at what seemed his want of spirit, sighed as she saw him from day to day lounging about in the long-skirted Lowland coat, which the legislature had imposed upon the Gael instead of their own romantic garb, and thought how much nearer he would have resembled her husband, had he been clad in the belted plaid and short hose, with his polished arms gleaming at his side.*

Besides these subjects for anxiety, Elspat had others arising from the engrossing impetuosity of her temper. Her love of MacTavish Mhor had been qualified by respect and sometimes even by fear; for the cateran was not the species of man who submits to female government; but over his son she had exerted, at first during childhood and afterwards in early youth, an imperious authority which gave her maternal love a character of jealousy. She could not bear when Hamish, with advancing life, made repeated steps towards independence, absented himself from her cottage at such season and for such length of time as he chose, and seemed to consider, although maintaining towards her every possible degree of respect and kindness, that the control and responsibility of his actions rested on himself alone. This would have been of little consequence could she have concealed her feelings within her own bosom; but the ardour and impatience of her passions made her frequently show her son that she conceived herself neglected and ill used.

When he was absent for any length of time from her cottage without giving intimation of his purpose, her resentment on his return used to be so unreasonable, that it naturally suggested to a young man, fond of independence and desirous to amend his situation in the world, to leave her, even for the very purpose of enabling him to provide for the parent whose egotistical demands on his filial attention tended to confine him to a desert, in which both were starving in hopeless and helpless indigence.

Upon one occasion, the son having been guilty of some independent excursion by which the mother felt herself affronted and disobliged, she had been more than usually violent on his return, and awakened in Hamish a sense of displeasure, which clouded his brow and cheek. At length, as she persevered in her unreasonable resentment, his patience became exhausted, and taking his gun from the chimney corner and muttering to himself the reply which his respect for his mother prevented him from speaking aloud, he was about to leave the hut which he had but barely entered.

'Hamish,' said his mother, 'are you again about to leave me?' But Hamish only replied by looking at, and rubbing the lock of his gun.

'Ay, rub the lock of your gun,' said his parent, bitterly; 'I am glad you have courage enough to fire it, though it be but at a roe-deer.' Hamish started at this undeserved taunt, and cast a look of anger at her in reply. She saw that she had found the means of giving him pain.

'Yes,' she said, 'look fierce as you will at an old woman, and your mother; it would be long ere you bent your brow on the angry countenance of a bearded man.'

'Be silent, mother, or speak of what you understand,' said Hamish, much irritated, 'and that is of the distaff and the spindle.'

'And was it of spindle and distaff that I was thinking when I bore you away on my back through the fire of six of the Saxon soldiers, and you a wailing child? I tell you, Hamish, I know a hundred-fold more of swords and guns than ever you will; and you will never learn so much of noble war by yourself, as you have seen when you were wrapped up in my plaid.'

'You are determined at least to allow me no peace at home, mother; but this shall have an end,' said Hamish, as, resuming his purpose of leaving the hut, he rose and went towards the door.

'Stay, I command you,' said his mother; 'stay, or may the gun you carry be the means of your ruin—may the road you are going be the track of your funeral!'

'What makes you use such words, mother?' said the young man, turning a little back—'they are not good, and good cannot come of them. Farewell just now, we are too angry to speak together—farewell; it will be long ere you see me again.' And he departed, his mother, in the first burst of her impatience, showering after him her maledictions, and in the next invoking them on her own head so that they might spare her son's. She passed that day and the next in all the vehemence of impotent and yet unrestrained passion, now entreating Heaven and such powers as were familiar to her by rude tradition to restore her

dear son, 'the calf of her heart'; now in impatient
resentment meditating with what bitter terms
she should rebuke his filial disobedience upon
his return, and now studying the most tender
language to attach him to the cottage, which,
when her boy was present, she would not, in the
rapture of her affection, have exchanged for the
apartments of Taymouth Castle.*

Two days passed, during which, neglecting
even the slender means of supporting nature
which her situation afforded, nothing but the
strength of a frame accustomed to hardships and
privations of every kind could have kept her in
existence, notwithstanding the anguish of her
mind prevented her being sensible of her personal
weakness. Her dwelling, at this period, was the
same cottage near which I had found her, but
then more habitable by the exertions of Hamish,
by whom it had been in a great measure built
and repaired.

It was on the third day after her son had disappeared, as she sat at the door rocking herself
after the fashion of her countrywomen when in
distress or in pain, that the then unwonted circumstance occurred of a passenger being seen on
the highroad above the cottage. She cast but
one glance at him—he was on horseback, so that
it could not be Hamish, and Elspat cared not
enough for any other being on earth, to make her
turn her eyes towards him a second time. The
stranger, however, paused opposite to her cottage,
and dismounting from his pony, led it down the
steep and broken path which conducted to her
door.

'God bless you, Elspat MacTavish!'—She

looked at the man as he addressed her in her native language with the displeased air of one whose reverie is interrupted; but the traveller went on to say, 'I bring you tidings of your son Hamish.' At once, from being the most uninteresting object, in respect to Elspat, that could exist, the form of the stranger became awful in her eyes, as that of a messenger descended from Heaven expressly to pronounce upon her death or life. She started from her seat, and with hands convulsively clasped together and held up to Heaven, eyes fixed on the stranger's countenance, and person stooping forward to him, she looked those inquiries which her faltering tongue could not articulate. 'Your son sends you his dutiful remembrance and this,' said the messenger, putting into Elspat's hand a small purse containing four or five dollars.

'He is gone, he is gone!' exclaimed Elspat; 'he has sold himself to be the servant of the Saxons, and I shall never more behold him! Tell me, Miles MacPhadraick, for now I know you, is it the price of the son's blood that you have put into the mother's hand?'

'Now God forbid!' answered MacPhadraick, who was a tacksman*and had possession of a considerable tract of ground under his chief, a proprietor who lived about twenty miles off—'God forbid I should do wrong, or say wrong, to you or to the son of MacTavish Mhor! I swear to you by the hand of my chief, that your son is well and will soon see you, and the rest he will tell you himself.' So saying, MacPhadraick hastened back up the pathway, gained the road, mounted his pony, and rode upon his way.

CHAPTER III

ELSPAT MACTAVISH remained gazing on the money, as if the impress of the coin could have conveyed information how it was procured.

'I love not this MacPhadraick,' she said to herself; 'it was his race of whom the bard hath spoken, saying, Fear them not when their words are loud as the winter's wind, but fear them when they fall on you like the sound of the thrush's song.' And yet this riddle can be read but one way: My son hath taken the sword, to win that with strength like a man, which churls would keep him from with the words that frighten children.' This idea, when once it occurred to her, seemed the more reasonable, that MacPhadraick, as she well knew, himself a cautious man, had so far encouraged her husband's practices as occasionally to buy cattle of MacTavish, although he must have well known how they were come by, taking care, however, that the transaction was so made as to be accompanied with great profit and absolute safety. Who so likely as MacPhadraick to indicate to a young cateran the glen in which he could commence his perilous trade with most prospect of success? who so likely to convert his booty into money? The feelings which another might have experienced on believing that an only son had rushed forward on the same path in which his father had perished, were scarce known to the Highland mothers of that day. She thought of the death of MacTavish Mhor as that of a hero who had fallen in his proper trade of war, and who had not fallen unavenged. She feared less for her son's life than for his dishonour. She dreaded on his account the subjection to strangers, and the death-sleep of the soul which is brought on by what she regarded as slavery.

The moral principle which so naturally and so justly occurs to the mind of those who have been educated under a settled government of laws that protect the property of the weak against the incursions of the strong, was to poor Elspat a book sealed and a fountain closed.* She had been taught to consider those whom they called Saxons, as a race with whom the Gael were constantly at war, and she regarded every settlement of theirs within the reach of Highland incursion, as affording a legitimate object of attack and plunder. Her feelings on this point had been strengthened and confirmed, not only by the desire of revenge for the death of her husband, but by the sense of general indignation entertained, not unjustly, through the Highlands of Scotland, on account of the barbarous and violent conduct of the victors after the battle of Culloden.* Other Highland clans, too, she regarded as the fair objects of plunder when that was possible, upon the score of ancient enmities and deadly feuds.

The prudence that might have weighed the slender means which the times afforded for resisting the efforts of a combined government, which had, in its less compact and established authority, been unable to put down the ravages of such lawless caterans as MacTavish Mhor, was unknown to a solitary woman whose ideas still dwelt upon her own early times. She imagined that her son had only to proclaim himself his father's successor in adventure and enterprise, and that a force of men as gallant as those who had followed his father's banner would crowd around to support it when again displayed. To her, Hamish was the eagle who had only to soar aloft and resume his native place in the skies, without her being able to comprehend how many additional eyes would have watched his flight, how many additional bullets would have been directed at his bosom. To be brief, Elspat was one who viewed the present state of society with the same feelings with which she regarded the times that had passed away. She had been indigent, neglected, oppressed, since the days that her husband had no longer been feared and powerful, and she thought that the term of her ascendance would return when her son had determined to play the part of his father. If she permitted her eye to glance farther into futurity, it was but to anticipate that she must be for many a day cold in the grave, with the coronach of her tribe cried duly over her, before her fair-haired Hamish could, according to her calculation, die with his hand on the basket-hilt of the red claymore. His father's hair was grey, ere, after a hundred dangers, he had fallen with his arms in his hands. That she should have seen and survived the sight was a natural consequence of the manners of that age. And better it was—such was her proud thought—that she had seen him so die, than to have witnessed his departure from life in a smoky hovel—on a bed of rotten straw, like an over-worn hound or a bullock which died of disease. But the hour of her young, her brave Hamish, was yet far distant. He must succeed—he must conquer, like his father. And when he fell at length,—for she anticipated for him no bloodless death,—Elspat would ere then have lain long in the grave, and could neither see his death-struggle nor mourn over his grave-sod.

With such wild notions working in her brain, the spirit of Elspat rose to its usual pitch, or rather to one which seemed higher. In the emphatic language of Scripture, which in that idiom does not greatly differ from her own, she arose, she washed and changed her apparel, and ate bread, and was refreshed.*

She longed eagerly for the return of her son, but she now longed not with the bitter anxiety of doubt and apprehension. She said to herself that much must be done ere he could, in these times, arise to be an eminent and dreaded leader. Yet when she saw him again, she almost expected him at the head of a daring band, with pipes playing and banners flying, the noble tartans fluttering free in the wind, in despite of the laws which had suppressed, under severe penalties, the use of the national garb, and all the appurtenances of Highland chivalry. For all this, her eager imagination was content only to allow the interval of some days.

From the moment this opinion had taken deep and serious possession of her mind, her thoughts were bent upon receiving her son at the head of his adherents, in the manner in which she used to adorn her hut for the return of his father.

The substantial means of subsistence she had not the power of providing, nor did she consider that of importance. The successful caterans would bring with them herds and flocks. But the interior of her hut was arranged for their reception—the usquebaugh was brewed, or distilled, in a larger quantity than it could have been supposed one lone woman could have made ready. Her hut was put into such order as might, in some degree, give it the appearance of a day of rejoicing. It was swept and decorated with boughs of various kinds, like the house of a Jewess upon what is termed the Feast of the Tabernacles.* The produce of the milk of her little flock was prepared in as great variety of forms as her skill admitted, to entertain her son and his associates whom she expected to receive along with him.

But the principal decoration, which she sought with the greatest toil, was the cloud-berry, a scarlet fruit,* which is only found on very high hills, and there only in small quantities. Her husband, or perhaps one of his forefathers, had chosen this as the emblem of his family, because it seemed at once to imply by its scarcity the smallness of their clan, and by the places in which it was found, the ambitious height of their pretensions.

For the time that these simple preparations of welcome endured, Elspat was in a state of troubled happiness. In fact, her only anxiety was that she might be able to complete all that she could do to welcome Hamish and the friends who she supposed must have attached themselves to his band before they should arrive, and find her unprovided for their reception.

But when such efforts as she could make had been accomplished, she once more had nothing left to engage her save the trifling care of her goats; and when these had been attended to, she

had only to review her little preparations, renew
such as were of a transitory nature, replace
decayed branches and fading boughs, and then
to sit down at her cottage door and watch the
road, as it ascended on the one side from the
banks of the Awe and on the other wound round
the heights of the mountain with such a degree
of accommodation to hill and level as the plan
of the military engineer permitted. While so
occupied, her imagination, anticipating the
future from recollections of the past, formed out
of the morning-mist, or the evening-cloud, the
wild forms of an advancing band, which were
then called 'Sidier Dhu,'—dark soldiers—dressed
in their native tartan, and so named to distinguish
them from the scarlet ranks of the British army.
In this occupation she spent many hours of each
morning and evening.

CHAPTER IV

IT was in vain that Elspat's eyes surveyed the
distant path, by the earliest light of the dawn and
the latest glimmer of the twilight. No rising dust
awakened the expectation of nodding plumes or
flashing arms; the solitary traveller trudged list-
lessly along in his brown lowland greatcoat, his
tartans dyed black or purple, to comply with or
evade the law, which prohibited their being
worn in their variegated hues. The spirit of the
Gael, sunk and broken by the severe though perhaps necessary laws that proscribed the dress and
arms which he considered as his birthright, was
intimated by his drooping head and dejected
appearance. Not in such depressed wanderers

did Elspat recognize the light and free step of her son, now, as she concluded, regenerated from every sign of Saxon thraldom. Night by night, as darkness came, she removed from her unclosed door to throw herself on her restless pallet, not to sleep but to watch. The brave and the terrible, she said, walk by night—their steps are heard in darkness, when all is silent save the whirlwind and the cataract—the timid deer comes only forth when the sun is upon the mountain's peak; but the bold wolf walks in the red light of the harvest-moon. She reasoned in vain—her son's expected summons did not call her from the lowly couch, where she lay dreaming of his approach. Hamish came not.

'Hope deferred', saith the royal sage, 'maketh the heart sick'; and strong as was Elspat's constitution, she began to experience that it was unequal to the toils to which her anxious and immoderate affection subjected her, when early one morning the appearance of a traveller on the lonely mountain-road revived hopes which had begun to sink into listless despair. There was no sign of Saxon subjugation about the stranger. At a distance she could see the flutter of the belted plaid that drooped in graceful folds behind him, and the plume that, placed in the bonnet, showed rank and gentle birth. He carried a gun over his shoulder, the claymore was swinging by his side, with its usual appendages, the dirk, the pistol, and the *sporran mollach*.[1] Ere yet her eye had scanned all these particulars the light step of the traveller was hastened, his arm was waved in

[1] The goat-skin pouch, worn by the Highlanders round their waist.

token of recognition—a moment more, and
Elspat held in her arms her darling son, dressed
in the garb of his ancestors, and looking in her
maternal eyes, the fairest among ten thousand!

The first outpouring of affection it would be
impossible to describe. Blessings mingled with
the most endearing epithets which her energetic
language affords, in striving to express the wild
rapture of Elspat's joy. Her board was heaped
hastily with all she had to offer; and the mother
watched the young soldier, as he partook of the
refreshment, with feelings how similar to, yet how
different from, those with which she had seen
him draw his first sustenance from her bosom!

When the tumult of joy was appeased, Elspat
became anxious to know her son's adventures
since they parted, and could not help greatly
censuring his rashness for traversing the hill in
the Highland dress in the broad sunshine, when
the penalty was so heavy, and so many red soldiers
were abroad in the country.

'Fear not for me, mother,' said Hamish, in a
tone designed to relieve her anxiety, and yet
somewhat embarrassed; 'I may wear the *breacan*[1]
at the gate of Fort Augustus, if I like it.'

'Oh, be not too daring, my beloved Hamish,
though it be the fault which best becomes thy
father's son—yet be not too daring! Alas, they
fight not now as in former days, with fair weapons
and on equal terms, but take odds of numbers
and of arms, so that the feeble and the strong are
alike levelled by the shot of a boy. And do not
think me unworthy to be called your father's
widow, and your mother, because I speak thus;

[1] That which is variegated, i.e. the tartan.

for God knoweth that, man to man, I would peril
thee against the best in Breadalbane, and broad
Lorn besides.'

'I assure you, my dearest mother,' replied
Hamish, 'that I am in no danger. But have you
seen MacPhadraick, mother, and what has he
said to you on my account?'

'Silver he left me in plenty, Hamish; but the
best of his comfort was that you were well and
would see me soon. But beware of MacPhadraick,
my son; for when he called himself the friend of
your father, he better loved the most worthless
stirk in his herd than he did the life-blood of
MacTavish Mhor. Use his services, therefore,
and pay him for them—for it is thus we should
deal with the unworthy; but take my counsel,
and trust him not.'

Hamish could not suppress a sigh, which
seemed to Elspat to intimate that the caution
came too late. 'What have you done with him?'
she continued, eager and alarmed. 'I had money
of him, and he gives not that without value—he
is none of those who exchange barley for chaff.
Oh, if you repent you of your bargain, and if it
be one which you may break off without disgrace
to your truth or your manhood, take back his
silver and trust not to his fair words.'

'It may not be, mother,' said Hamish; 'I do
not repent my engagement, unless that it must
make me leave you soon.'

'Leave me! how leave me? Silly boy, think
you I know not what duty belongs to the wife or
mother of a daring man? Thou art but a boy
yet; and when thy father had been the dread of
the country for twenty years, he did not despise

my company and assistance, but often said my help was worth that of two strong gillies.'

'It is not on that score, mother; but since I must leave the country——'

'Leave the country!' replied his mother, interrupting him; 'and think you that I am like a bush, that is rooted to the soil where it grows and must die if carried elsewhere? I have breathed other winds than these of Ben Cruachan—I have followed your father to the wilds of Ross, and the impenetrable deserts of Y Mac Y Mhor—Tush, man, my limbs, old as they are, will bear me as far as your young feet can trace the way.'

'Alas, mother,' said the young man, with a faltering accent, 'but to cross the sea——'

'The sea! who am I that I should fear the sea! Have I never been in a birling in my life—never known the Sound of Mull, the Isles of Treshornish, and the rough rocks of Harris?'

'Alas, mother, I go far, far from all of these—I am enlisted in one of the new regiments, and we go against the French in America.'*

'Enlisted!' uttered the astonished mother—'against *my* will—without *my* consent—you could not, you would not,'—then rising up and assuming a posture of almost imperial command, 'Hamish, you DARED not!'

'Despair, mother, dares everything,' answered Hamish, in a tone of melancholy resolution. 'What should I do here, where I can scarce get bread for myself and you and when the times are growing daily worse? Would you but sit down and listen, I would convince you I have acted for the best.'

With a bitter smile Elspat sat down, and the

same severe ironical expression was on her features as, with her lips firmly closed, she listened to his vindication.

Hamish went on, without being disconcerted by her expected displeasure. 'When I left you, dearest mother, it was to go to MacPhadraick's house; for although I knew he is crafty and worldly after the fashion of the Sassenach, yet he is wise, and I thought how he would teach me, as it would cost him nothing, in which way I could mend our estate in the world.'

'Our estate in the world!' said Elspat, losing patience at the word; 'and went you to a base fellow, with a soul no better than that of a cowherd, to ask counsel about your conduct? Your father asked none, save of his courage and his sword.'

'Dearest mother,' answered Hamish, 'how shall I convince you that you live in this land of our fathers, as if our fathers were yet living? You walk as it were in a dream, surrounded by the phantoms of those who have been long with the dead. When my father lived and fought, the great respected the man of the strong right hand, and the rich feared him. He had protection from MacAllan Mhor,* and from Caberfae,[1] and tribute from meaner men. That is ended, and his son would only earn a disgraceful and unpitied death, by the practices which gave his father credit and power among those who wear the breacan. The land is conquered—its lights are quenched,—Glengary, Lochiel, Perth, Lord Lewis,* all the high chiefs are dead or in exile—

---

[1] Caberfae—*Anglice*, the Stag's head, the Celtic designation for the arms of the family of the high Chief of Seaforth.*

We may mourn for it, but we cannot help it. Bonnet, broadsword, and sporran—power, strength, and wealth, were all lost on Drum-mossie-muir.'*

'It is false!' said Elspat, fiercely; 'you and such-like dastardly spirits are quelled by your own faint hearts, not by the strength of the enemy; you are like the fearful waterfowl, to whom the least cloud in the sky seems the shadow of the eagle.'

'Mother,' said Hamish, proudly, 'lay not faint heart to my charge. I go where men are wanted who have strong arms and bold hearts too. I leave a desert for a land where I may gather fame.'

'And you leave your mother to perish in want, age, and solitude,' said Elspat, essaying succes-sively every means of moving a resolution which she began to see was more deeply rooted than she had at first thought.

'Not so, neither,' he answered; 'I leave you to comfort and certainty, which you have yet never known. Barcaldine's son* is made a leader, and with him I have enrolled myself; MacPhadraick acts for him, and raises men, and finds his own good in it.'

'That is the truest word of the tale, were all the rest as false as hell,' said the old woman bitterly.

'But we are to find our good in it also,' con-tinued Hamish; 'for Barcaldine is to give you a shieling in his wood of Letterfindreight, with grass for your goats, and a cow, when you please to have one, on the common; and my own pay, dearest mother, though I am far away, will do more than provide you with meal, and with all else you can want. Do not fear for me. I enter a private gentleman; but I will return, if hard fighting and regular duty can deserve it, an officer, and with half a dollar a day.'

'Poor child!' replied Elspat, in a tone of pity mingled with contempt, 'and you trust MacPhadraick?'

'I might, mother,' said Hamish, the dark red colour of his race crossing his forehead and cheeks, 'for MacPhadraick knows the blood which flows in my veins, and is aware that should he break trust with you, he might count the days which could bring Hamish back to Breadalbane, and number those of his life within three suns more. I would kill him at his own hearth, did he break his word with me—I would, by the great Being who made us both!'

The look and attitude of the young soldier for a moment overawed Elspat; she was unused to see him express a deep and bitter mood, which reminded her so strongly of his father, but she resumed her remonstrances in the same taunting manner in which she had commenced them.

'Poor boy!' she said; 'and you think that at the distance of half the world your threats will be heard or thought of! But go—go—place your neck under him of Hanover's yoke, against whom every true Gael fought to the death.—Go, disown the royal Stuart,* for whom your father, and his fathers, and your mother's fathers, have crimsoned many a field with their blood.—Go, put your head under the belt of one of the race of Dermid,* whose children murdered—yes,' she added, with a wild shriek, 'murdered your mother's fathers in their peaceful dwellings in

Glencoe!*—Yes,' she again exclaimed, with a wilder and shriller scream, 'I was then unborn, but my mother has told me—and I attended to the voice of *my* mother—Well I remember her words!—They came in peace, and were received in friendship, and blood and fire arose, and screams, and murder!'

'Mother,' answered Hamish, mournfully, but with a decided tone, 'all that I have thought over—there is not a drop of the blood of Glencoe on the noble hand of Barcaldine—with the unhappy house of Glenlyon, the curse remains, and on them God hath avenged it.'

'You speak like the Saxon priest already,' replied his mother; 'will you not better stay and ask a kirk from MacAllan Mhor, that you may preach forgiveness to the race of Dermid?'

'Yesterday was yesterday,' answered Hamish, 'and to-day is to-day. When the clans are crushed and confounded together, it is well and wise that their hatreds and their feuds should not survive their independence and their power. He that cannot execute vengeance like a man should not harbour useless enmity like a craven. Mother, young Barcaldine is true and brave; I know that MacPhadraick counselled him that he should not let me take leave of you, lest you dissuaded me from my purpose; but he said, "Hamish MacTavish is the son of a brave man, and he will not break his word." Mother, Barcaldine leads an hundred of the bravest of the sons of the Gael in their native dress, and with their fathers' arms—heart to heart—shoulder to shoulder. I have sworn to go with him—He has trusted me, and I will trust him.'

At this reply, so firmly and resolvedly pronounced, Elspat remained like one thunderstruck, and sunk in despair. The arguments which she had considered so irresistibly conclusive had recoiled like a wave from a rock. After a long pause, she filled her son's quaigh, and presented it to him with an air of dejected deference and submission.

'Drink', she said, 'to thy father's roof-tree, ere you leave it for ever; and tell me, since the chains of a new king, and of a new chief, whom your fathers knew not save as mortal enemies, are fastened upon the limbs of your father's son,—tell me how many links you count upon them?'

Hamish took the cup, but looked at her as if uncertain of her meaning. She proceeded in a raised voice. 'Tell me,' she said, 'for I have a right to know, for how many days the will of those you have made your masters permits me to look upon you?—In other words, how many are the days of my life—for when you leave me, the earth has nought besides worth living for!'

'Mother,' replied Hamish MacTavish, 'for six days I may remain with you, and if you will set out with me on the fifth, I will conduct you in safety to your new dwelling. But if you remain here, then I will depart on the seventh by daybreak—then, as at the last moment, I MUST set out for Dunbarton, for if I appear not on the eighth day, I am subject to punishment as a deserter, and am dishonoured as a soldier and a gentleman.'

'Your father's foot', she answered, 'was free as the wind on the heath—it were as vain to say to him, "Where goest thou?" as to ask that viewless driver of the clouds, "Wherefore blowest thou?" Tell me under what penalty thou must—since go thou must and go thou wilt—return to thy thraldom?'

'Call it not thraldom, mother, it is the service of an honourable soldier—the only service which is now open to the son of MacTavish Mhor.'

'Yet say what is the penalty if thou shouldst not return!' replied Elspat.

'Military punishment as a deserter,' answered Hamish; writhing, however, as his mother failed not to observe, under some internal feelings, which she resolved to probe to the uttermost.

'And that', she said, with assumed calmness, which her glancing eye disowned, 'is the punishment of a disobedient hound, is it not?'

'Ask me no more, mother,' said Hamish; 'the punishment is nothing to one who will never deserve it.'

'To me it is something,' replied Elspat, 'since I know better than thou, that where there is power to inflict, there is often the will to do so without cause. I would pray for thee, Hamish, and I must know against what evils I should beseech Him who leaves none unguarded, to protect thy youth and simplicity.'

'Mother,' said Hamish, 'it signifies little to what a criminal may be exposed, if a man is determined not to be such. Our Highland chiefs used also to punish their vassals, and, as I have heard, severely. Was it not Lachlan MacIan, whom we remember of old, whose head was struck off by order of his chieftain for shooting at the stag before him?'

'Ay,' said Elspat, 'and right he had to lose it,

since he dishonoured the father of the people even in the face of the assembled clan. But the chiefs were noble in their ire—they punished with the sharp blade, and not with the baton. Their punishments drew blood, but they did not infer dishonour. Canst thou say the same for the laws under whose yoke thou hast placed thy freeborn neck?'

'I cannot, mother, I cannot,' said Hamish, mournfully. 'I saw them punish a Sassenach for deserting, as they called it, his banner. He was scourged—I own it—scourged like a hound who has offended an imperious master. I was sick at the sight—I confess it. But the punishment of dogs is only for those worse than dogs, who know not how to keep their faith.'

'To this infamy, however, thou hast subjected thyself, Hamish,' replied Elspat, 'if thou shouldest give, or thy officers take, measure of offence against thee.—I speak no more to thee on thy purpose.—Were the sixth day from this morning's sun my dying day, and thou wert to stay to close mine eyes, thou wouldst run the risk of being lashed like a dog at a post—yes! unless thou hadst the gallant heart to leave me to die alone, and upon my desolate hearth, the last spark of thy father's fire and of thy forsaken mother's life, to be extinguished together!'—Hamish traversed the hut with an impatient and angry pace.

'Mother,' he said at length, 'concern not yourself about such things. I cannot be subjected to such infamy, for never will I deserve it; and were I threatened with it, I should know how to die before I was so far dishonoured.'

'There spoke the son of the husband of my

heart!' replied Elspat; and she changed the discourse, and seemed to listen in melancholy acquiescence, when her son reminded her how short the time was which they were permitted to pass in each other's society, and entreated that it might be spent without useless and unpleasant recollections respecting the circumstances under which they must soon be separated.

Elspat was now satisfied that her son, with some of his father's other properties, preserved the haughty masculine spirit which rendered it impossible to divert him from a resolution which he had deliberately adopted. She assumed, therefore, an exterior of apparent submission to their inevitable separation; and if she now and then broke out into complaints and murmurs, it was either that she could not altogether suppress the natural impetuosity of her temper, or because she had the wit to consider that a total and unreserved acquiescence might have seemed to her son constrained and suspicious, and induced him to watch and defeat the means by which she still hoped to prevent his leaving her. Her ardent though selfish affection for her son, incapable of being qualified by a regard for the true interests of the unfortunate object of her attachment, resembled the instinctive fondness of the animal race for their offspring; and diving little farther into futurity than one of the inferior creatures, she only felt that to be separated from Hamish was to die.

In the brief interval permitted them, Elspat exhausted every art which affection could devise, to render agreeable to him the space which they were apparently to spend with each other. Her memory carried her far back into former days, and her stores of legendary history, which furnish at all times a principal amusement of the High-lander in his moments of repose, were augmented by an unusual acquaintance with the songs of ancient bards, and traditions of the most ap-proved seannachies* and tellers of tales. Her officious attentions to her son's accommodation, indeed, were so unremitted as almost to give him pain; and he endeavoured quietly to prevent her from taking so much personal toil in selecting the blooming heath for his bed or preparing the meal for his refreshment. 'Let me alone, Hamish,' she would reply on such occasions; 'you follow your own will in departing from your mother, let your mother have hers in doing what gives her pleasure while you remain.'

So much she seemed to be reconciled to the arrangements which he had made in her behalf, that she could hear him speak to her of her re-moving to the lands of Green Colin,* as the gentle-man was called on whose estate he had provided her an asylum. In truth, however, nothing could be farther from her thoughts. From what he had said during their first violent dispute, Elspat had gathered that if Hamish returned not by the appointed time permitted by his furlough, he would incur the hazard of corporal punishment. Were he placed within the risk of being thus dis-honoured, she was well aware that he would never submit to the disgrace by a return to the regiment where it might be inflicted. Whether she looked to any farther probable consequences of her unhappy scheme, cannot be known; but the partner of MacTavish Mhor, in all his perils and wanderings, was familiar with an hundred instances of resistance or escape, by which one brave man, amidst a land of rocks, lakes, and mountains, dangerous passes, and dark forests, might baffle the pursuit of hundreds. For the future, therefore, she feared nothing; her sole engrossing object was to prevent her son from keeping his word with his commanding officer.

With this secret purpose, she evaded the proposal which Hamish repeatedly made, that they should set out together to take possession of her new abode; and she resisted it upon grounds apparently so natural to her character, that her son was neither alarmed nor displeased. 'Let me not,' she said, 'in the same short week, bid farewell to my only son, and to the glen in which I have so long dwelt. Let my eye, when dimmed with weeping for thee, still look around, for a while at least, upon Loch Awe and on Ben Cruachan.'

Hamish yielded the more willingly to his mother's humour in this particular, that one or two persons who resided in a neighbouring glen, and had given their sons to Barcaldine's levy, were also to be provided for on the estate of the chieftain, and it was apparently settled that Elspat was to take her journey along with them when they should remove to their new residence. Thus Hamish believed that he had at once indulged his mother's humour, and ensured her safety and accommodation. But she nourished in her mind very different thoughts and projects!

The period of Hamish's leave of absence was fast approaching, and more than once he proposed to depart, in such time as to ensure his gaining easily and early Dunbarton, the town where were the head-quarters of his regiment. But still his mother's entreaties, his own natural disposition to linger among scenes long dear to him, and above all, his firm reliance in his speed and activity, induced him to protract his departure till the sixth day, being the very last which he could possibly afford to spend with his mother, if indeed he meant to comply with the conditions of his furlough.

CHAPTER V

But, for your son,—believe it, oh, believe it
Most dangerously you have with him prevailed,
If not most mortal to him.

Coriolanus.

ON the evening which preceded his proposed departure, Hamish walked down to the river with his fishing-rod, to practise in the Awe, for the last time, a sport in which he excelled, and to find, at the same time, the means for making one social meal with his mother, on something better than their ordinary cheer. He was as successful as usual, and soon killed a fine salmon. On his return homeward an incident befell him which he afterwards related as ominous, though probably his heated imagination, joined to the universal turn of his countrymen for the marvellous, exaggerated into superstitious importance some very ordinary and accidental circumstance.

In the path which he pursued homeward, he was surprised to observe a person, who, like himself, was dressed and armed after the old Highland fashion. The first idea that struck him was that the passenger belonged to his own corps,

who, levied by government, and bearing arms
under royal authority, were not amenable for
breach of the statutes against the use of the Highland garb or weapons. But he was struck on
perceiving, as he mended his pace to make up to
his supposed comrade, meaning to request his
company for the next day's journey, that the
stranger wore a white cockade, the fatal badge
which was proscribed in the Highlands. The
stature of the man was tall, and there was something shadowy in the outline, which, added to
his size, and his mode of motion which rather
resembled gliding than walking, impressed
Hamish with superstitious fears concerning the
character of the being which thus passed before
him in the twilight. He no longer strove to make
up to the stranger, but contented himself with
keeping him in view; under the superstition,
common to the Highlanders, that you ought
neither to intrude yourself on such supernatural
apparitions as you may witness nor avoid their
presence, but leave it to themselves to withhold
or extend their communication, as their power
may permit or the purpose of their commission
require.

Upon an elevated knoll by the side of the road,
just where the pathway turned down to Elspat's
hut, the stranger made a pause and seemed to
await Hamish's coming up. Hamish, on his part,
seeing it was necessary he should pass the object
of his suspicion, mustered up his courage, and
approached the spot where the stranger had
placed himself; who first pointed to Elspat's hut,
and made with arm and head a gesture pro-
hibiting Hamish to approach it, then stretched

his hand to the road which led to the southward, with a motion which seemed to enjoin his
instant departure in that direction. In a moment
afterwards the plaided form was gone—Hamish
did not exactly say vanished, because there were
rocks and stunted trees enough to have concealed
him; but it was his own opinion that he had seen
the spirit of MacTavish Mhor, warning him to
commence his instant journey to Dunbarton,
without waiting till morning or again visiting
his mother's hut.

In fact, so many accidents might arise to delay
his journey, especially where there were many
ferries, that it became his settled purpose, though
he could not depart without bidding his mother
adieu, that he neither could nor would abide
longer than for that object; and that the first
glimpse of next day's sun should see him many
miles advanced towards Dunbarton. He descended the path, therefore, and entering the cottage, he communicated, in a hasty and troubled
voice, which indicated mental agitation, his
determination to take his instant departure.
Somewhat to his surprise, Elspat appeared not
to combat his purpose, but she urged him to take
some refreshment ere he left her for ever. He did
so hastily and in silence, thinking on the approaching separation, and scarce yet believing
it would take place without a final struggle with
his mother's fondness. To his surprise, she filled
the quaigh with liquor for his parting cup.

'Go,' she said, 'my son, since such is thy settled
purpose; but first stand once more on thy mother's
hearth, the flame on which will be extinguished
long ere thy foot shall again be placed there.'

'To your health, mother!' said Hamish, 'and
may we meet again in happiness, in spite of your
ominous words.'

'It were better not to part,' said his mother,
watching him as he quaffed the liquor, of which
he would have held it ominous to have left a drop.

'And now,' she said, muttering the words to
herself, 'go—if thou canst go.'

'Mother,' said Hamish, as he replaced on the
table the empty quaigh, 'thy drink is pleasant to
the taste, but it takes away the strength which it
ought to give.'

'Such is its first effect, my son,' replied Elspat;
'but lie down upon that soft heather couch, shut
your eyes but for a moment, and, in the sleep of
an hour, you shall have more refreshment than
in the ordinary repose of three whole nights,
could they be blended into one.'

'Mother,' said Hamish, upon whose brain the
potion was now taking rapid effect, 'give me my
bonnet—I must kiss you and begone—yet it
seems as if my feet were nailed to the floor.'

'Indeed,' said his mother, 'you will be instantly
well, if you will sit down for half an hour—but
half an hour; it is eight hours to dawn, and dawn
were time enough for your father's son to begin
such a journey.'

'I must obey you, mother—I feel I must,' said
Hamish, inarticulately; 'but call me when the
moon rises.'

He sat down on the bed—reclined back, and
almost instantly was fast asleep. With the throbbing glee of one who has brought to an end a
difficult and troublesome enterprise, Elspat proceeded tenderly to arrange the plaid of the un-

conscious slumberer, to whom her extravagant
affection was doomed to be so fatal, expressing,
while busied in her office, her delight in tones of
mingled tenderness and triumph. 'Yes,' she said,
'calf of my heart, the moon shall arise and set to
thee, and so shall the sun; but not to light thee
from the land of thy fathers, or tempt thee to
serve the foreign prince or the feudal enemy! To
no son of Dermid shall I be delivered, to be fed
like a bondswoman; but he who is my pleasure
and my pride shall be my guard and my pro-
tector. They say the Highlands are changed;
but I see Ben Cruachan rear his crest as high as
ever into the evening sky—no one hath yet
herded his kine on the depth of Loch Awe—and
yonder oak does not yet bend like a willow. The
children of the mountains will be such as their
fathers, until the mountains themselves shall be
levelled with the strath. In these wild forests
which used to support thousands of the brave,
there is still surely subsistence and refuge left for
one aged woman, and one gallant youth, of the
ancient race and the ancient manners.'

While the misjudging mother thus exulted in
the success of her stratagem, we may mention to
the reader that it was founded on the acquaintance with drugs and simples, which Elspat,
accomplished in all things belonging to the wild
life which she had led, possessed in an uncommon
degree, and which she exercised for various
purposes. With the herbs, which she knew how
to select as well as how to distil, she could relieve
more diseases than a regular medical person
could easily believe. She applied some to dye the
bright colours of the tartan—from others she

compounded draughts of various powers, and unhappily possessed the secret of one which was strongly soporific. Upon the effects of this last concoction, as the reader doubtless has anticipated, she reckoned with security on delaying Hamish beyond the period for which his return was appointed; and she trusted to his horror for the apprehended punishment to which he was thus rendered liable, to prevent him from returning at all.

Sound and deep, beyond natural rest, was the sleep of Hamish MacTavish on that eventful evening, but not such the repose of his mother. Scarce did she close her eyes from time to time, but she awakened again with a start, in the terror that her son had arisen and departed; and it was only on approaching his couch, and hearing his deep-drawn and regular breathing, that she reassured herself of the security of the repose in which he was plunged.

Still, dawning, she feared, might awaken him, notwithstanding the unusual strength of the potion with which she had drugged his cup. If there remained a hope of mortal man accomplishing the journey, she was aware that Hamish would attempt it, though he were to die from fatigue upon the road. Animated by this new fear, she studied to exclude the light by stopping all the crannies and crevices through which, rather than through any regular entrance, the morning beams might find access to her miserable dwelling; and this in order to detain amid its wants and wretchedness the being on whom, if the world itself had been at her disposal, she would have joyfully conferred it.

Her pains were bestowed unnecessarily. The sun rose high above the heavens, and not the fleetest stag in Breadalbane, were the hounds at his heels, could have sped, to save his life, so fast as would have been necessary to keep Hamish's appointment. Her purpose was fully attained— her son's return within the period assigned was impossible. She deemed it equally impossible that he would ever dream of returning, standing, as he must now do, in the danger of an infamous punishment. By degrees, and at different times, she had gained from him a full acquaintance with the predicament in which he would be placed by failing to appear on the day appointed, and the very small hope he could entertain of being treated with lenity. It is well known that the great and wise Earl of Chatham*prided himself on the scheme by which he drew together for the defence of the colonies, those hardy Highlanders, who, until his time, had been the objects of doubt, fear, and suspicion on the part of each successive administration. But some obstacles occurred, from the peculiar habits and temper of this people, to the execution of his patriotic project. By nature and habit, every Highlander was accustomed to the use of arms, but at the same time totally unaccustomed to, and impatient of, the restraints imposed by discipline upon regular troops. They were a species of militia, who had no conception of a camp as their only home. If a battle was lost, they dispersed to save themselves, and look out for the safety of their families; if won, they went back to their glens to hoard up their booty, and attend to their cattle and their farms. This privilege of

going and coming at pleasure, they would not be
deprived of even by their chiefs, whose authority
was in most other respects so despotic. It followed
as a matter of course, that the new-levied Highland recruits could scarce be made to comprehend the nature of a military engagement, which
compelled a man to serve in the army longer than
he pleased; and perhaps, in many instances,
sufficient care was not taken at enlisting to explain to them the permanency of the engagement
which they came under, lest such a disclosure
should induce them to change their mind. Deser-
tions were therefore become numerous from the
newly-raised regiment, and the veteran general
who commanded at Dunbarton saw no better
way of checking them than by causing an unusually severe example to be made of a deserter
from an English corps. The young Highland
regiment was obliged to attend upon the punishment, which struck a people peculiarly jealous
of personal honour with equal horror and disgust,
and not unnaturally indisposed some of them to
the service. The old general, however, who had
been regularly bred in the German wars, stuck
to his own opinion, and gave out in orders that
the first Highlander who might either desert, or
fail to appear at the expiry of his furlough, should
be brought to the halberds and punished like the
culprit whom they had seen in that condition.
No man doubted that General —— would keep
his word rigorously whenever severity was required, and Elspat, therefore, knew that her son,
when he perceived that due compliance with his
orders was impossible, must at the same time
consider the degrading punishment denounced

against his defection as inevitable, should he place himself within the General's power.*

When noon was well passed, new apprehensions came on the mind of the lonely woman. Her son still slept under the influence of the draught; but what if, being stronger than she had ever known it administered, his health or his reason should be affected by its potency? For the first time, likewise, notwithstanding her high ideas on the subject of parental authority, she began to dread the resentment of her son, whom her heart told her she had wronged. Of late, she had observed that his temper was less docile, and his determinations, especially upon this late occasion of his enlistment, independently formed, and then boldly carried through. She remembered the stern wilfulness of his father when he accounted himself ill-used, and began to dread that Hamish, upon finding the deceit she had put upon him, might resent it even to the extent of casting her off, and pursuing his own course through the world alone. Such were the alarming and yet the reasonable apprehensions which began to crowd upon the unfortunate woman, after the apparent success of her ill-advised stratagem.

It was near evening when Hamish first awoke, and then he was far from being in the full possession either of his mental or bodily powers. From his vague expressions and disordered pulse, Elspat at first experienced much apprehension; but she used such expedients as her medical knowledge suggested; and in the course of the night she had the satisfaction to see him sink once more into a deep sleep, which probably carried off the greater part of the effects of the drug, for about sunrising she heard him arise, and call to her for his bonnet. This she had purposely removed, from a fear that he might awaken and depart in the night-time, withou' her knowledge.

'My bonnet—my bonnet,' cried Hamish, 'it is time to take farewell. Mother, your drink was too strong—the sun is up—but with the next morning I will still see the double summit of the ancient Dun. My bonnet—my bonnet! mother, I must be instant in my departure.' These expressions made it plain that poor Hamish was unconscious that two nights and a day had passed since he had drained the fatal quaigh, and Elspat had now to venture on what she felt as the almost perilous, as well as painful task, of explaining her machinations.

'Forgive me, my son,' she said, approaching Hamish, and taking him by the hand with an air of deferential awe, which perhaps she had not always used to his father, even when in his moody fits.

'Forgive you, mother—for what?' said Hamish, laughing; 'for giving me a dram that was too strong, and which my head still feels this morning, or for hiding my bonnet to keep me an instant longer? Nay, do *you* forgive *me*. Give me the bonnet, and let that be done which now must be done. Give me my bonnet, or I go without it; surely I am not to be delayed by so trifling a want as that—I, who have gone for years with only a strap of deer's hide to tie back my hair. Trifle not, but give it me, or I must go bareheaded, since to stay is impossible.'

'My son,' said Elspat, keeping fast hold of his hand, 'what is done cannot be recalled; could you borrow the wings of yonder eagle, you would arrive at the Dun too late for what you purpose, —too soon for what awaits you there. You believe you see the sun rising for the first time since you have seen him set, but yesterday beheld him climb Ben Cruachan, though your eyes were closed to his light.'

Hamish cast upon his mother a wild glance of extreme terror, then instantly recovering himself, said—'I am no child to be cheated out of my purpose by such tricks as these—Farewell, mother, each moment is worth a lifetime.'

'Stay,' she said, 'my dear—my deceived son! rush not on infamy and ruin—Yonder I see the priest upon the highroad on his white horse—ask him the day of the month and week—let him decide between us.'

With the speed of an eagle, Hamish darted up the acclivity and stood by the minister of Glenorquhy, who was pacing out thus early to administer consolation to a distressed family near Bunawe.

The good man was somewhat startled to behold an armed Highlander, then so unusual a sight, and apparently much agitated, stop his horse by the bridle, and ask him with a faltering voice the day of the week and month. 'Had you been where you should have been yesterday, young man,' replied the clergyman, 'you would have known that it was God's Sabbath; and that this is Monday, the second day of the week, and twenty-first of the month.'

'And this is true?' said Hamish.

'As true', answered the surprised minister, 'as that I yesterday preached the word of God to this parish.—What ails you, young man?—are you sick?—are you in your right mind?'

Hamish made no answer, only repeated to himself the first expression of the clergyman— 'Had you been where you should have been yesterday'; and so saying, he let go the bridle, turned from the road, and descended the path towards the hut with the look and pace of one who was going to execution. The minister looked after him with surprise; but although he knew the inhabitant of the hovel, the character of Elspat had not invited him to open any communication with her, because she was generally reputed a Papist, or rather one indifferent to all religion, except some superstitious observances which had been handed down from her parents. On Hamish the Reverend Mr. Tyrie had bestowed instructions when he was occasionally thrown in his way, and if the seed fell among the brambles and thorns*of a wild and uncultivated disposition, it had not yet been entirely checked or destroyed. There was something so ghastly in the present expression of the youth's features, that the good man was tempted to go down to the hovel, and inquire whether any distress had befallen the inhabitants in which his presence might be consoling, and his ministry useful. Unhappily he did not persevere in this resolution, which might have saved a great misfortune, as he would have probably become a mediator for the unfortunate young man; but a recollection of the wild moods of such Highlanders as had been educated after the old fashion of the country, prevented his interesting himself in the widow and son of the far-dreaded robber, MacTavish Mhor; and he thus missed an opportunity, which he afterwards sorely repented, of doing much good.

When Hamish MacTavish entered his mother's hut, it was only to throw himself on the bed he had left, and exclaiming, 'Undone, undone!' to give vent, in cries of grief and anger, to his deep sense of the deceit which had been practised on him, and of the cruel predicament to which he was reduced.

Elspat was prepared for the first explosion of her son's passion, and said to herself, 'It is but the mountain torrent, swelled by the thunder shower. Let us sit and rest us by the bank; for all its present tumult, the time will soon come when we may pass it dryshod.' She suffered his complaints and his reproaches, which were, even in the midst of his agony, respectful and affectionate, to die away without returning any answer; and when, at length, having exhausted all the exclamations of sorrow which his language, copious in expressing the feelings of the heart, affords to the sufferer, he sunk into a gloomy silence, she suffered the interval to continue near an hour ere she approached her son's couch.

'And now', she said at length, with a voice in which the authority of the mother was qualified by her tenderness, 'have you exhausted your idle sorrows, and are you able to place what you have gained against what you have lost? Is the false son of Dermid your brother, or the father of your tribe, that you weep because you cannot bind yourself to his belt, and become one of those who must do his bidding? Could you find in yonder distant country the lakes and the mountains that you leave behind you here? Can you hunt the deer of Breadalbane in the forests of America, or will the ocean afford you the silver-scaled salmon of the Awe? Consider, then, what is your loss, and like a wise man, set it against what you have won.'

'I have lost all, mother,' replied Hamish, 'since I have broken my word and lost my honour. I might tell my tale, but who, oh, who would believe me?' The unfortunate young man again clasped his hands together, and pressing them to his forehead, hid his face upon the bed.

Elspat was now really alarmed, and perhaps wished the fatal deceit had been left unattempted. She had no hope or refuge saving in the eloquence of persuasion, of which she possessed no small share, though her total ignorance of the world as it actually existed rendered its energy unavailing. She urged her son, by every tender epithet which a parent could bestow, to take care for his own safety.

'Leave me,' she said, 'to baffle your pursuers. I will save your life—I will save your honour— I will tell them that my fair-haired Hamish fell from the Corrie dhu (black precipice)* into the gulf, of which human eye never beheld the bottom. I will tell them this, and I will fling your plaid on the thorns which grow on the brink of the precipice, that they may believe my words. They will believe, and they will return to the Dun of the double-crest;* for though the Saxon drum can call the living to die, it cannot recall the dead to their slavish standard. Then will we travel together far northward to the salt

lakes of Kintail, and place glens and mountains
betwixt us and the sons of Dermid. We will visit
the shores of the dark lake, and my kinsmen—(for
was not my mother of the children of Kenneth,*
and will they not remember us with the old
love?)—my kinsmen will receive us with the
affection of the olden time, which lives in those
distant glens, where the Gael still dwell in their
nobleness, unmingled with the churl Saxons, or
with the base brood that are their tools and their
slaves.'

The energy of the language, somewhat allied
to hyperbole, even in its most ordinary expressions, now seemed almost too weak to afford
Elspat the means of bringing out the splendid
picture which she presented to her son of the land
in which she proposed to him to take refuge.
Yet the colours were few with which she could
paint her Highland paradise. 'The hills', she
said, 'were higher and more magnificent than
those of Breadalbane—Ben Cruachan was but
a dwarf to Skooroora. The lakes were broader
and larger, and abounded not only with fish, but
with the enchanted and amphibious animal
which gives oil to the lamp.[1] The deer were
larger and more numerous—the white-tusked
boar, the chase of which the brave loved best,
was yet to be roused in those western solitudes—
the men were nobler, wiser, and stronger than
the degenerate brood who lived under the Saxon
banner. The daughters of the land were beautiful, with blue eyes and fair hair and bosoms of
snow, and out of these she would choose a wife

[1] The seals are considered by the Highlanders as enchanted princes.

for Hamish, of blameless descent, spotless fame,
fixed and true affection, who should be in their
summer bothy as a beam of the sun, and in their
winter abode as the warmth of the needful fire.'

Such were the topics with which Elspat strove
to soothe the despair of her son, and to determine
him, if possible, to leave the fatal spot, on which
he seemed resolved to linger. The style of her
rhetoric was poetical, but in other respects resembled that which, like other fond mothers, she
had lavished on Hamish, while a child or a boy,
in order to gain his consent to do something he
had no mind to; and she spoke louder, quicker,
and more earnestly, in proportion as she began
to despair of her words carrying conviction.

On the mind of Hamish her eloquence made
no impression. He knew far better than she did
the actual situation of the country, and was
sensible that, though it might be possible to hide
himself as a fugitive among more distant mountains, there was now no corner in the Highlands
in which his father's profession could be practised,
even if he had not adopted, from the improved
ideas of the time when he lived, the opinion that
the trade of the cateran was no longer the road
to honour and distinction. Her words were
therefore poured into regardless ears, and she
exhausted herself in vain in the attempt to paint
the regions of her mother's kinsmen in such
terms as might tempt Hamish to accompany her
thither. She spoke for hours, but she spoke in
vain. She could extort no answer, save groans,
and sighs, and ejaculations, expressing the extremity of despair.

At length, starting on her feet, and changing

the monotonous tone in which she had chanted, as it were, the praises of the province of refuge, into the short, stern language of eager passion—'I am a fool', she said, 'to spend my words upon an idle, poor-spirited, unintelligent boy, who crouches like a hound to the lash. Wait here, and receive your task-masters and abide your chastisement at their hands; but do not think your mother's eyes will behold it. I could not see it and live. My eyes have looked often upon death, but never upon dishonour. Farewell, Hamish!—We never meet again.'

She dashed from the hut like a lapwing, and perhaps for the moment actually entertained the purpose which she expressed, of parting with her son for ever. A fearful sight she would have been that evening to any who might have met her wandering through the wilderness like a restless spirit, and speaking to herself in language which will endure no translation. She rambled for hours, seeking rather than shunning the most dangerous paths. The precarious track through the morass, the dizzy path along the edge of the precipice, or by the banks of the gulfing river, were the roads which, far from avoiding, she sought with eagerness, and traversed with reckless haste. But the courage arising from despair was the means of saving the life, which (though deliberate suicide was rarely practised in the Highlands) she was perhaps desirous of terminating. Her step on the verge of the precipice was firm as that of the wild goat. Her eye, in that state of excitement, was so keen as to discern, even amid darkness, the perils which noon would not have enabled a stranger to avoid.

Elspat's course was not directly forward, else she had soon been far from the bothy in which she had left her son. It was circuitous, for that hut was the centre to which her heartstrings were chained, and though she wandered around it, she felt it impossible to leave the vicinity. With the first beams of morning, she returned to the hut. A while she paused at the wattled door, as if ashamed that lingering fondness should have brought her back to the spot which she had left with the purpose of never returning; but there was yet more of fear and anxiety in her hesitation —of anxiety, lest her fair-haired son had suffered from the effects of her potion—of fear, lest his enemies had come upon him in the night. She opened the door of the hut gently, and entered with noiseless step. Exhausted with his sorrow and anxiety, and not entirely relieved perhaps from the influence of the powerful opiate, Hamish Bean again slept the stern sound sleep, by which the Indians are said to be overcome during the interval of their torments. His mother was scarcely sure that she actually discerned his form on the bed, scarce certain that her ear caught the sound of his breathing. With a throbbing heart, Elspat went to the fireplace in the centre of the hut, where slumbered, covered with a piece of turf, the glimmering embers of the fire, never extinguished on a Scottish hearth until the indwellers leave the mansion for ever.

'Feeble greishogh,'[1] she said, as she lighted, by the help of a match, a splinter of bog pine which was to serve the place of a candle; 'weak greishogh, soon shalt thou be put out for ever,

[1] Greishogh, a glowing ember.

and may Heaven grant that the life of Elspat MacTavish have no longer duration than thine!'

While she spoke she raised the blazing light towards the bed, on which still lay the prostrate limbs of her son, in a posture that left it doubtful whether he slept or swooned. As she advanced towards him, the light flashed upon his eyes— he started up in an instant, made a stride forward with his naked dirk in his hand, like a man armed to meet a mortal enemy, and exclaimed, 'Stand off!—on thy life, stand off!'

'It is the word and the action of my husband,' answered Elspat; 'and I know by his speech and his step the son of MacTavish Mhor.'

'Mother,' said Hamish, relapsing from his tone of desperate firmness into one of melancholy expostulation; 'oh, dearest mother, wherefore have you returned hither?'

'Ask why the hind comes back to the fawn,' said Elspat; 'why the cat of the mountain returns to her lodge and her young. Know you, Hamish, that the heart of the mother only lives in the bosom of the child.'

'Then will it soon cease to throb,' said Hamish, 'unless it can beat within a bosom that lies beneath the turf. Mother, do not blame me; if I weep, it is not for myself, but for you, for my sufferings will soon be over; but yours——Oh, who but Heaven shall set a boundary to them!'

Elspat shuddered and stepped backward, but almost instantly resumed her firm and upright position, and her dauntless bearing.

'I thought thou wert a man but even now,' she said, 'and thou art again a child. Hearken to me yet, and let us leave this place together. Have

I done thee wrong or injury? if so, yet do not avenge it so cruelly—See, Elspat MacTavish, who never kneeled before even to a priest, falls prostrate before her own son and craves his forgiveness.' And at once she threw herself on her knees before the young man, seized on his hand, and kissing it an hundred times, repeated as often, in heart-breaking accents, the most earnest entreaties for forgiveness. 'Pardon,' she exclaimed, 'pardon, for the sake of your father's ashes—pardon, for the sake of the pain with which I bore thee, the care with which I nurtured thee!—Hear it, Heaven, and behold it, Earth—the mother asks pardon of her child, and she is refused!'

It was in vain that Hamish endeavoured to stem this tide of passion, by assuring his mother, with the most solemn asseverations, that he forgave entirely the fatal deceit which she had practised upon him.

'Empty words,' she said; 'idle protestations, which are but used to hide the obduracy of your resentment. Would you have me believe you, then leave the hut this instant, and retire from a country which every hour renders more dangerous—Do this, and I may think you have forgiven me—refuse it, and again I call on moon and stars, heaven and earth, to witness the unrelenting resentment with which you prosecute your mother for a fault, which, if it be one, arose out of love to you.'

'Mother,' said Hamish, 'on this subject you move me not. I will fly before no man. If Barcaldine should send every Gael that is under his banner, here, and in this place, will I abide them;

and when you bid me fly, you may as well command yonder mountain to be loosened from its foundations. Had I been sure of the road by which they are coming hither, I had spared them the pains of seeking me; but I might go by the mountain, while they perchance came by the lake. Here I will abide my fate; nor is there in Scotland a voice of power enough to bid me stir from hence, and be obeyed.'

'Here, then, I also stay,' said Elspat, rising up and speaking with assumed composure. 'I have seen my husband's death—my eyelids shall not grieve to look on the fall of my son. But MacTavish Mhor died as became the brave, with his good sword in his right hand; my son will perish like the bullock that is driven to the shambles by the Saxon owner, who has bought him for a price.'

'Mother,' said the unhappy young man, 'you have taken my life; to that you have a right, for you gave it; but touch not my honour! It came to me from a brave train of ancestors, and should be sullied neither by man's deed nor woman's speech. What I shall do, perhaps I myself yet know not; but tempt me no farther by reproachful words; you have already made wounds more than you can ever heal.'

'It is well, my son,' said Elspat, in reply. 'Expect neither farther complaint nor remonstrance from me; but let us be silent, and wait the chance which Heaven shall send us.'

The sun arose on the next morning, and found the bothy silent as the grave. The mother and son had arisen, and were engaged each in their separate task—Hamish in preparing and cleaning his arms with the greatest accuracy, but with an air of deep dejection. Elspat, more restless in her agony of spirit, employed herself in making ready the food which the distress of yesterday had induced them both to dispense with for an unusual number of hours. She placed it on the board before her son so soon as it was prepared, with the words of a Gaelic poet, 'Without daily food, the husbandman's ploughshare stands still in the furrow; without daily food, the sword of the warrior is too heavy for his hand. Our bodies are our slaves, yet they must be fed if we would have their service. So spake, in ancient days, the Blind Bard to the warriors of Fion.'*

The young man made no reply, but he fed on what was placed before him, as if to gather strength for the scene which he was to undergo. When his mother saw that he had eaten what sufficed him, she again filled the fatal quaigh, and proffered it as the conclusion of the repast. But he started aside with a convulsive gesture, expressive at once of fear and abhorrence.

'Nay, my son,' she said, 'this time, surely, thou hast no cause of fear.'

'Urge me not, mother,' answered Hamish; 'or put the leprous toad into a flagon, and I will drink; but from that accursed cup and of that mind-destroying potion never will I taste more!'

'At your pleasure, my son,' said Elspat, haughtily; and began, with much apparent assiduity, the various domestic tasks which had been interrupted during the preceding day. Whatever was at her heart, all anxiety seemed banished from her looks and demeanour. It was but from an over-activity of bustling exertion that it might have been perceived, by a close observer, that her actions were spurred by some internal cause of painful excitement; and such a spectator, too, might also have observed how often she broke off the snatches of songs or tunes which she hummed, apparently without knowing what she was doing, in order to cast a hasty glance from the door of the hut. Whatever might be in the mind of Hamish, his demeanour was directly the reverse of that adopted by his mother. Having finished the task of cleaning and preparing his arms, which he arranged within the hut, he sat himself down before the door of the bothy, and watched the opposite hill, like the fixed sentinel who expects the approach of an enemy. Noon found him in the same unchanged posture, and it was an hour after that period, when his mother, standing beside him, laid her hand on his shoulder, and said, in a tone indifferent as if she had been talking of some friendly visit, 'When dost thou expect them?'

'They cannot be here till the shadows fall long to the eastward,' replied Hamish; 'that is, even supposing the nearest party, commanded by Sergeant Allan Breack Cameron, has been commanded hither by express from Dunbarton, as it is most likely they will.'

'Then enter beneath your mother's roof once more; partake the last time of the food which she has prepared; after this, let them come, and thou shalt see if thy mother is a useless encumbrance in the day of strife. Thy hand, practised as it is, cannot fire these arms so fast as I can load them; nay, if it is necessary, I do not myself fear the flash or the report, and my aim has been held fatal.'

'In the name of Heaven, mother, meddle not with this matter!' said Hamish. 'Allan Breack is a wise man and a kind one, and comes of a good stem. It may be, he can promise for our officers that they will touch me with no infamous punishment; and if they offer me confinement in the dungeon, or death by the musket, to that I may not object.'

'Alas! and wilt thou trust to their word, my foolish child? Remember the race of Dermid were ever fair and false, and no sooner shall they have gyves on thy hands, than they will strip thy shoulders for the scourge.'

'Save your advice, mother,' said Hamish, sternly; 'for me, my mind is made up.'

But though he spoke thus, to escape the almost persecuting urgency of his mother, Hamish would have found it, at that moment, impossible to say upon what course of conduct he had thus fixed. On one point alone he was determined, namely, to abide his destiny, be what it might, and not to add to the breach of his word, of which he had been involuntarily rendered guilty, by attempting to escape from punishment. This act of self-devotion he conceived to be due to his own honour, and that of his countrymen. Which of his comrades would in future be trusted, if he should be considered as having broken his word, and betrayed the confidence of his officers? and whom but Hamish Bean MacTavish would the Gael accuse, for having verified and confirmed the suspicions which the Saxon general was well known to entertain against the good faith of the Highlanders? He was, therefore, bent firmly to abide his fate. But whether his intention was to yield himself peaceably into the hands of the party who should come to apprehend him, or whether he purposed, by a show of resistance, to provoke them to kill him on the spot, was a question which he could not himself have answered. His desire to see Barcaldine, and explain the cause of his absence at the appointed time, urged him to the one course; his fear of the degrading punishment, and of his mother's bitter upbraidings, strongly instigated the latter and the more dangerous purpose. He left it to chance to decide when the crisis should arrive; nor did he tarry long in expectation of the catastrophe.

Evening approached, the gigantic shadows of the mountains streamed in darkness towards the east, while their western peaks were still glowing with crimson and gold. The road which winds round Ben Cruachan was fully visible from the door of the bothy, when a party of five Highland soldiers, whose arms glanced in the sun, wheeled suddenly into sight from the most distant extremity where the highway is hidden behind the mountain. One of the party walked a little before the other four, who marched regularly and in files, according to the rules of military discipline. There was no dispute, from the firelocks which they carried, and the plaids and bonnets which they wore, that they were a party of Hamish's regiment, under a non-commissioned officer; and there could be as little doubt of the purpose of their appearance on the banks of Loch Awe.

'They come briskly forward,' said the widow of MacTavish Mhor,—'I wonder how fast or how slow some of them will return again! But they

are five, and it is too much odds for a fair field.
Step back, within the hut, my son, and shoot
from the loophole beside the door. Two you
may bring down ere they quit the highroad for
the footpath—there will remain but three; and
your father, with my aid, has often stood against
that number.'

Hamish Bean took the gun which his mother
offered, but did not stir from the door of the hut.
He was soon visible to the party on the highroad,
as was evident from their increasing their pace
to a run; the files, however, still keeping together,
like coupled greyhounds, and advancing with
great rapidity. In far less time than would have
been accomplished by men less accustomed to the
mountains, they had left the highroad, traversed
the narrow path, and approached within pistol-
shot of the bothy, at the door of which stood
Hamish, fixed like a statue of stone, with his
firelock in his hand, while his mother, placed
behind him, and almost driven to frenzy by the
violence of her passions, reproached him in the
strongest terms which despair could invent, for
his want of resolution and faintness of heart.
Her words increased the bitter gall which was
arising in the young man's own spirit, as he
observed the unfriendly speed with which his
late comrades were eagerly making towards him,
like hounds towards the stag when he is at bay.
The untamed and angry passions which he inherited from father and mother were awakened
by the supposed hostility of those who pursued
him; and the restraint under which these passions
had been hitherto held by his sober judgement
began gradually to give way. The sergeant now

called to him, 'Hamish Bean MacTavish, lay down your arms, and surrender.'

'Do *you* stand, Allan Breack Cameron, and command your men to stand, or it will be the worse for us all.'

'Halt, men!'—said the sergeant, but continuing himself to advance. 'Hamish, think what you do, and give up your gun; you may spill blood, but you cannot escape punishment.'

'The scourge—the scourge!—My son, beware the scourge!' whispered his mother.

'Take heed, Allan Breack,' said Hamish. 'I would not hurt you willingly,—but I will not be taken unless you can assure me against the Saxon lash.'

'Fool!' answered Cameron, 'you know I cannot; yet I will do all I can. I will say I met you on your return, and the punishment will be light —But give up your musket.—Come on, men.'

Instantly he rushed forward, extending his arm as if to push aside the young man's levelled firelock. Elspat exclaimed, 'Now, spare not your father's blood to defend your father's hearth!' Hamish fired his piece, and Cameron dropped dead. All these things happened, it might be said, in the same moment of time. The soldiers rushed forward and seized Hamish, who, seeming petrified with what he had done, offered not the least resistance. Not so his mother; who, seeing the men about to put handcuffs on her son, threw herself on the soldiers with such fury, that it required two of them to hold her, while the rest secured the prisoner.

'Are you not an accursed creature,' said one of the men to Hamish, 'to have slain your best friend, who was contriving, during the whole march, how he could find some way of getting you off without punishment for your desertion?'

'Do you hear *that*, mother?' said Hamish, turning himself as much towards her as his bonds would permit—but the mother heard nothing, and saw nothing. She had fainted on the floor of her hut. Without waiting for her recovery, the party almost immediately began their homeward march towards Dunbarton, leading along with them their prisoner. They thought it necessary, however, to stay for a little space at the village of Dalmally, from which they dispatched a party of the inhabitants to bring away the body of their unfortunate leader, while they themselves repaired to a magistrate to state what had happened, and require his instructions as to the farther course to be pursued. The crime being of a military character, they were instructed to march the prisoner to Dunbarton without delay.

The swoon of the mother of Hamish lasted for a length of time; the longer perhaps that her constitution, strong as it was, must have been much exhausted by her previous agitation of three days' endurance. She was roused from her stupor at length by female voices, which cried the coronach, or lament for the dead, with clapping of hands and loud exclamations; while the melancholy note of a lament, appropriate to the clan Cameron, played on the bagpipe, was heard from time to time.

Elspat started up like one awakened from the dead, and without any accurate recollection of the scene which had passed before her eyes. There were females in the hut who were swathing the corpse in its bloody plaid before carrying it from the fatal spot. 'Women,' she said, starting up and interrupting their chant at once and their labour—'Tell me, women, why sing you the dirge of MacDhonuil Dhu*in the house of MacTavish Mhor?'

'She-wolf, be silent with thine ill-omened yell,' answered one of the females, a relation of the deceased, 'and let us do our duty to our beloved kinsman! There shall never be coronach cried, or dirge played, for thee or thy bloody wolf-burd.[1] The ravens shall eat him from the gibbet, and the foxes and wild-cats shall tear thy corpse upon the hill. Cursed be he that would sain your bones, or add a stone to your cairn!"*

'Daughter of a foolish mother,' answered the widow of MacTavish Mhor, 'know that the gibbet with which you threaten us is no portion of our inheritance. For thirty years the Black Tree of the Law, whose apples are dead men's bodies, hungered after the beloved husband of my heart; but he died like a brave man, with the sword in his hand, and defrauded it of its hopes and its fruit.'

'So shall it not be with thy child, bloody sorceress,' replied the female mourner, whose passions were as violent as those of Elspat herself. 'The ravens shall tear his fair hair to line their nests, before the sun sinks beneath the Treshornish islands.'

These words recalled to Elspat's mind the whole history of the last three dreadful days. At first, she stood fixed as if the extremity of distress had converted her into stone; but in a minute,

[1] Wolf-brood, i.e. wolf-cub.

the pride and violence of her temper, outbraved as she thought herself on her own threshold, enabled her to reply—'Yes, insulting hag, my fair-haired boy may die, but it will not be with a white hand—it has been dyed in the blood of his enemy, in the best blood of a Cameron— remember that; and when you lay your dead in his grave, let it be his best epitaph, that he was killed by Hamish Bean for essaying to lay hands on the son of MacTavish Mhor on his own threshold. Farewell—the shame of defeat, loss, and slaughter remain with the clan that has endured it.'

The relative of the slaughtered Cameron raised her voice in reply; but Elspat, disdaining to continue the objurgation, or perhaps feeling her grief likely to overmaster her power of expressing her resentment, had left the hut, and was walking forth in the bright moonshine.

The females who were arranging the corpse of the slaughtered man hurried from their melancholy labour to look after her tall figure as it glided away among the cliffs. 'I am glad she is gone,' said one of the younger persons who assisted. 'I would as soon dress a corpse when the great Fiend himself—God sain us—stood visibly before us, as when Elspat of the Tree is amongst us.—Ay—ay, even overmuch intercourse hath she had with the Enemy in her day.'

'Silly woman,' answered the female who had maintained the dialogue with the departed Elspat, 'thinkest thou that there is a worse fiend on earth, or beneath it, than the pride and fury of an offended woman, like yonder bloody-minded hag? Know that blood has been as familiar to her as the dew to the mountain daisy. Many and many a brave man has she caused to breathe their last for little wrong they had done to her or hers. But her hough-sinews are cut, now that her wolf-burd must, like a murderer as he is, make a murderer's end.'

Whilst the women thus discoursed together as they watched the corpse of Allan Breack Cameron, the unhappy cause of his death pursued her lonely way across the mountain. While she remained within sight of the bothy, she put a strong constraint on herself, that by no alteration of pace or gesture she might afford to her enemies the triumph of calculating the excess of her mental agitation, nay, despair. She stalked, therefore, with a slow rather than a swift step, and, holding herself upright, seemed at once to endure with firmness that woe which was passed, and bid defiance to that which was about to come. But when she was beyond the sight of those who remained in the hut, she could no longer suppress the extremity of her agitation. Drawing her mantle wildly round her, she stopped at the first knoll, and climbing to its summit, extended her arms up to the bright moon, as if accusing heaven and earth for her misfortunes, and uttered scream on scream, like those of an eagle whose nest has been plundered of her brood. Awhile she vented her grief in these inarticulate cries, then rushed on her way with a hasty and unequal step, in the vain hope of overtaking the party which was conveying her son a prisoner to Dunbarton. But her strength, superhuman as it seemed, failed her in the trial, nor was it possible for her, with her utmost efforts, to accomplish her purpose.

Yet she pressed onward, with all the speed which her exhausted frame could exert. When food became indispensable, she entered the first cottage: 'Give me to eat,' she said; 'I am the widow of MacTavish Mhor—I am the mother of Hamish MacTavish Bean,—give me to eat, that I may once more see my fair-haired son.' Her demand was never refused, though granted in many cases with a kind of struggle between compassion and aversion in some of those to whom she applied, which was in others qualified by fear. The share she had had in occasioning the death of Allan Breack Cameron, which must probably involve that of her own son, was not accurately known; but, from a knowledge of her violent passions and former habits of life, no one doubted that in one way or other she had been the cause of the catastrophe; and Hamish Bean was considered, in the slaughter which he had committed, rather as the instrument than as the accomplice of his mother.

This general opinion of his countrymen was of little service to the unfortunate Hamish. As his captain, Green Colin, understood the manners and habits of his country, he had no difficulty in collecting from Hamish the particulars accompanying his supposed desertion, and the subsequent death of the non-commissioned officer. He felt the utmost compassion for a youth who had thus fallen a victim to the extravagant and fatal fondness of a parent. But he had no excuse to plead which could rescue his unhappy recruit from the doom which military discipline and the award of a court martial denounced against him for the crime he had committed.

No time had been lost in their proceedings, and as little was interposed betwixt sentence and execution. General —— had determined to make a severe example of the first deserter who should fall into his power, and here was one who had defended himself by main force, and slain in the affray the officer sent to take him into custody. A fitter subject for punishment could not have occurred, and Hamish was sentenced to immediate execution. All which the interference of his captain in his favour could procure was that he should die a soldier's death; for there had been a purpose of executing him upon the gibbet.

The worthy clergyman of Glenorquhy chanced to be at Dunbarton, in attendance upon some church courts, at the time of this catastrophe. He visited his unfortunate parishioner in his dungeon, found him ignorant indeed but not obstinate, and the answers which he received from him, when conversing on religious topics, were such as induced him doubly to regret that a mind naturally pure and noble should have remained unhappily so wild and uncultivated.

When he ascertained the real character and disposition of the young man, the worthy pastor made deep and painful reflections on his own shyness and timidity, which, arising out of the evil fame that attached to the lineage of Hamish, had restrained him from charitably endeavouring to bring this strayed sheep within the great fold. While the good minister blamed his cowardice in times past, which had deterred him from risking his person to save, perhaps, an immortal soul, he resolved no longer to be governed by

such timid counsels, but to endeavour, by application to his officers, to obtain a reprieve at least,
if not a pardon, for the criminal in whom he felt
so unusually interested at once from his docility
of temper and his generosity of disposition.

Accordingly, the divine sought out Captain
Campbell at the barracks within the garrison.
There was a gloomy melancholy on the brow of
Green Colin, which was not lessened, but increased, when the clergyman stated his name,
quality, and errand. 'You cannot tell me better
of the young man than I am disposed to believe,'
answered the Highland officer; 'you cannot ask
me to do more in his behalf than I am of myself
inclined, and have already endeavoured to do.
But it is all in vain. General —— is half a Lowlander, half an Englishman. He has no idea of
the high and enthusiastic character which, in
these mountains, often brings exalted virtues in
contact with great crimes, which, however, are
less offences of the heart than errors of the understanding. I have gone so far as to tell him that
in this young man he was putting to death the
best and the bravest of my company, where all,
or almost all, are good and brave. I explained
to him by what strange delusion the culprit's
apparent desertion was occasioned, and how
little his heart was accessory to the crime which
his hand unhappily committed. His answer was,
"These are Highland visions, Captain Campbell,
as unsatisfactory and vain as those of the second
sight. An act of gross desertion may, in any case,
be palliated under the plea of intoxication; the
murder of an officer may be as easily coloured
over with that of temporary insanity. The

example must be made; and if it has fallen on a man otherwise a good recruit, it will have the greater effect."—Such being the general's unalterable purpose,' continued Captain Campbell, with a sigh, 'be it your care, reverend sir, that your penitent prepare, by break of day tomorrow, for that great change which we shall all one day be subjected to.'

'And for which,' said the clergyman, 'may God prepare us all, as I in my duty will not be wanting to this poor youth.'

Next morning, as the very earliest beams of sunrise saluted the grey towers which crown the summit of that singular and tremendous rock, the soldiers of the new Highland regiment appeared on the parade within the Castle of Dunbarton, and having fallen into order, began to move downward by steep staircases and narrow passages towards the external barrier-gate which is at the very bottom of the rock. The wild wailings of the pibroch were heard at times, interchanged with the drums and fifes, which beat the Dead March.

The unhappy criminal's fate did not, at first, excite that general sympathy in the regiment which would probably have arisen had he been executed for desertion alone. The slaughter of the unfortunate Allan Breack had given a different colour to Hamish's offence; for the deceased was much beloved, and besides belonged to a numerous and powerful clan, of whom there were many in the ranks. The unfortunate criminal, on the contrary, was little known to, and scarcely connected with, any of his regimental companions. His father had been, indeed, distinguished for his strength and manhood, but he was of a broken clan, as those names were called who had no chief to lead them to battle.

It would have been almost impossible, in another case, to have turned out of the ranks of the regiment the party necessary for execution of the sentence; but the six individuals selected for that purpose were friends of the deceased, descended, like him, from the race of MacDhonuil Dhu; and while they prepared for the dismal task which their duty imposed, it was not without a stern feeling of gratified revenge. The leading company of the regiment began now to defile from the barrier-gate, and was followed by the others, each successively moving and halting according to the orders of the adjutant, so as to form three sides of an oblong square, with the ranks faced inwards. The fourth, or blank side of the square, was closed up by the huge and lofty precipice on which the castle rises. About the centre of the procession, bareheaded, disarmed, and with his hands bound, came the unfortunate victim of military law. He was deadly pale, but his step was firm and his eye as bright as ever. The clergyman walked by his side—the coffin, which was to receive his mortal remains, was borne before him. The looks of his comrades were still, composed, and solemn. They felt for the youth, whose handsome form and manly yet submissive deportment had, as soon as he was distinctly visible to them, softened the hearts of many, even of some who had been actuated by vindictive feelings.

The coffin destined for the yet living body of

Hamish Bean was placed at the bottom of the hollow square, about two yards distant from the foot of the precipice, which rises in that place as steep as a stone wall to the height of three or four hundred feet. Thither the prisoner was also led, the clergyman still continuing by his side, pouring forth exhortations of courage and consolation, to which the youth appeared to listen with respectful devotion. With slow and, it seemed, almost unwilling steps, the firing party entered the square, and were drawn up facing the prisoner, about ten yards distant. The clergyman was now about to retire—'Think, my son,' he said, 'on what I have told you, and let your hope be rested on the anchor which I have given. You will then exchange a short and miserable existence here for a life in which you will experience neither sorrow nor pain.—Is there aught else which you can entrust to me to execute for you?'

The youth looked at his sleeve buttons. They were of gold, booty perhaps which his father had taken from some English officer during the civil wars.* The clergyman disengaged them from his sleeves.

'My mother!' he said with some effort, 'give them to my poor mother!—See her, good father, and teach her what she should think of all this. Tell her Hamish Bean is more glad to die than ever he was to rest after the longest day's hunting. Farewell, sir—Farewell!'

The good man could scarce retire from the fatal spot. An officer afforded him the support of his arm. At his last look towards Hamish, he beheld him alive and kneeling on the coffin; the few that were around him had all withdrawn. The fatal word was given, the rock rang sharp to the sound of the discharge, and Hamish, falling forward with a groan, died, it may be supposed, without almost a sense of the passing agony.

Ten or twelve of his own company then came forward, and laid with solemn reverence the remains of their comrade in the coffin, while the Dead March was again struck up, and the several companies, marching in single files, passed the coffin one by one, in order that all might receive from the awful spectacle the warning which it was peculiarly intended to afford. The regiment was then marched off the ground, and reascended the ancient cliff, their music, as usual on such occasions, striking lively strains, as if sorrow, or even deep thought, should as short a while as possible be the tenant of the soldier's bosom.

At the same time the small party, which we before mentioned, bore the bier of the ill-fated Hamish to his humble grave, in a corner of the churchyard of Dunbarton usually assigned to criminals. Here, among the dust of the guilty, lies a youth, whose name, had he survived the ruin of the fatal events by which he was hurried into crime, might have adorned the annals of the brave.

The minister of Glenorquhy left Dunbarton immediately after he had witnessed the last scene of this melancholy catastrophe. His reason acquiesced in the justice of the sentence, which required blood for blood, and he acknowledged that the vindictive character of his countrymen required to be powerfully restrained by the strong curb of social law. But still he mourned over the individual victim. Who may arraign the bolt of Heaven when it bursts among the sons of the forest; yet who can refrain from mourning, when it selects for the object of its blighting aim the fair stem of a young oak that promised to be the pride of the dell in which it flourished? Musing on these melancholy events, noon found him engaged in the mountain passes, by which he was to return to his still distant home.

Confident in his knowledge of the country, the clergyman had left the main road, to seek one of those shorter paths which are only used by pedestrians, or by men, like the minister, mounted on the small but sure-footed, hardy, and sagacious horses of the country. The place which he now traversed was in itself gloomy and desolate, and tradition had added to it the terror of superstition, by affirming it was haunted by an evil spirit, termed *Cloght-dearg*,* that is, Red-mantle, who at all times, but especially at noon and at midnight, traversed the glen, in enmity both to man and the inferior creation, did such evil as her power was permitted to extend to, and afflicted with ghastly terrors those whom she had not licence otherwise to hurt.

The minister of Glenorquhy had set his face in opposition to many of these superstitions, which he justly thought were derived from the dark ages of Popery, perhaps even from those of paganism, and unfit to be entertained or believed by the Christians of an enlightened age. Some of his more attached parishioners considered him as too rash in opposing the ancient faith of their fathers; and though they honoured the moral intrepidity of their pastor, they could not avoid entertaining and expressing fears that he would one day fall a victim to his temerity, and be torn to pieces in the glen of the Cloght-dearg, or some of those other haunted wilds, which he appeared rather to have a pride and pleasure in traversing alone on the days and hours when the wicked spirits were supposed to have especial power over man and beast.

These legends came across the mind of the clergyman; and, solitary as he was, a melancholy smile shaded his cheek, as he thought of the inconsistency of human nature, and reflected how many brave men, whom the yell of the pibroch would have sent headlong against fixed bayonets as the wild bull rushes on his enemy, might have yet feared to encounter those visionary terrors, which he himself, a man of peace, and in ordinary perils no way remarkable for the firmness of his nerves, was now risking without hesitation.

As he looked around the scene of desolation, he could not but acknowledge in his own mind that it was not ill chosen for the haunt of those spirits which are said to delight in solitude and desolation. The glen was so steep and narrow, that there was but just room for the meridian sun to dart a few scattered rays upon the gloomy and precarious stream which stole through its recesses, for the most part in silence, but occasionally murmuring sullenly against the rocks and large stones which seemed determined to bar its further progress. In winter or in the rainy season, this small stream was a foaming torrent of the most formidable magnitude, and it was at such periods that it had torn open and laid bare the broad-faced and huge fragments of rock, which, at the season of which we speak, hid its course from the eye, and seemed disposed totally to interrupt its course. 'Undoubtedly', thought the clergyman, 'this mountain rivulet, suddenly swelled by a water-spout, or thunder-storm, has often been the cause of those accidents which, happening in the glen called by her name, have been ascribed to the agency of the Cloght-dearg.'

Just as this idea crossed his mind, he heard a female voice exclaim, in a wild and thrilling accent, 'Michael Tyrie—Michael Tyrie!' He looked round in astonishment, and not without some fear. It seemed for an instant as if the Evil Being, whose existence he had disowned, was about to appear for the punishment of his incredulity. This alarm did not hold him more than an instant, nor did it prevent his replying in a firm voice, 'Who calls—and where are you?'

'One who journeys in wretchedness, between life and death,' answered the voice; and the speaker, a tall female, appeared from among the fragments of rocks which had concealed her from view.

As she approached more closely, her mantle of bright tartan, in which the red colour much predominated, her stature, the long stride with which she advanced, and the writhen features and wild eyes which were visible from under her curch, would have made her no inadequate representative of the spirit which gave name to the valley. But Mr. Tyrie instantly knew her as the Woman of the Tree, the widow of MacTavish Mhor, the now childless mother of Hamish Bean.

I am not sure whether the minister would not have endured the visitation of the Cloght-dearg herself rather than the shock of Elspat's presence, considering her crime and her misery. He drew up his horse instinctively, and stood endeavouring to collect his ideas, while a few paces brought her up to his horse's head.

'Michael Tyrie,' said she, 'the foolish women of the clachan[1] hold thee as a god—be one to me, and say that my son lives. Say this, and I too will be of thy worship—I will bend my knees on the seventh day in thy house of worship, and thy God shall be my God.'

'Unhappy woman,' replied the clergyman, 'man forms not pactions with his Maker as with a creature of clay like himself. Thinkest thou to chaffer with Him who formed the earth and spread out the heavens, or that thou canst offer aught of homage or devotion that can be worth acceptance in His eyes? He hath asked obedience, not sacrifice; patience under the trials with which He afflicts us, instead of vain bribes such as man offers to his changeful brother of clay that he may be moved from his purpose.'

'Be silent, priest!' answered the desperate woman; 'speak not to me the words of thy white book. Elspat's kindred were of those who crossed themselves and knelt when the sacring bell was rung; and she knows that atonement can be made on the altar for deeds done in the field. Elspat had once flocks and herds, goats upon the cliffs, and cattle in the strath. She wore gold around her neck and on her hair—thick twists as those worn by the heroes of old. All these

[1] i.e. the village, literally the stones.

would she have resigned to the priest—all these; and if he wished for the ornaments of a gentle lady, or the sporran of a high chief, though they had been great as Macallanmore himself, Mac-Tavish Mhor would have procured them if Elspat had promised them. Elspat is now poor and has nothing to give. But the Black Abbot of Inchaffray*would have bidden her scourge her shoulders and macerate her feet by pilgrimage, and he would have granted his pardon to her when he saw that her blood had flowed and that her flesh had been torn. These were the priests who had indeed power even with the most power-ful—they threatened the great men of the earth with the word of their mouth, the sentence of their book, the blaze of their torch, the sound of their sacring bell. The mighty bent to their will, and unloosed at the word of the priests those whom they had bound in their wrath, and set at liberty, unharmed, him whom they had sentenced to death, and for whose blood they had thirsted. These were a powerful race, and might well ask the poor to kneel, since their power could humble the proud. But you!—against whom are ye strong, but against women who have been guilty of folly, and men who never wore sword? The priests of old were like the winter torrent which fills this hollow valley, and rolls these massive rocks against each other as easily as the boy plays with the ball which he casts before him—But you! you do but resemble the summer-stricken stream, which is turned aside by the rushes, and stemmed by a bush of sedges—Woe worth you, for there is no help in you!'

The clergyman was at no loss to conceive that

Elspat had lost the Roman Catholic faith without gaining any other, and that she still retained a vague and confused idea of the composition with the priesthood, by confession, alms, and penance, and of their extensive power, which, according to her notion, was adequate, if duly propitiated, even to effecting her son's safety. Compassionating her situation, and allowing for her errors and ignorance, he answered her with mildness.

'Alas, unhappy woman! Would to God I could convince thee as easily where thou oughtest to seek, and art sure to find consolation, as I can assure you with a single word that, were Rome and all her priesthood once more in the plenitude of their power, they could not, for largesse or penance, afford to thy misery an atom of aid or comfort.—Elspat MacTavish, I grieve to tell you the news.'

'I know them without thy speech,' said the unhappy woman—'My son is doomed to die.'

'Elspat,' resumed the clergyman, 'he *was* doomed, and the sentence has been executed.' The hapless mother threw her eyes up to heaven, and uttered a shriek so unlike the voice of a human being, that the eagle which soared in middle air answered it as she would have done the call of her mate.

'It is impossible!' she exclaimed, 'it is impossible! Men do not condemn and kill on the same day! Thou art deceiving me.—The people call thee holy—hast thou the heart to tell a mother she has murdered her only child?'

'God knows', said the priest, the tears falling fast from his eyes, 'that, were it in my power, I would gladly tell better tidings—but these which I bear are as certain as they are fatal—My own ears heard the death-shot, my own eyes beheld thy son's death—thy son's funeral.—My tongue bears witness to what my ears heard and my eyes saw.'

The wretched female clasped her hands close together, and held them up towards heaven like a sibyl announcing war and desolation; while, in impotent yet frightful rage, she poured forth a tide of the deepest imprecations.—'Base Saxon churl!' she exclaimed, 'vile hypocritical juggler! May the eyes that looked tamely on the death of my fair-haired boy be melted in their sockets with ceaseless tears, shed for those that are nearest and most dear to thee! May the ears that heard his death-knell be dead hereafter to all other sounds save the screech of the raven and the hissing of the adder! May the tongue that tells me of his death and of my own crime be withered in thy mouth—or, better, when thou wouldst pray with thy people, may the Evil One guide it, and give voice to blasphemies instead of blessings, until men shall fly in terror from thy presence, and the thunder of heaven be launched against thy head and stop for ever thy cursing and accursed voice!—begone, with this malison! Elspat will never, never again bestow so many words upon living man.'

She kept her word. From that day the world was to her a wilderness, in which she remained, without thought, care, or interest, absorbed in her own grief—indifferent to everything else.

With her mode of life, or rather of existence, the reader is already as far acquainted as I have the power of making him. Of her death, I can tell him nothing. It is supposed to have happened several years after she had attracted the attention of my excellent friend Mrs. Bethune Baliol. Her benevolence, which was never satisfied with dropping a sentimental tear when there was room for the operation of effective charity, induced her to make various attempts to alleviate the condition of this most wretched woman. But all her exertions could only render Elspat's means of subsistence less precarious, a circumstance which, though generally interesting even to the most wretched outcasts, seemed to her a matter of total indifference. Every attempt to place any person in her hut to take charge of her miscarried, through the extreme resentment with which she regarded all intrusion on her solitude, or by the timidity of those who had been pitched upon to be inmates with the terrible Woman of the Tree. At length, when Elspat became totally unable (in appearance at least) to turn herself on the wretched settle which served her for a couch, the humanity of Mr. Tyrie's successor sent two women to attend upon the last moments of the solitary, which could not, it was judged, be far distant, and to avert the possibility that she might perish for want of assistance or food, before she sunk under the effects of extreme age, or mortal malady.

It was on a November evening that the two women appointed for this melancholy purpose arrived at the miserable cottage which we have already described. Its wretched inmate lay stretched upon the bed, and seemed almost already a lifeless corpse, save for the wandering of the fierce dark eyes, which rolled in their sockets in a manner terrible to look upon, and seemed to watch with surprise and indignation the motions of the strangers, as persons whose presence was alike unexpected and unwelcome. They were frightened at her looks; but, assured in each other's company, they kindled a fire, lighted a candle, prepared food, and made other arrangements for the discharge of the duty assigned them.

The assistants agreed they should watch the bedside of the sick person by turns; but, about midnight, overcome by fatigue (for they had walked far that morning), both of them fell fast asleep. When they awoke, which was not till after the interval of some hours, the hut was empty, and the patient gone. They rose in terror, and went to the door of the cottage, which was latched as it had been at night. They looked out into the darkness, and called upon their charge by her name. The night-raven screamed from the old oak-tree; the fox howled on the hill; the hoarse waterfall replied with its echoes; but there was no human answer. The terrified women did not dare to make further search till morning should appear; for the sudden disappearance of a creature so frail as Elspat, together with the wild tenor of her history, intimidated them from stirring from the hut. They remained, therefore, in dreadful terror, sometimes thinking they heard her voice without, and at other times that sounds of a different description were mingled with the mournful sigh of the night-breeze or the dash of the cascade. Sometimes, too, the latch rattled, as if some frail and impotent hand were in vain attempting to lift it, and ever and anon they expected the entrance of their terrible patient, animated by supernatural strength, and in the company, perhaps, of some being more dreadful than herself. Morning came at length. They sought brake, rock, and thicket in vain. Two hours after daylight the minister himself appeared; and, on the report of the watchers, caused the country to be alarmed, and a general and exact search to be made through the whole neighbourhood of the cottage, and the oak-tree. But it was all in vain. Elspat MacTavish was never found, whether dead or alive; nor could there ever be traced the slightest circumstance to indicate her fate.

The neighbourhood was divided concerning the cause of her disappearance. The credulous thought that the Evil Spirit, under whose influence she seemed to have acted, had carried her away in the body; and there are many who are still unwilling, at untimely hours, to pass the oak-tree, beneath which as they allege she may still be seen seated according to her wont. Others less superstitious supposed that, had it been possible to search the gulf of the Corri Dhu, the profound depths of the lake, or the whelming eddies of the river, the remains of Elspat MacTavish might have been discovered; as nothing was more natural, considering her state of body and mind, than that she should have fallen in by accident, or precipitated herself intentionally into one or other of those places of sure destruction. The clergyman entertained an opinion of his own. He thought that, impatient of the watch which was placed over her, this unhappy woman's instinct had taught her, as it directs various domestic animals, to withdraw herself from the sight of her own race, that the death-struggle might take place in some secret den, where, in all probability, her mortal relics would never meet the eyes of mortals. This species of instinctive feeling seemed to him of a tenor with the whole course of her unhappy life, and most likely to influence her when it drew to a conclusion.

CHRONICLES OF THE CANONGATE

MR. CROFTANGRY INTRODUCES ANOTHER TALE

> Together both on the high lawns appear'd.
> Under the opening eyelids of the morn
> They drove afield.
>
> *Elegy on Lycidas.*

I HAVE sometimes wondered why all the favourite occupations and pastimes of mankind go to the disturbance of that happy state of tranquillity, that *Otium*, as Horace terms it, which he says is the object of all men's prayers, whether preferred from sea or land, and that the undisturbed repose, of which we are so tenacious when duty or necessity compels us to abandon it, is precisely what we long to exchange for a state of excitation, as soon as we may prolong it at our own pleasure. Briefly, you have only to say to a man, 'remain at rest', and you instantly inspire the love of labour. The sportsman toils like his gamekeeper, the master of the pack takes as severe exercise as his whipper-in, the statesman or politician drudges more than the professional lawyer; and to come to my own case, the volunteer author subjects himself to the risk of painful criticism, and the assured certainty of mental and manual labour, just as completely as his needy brother, whose necessities compel him to assume the pen.

These reflections have been suggested by an annunciation on the part of Janet, 'that the little

Gillie-whitefoot* was come from the printing-office.'

'Gillie-blackfoot you should call him, Janet,' was my response, 'for he is neither more nor less than an imp of the devil,* come to torment me for *copy*, for so the printers call a supply of manuscript for the press.'

'Now, Cot forgie your honour,' said Janet; 'for it is no like your ainsell to give such names to a faitherless bairn.'

'I have got nothing else to give him, Janet—he must wait a little.'

'Then I have got some breakfast to give the bit gillie,' said Janet; 'and he can wait by the fireside in the kitchen, till your honour's ready; and cood enough for the like of him, if he was to wait your honour's pleasure all day.'

'But, Janet,' said I to my little active super-intendent, on her return to the parlour, after having made her hospitable arrangements, 'I begin to find this writing our Chronicles is rather more tiresome than I expected, for here comes this little fellow to ask for manuscript—that is, for something to print—and I have got none to give him.'

'Your honour can be at nae loss; I have seen you write fast and fast enough; and for subjects, you have the whole Highlands to write about, and I am sure you know a hundred tales better than that about Hamish MacTavish, for it was but about a young cateran and an auld carline, when all's done; and if they had burned the rudas queen* for a witch, I am thinking, may be, they would not have tyned their coals—and her to gar her neer-do-weel son shoot a gentleman

Cameron! I am third cousin to the Camerons mysell—my blood warms to them—And if you want to write about deserters, I am sure there were deserters enough on the top of Arthur's Seat, when the MacRaas*broke out, and on that woful day beside Leith Pier*—Ohonari!'—

Here Janet began to weep, and to wipe her eyes with her apron. For my part, the idea I wanted was supplied, but I hesitated to make use of it. Topics, like times, are apt to become common by frequent use. It is only an ass like Justice Shallow, who would pitch upon the overscutched tunes which the carmen whistled, and try to pass them off as his *fancies* and his *goodnights*.* Now, the Highlands, though formerly a rich mine for original matter, are, as my friend Mrs. Bethune Baliol warned me, in some degree worn out by the incessant labour of modern romancers and novelists who, finding in those remote regions primitive habits and manners, have vainly imagined that the public can never tire of them; and so kilted Highlanders are to be found as frequently, and nearly of as genuine descent, on the shelves of a circulating library, as at a Caledonian ball.* Much might have been made at an earlier time out of the history of a Highland regiment, and the singular revolution of ideas which must have taken place in the minds of those who composed it, when exchanging their native hills for the battle-fields of the Continent, and their simple, and sometimes indolent domestic habits, for the regular exertions demanded by modern discipline. But the market is forestalled. There is Mrs. Grant of Laggan*has drawn the manners, customs, and superstitions of the mountains in their natural unsophisticated state;[1] and my friend, General Stewart of Garth,[2] in giving the real history of the Highland regiments, has rendered any attempt to fill up the sketch with fancy-colouring extremely rash and precarious. Yet I, too, have still a lingering fancy to add a stone to the cairn;* and without calling in imagination to aid the impressions of juvenile recollection, I may just attempt to embody one or two scenes illustrative of the Highland character, and which belong peculiarly to the Chronicles of the Canongate, to the grey-headed eld of whom they are as familiar as to Chrystal Croftangry. Yet I will not go back to the days of clanship and claymores. Have at you, gentle reader, with a tale of Two Drovers.* An oyster may be crossed in love, says the gentle Tilburina*—and a drover may be touched on a point of honour, says the Chronicler of the Canongate.

[1] Letters from the Mountains, 3 vols.—Essays on the Superstitions of the Highlanders. —The Highlanders, and other Poems, &c.
[2] The gallant and amiable author of the History of the Highland Regiments, in whose glorious services his own share had been great, went out Governor of St. Lucie in 1828, and died in that island on December 18, 1829,—no man more regretted, or perhaps by a wider circle of friends and acquaintance.

THE TWO DROVERS

CHAPTER I

IT was the day after Doune Fair* when my story commences. It had been a brisk market; several dealers had attended from the northern and midland counties in England, and English money had flown so merrily about as to gladden the hearts of the Highland farmers. Many large droves were about to set off for England, under the protection of their owners, or of the topsmen whom they employed in the tedious, laborious, and responsible office of driving the cattle for many hundred miles, from the market where they had been purchased, to the fields or farm-yards where they were to be fattened for the shambles.

The Highlanders, in particular, are masters of this difficult trade of driving, which seems to suit them as well as the trade of war. It affords exercise for all their habits of patient endurance and active exertion. They are required to know perfectly the drove-roads,* which lie over the wildest tracts of the country, and to avoid as much as possible the highways, which distress the feet of the bullocks, and the turnpikes, which annoy the spirit of the drover; whereas, on the broad green or grey track, which leads across the pathless moor, the herd not only move at ease and without taxation, but, if they mind their business, may pick up a mouthful of food by the way. At night, the drovers usually sleep along with their cattle, let the weather be what it will; and many of these hardy men do not once rest under a roof during a journey on foot from Lochaber to Lincolnshire. They are paid very highly, for the trust reposed is of the last importance, as it depends on their prudence, vigilance, and honesty, whether the cattle reach the final market in good order, and afford a profit to the grazier. But as they maintain themselves at their own expense, they are especially economical in that particular. At the period we speak of, a Highland drover was victualled for his long and toilsome journey with a few handfuls of oatmeal, and two or three onions, renewed from time to time, and a ram's horn filled with whisky, which he used regularly, but sparingly, every night and morning. His dirk, or *skene-dhu* (i.e. black-knife), so worn as to be concealed beneath the arm, or by the folds of the plaid, was his only weapon, excepting the cudgel with which he directed the movements of the cattle. A Highlander was never so happy as on these occasions. There was a variety in the whole journey, which exercised the Celt's natural curiosity and love of motion; there were the constant change of place and scene, the petty adventures incidental to the traffic, and the intercourse with the various farmers, graziers, and traders, intermingled with occasional merry-makings, not the less acceptable to Donald*that they were void of expense;—and there was the consciousness of superior skill; for the Highlander, a child amongst flocks, is a prince amongst herds, and his natural habits induce him to disdain the shepherd's slothful life, so that he feels himself nowhere more at home than when following a gallant drove of his country cattle in the character of their guardian.

Of the number who left Doune in the morning, and with the purpose we have described, not a *Glunamie**of them all cocked his bonnet more briskly, or gartered his tartan hose under knee over a pair of more promising *spiogs* (legs) than did Robin Oig M'Combich, called familiarly Robin Oig, that is, Young, or the Lesser, Robin. Though small of stature as the epithet Oig implies, and not very strongly limbed, he was as light and alert as one of the deer of his mountains. He had an elasticity of step which, in the course of a long march, made many a stout fellow envy him; and the manner in which he busked his plaid and adjusted his bonnet, argued a consciousness that so smart a John Highlandman* as himself would not pass unnoticed among the Lowland lasses. The ruddy cheek, red lips, and white teeth, set off a countenance which had gained by exposure to the weather a healthful and hardy rather than a rugged hue. If Robin Oig did not laugh, or even smile frequently, as indeed is not the practice among his countrymen, his bright eyes usually gleamed from under his bonnet with an expression of cheerfulness ready to be turned into mirth.

The departure of Robin Oig was an incident in the little town, in and near which he had many friends, male and female. He was a topping person in his way, transacted considerable business on his own behalf, and was entrusted by the best farmers in the Highlands in preference to any other drover in that district. He might have increased his business to any extent had he condescended to manage it by deputy; but except a lad or two, sister's sons of his own, Robin rejected the idea of assistance, conscious, perhaps, how much his reputation depended upon his attending in person to the practical discharge of his duty in every instance. He remained, therefore, contented with the highest premium given to persons of his description, and comforted himself with the hopes that a few journeys to England might enable him to conduct business on his own account, in a manner becoming his birth. For Robin Oig's father, Lachlan M'Combich (or *son of my friend*, his actual clan-surname being M'Gregor), had been so called by the celebrated Rob Roy,* because of the particular friendship which had subsisted between the grandsire of Robin and that renowned cateran. Some people even say that Robin Oig derived his Christian name from one as renowned in the wilds of Loch Lomond as ever was his namesake Robin Hood, in the precincts of merry Sherwood. 'Of such ancestry,' as James Boswell says, 'who would not be proud?'* Robin Oig was proud accordingly; but his frequent visits to England and to the Lowlands had given him tact enough to know that pretensions, which still gave him a little right to distinction in his own lonely glen, might be both obnoxious and ridiculous if preferred elsewhere. The pride of birth, therefore, was like the miser's treasure, the secret subject of his contemplation, but never exhibited to strangers as a subject of boasting.

Many were the words of gratulation and good luck which were bestowed on Robin Oig. The judges commended his drove, especially Robin's own property, which were the best of them. Some thrust out their snuff-mulls for the parting pinch—others tendered the *doch-an-dorrach* or parting cup. All cried—'Good luck travel out with you and come home with you.—Give you luck in the Saxon market—brave notes in the *leabhar-dhu*' (black pocket-book) 'and plenty of English gold in the *sporran*' (pouch of goatskin).

The bonny lasses made their adieus more modestly, and more than one, it was said, would have given her best brooch to be certain that it was upon her that his eye last rested as he turned towards the road.

Robin Oig had just given the preliminary '*Hoo-hoo!*' to urge forward the loiterers of the drove, when there was a cry behind him.

'Stay, Robin—bide a blink. Here is Janet of Tomahourich—auld Janet, your father's sister.'

'Plague on her, for an auld Highland witch and spaewife,' said a farmer from the Carse of Stirling;*'she'll cast some of her cantrips on the cattle.'

'She canna do that,' said another sapient of the same profession—'Robin Oig is no the lad to leave any of them without tying St. Mungo's knot*on their tails, and that will put to her speed the best witch that ever flew over Dimayet*upon a broomstick.'

It may not be indifferent to the reader to know that the Highland cattle are peculiarly liable to be *taken*, or infected, by spells and witchcraft; which judicious people guard against by knitting knots of peculiar complexity on the tuft of hair which terminates the animal's tail.

But the old woman who was the object of the farmer's suspicion seemed only busied about the drover, without paying any attention to the drove. Robin, on the contrary, appeared rather impatient of her presence.

'What auld-world fancy', he said, 'has brought you so early from the ingle-side this morning, Muhme?* I am sure I bid you good-even, and had your God-speed, last night.'

'And left me more siller than the useless old woman will use till you come back again, bird of my bosom,' said the sibyl. 'But it is little I would care for the food that nourishes me, or the fire that warms me, or for God's blessed sun itself, if aught but weal should happen to the grandson of my father. So let me walk the *deasil* round you, that you may go safe out into the far foreign land, and come safe home.'

Robin Oig stopped, half embarrassed, half laughing, and signing to those around that he only complied with the old woman to soothe her humour. In the meantime she traced around him, with wavering steps, the propitiation, which some have thought has been derived from the Druidical mythology. It consists, as is well known, in the person who makes the *deasil* walking three times round the person who is the object of the ceremony, taking care to move according to the course of the sun. At once, however, she stopped short, and exclaimed, in a voice of alarm and horror, 'Grandson of my father, there is blood on your hand.'

'Hush, for God's sake, aunt,' said Robin Oig; 'you will bring more trouble on yourself with this *taishataragh*' (second sight) 'than you will be able to get out of for many a day.'

The old woman only repeated, with a ghastly look, 'There is blood on your hand, and it is

English blood. The blood of the Gael is richer and redder. Let us see—let us——'

Ere Robin Oig could prevent her, which, indeed, could only have been by positive violence, so hasty and peremptory were her proceedings, she had drawn from his side the dirk which lodged in the folds of his plaid, and held it up, exclaiming, although the weapon gleamed clear and bright in the sun, 'Blood, blood— Saxon blood again. Robin Oig M'Combich, go not this day to England!'

'Prutt trutt,' answered Robin Oig, 'that will never do neither—it would be next thing to running the country. For shame, Muhme—give me the dirk. You cannot tell by the colour the difference betwixt the blood of a black bullock and a white one, and you speak of knowing Saxon from Gaelic blood. All men have their blood from Adam, Muhme. Give me my skene-dhu, and let me go on my road. I should have been half-way to Stirling Brig* by this time.— Give me my dirk, and let me go.'

'Never will I give it to you,' said the old woman —'Never will I quit my hold on your plaid, unless you promise me not to wear that unhappy weapon.'

The women around him urged him also, saying few of his aunt's words fell to the ground; and as the Lowland farmers continued to look moodily on the scene, Robin Oig determined to close it at any sacrifice.

'Well, then,' said the young drover, giving the scabbard of the weapon to Hugh Morrison, 'you Lowlanders care nothing for these freats. Keep my dirk for me. I cannot give it you, because it was my father's; but your drove follows ours, and I am content it should be in your keeping, not in mine.—Will this do, Muhme?'

'It must,' said the old woman—'that is, if the Lowlander is mad enough to carry the knife.'

The strong westlandman laughed aloud.

'Goodwife,' said he, 'I am Hugh Morrison from Glenae, come of the Manly Morrisons* of auld langsyne, that never took short weapon against a man in their lives. And neither needed they. They had their broadswords, and I have this bit supple,' showing a formidable cudgel— 'for dirking ower the board, I leave that to John Highlandman—Ye needna snort, none of you Highlanders, and you in especial, Robin. I'll keep the bit knife, if you are feared for the auld spaewife's tale, and give it back to you whenever you want it.'

Robin was not particularly pleased with some part of Hugh Morrison's speech; but he had learned in his travels more patience than belonged to his Highland constitution originally, and he accepted the service of the descendant of the Manly Morrisons without finding fault with the rather depreciating manner in which it was offered.

'If he had not had his morning in his head, and been but a Dumfriesshire hog into the boot, he would have spoken more like a gentleman. But you cannot have more of a sow than a grumph.* It's shame my father's knife should ever slash a haggis for the like of him.'

Thus saying (but saying it in Gaelic) Robin drove on his cattle, and waved farewell to all behind him. He was in the greater haste, because

he expected to join at Falkirk* a comrade and
brother in profession, with whom he proposed to
travel in company.

Robin Oig's chosen friend was a young Englishman, Harry Wakefield by name, well known at
every northern market, and in his way as much
famed and honoured as our Highland driver of
bullocks. He was nearly six feet high, gallantly
formed to keep the rounds at Smithfield,* or
maintain the ring at a wrestling match; and
although he might have been overmatched, perhaps, among the regular professors of the Fancy,
yet, as a yokel, or rustic, or a chance customer,
he was able to give a bellyful to any amateur of
the pugilistic art. Doncaster races saw him in
his glory, betting his guinea, and generally successfully; nor was there a main fought in Yorkshire, the feeders being persons of celebrity, at
which he was not to be seen, if business permitted.
But though a *sprack* lad, and fond of pleasure and
its haunts, Harry Wakefield was steady, and not
the cautious Robin Oig M'Combich himself was
more attentive to the main chance. His holidays
were holidays indeed; but his days of work were
dedicated to steady and persevering labour. In
countenance and temper, Wakefield was the
model of Old England's merry yeomen, whose
clothyard shafts, in so many hundred battles,
asserted her superiority over the nations, and
whose good sabres in our own time are her
cheapest and most assured defence. His mirth
was readily excited; for, strong in limb and constitution, and fortunate in circumstances, he was
disposed to be pleased with everything about
him; and such difficulties as he might occasionally

encounter were, to a man of his energy, rather matter of amusement than serious annoyance. With all the merits of a sanguine temper, our young English drover was not without his defects. He was irascible, sometimes to the verge of being quarrelsome; and perhaps not the less inclined to bring his disputes to a pugilistic decision, because he found few antagonists able to stand up to him in the boxing ring.

It is difficult to say how Harry Wakefield and Robin Oig first became intimates; but it is certain a close acquaintance had taken place betwixt them, although they had apparently few common subjects of conversation or of interest, so soon as their talk ceased to be of bullocks. Robin Oig, indeed, spoke the English language rather imperfectly upon any other topics but stots and kyloes, and Harry Wakefield could never bring his broad Yorkshire tongue to utter a single word of Gaelic. It was in vain Robin spent a whole morning, during a walk over Minch Moor in attempting to teach his companion to utter, with true precision, the shibboleth *Llhu*, which is the Gaelic for a calf.* From Traquair to Murdercairn, the hill rang with the discordant attempts of the Saxon upon the unmanageable monosyllable, and the heartfelt laugh which followed every failure. They had, however, better modes of awakening the echoes; for Wakefield could sing many a ditty to the praise of Moll, Susan, and Cicely, and Robin Oig had a particular gift at whistling interminable pibrochs through all their involutions, and what was more agreeable to his companion's southern ear, knew many of the northern airs, both lively and pathetic, to

which Wakefield learned to pipe a bass. Thus,
though Robin could hardly have comprehended
his companion's stories about horse-racing, and
cock-fighting or fox-hunting, and although his
own legends of clan-fights and *creaghs*, varied
with talk of Highland goblins and fairy folk,
would have been caviare to his companion, they
contrived nevertheless to find a degree of pleasure
in each other's company, which had for three
years back induced them to join company and
travel together, when the direction of their
journey permitted. Each, indeed, found his
advantage in this companionship; for where
could the Englishman have found a guide through
the Western Highlands like Robin Oig M'Combich? and when they were on what Harry called
the *right* side of the Border, his patronage, which
was extensive, and his purse, which was heavy,
were at all times at the service of his Highland
friend, and on many occasions his liberality did
him genuine yeoman's service.

CHAPTER II

Were ever two such loving friends!—
    How could they disagree?
Oh thus it was, he loved him dear,
    And thought how to requite him,
And having no friend left but he,
    He did resolve to fight him.   *Duke upon Duke*.

THE pair of friends had traversed with their
usual cordiality the grassy wilds of Liddesdale,
and crossed the opposite part of Cumberland,
emphatically called The Waste. In these solitary
regions, the cattle under the charge of our drovers

derived their subsistence chiefly by picking their food as they went along the drove-road, or sometimes by the tempting opportunity of a *start and owerloup*, or invasion of the neighbouring pasture, where an occasion presented itself. But now the scene changed before them; they were descending towards a fertile and enclosed country, where no such liberties could be taken with impunity, or without a previous arrangement and bargain with the possessors of the ground. This was more especially the case, as a great northern fair was upon the eve of taking place, where both the Scotch and English drover expected to dispose of a part of their cattle, which it was desirable to produce in the market, rested and in good order. Fields were therefore difficult to be obtained, and only upon high terms. This necessity occasioned a temporary separation betwixt the two friends, who went to bargain, each as he could, for the separate accommodation of his herd. Unhappily it chanced that both of them, unknown to each other, thought of bargaining for the ground they wanted on the property of a country gentleman of some fortune, whose estate lay in the neighbourhood. The English drover applied to the bailiff on the property, who was known to him. It chanced that the Cumbrian squire, who had entertained some suspicions of his manager's honesty, was taking occasional measures to ascertain how far they were well founded, and had desired that any inquiries about his enclosures, with a view to occupy them for a temporary purpose, should be referred to himself. As, however, Mr. Ireby had gone the day before upon a journey of some miles' distance to the northward, the bailiff chose to consider the check upon his full powers as for the time removed, and concluded that he should best consult his master's interest, and perhaps his own, in making an agreement with Harry Wakefield. Meanwhile, ignorant of what his comrade was doing, Robin Oig, on his side, chanced to be overtaken by a good-looking smart little man upon a pony, most knowingly hogged and cropped, as was then the fashion, the rider wearing tight leather breeches and long-necked bright spurs. This cavalier asked one or two pertinent questions about markets and the price of stock. So Robin, seeing him a well-judging civil gentleman, took the freedom to ask him whether he could let him know if there was any grass-land to be let in that neighbourhood, for the temporary accommodation of his drove. He could not have put the question to more willing ears. The gentleman of the buckskins was the proprietor with whose bailiff Harry Wakefield had dealt or was in the act of dealing.

'Thou art in good luck, my canny Scot,' said Mr. Ireby, 'to have spoken to me, for I see thy cattle have done their day's work, and I have at my disposal the only field within three miles that is to be let in these parts.'

'The drove can pe gang two, three, four miles very pratty weel indeed,' said the cautious Highlander; 'put what would his honour pe axing for the peasts pe the head, if she was to tak the park for twa or three days?'

'We won't differ, Sawney, if you let me have six stots for winterers, in the way of reason.'

'And which peasts wad your honour pe for having?'

'Why—let me see—the two black—the dun one—yon doddy—him with the twisted horn—the brocket—How much by the head?'

'Ah,' said Robin, 'your honour is a shudge—a real shudge—I couldna have set off the pest six peasts petter mysell, me that ken them as if they were my pairns, puir things.'

'Well, how much per head, Sawney?' continued Mr. Ireby.

'It was high markets at Doune and Falkirk,' answered Robin.

And thus the conversation proceeded, until they had agreed on the *prix juste* for the bullocks, the squire throwing in the temporary accommodation of the enclosure for the cattle into the boot, and Robin making, as he thought, a very good bargain, provided the grass was but tolerable. The squire walked his pony alongside of the drove, partly to show him the way, and see him put into possession of the field, and partly to learn the latest news of the northern markets.

They arrived at the field, and the pasture seemed excellent. But what was their surprise when they saw the bailiff quietly inducting the cattle of Harry Wakefield into the grassy Goshen* which had just been assigned to those of Robin Oig M'Combich by the proprietor himself! Squire Ireby set spurs to his horse, dashed up to his servant, and learning what had passed between the parties, briefly informed the English drover that his bailiff had let the ground without his authority, and that he might seek grass for his cattle wherever he would, since he was to get none there. At the same time he rebuked his servant severely for having transgressed his commands, and ordered him instantly to assist in ejecting the hungry and weary cattle of Harry Wakefield, which were just beginning to enjoy a meal of unusual plenty, and to introduce those of his comrade, whom the English drover now began to consider as a rival.

The feelings which arose in Wakefield's mind would have induced him to resist Mr. Ireby's decision; but every Englishman has a tolerably accurate sense of law and justice, and John Fleecebumpkin, the bailiff, having acknowledged that he had exceeded his commission, Wakefield saw nothing else for it than to collect his hungry and disappointed charge, and drive them on to seek quarters elsewhere. Robin Oig saw what had happened with regret, and hastened to offer to his English friend to share with him the disputed possession. But Wakefield's pride was severely hurt, and he answered disdainfully, 'Take it all, man—take it all—never make two bites of a cherry—thou canst talk over the gentry, and blear a plain man's eye—Out upon you, man—I would not kiss any man's dirty latchets for leave to bake in his oven.'

Robin Oig, sorry but not surprised at his comrade's displeasure, hastened to entreat his friend to wait but an hour till he had gone to the squire's house to receive payment for the cattle he had sold, and he would come back and help him to drive the cattle into some convenient place of rest, and explain to him the whole mistake they had both of them fallen into. But the Englishman continued indignant: 'Thou hast been selling, hast thou? Ay, ay,—thou is a cunning lad for kenning the hours of bargaining. Go to the devil with thyself, for I will ne'er see thy fause loon's visage again—thou should be ashamed to look me in the face.'

'I am ashamed to look no man in the face,' said Robin Oig, something moved; 'and, moreover, I will look you in the face this blessed day, if you will bide at the clachan down yonder.'

'Mayhap you had as well keep away,' said his comrade; and turning his back on his former friend, he collected his unwilling associates, assisted by the bailiff, who took some real and some affected interest in seeing Wakefield accommodated.

After spending some time in negotiating with more than one of the neighbouring farmers, who could not, or would not, afford the accommodation desired, Henry Wakefield at last, and in his necessity, accomplished his point by means of the landlord of the alehouse at which Robin Oig and he had agreed to pass the night, when they first separated from each other. Mine host was content to let him turn his cattle on a piece of barren moor, at a price little less than the bailiff had asked for the disputed enclosure; and the wretchedness of the pasture, as well as the price paid for it, were set down as exaggerations of the breach of faith and friendship of his Scottish crony. This turn of Wakefield's passions was encouraged by the bailiff (who had his own reasons for being offended against poor Robin, as having been the unwitting cause of his falling into disgrace with his master), as well as by the innkeeper, and two or three chance guests, who stimulated the drover in his resentment against his quondam associate,—some from the ancient grudge against the Scots which, when it exists anywhere, is to be found lurking in the Border counties, and some from the general love of mischief, which characterizes mankind in all ranks of life, to the honour of Adam's children be it spoken. Good John Barleycorn also, who always heightens and exaggerates the prevailing passions, be they angry or kindly, was not wanting in his offices on this occasion; and confusion to false friends and hard masters was pledged in more than one tankard.

In the meanwhile Mr. Ireby found some amusement in detaining the northern drover at his ancient hall. He caused a cold round of beef to be placed before the Scot in the butler's pantry, together with a foaming tankard of home-brewed, and took pleasure in seeing the hearty appetite with which these unwonted edibles were discussed by Robin Oig M'Combich. The squire himself lighting his pipe, compounded between his patrician dignity and his love of agricultural gossip, by walking up and down while he conversed with his guest.

'I passed another drove,' said the squire, 'with one of your countrymen behind them—they were something less beasts than your drove, doddies most of them—a big man was with them —none of your kilts though, but a decent pair of breeches—D'ye know who he may be?'

'Hout aye—that might, could, and would be Hughie Morrison—I didna think he could hae peen sae weel up. He has made a day on us; but his Argyleshires will have wearied shanks. How far was he pehind?'

'I think about six or seven miles,' answered the squire, 'for I passed them at the Christenbury Crag,* and I overtook you at the Hollan Bush. If his beasts be leg-weary, he will be maybe selling bargains.'

'Na, na, Hughie Morrison is no the man for pargains—ye maun come to some Highland body like Robin Oig hersell for the like of these—put I maun pe wishing you goot night, and twenty of them let alane ane, and I maun down to the clachan to see if the lad Harry Waakfelt is out of his humdudgeons yet.'

The party at the alehouse were still in full talk, and the treachery of Robin Oig still the theme of conversation, when the supposed culprit entered the apartment. His arrival, as usually happens in such a case, put an instant stop to the discussion of which he had furnished the subject, and he was received by the company assembled with that chilling silence which, more than a thousand exclamations, tells an intruder that he is unwelcome. Surprised and offended, but not appalled by the reception which he experienced, Robin entered with an undaunted and even a haughty air, attempted no greeting as he saw he was received with none, and placed himself by the side of the fire, a little apart from a table at which Harry Wakefield, the bailiff, and two or three other persons were seated. The ample Cumbrian kitchen would have afforded plenty of room, even for a larger separation.

Robin, thus seated, proceeded to light his pipe, and call for a pint of twopenny.

'We have no twopence ale,' answered Ralph Heskett, the landlord; 'but as thou findest thy own tobacco, it's like thou mayest find thy own liquor too—it's the wont of thy country, I wot.'

'Shame, goodman,' said the landlady, a blithe bustling house-wife, hastening herself to supply the guest with liquor—'Thou knowest well enow what the strange man wants, and it's thy trade to be civil, man. Thou shouldst know, that if the Scot likes a small pot, he pays a sure penny.'

Without taking any notice of this nuptial dialogue, the Highlander took the flagon in his hand, and addressing the company generally, drank the interesting toast of 'Good markets', to the party assembled.

'The better that the wind blew fewer dealers from the north,' said one of the farmers, 'and fewer Highland runts to eat up the English meadows.'

'Saul of my pody, put you are wrang there, my friend,' answered Robin, with composure, 'it is your fat Englishmen that eat up our Scots cattle, puir things.'

'I wish there was a summat to eat up their drovers,' said another; 'a plain Englishman canna make bread within a kenning of them.'

'Or an honest servant keep his master's favour, but they will come sliding in between him and the sunshine,' said the bailiff.

'If these pe jokes,' said Robin Oig, with the same composure, 'there is ower mony jokes upon one man.'

'It is no joke, but downright earnest,' said the bailiff. 'Harkye, Mr. Robin Ogg, or whatever is your name, it's right we should tell you that we are all of one opinion, and that is that you,

Mr. Robin Ogg, have behaved to our friend
Mr. Harry Wakefield here, like a raff and a
blackguard.'

'Nae doubt, nae doubt,' answered Robin, with
great composure; 'and you are a set of very pretty
judges, for whose prains or pehaviour I wad not
gie a pinch of sneeshing. If Mr. Harry Waakfelt
kens where he is wranged, he kens where he may
be righted.'

'He speaks truth,' said Wakefield, who had
listened to what passed, divided between the
offence which he had taken at Robin's late
behaviour, and the revival of his habitual feelings
of regard.

He now rose, and went towards Robin, who
got up from his seat as he approached, and held
out his hand.

'That's right, Harry—go it—serve him out,'
resounded on all sides—'tip him the nailer—
show him the mill.'

'Hold your peace all of you, and be——,' said
Wakefield; and then addressing his comrade, he
took him by the extended hand, with something
alike of respect and defiance. 'Robin,' he said,
'thou hast used me ill enough this day; but if you
mean, like a frank fellow, to shake hands, and
take a tussle for love on the sod, why I'll forgie
thee, man, and we shall be better friends than
ever.'

'And would it not pe petter to pe cood friends
without more of the matter?' said Robin; 'we will
be much petter friendships with our panes hale
than proken.'

Harry Wakefield dropped the hand of his
friend, or rather threw it from him.

'I did not think I had been keeping company for three years with a coward.'

'Coward pelongs to none of my name,' said Robin, whose eyes began to kindle, but keeping the command of his temper. 'It was no coward's legs or hands, Harry Waakfelt, that drew you out of the fords of Frew,* when you was drifting ower the plack rock, and every eel in the river expected his share of you.'

'And that is true enough, too,' said the Englishman, struck by the appeal.

'Adzooks!' exclaimed the bailiff—'sure Harry Wakefield, the nattiest lad at Whitson Tryste, Wooler Fair, Carlisle Sands, or Stagshaw Bank,* is not going to show white feather? Ah, this comes of living so long with kilts and bonnets— men forget the use of their daddles.'

'I may teach you, Master Fleecebumpkin, that I have not lost the use of mine,' said Wakefield, and then went on. 'This will never do, Robin. We must have a turn-up, or we shall be the talk of the country-side. I'll be d——d if I hurt thee —I'll put on the gloves gin thou like. Come, stand forward like a man.'

'To pe peaten like a dog,' said Robin; 'is there any reason in that? If you think I have done you wrong, I'll go before your shudge, though I neither know his law nor his language.'

A general cry of 'No, no—no law, no lawyer! a bellyful and be friends,' was echoed by the bystanders.

'But,' continued Robin, 'if I am to fight, I've no skill to fight like a jackanapes, with hands and nails.'

'How would you fight, then?' said his antagonist; 'though I am thinking it would be hard to bring you to the scratch anyhow.'

'I would fight with proadswords, and sink point on the first plood drawn, like a gentlemans.'

A loud shout of laughter followed the proposal, which indeed had rather escaped from poor Robin's swelling heart, than been the dictate of his sober judgement.

'Gentleman, quotha!' was echoed on all sides, with a shout of unextinguishable laughter; 'a very pretty gentleman, God wot—Canst get two swords for the gentlemen to fight with, Ralph Heskett?'

'No, but I can send to the armoury at Carlisle, and lend them two forks, to be making shift with in the meantime.'

'Tush, man,' said another, 'the bonny Scots come into the world with the blue bonnet on their heads, and dirk and pistol at their belt.'

'Best send post', said Mr. Fleecebumpkin, 'to the squire of Corby Castle,* to come and stand second to the *gentleman*.'

In the midst of this torrent of general ridicule, the Highlander instinctively griped beneath the folds of his plaid.

'But it's better not,' he said in his own language. 'A hundred curses on the swine-eaters,* who know neither decency nor civility!'

'Make room, the pack of you,' he said, advancing to the door.

But his former friend interposed his sturdy bulk, and opposed his leaving the house; and when Robin Oig attempted to make his way by force, he hit him down on the floor, with as much ease as a boy bowls down a nine-pin.

'A ring, a ring!' was now shouted, until the dark rafters, and the hams that hung on them, trembled again, and the very platters on the *bink* clattered against each other. 'Well done, Harry,' —'Give it him home, Harry,'—'Take care of him now,—he sees his own blood!'

Such were the exclamations, while the Highlander, starting from the ground, all his coldness and caution lost in frantic rage, sprung at his antagonist with the fury, the activity, and the vindictive purpose of an incensed tiger-cat. But when could rage encounter science and temper? Robin Oig again went down in the unequal contest; and as the blow was necessarily a severe one, he lay motionless on the floor of the kitchen. The landlady ran to offer some aid, but Mr. Fleecebumpkin would not permit her to approach.

'Let him alone,' he said, 'he will come to within time, and come up to the scratch again. He has not got half his broth yet.'

'He has got all I mean to give him, though,' said his antagonist, whose heart began to relent towards his old associate; 'and I would rather by half give the rest to yourself, Mr. Fleecebumpkin, for you pretend to know a thing or two, and Robin had not art enough even to peel before setting to, but fought with his plaid dangling about him.—Stand up, Robin, my man! all friends now; and let me hear the man that will speak a word against you, or your country, for your sake.'

Robin Oig was still under the dominion of his passion, and eager to renew the onset; but being withheld on the one side by the peace-making Dame Heskett, and on the other, aware that

Wakefield no longer meant to renew the combat, his fury sank into gloomy sullenness.

'Come, come, never grudge so much at it, man,' said the brave-spirited Englishman, with the placability of his country, 'shake hands, and we will be better friends than ever.'

'Friends!' exclaimed Robin Oig, with strong emphasis—'friends!—Never. Look to yourself, Harry Waakfelt.'

'Then the curse of Cromwell on your proud Scots stomach, as the man says in the play; and you may do your worst, and be d——d; for one man can say nothing more to another after a tussle, than that he is sorry for it.'

On these terms the friends parted; Robin Oig drew out, in silence, a piece of money, threw it on the table, and then left the alehouse. But turning at the door, he shook his hand at Wakefield, pointing with his forefinger upwards, in a manner which might imply either a threat or a caution. He then disappeared in the moonlight.

Some words passed after his departure between the bailiff, who piqued himself on being a little of a bully, and Harry Wakefield, who, with generous inconsistency, was now not indisposed to begin a new combat in defence of Robin Oig's reputation, 'although he could not use his daddles like an Englishman, as it did not come natural to him.' But Dame Heskett prevented this second quarrel from coming to a head by her peremptory interference. 'There should be no more fighting in her house,' she said; 'there had been too much already.—And you, Mr. Wakefield, may live to learn', she added, 'what it is to make a deadly enemy out of a good friend.'

'Pshaw, dame! Robin Oig is an honest fellow, and will never keep malice.'

'Do not trust to that—you do not know the dour temper of the Scots, though you have dealt with them so often. I have a right to know them, my mother being a Scot.'

'And so is well seen on her daughter,' said Ralph Heskett.

This nuptial sarcasm gave the discourse another turn; fresh customers entered the tap-room or kitchen, and others left it. The conversation turned on the expected markets, and the report of prices from different parts both of Scotland and England—treaties were commenced, and Harry Wakefield was lucky enough to find a chap for a part of his drove, and at a very considerable profit; an event of consequence more than sufficient to blot out all remembrances of the unpleasant scuffle in the earlier part of the day. But there remained one party from whose mind that recollection could not have been wiped away by the possession of every head of cattle betwixt Esk and Eden.

This was Robin Oig M'Combich.—'That I should have had no weapon,' he said, 'and for the first time in my life!—Blighted be the tongue that bids the Highlander part with the dirk— the dirk—ha! the English blood!—My Muhme's word—when did her word fall to the ground?'

The recollection of the fatal prophecy confirmed the deadly intention which instantly sprang up in his mind.

'Ha! Morrison cannot be many miles behind; and if it were a hundred, what then?'

His impetuous spirit had now a fixed purpose

and motive of action, and he turned the light foot
of his country towards the wilds, through which
he knew, by Mr. Ireby's report, that Morrison
was advancing. His mind was wholly engrossed
by the sense of injury—injury sustained from
a friend; and by the desire of vengeance on one
whom he now accounted his most bitter enemy.
The treasured ideas of self-importance and self-
opinion—of ideal birth and quality, had become
more precious to him, like the hoard to the miser,
because he could only enjoy them in secret. But
that hoard was pillaged, the idols which he had
secretly worshipped had been desecrated and
profaned. Insulted, abused, and beaten, he was
no longer worthy, in his own opinion, of the
name he bore or the lineage which he belonged
to—nothing was left to him—nothing but revenge;
and, as the reflection added a galling spur to
every step, he determined it should be as sudden
and signal as the offence.

When Robin Oig left the door of the ale-house,
seven or eight English miles at least lay betwixt
Morrison and him. The advance of the former
was slow, limited by the sluggish pace of his
cattle; the last left behind him stubble-field and
hedge-row, crag and dark heath, all glittering
with frost-rime in the broad November moonlight, at the rate of six miles an hour. And now
the distant lowing of Morrison's cattle is heard;
and now they are seen creeping like moles in size
and slowness of motion on the broad face of the
moor; and now he meets them—passes them,
and stops their conductor.

'May good betide us,' said the Southlander.
'Is this you, Robin M'Combich, or your wraith?'

'It is Robin Oig M'Combich,' answered the Highlander, 'and it is not.—But never mind that, put pe giving me the skene-dhu.'

'What! you are for back to the Highlands— The devil!—Have you selt all off before the fair? This beats all for quick markets!'

'I have not sold—I am not going north—May pe I will never go north again.—Give me pack my dirk, Hugh Morrison, or there will pe words petween us.'

'Indeed, Robin, I'll be better advised before I gie it back to you—it is a wanchancy weapon in a Highlandman's hand, and I am thinking you will be about some barns-breaking.'

'Prutt, trutt! let me have my weapon,' said Robin Oig, impatiently.

'Hooly, and fairly,' said his well-meaning friend. 'I'll tell you what will do better than these dirking doings—Ye ken Highlander, and Lowlander, and Border-men, are a' ae man's bairns when you are over the Scots dyke. See, the Eskdale callants, and fighting Charlie of Liddesdale, and the Lockerby lads, and the four Dandies of Lustruther, and a wheen mair grey plaids, are coming up behind, and if you are wranged, there is the hand of a Manly Morrison, we'll see you righted, if Carlisle and Stanwix baith took up the feud.'

'To tell you the truth,' said Robin Oig, desirous of eluding the suspicions of his friend, 'I have enlisted with a party of the Black Watch, and must march off to-morrow morning.'

'Enlisted! Were you mad or drunk?—You must buy yourself off—I can lend you twenty notes, and twenty to that, if the drove sell.'

'I thank you—thank ye, Hughie; but I go with good will the gate that I am going,—so the dirk—the dirk!'

'There it is for you then, since less wunna serve. But think on what I was saying.—Waes me, it will be sair news in the braes of Balquidder, that Robin Oig M'Combich should have run an ill gate, and ta'en on.'

'Ill news in Balquidder, indeed!' echoed poor Robin. 'But Cot speed you, Hughie, and send you good marcats. Ye winna meet with Robin Oig again, either at tryste or fair.'

So saying, he shook hastily the hand of his acquaintance, and set out in the direction from which he had advanced, with the spirit of his former pace.

'There is something wrang with the lad,' muttered the Morrison to himself, 'but we will maybe see better into it the morn's morning.'

But long ere the morning dawned, the catastrophe of our tale had taken place. It was two hours after the affray had happened, and it was totally forgotten by almost every one, when Robin Oig returned to Heskett's inn. The place was filled at once by various sorts of men, and with noises corresponding to their character. There were the grave low sounds of men engaged in busy traffic, with the laugh, the song, and the riotous jest of those who had nothing to do but to enjoy themselves. Among the last was Harry Wakefield, who, amidst a grinning group of smock-frocks, hobnailed shoes, and jolly English physiognomies, was trolling forth the old ditty,

What though my name be Roger,
Who drives the plough and cart—*

when he was interrupted by a well-known voice saying in a high and stern voice, marked by the sharp Highland accent, 'Harry Waakfelt—if you be a man, stand up!'

'What is the matter?—what is it?' the guests demanded of each other.

'It is only a d——d Scotsman,' said Fleece-bumpkin, who was by this time very drunk, 'whom Harry Wakefield helped to his broth today, who is now come to have *his cauld kail* het again.'*

'Harry Waakfelt,' repeated the same ominous summons, 'stand up, if you be a man!'

There is something in the tone of deep and con-centrated passion, which attracts attention and imposes awe, even by the very sound. The guests shrunk back on every side, and gazed at the High-lander as he stood in the middle of them, his brows bent, and his features rigid with resolution.

'I will stand up with all my heart, Robin, my boy, but it shall be to shake hands with you, and drink down all unkindness. It is not the fault of your heart, man, that you don't know how to clench your hands.'

By this time he stood opposite to his antagonist; his open and unsuspecting look strangely con-trasted with the stern purpose, which gleamed wild, dark, and vindictive in the eyes of the Highlander.

''Tis not thy fault, man, that, not having the luck to be an Englishman, thou canst not fight more than a schoolgirl.'

'I *can* fight,' answered Robin Oig sternly, but calmly, 'and you shall know it. You, Harry Waakfelt, showed me to-day how the Saxon

churls fight—I show you now how the Highland
Dunniè-wassel fights.'

He seconded the word with the action, and
plunged the dagger, which he suddenly displayed,
into the broad breast of the English yeoman,
with such fatal certainty and force, that the hilt
made a hollow sound against the breast-bone,
and the double-edged point split the very heart
of his victim. Harry Wakefield fell and expired
with a single groan. His assassin next seized the
bailiff by the collar, and offered the bloody
poniard to his throat, whilst dread and surprise
rendered the man incapable of defence.

'It were very just to lay you beside him,' he
said, 'but the blood of a base pickthank shall
never mix on my father's dirk with that of a
brave man.'

As he spoke, he cast the man from him with so
much force that he fell on the floor, while Robin,
with his other hand, threw the fatal weapon into
the blazing turf-fire.

'There,' he said, 'take me who likes—and let
fire cleanse blood if it can.'

The pause of astonishment still continuing,
Robin Oig asked for a peace-officer, and a constable having stepped out, he surrendered himself to his custody.

'A bloody night's work you have made of it,'
said the constable.

'Your own fault,' said the Highlander. 'Had
you kept his hands off me twa hours since, he
would have been now as well and merry as he
was twa minutes since.'

'It must be sorely answered,' said the peace-
officer.

'Never you mind that—death pays all debts; it will pay that too.'

The horror of the bystanders began now to give way to indignation; and the sight of a favourite companion murdered in the midst of them, the provocation being, in their opinion, so utterly inadequate to the excess of vengeance, might have induced them to kill the perpetrator of the deed even upon the very spot. The constable, however, did his duty on this occasion, and with the assistance of some of the more reasonable persons present, procured horses to guard the prisoner to Carlisle, to abide his doom at the next assizes. While the escort was preparing, the prisoner neither expressed the least interest nor attempted the slightest reply. Only, before he was carried from the fatal apartment, he desired to look at the dead body, which, raised from the floor, had been deposited upon the large table (at the head of which Harry Wakefield had presided but a few minutes before, full of life, vigour, and animation) until the surgeons should examine the mortal wound. The face of the corpse was decently covered with a napkin. To the surprise and horror of the bystanders, which displayed itself in a general *Ah!* drawn through clenched teeth and half-shut lips, Robin Oig removed the cloth, and gazed with a mournful but steady eye on the lifeless visage, which had been so lately animated that the smile of good-humoured confidence in his own strength, of conciliation at once and contempt towards his enemy, still curled his lip. While those present expected that the wound, which had so lately flooded the apartment with gore, would send forth fresh streams at the touch of the homicide, Robin Oig replaced the covering, with the brief exclamation—'He was a pretty man!'

My story is nearly ended. The unfortunate Highlander stood his trial at Carlisle. I was myself present, and as a young Scottish lawyer, or barrister at least, and reputed a man of some quality, the politeness of the Sheriff of Cumberland offered me a place on the bench. The facts of the case were proved in the manner I have related them; and whatever might be at first the prejudice of the audience against a crime so un-English as that of assassination from revenge, yet when the rooted national prejudices of the prisoner had been explained, which made him consider himself as stained with indelible dishonour when subjected to personal violence; when his previous patience, moderation, and endurance were considered, the generosity of the English audience was inclined to regard his crime as the wayward aberration of a false idea of honour rather than as flowing from a heart naturally savage, or perverted by habitual vice. I shall never forget the charge of the venerable judge to the jury, although not at that time liable to be much affected either by that which was eloquent or pathetic.

'We have had', he said, 'in the previous part of our duty' (alluding to some former trials) 'to discuss crimes which infer disgust and abhorrence, while they call down the well-merited vengeance of the law. It is now our still more melancholy task to apply its salutary though severe enactments to a case of a very singular character, in which the crime (for a crime it is, and a deep one) arose less out of the malevolence of the heart, than the error of the understanding—less from any idea of committing wrong, than from an unhappily perverted notion of that which is right. Here we have two men, highly esteemed, it has been stated, in their rank of life, and attached, it seems, to each other as friends, one of whose lives has been already sacrificed to a punctilio, and the other is about to prove the vengeance of the offended laws; and yet both may claim our commiseration at least, as men acting in ignorance of each other's national prejudices, and unhappily misguided rather than voluntarily erring from the path of right conduct.

'In the original cause of the misunderstanding, we must in justice give the right to the prisoner at the bar. He had acquired possession of the enclosure, which was the object of competition, by a legal contract with the proprietor, Mr. Ireby; and yet, when accosted with reproaches undeserved in themselves, and galling doubtless to a temper at least sufficiently susceptible of passion, he offered notwithstanding to yield up half his acquisition for the sake of peace and good neighbourhood, and his amicable proposal was rejected with scorn. Then follows the scene at Mr. Heskett the publican's, and you will observe how the stranger was treated by the deceased, and, I am sorry to observe, by those around, who seem to have urged him in a manner which was aggravating in the highest degree. While he asked for peace and for composition, and offered submission to a magistrate, or to a mutual arbiter, the prisoner was insulted by a whole company, who seem on this occasion to have forgotten the national maxim of "fair play"; and while attempting to escape from the place in peace, he was intercepted, struck down, and beaten to the effusion of his blood.

'Gentlemen of the jury, it was with some impatience that I heard my learned brother, who opened the case for the crown, give an unfavourable turn to the prisoner's conduct on this occasion. He said the prisoner was afraid to encounter his antagonist in fair fight, or to submit to the laws of the ring; and that therefore, like a cowardly Italian, he had recourse to his fatal stiletto, to murder the man whom he dared not meet in manly encounter. I observed the prisoner shrink from this part of the accusation with the abhorrence natural to a brave man; and as I would wish to make my words impressive when I point his real crime, I must secure his opinion of my impartiality, by rebutting everything that seems to me a false accusation. There can be no doubt that the prisoner is a man of resolution—too much resolution—I wish to Heaven that he had less, or rather that he had had a better education to regulate it.

'Gentlemen, as to the laws my brother talks of, they may be known in the bull-ring, or the bear-garden, or the cockpit, but they are not known here. Or, if they should be so far admitted as furnishing a species of proof that no malice was intended in this sort of combat, from which fatal accidents do sometimes arise, it can only be so admitted when both parties are *in pari casu*, equally acquainted with, and equally willing to refer themselves to, that species of arbitrament. But will it be contended that a man of superior

rank and education is to be subjected, or is
obliged to subject himself, to this coarse and
brutal strife, perhaps in opposition to a younger,
stronger, or more skilful opponent? Certainly
even the pugilistic code, if founded upon the fair
play of Merry Old England, as my brother alleges
it to be, can contain nothing so preposterous.
And, gentlemen of the jury, if the laws would
support an English gentleman, wearing, we will
suppose, his sword, in defending himself by force
against a violent personal aggression of the nature
offered to this prisoner, they will not less protect
a foreigner and a stranger, involved in the same
unpleasing circumstances. If, therefore, gentlemen of the jury, when thus pressed by a *vis major*,
the object of obloquy to a whole company, and
of direct violence from one at least, and, as he
might reasonably apprehend, from more, the
panel had produced the weapon which his
countrymen, as we are informed, generally carry
about their persons, and the same unhappy
circumstance had ensued which you have heard
detailed in evidence, I could not in my conscience
have asked from you a verdict of murder. The
prisoner's personal defence might, indeed, even
in that case, have gone more or less beyond the
Moderamen inculpatae tutelae,* spoken of by lawyers,
but the punishment incurred would have been
that of manslaughter, not of murder. I beg leave
to add that I should have thought this milder
species of charge was demanded in the case supposed, notwithstanding the statute of James I
cap. 8, which takes the case of slaughter by
stabbing with a short weapon, even without
malice prepense, out of the benefit of clergy.*

For this statute of stabbing, as it is termed, arose out of a temporary cause; and as the real guilt is the same, whether the slaughter be committed by the dagger, or by sword or pistol, the benignity of the modern law places them all on the same, or nearly the same footing.

'But, gentlemen of the jury, the pinch of the case lies in the interval of two hours interposed betwixt the reception of the injury and the fatal retaliation. In the heat of affray and *chaude mêlée*, law, compassionating the infirmities of humanity, makes allowance for the passions which rule such a stormy moment—for the sense of present pain, for the apprehension of further injury, for the difficulty of ascertaining with due accuracy the precise degree of violence which is necessary to protect the person of the individual, without annoying or injuring the assailant more than is absolutely necessary. But the time necessary to walk twelve miles, however speedily performed, was an interval sufficient for the prisoner to have recollected himself; and the violence with which he carried his purpose into effect, with so many circumstances of deliberate determination, could neither be induced by the passion of anger, nor that of fear. It was the purpose and the act of predetermined revenge, for which law neither can, will, nor ought to have sympathy or allowance.

'It is true, we may repeat to ourselves, in alleviation of this poor man's unhappy action, that his case is a very peculiar one. The country which he inhabits was, in the days of many now alive, inaccessible to the laws, not only of England, which have not even yet penetrated thither, but to those to which our neighbours of Scotland are subjected, and which must be supposed to be, and no doubt actually are, founded upon the general principles of justice and equity which pervade every civilized country. Amongst their mountains, as among the North American Indians, the various tribes were wont to make war upon each other, so that each man was obliged to go armed for his own protection. These men, from the ideas which they entertained of their own descent and of their own consequence, regarded themselves as so many cavaliers or men-at-arms, rather than as the peasantry of a peaceful country. Those laws of the ring, as my brother terms them, were unknown to the race of warlike mountaineers; that decision of quarrels by no other weapons than those which nature has given every man, must to them have seemed as vulgar and as preposterous as to the noblesse of France. Revenge, on the other hand, must have been as familiar to their habits of society as to those of the Cherokees or Mohawks. It is indeed, as described by Bacon, at bottom a kind of wild untutored justice; for the fear of retaliation must withhold the hands of the oppressor where there is no regular law to check daring violence. But though all this may be granted, and though we may allow that, such having been the case of the Highlands in the days of the prisoner's fathers, many of the opinions and sentiments must still continue to influence the present generation, it cannot, and ought not, even in this most painful case, to alter the administration of the law, either in your hands, gentlemen of the jury, or in mine. The first object of civilization is to place the general protection of the law, equally administered, in the room of that wild justice, which every man cut and carved for himself, according to the length of his sword and the strength of his arm. The law says to the subjects, with a voice only inferior to that of the Deity, 'Vengeance is mine.'* The instant that there is time for passion to cool, and reason to interpose, an injured party must become aware that the law assumes the exclusive cognizance of the right and wrong betwixt the parties, and opposes her inviolable buckler to every attempt of the private party to right himself. I repeat, that this unhappy man ought personally to be the object rather of our pity than our abhorrence, for he failed in his ignorance, and from mistaken notions of honour. But his crime is not the less that of murder, gentlemen, and, in your high and important office, it is your duty so to find. Englishmen have their angry passions as well as Scots; and should this man's action remain unpunished, you may unsheath, under various pretences, a thousand daggers betwixt the Land's-end and the Orkneys.'

The venerable judge thus ended what, to judge by his apparent emotion, and by the tears which filled his eyes, was really a painful task. The jury, according to his instructions, brought in a verdict of Guilty; and Robin Oig M'Combich, *alias* M'Gregor, was sentenced to death and left for execution, which took place accordingly. He met his fate with great firmness, and acknowledged the justice of his sentence. But he repelled indignantly the observations of those who accused him of attacking an unarmed man. 'I give a life for the life I took,'*he said, 'and what can I do more?'*

MY AUNT MARGARET'S MIRROR

INTRODUCTION

THE species of publication which has come to be generally known by the title of *Annual*, being a miscellany of prose and verse equipped with numerous engravings, and put forth every year about Christmas, had flourished for a long while in Germany, before it was imitated in this country by an enterprising bookseller, a German by birth, Mr. Ackermann*. The rapid success of his work, as is the custom of the time, gave birth to a host of rivals, and, among others, to an annual styled *The Keepsake*,* the first volume of which appeared in 1828, and attracted much notice, chiefly in consequence of the very uncommon splendour of its illustrative accompaniments. The expenditure which the spirited proprietors lavished on this magnificent volume is understood to have been not less than from ten to twelve thousand pounds sterling!

Various gentlemen, of such literary reputation that any one might think it an honour to be associated with them, had been announced as contributors to this annual, before application was made to me to assist in it; and I accordingly placed with much pleasure at the editor's disposal a few fragments, originally designed to have been worked into the Chronicles of the Canongate, besides a MS. drama, the long-neglected performance of my youthful days,— The House of Aspen.

The Keepsake for 1828 included, however, only

three of these little prose tales—of which the first in order was that entitled 'My Aunt Margaret's Mirror'. By way of *introduction* to this, when now included in a general collection of my lucubrations, I have only to say that it is a mere transcript, or at least with very little embellishment, of a story that I remembered being struck with in my childhood, when told at the fireside by a lady of eminent virtues and no inconsiderable share of talent, one of the ancient and honourable house of Swinton.* She was a kind relation of my own, and met her death in a manner so shocking, being killed in a fit of insanity by a female attendant who had been attached to her person for half a lifetime, that I cannot now recall her memory, child as I was when the catastrophe occurred, without a painful re-awakening of perhaps the first images of horror that the scenes of real life stamped on my mind.

This good spinster had in her composition a strong vein of the superstitious, and was pleased, among other fancies, to read alone in her chamber by a taper fixed in a candlestick which she had formed out of a human skull. One night, this strange piece of furniture acquired suddenly the power of locomotion, and, after performing some odd circles on her chimney-piece, fairly leaped on the floor, and continued to roll about the apartment. Mrs. Swinton calmly proceeded to the adjoining room for another light, and had the satisfaction to penetrate the mystery on the spot. Rats abounded in the ancient building she inhabited, and one of these had managed to ensconce itself within her favourite *memento mori*. Though thus endowed with a more than feminine

share of nerve, she entertained largely that belief
in supernaturals, which in those times was not
considered as sitting ungracefully on the grave
and aged of her condition; and the story of the
Magic Mirror* was one for which she vouched
with particular confidence, alleging indeed that
one of her own family had been an eye-witness
of the incidents recorded in it.

I tell the tale as it was told to me.*

Stories enow of much the same cast will present
themselves to the recollection of such of my
readers as have ever dabbled in a species of lore
to which I certainly gave more hours, at one
period of my life, than I should gain any credit
by confessing.

August, 1831.

MY AUNT MARGARET'S MIRROR

There are times
When Fancy plays her gambols, in despite
Even of our watchful senses, when in sooth
Substance seems shadow, shadow substance seems,
When the broad, palpable, and mark'd partition,
'Twixt that which is and is not, seems dissolved,
As if the mental eye gain'd power to gaze
Beyond the limits of the existing world.
Such hours of shadowy dreams I better love
Than all the gross realities of life.—ANONYMOUS.*

MY Aunt Margaret was one of that respected sisterhood, upon whom devolve all the trouble and solicitude incidental to the possession of children, excepting only that which attends their entrance into the world. We were a large family, of very different dispositions and constitutions. Some were dull and peevish—they were sent to Aunt Margaret to be amused; some were rude, romping, and boisterous—they were sent to Aunt Margaret to be kept quiet, or rather that their noise might be removed out of hearing: those who were indisposed were sent with the prospect of being nursed—those who were stubborn, with the hope of their being subdued by the kindness of Aunt Margaret's discipline; in short, she had all the various duties of a mother, without the credit and dignity of the maternal character. The busy scene of her various cares is now over—of the invalids and the robust, the kind and the rough, the peevish and pleased children, who thronged her little parlour from morning to night, not one now remains alive but myself; who, afflicted by early infirmity, was one of the most delicate of her nurslings, yet nevertheless, have outlived them all.

It is still my custom, and shall be so while I have the use of my limbs, to visit my respected relation at least three times a week. Her abode is about half a mile from the suburbs of the town in which I reside; and is accessible, not only by the high road from which it stands at some distance, but by means of a greensward footpath, leading through some pretty meadows. I have so little left to torment me in life, that it is one of my greatest vexations to know that several of these sequestered fields have been devoted as sites for building. In that which is nearest the town, wheelbarrows have been at work for several weeks in such numbers that, I verily believe, its whole surface, to the depth of at least eighteen inches, was mounted in these monotrochs at the same moment, and in the act of being transported from one place to another. Huge triangular piles of planks are also reared in different parts of the devoted messuage; and a little group of trees, that still grace the eastern end which rises in a gentle ascent, have just received warning to quit expressed by a daub of white paint, and are to give place to a curious grove of chimneys.

It would, perhaps, hurt others in my situation to reflect that this little range of pasturage once belonged to my father (whose family was of some consideration in the world) and was sold by patches to remedy distresses in which he involved himself in an attempt by commercial adventure to redeem his diminished fortune. While the building scheme was in full operation, this circumstance was often pointed out to me by the

class of friends who are anxious that no part of
your misfortunes should escape your observation.
'Such pasture-ground!—lying at the very town's
end—in turnips and potatoes, the parks would
bring 20*l*. per acre, and if leased for building—
Oh, it was a gold mine!—And all sold for an old
song*out of the ancient possessor's hands!' My
comforters cannot bring me to repine much on
this subject. If I could be allowed to look back
on the past without interruption, I could willingly
give up the enjoyment of present income, and
the hope of future profit, to those who have
purchased what my father sold. I regret the
alteration of the ground only because it destroys
associations, and I would more willingly (I think)
see the Earl's Closes in the hands of strangers,
retaining their sylvan appearance, than know
them for my own, if torn up by agriculture, or
covered with buildings. Mine are the sensations
of poor Logan:

> The horrid plough has rased the green
>   Where yet a child I stray'd;
> The axe has fell'd the hawthorn screen,
>   The schoolboy's summer shade.*

I hope, however, the threatened devastation
will not be consummated in my day. Although
the adventurous spirit of times short while since
passed gave rise to the undertaking, I have been
encouraged to think that the subsequent changes
have so far damped the spirit of speculation, that
the rest of the woodland footpath leading to
Aunt Margaret's retreat will be left undisturbed
for her time and mine. I am interested in this,
for every step of the way, after I have passed
through the green already mentioned, has for me

something of early remembrance:—There is the
stile at which I can recollect a cross child's-maid
upbraiding me with my infirmity, as she lifted
me coarsely and carelessly over the flinty steps,
which my brothers traversed with shout and
bound.* I remember the suppressed bitterness of
the moment, and, conscious of my own inferiority,
the feeling of envy with which I regarded the
easy movements and elastic steps of my more
happily formed brethren. Alas! these goodly
barks have all perished on life's wide ocean, and
only that which seemed so little seaworthy, as the
naval phrase goes, has reached the port when
the tempest is over. Then there is the pool,
where, manœuvring our little navy, constructed
out of the broad water flags, my elder brother
fell in, and was scarce saved from the watery
element to die under Nelson's banner.* There is
the hazel copse also, in which my brother Henry
used to gather nuts, thinking little that he was to
die in an Indian jungle in quest of rupees.

There is so much more of remembrance about
the little walk that—as I stop, rest on my crutch-
headed cane, and look round with that species of
comparison between the thing I was and that
which I now am—it almost induces me to doubt
my own identity; until I find myself in face of the
honeysuckle porch of Aunt Margaret's dwelling,
with its irregularity of front, and its odd projecting latticed windows; where the workmen seem
to have made a study that no one of them should
resemble another, in form, size, or in the old-
fashioned stone entablature and labels which
adorn them. This tenement, once the manor-
house of Earl's Closes, we still retain a slight hold

upon; for, in some family arrangements, it had been settled upon Aunt Margaret during the term of her life. Upon this frail tenure depends, in a great measure, the last shadow of the family of Bothwell of Earl's Closes, and their last slight connexion with their paternal inheritance. The only representative will then be an infirm old man, moving not unwillingly to the grave, which has devoured all that were dear to his affections.

When I have indulged such thoughts for a minute or two, I enter the mansion which is said to have been the gatehouse only of the original building, and find one being on whom time seems to have made little impression; for the Aunt Margaret of to-day bears the same proportional age to the Aunt Margaret of my early youth, that the boy of ten years old does to the man of (by'r Lady!) some fifty-six years. The old lady's invariable costume has doubtless some share in confirming one in the opinion that time has stood still with Aunt Margaret.

The brown or chocolate-coloured silk gown, with ruffles of the same stuff at the elbow, within which are others of Mechlin lace—the black silk gloves, or mitts, the white hair combed back upon a roll, and the cap of spotless cambric, which closes around the venerable countenance, as they were not the costume of 1780, so neither were they that of 1826; they are altogether a style peculiar to the individual Aunt Margaret. There she still sits, as she sat thirty years since, with her wheel or the stocking, which she works by the fire in winter and by the window in summer; or, perhaps, venturing as far as the porch in an unusually fine summer evening. Her frame, like some well-constructed piece of mechanics, still performs the operations for which it had seemed destined; going its round with an activity which is gradually diminished, yet indicating no probability that it will soon come to a period.

The solicitude and affection which had made Aunt Margaret the willing slave to the inflictions of a whole nursery, have now for their object the health and comfort of one old and infirm man, the last remaining relative of her family, and the only one who can still find interest in the traditional stores which she hoards, as some miser hides the gold which he desires that no one should enjoy after his death.

My conversation with Aunt Margaret generally relates little either to the present or to the future: for the passing day we possess as much as we require, and we neither of us wish for more; and for that which is to follow we have on this side of the grave neither hopes, nor fears, nor anxiety. We therefore naturally look back to the past; and forget the present fallen fortunes and declined importance of our family, in recalling the hours when it was wealthy and prosperous.

With this slight introduction, the reader will know as much of Aunt Margaret and her nephew as is necessary to comprehend the following conversation and narrative.

Last week, when, late in a summer evening, I went to call on the old lady to whom my reader is now introduced, I was received by her with all her usual affection and benignity; while, at the same time, she seemed abstracted and disposed to silence. I asked her the reason. 'They have been clearing out the old chapel,' she said; 'John

Clayhudgeons having, it seems, discovered that the stuff within—being, I suppose, the remains of our ancestors—was excellent for top-dressing the meadows.'

Here I started up with more alacrity than I have displayed for some years; but sat down while my aunt added, laying her hand upon my sleeve, 'The chapel has been long considered as common ground, my dear, and used for a penfold, and what objection can we have to the man for employing what is his own, to his own profit? Besides, I did speak to him, and he very readily and civilly promised that, if he found bones or monuments, they should be carefully respected and reinstated; and what more could I ask? So, the first stone they found bore the name of Margaret Bothwell, 1585, and I have caused it to be laid carefully aside, as I think it betokens death; and having served my namesake two hundred years, it has just been cast up in time to do me the same good turn. My house has been long put in order, as far as the small earthly concerns require it, but who shall say that their account with Heaven is sufficiently revised?'

'After what you have said, aunt,' I replied, 'perhaps I ought to take my hat and go away, and so I should, but that there is on this occasion a little alloy mingled with our devotion. To think of death at all times is a duty—to suppose it nearer, from the finding an old gravestone, is superstition; and you, with your strong useful common sense which was so long the prop of a fallen family, are the last person whom I should have suspected of such weakness.'

'Neither would I deserve your suspicions,

kinsman,' answered Aunt Margaret, 'if we were speaking of any incident occurring in the actual business of human life. But for all this I have a sense of superstition about me, which I do not wish to part with. It is a feeling which separates me from this age, and links me with that to which I am hastening; and even when it seems, as now, to lead me to the brink of the grave, and bids me gaze on it, I do not love that it should be dispelled. It soothes my imagination, without influencing my reason or conduct.'

'I profess, my good lady,' replied I, 'that had any one but you made such a declaration, I should have thought it as capricious as that of the clergyman who, without vindicating his false reading, preferred, from habit's sake, his old Mumpsimus to the modern Sumpsimus.'*

'Well,' answered my aunt, 'I must explain my inconsistency in this particular, by comparing it to another. I am, as you know, a piece of that old-fashioned thing called a Jacobite, but I am so in sentiment and feeling only; for a more loyal subject never joined in prayers for the health and wealth of George the Fourth, whom God long preserve! But I dare say that kind-hearted sovereign would not deem that an old woman did him much injury if she leaned back in her arm-chair, just in such a twilight as this, and thought of the high-mettled men whose sense of duty called them to arms against his grandfather; and how, in a cause which they deemed that of their rightful prince and country,

They fought till their hand to the broadsword was glued, They fought against fortune with hearts unsubdued.*

Do not come at such a moment, when my head

is full of plaids, pibrochs, and claymores, and ask my reason to admit what, I am afraid, it cannot deny—I mean, that the public advantage peremptorily demanded that these things should cease to exist. I cannot, indeed, refuse to allow the justice of your reasoning; but yet, being convinced against my will, you will gain little by your motion. You might as well read to an infatuated lover the catalogue of his mistress's imperfections; for, when he has been compelled to listen to the summary, you will only get for answer, that "he lo'es her a' the better."'

I was not sorry to have changed the gloomy train of Aunt Margaret's thoughts, and replied in the same tone, 'Well, I can't help being persuaded that our good king is the more sure of Mrs. Bothwell's loyal affection, that he has the Stuart right of birth, as well as the Act of Succession in his favour'*.

'Perhaps my attachment, were its source of consequence, might be found warmer for the union of the rights you mention,' said Aunt Margaret; 'but, upon my word, it would be as sincere if the king's right were founded only on the will of the nation, as declared at the Revolution. I am none of your *jure divino**folks.'

'And a Jacobite notwithstanding.'

'And a Jacobite notwithstanding; or rather, I will give you leave to call me one of the party which, in Queen Anne's time, were called *Whimsicals*;*because they were sometimes operated upon by feelings, sometimes by principle. After all, it is very hard that you will not allow an old woman to be as inconsistent in her political sentiments as mankind in general show themselves in all the

various courses of life; since you cannot point out
one of them, in which the passions and prejudices
of those who pursue it are not perpetually carrying us away from the path which our reason
points out.'

'True, aunt; but you are a wilful wanderer,
who should be forced back into the right path.'

'Spare me, I entreat you,' replied Aunt Margaret. 'You remember the Gaelic song, though
I dare say I mispronounce the words—

> Hatil mohatil, na dowski mi.
> I am asleep, do not waken me.*

I tell you, kinsman, that the sort of waking
dreams which my imagination spins out, in what
your favourite Wordsworth calls 'moods of my
own mind'*, are worth all the rest of my more
active days. Then, instead of looking forwards
as I did in youth, and forming for myself fairy
palaces upon the verge of the grave, I turn my
eyes backward upon the days and manners of my
better time; and the sad, yet soothing recollections come so close and interesting, that I almost
think it sacrilege to be wiser, or more rational,
or less prejudiced, than those to whom I looked
up in my younger years.'

'I think I now understand what you mean,'
I answered, 'and can comprehend why you
should occasionally prefer the twilight of illusion
to the steady light of reason.'

'Where there is no task', she rejoined, 'to be
performed, we may sit in the dark if we like it—
if we go to work, we must ring for candles.'

'And amidst such shadowy and doubtful light,'
continued I, 'imagination frames her enchanted

and enchanting visions, and sometimes passes them upon the senses for reality.'

'Yes,' said Aunt Margaret, who is a well-read woman, 'to those who resemble the translator of Tasso,

> Prevailing poet, whose undoubting mind
> Believed the magic wonders which he sung.*

It is not required for this purpose, that you should be sensible of the painful horrors which an actual belief in such prodigies inflicts—such a belief, now-a-days, belongs only to fools and children. It is not necessary that your ears should tingle, and your complexion change, like that of Theodore, at the approach of the spectral huntsman.* All that is indispensable for the enjoyment of the milder feeling of supernatural awe is that you should be susceptible of the slight shuddering which creeps over you when you hear a tale of terror—that well-vouched tale which the narrator, having first expressed his general disbelief of all such legendary lore, selects and produces, as having something in it which he has been always obliged to give up as inexplicable. Another symptom is, a momentary hesitation to look round you when the interest of the narrative is at the highest; and the third, a desire to avoid looking into a mirror, when you are alone in your chamber for the evening. I mean such are signs which indicate the crisis, when a female imagination is in due temperature to enjoy a ghost story. I do not pretend to describe those which express the same disposition in a gentleman.'

'That last symptom, dear aunt, of shunning the mirror, seems likely to be a rare occurrence amongst the fair sex.'

'You are a novice in toilet fashions, my dear cousin. All women consult the looking-glass with anxiety before they go into company; but when they return home, the mirror has not the same charm. The die has been cast—the party has been successful or unsuccessful in the impression which she desired to make. But, without going deeper into the mysteries of the dressing-table, I will tell you that I myself, like many other honest folks, do not like to see the blank black front of a large mirror in a room dimly lighted, and where the reflection of the candle seems rather to lose itself in the deep obscurity of the glass, than to be reflected back again into the apartment. That space of inky darkness seems to be a field for fancy to play her revels in. She may call up other features to meet us, instead of the reflection of our own; or, as in the spells of Hallowe'en, which we learned in childhood,* some unknown form may be seen peeping over our shoulder. In short, when I am in a ghost-seeing humour, I make my handmaiden draw the green curtains over the mirror before I go into the room, so that she may have the first shock of the apparition, if there be any to be seen. But, to tell you the truth, this dislike to look into a mirror in particular times and places, has, I believe, its original foundation in a story which came to me by tradition from my grandmother, who was a party concerned in the scene of which I will now tell you.'

THE MIRROR

CHAPTER I

YOU are fond (said my aunt) of sketches of the society which has passed away. I wish I could describe to you Sir Philip Forester, the 'chartered libertine' of Scottish good company, about the end of the last century. I never saw him indeed; but my mother's traditions were full of his wit, gallantry, and dissipation. This gay knight flourished about the end of the seventeenth and beginning of the eighteenth century. He was the Sir Charles Easy and the Lovelace of his day*and country: renowned for the number of duels he had fought, and the successful intrigues which he had carried on. The supremacy which he had attained in the fashionable world was absolute; and when we combine it with one or two anecdotes, for which, 'if laws were made for every degree,'* he ought certainly to have been hanged, the popularity of such a person really serves to show, either that the present times are much more decent, if not more virtuous, than they formerly were; or that high breeding then was of more difficult attainment than that which is now so called; and, consequently, entitled the successful professor to a proportional degree of plenary indulgences and privileges. No beau of this day could have borne out so ugly a story as that of Pretty Peggy Grindstone, the miller's daughter at Sillermills*—it had wellnigh made work for the Lord Advocate.* But it hurt Sir Philip Forester no more than the hail hurts the hearthstone. He was as well received in society as ever, and dined with the Duke of A——* the day the poor girl was buried. She died of heartbreak. But that has nothing to do with my story.

Now, you must listen to a single word upon kith, kin, and ally; I promise you I will not be prolix. But it is necessary to the authenticity of my legend that you should know that Sir Philip Forester, with his handsome person, elegant accomplishments, and fashionable manners, married the younger Miss Falconer of King's Copland. The elder sister of this lady had previously become the wife of my grandfather, Sir Geoffrey Bothwell, and brought into our family a good fortune. Miss Jemima, or Miss Jemmie Falconer, as she was usually called, had also about ten thousand pounds sterling—then thought a very handsome portion indeed.

The two sisters were extremely different, though each had their admirers while they remained single. Lady Bothwell had some touch of the old King's-Copland blood about her. She was bold, though not to the degree of audacity; ambitious, and desirous to raise her house and family; and was, as has been said, a considerable spur to my grandfather, who was otherwise an indolent man; but whom, unless he has been slandered, his lady's influence involved in some political matters which had been more wisely let alone. She was a woman of high principle, however, and masculine good sense, as some of her letters testify, which are still in my wainscot cabinet.

Jemmie Falconer was the reverse of her sister in every respect. Her understanding did not reach above the ordinary pitch, if, indeed, she could be said to have attained it. Her beauty, while it lasted, consisted, in a great measure, of delicacy of complexion and regularity of features, without any peculiar force of expression. Even these charms faded under the sufferings attendant on an ill-sorted match. She was passionately attached to her husband, by whom she was treated with a callous, yet polite indifference, which, to one whose heart was as tender as her judgement was weak, was more painful perhaps than absolute ill-usage. Sir Philip was a voluptuary, that is, a completely selfish egotist, whose disposition and character resembled the rapier he wore, polished, keen, and brilliant, but inflexible and unpitying. As he observed carefully all the usual forms towards his lady, he had the art to deprive her even of the compassion of the world; and useless and unavailing as that may be while actually possessed by the sufferer, it is, to a mind like Lady Forester's, most painful to know she has it not.

The tattle of society did its best to place the peccant husband above the suffering wife. Some called her a poor spiritless thing, and declared that, with a little of her sister's spirit, she might have brought to reason any Sir Philip whatsoever, were it the termagant Falconbridge*himself. But the greater part of their acquaintance affected candour, and saw faults on both sides; though, in fact, there only existed the oppressor and the oppressed. The tone of such critics was—'To be sure, no one will justify Sir Philip Forester, but then we all know Sir Philip, and Jemmie Falconer might have known what she had to expect from

the beginning.—What made her set her cap at
Sir Philip?—He would never have looked at her
if she had not thrown herself at his head, with
her poor ten thousand pounds. I am sure, if it
is money he wanted, she spoiled his market. I
know where Sir Philip could have done much
better.—And then, if she *would* have the man,
could not she try to make him more comfortable
at home, and have his friends oftener, and not
plague him with the squalling children, and take
care all was handsome and in good style about
the house? I declare I think Sir Philip would
have made a very domestic man, with a woman
who knew how to manage him.'

Now these fair critics, in raising their profound
edifice of domestic felicity, did not recollect that
the corner-stone was wanting; and that to receive
good company with good cheer, the means of
the banquet ought to have been furnished by
Sir Philip; whose income (dilapidated as it was)
was not equal to the display of the hospitality required, and, at the same time, to the supply of
the good knight's *menus plaisirs*. So, in spite of all
that was so sagely suggested by female friends,
Sir Philip carried his good-humour everywhere
abroad, and left at home a solitary mansion and
a pining spouse.

At length, inconvenienced in his money affairs,
and tired even of the short time which he spent
in his own dull house, Sir Philip Forester determined to take a trip to the Continent, in the
capacity of a volunteer. It was then common for
men of fashion to do so; and our knight perhaps
was of opinion that a touch of the military character, just enough to exalt, but not render pedantic,

his qualities as a *beau garçon*, was necessary to maintain possession of the elevated situation which he held in the ranks of fashion.

Sir Philip's resolution threw his wife into agonies of terror, by which the worthy baronet was so much annoyed that, contrary to his wont, he took some trouble to soothe her apprehensions; and once more brought her to shed tears, in which sorrow was not altogether unmingled with pleasure. Lady Bothwell asked, as a favour, Sir Philip's permission to receive her sister and her family into her own house during his absence on the Continent. Sir Philip readily assented to a proposition which saved expense, silenced the foolish people who might have talked of a deserted wife and family, and gratified Lady Bothwell, for whom he felt some respect, as for one who often spoke to him, always with freedom, and sometimes with severity, without being deterred either by his raillery, or the prestige of his reputation.

A day or two before Sir Philip's departure, Lady Bothwell took the liberty of asking him, in her sister's presence, the direct question, which his timid wife had often desired, but never ventured, to put to him.

'Pray, Sir Philip, what route do you take when you reach the Continent?'

'I go from Leith to Helvoet*by a packet with advices.'

'That I comprehend perfectly,' said Lady Bothwell dryly; 'but you do not mean to remain long at Helvoet, I presume, and I should like to know what is your next object?'

'You ask me, my dear lady,' answered Sir

Philip, 'a question which I have not dared to ask myself. The answer depends on the fate of war. I shall, of course, go to head-quarters, wherever they may happen to be for the time; deliver my letters of introduction; learn as much of the noble art of war as may suffice a poor interloping amateur; and then take a glance at the sort of thing of which we read so much in the *Gazette*.'*

'And I trust, Sir Philip,' said Lady Bothwell, 'that you will remember that you are a husband and a father; and that though you think fit to indulge this military fancy, you will not let it hurry you into dangers which it is certainly unnecessary for any save professional persons to encounter?'

'Lady Bothwell does me too much honour,' replied the adventurous knight, 'in regarding such a circumstance with the slightest interest. But to soothe your flattering anxiety, I trust your ladyship will recollect that I cannot expose to hazard the venerable and paternal character which you so obligingly recommend to my protection, without putting in some peril an honest fellow called Philip Forester, with whom I have kept company for thirty years, and with whom, though some folks consider him a coxcomb, I have not the least desire to part.'

'Well, Sir Philip, you are the best judge of your own affairs; I have little right to interfere—you are not my husband.'

'God forbid!'—said Sir Philip hastily; instantly adding, however, 'God forbid that I should deprive my friend Sir Geoffrey of so inestimable a treasure.'

'But you are my sister's husband,' replied the

lady; 'and I suppose you are aware of her present distress of mind——'

'If hearing of nothing else from morning to night can make me aware of it,' said Sir Philip, 'I should know something of the matter.'

'I do not pretend to reply to your wit, Sir Philip,' answered Lady Bothwell; 'but you must be sensible that all this distress is on account of apprehensions for your personal safety.'

'In that case, I am surprised that Lady Bothwell, at least, should give herself so much trouble upon so insignificant a subject.'

'My sister's interest may account for my being anxious to learn something of Sir Philip Forester's motions; about which otherwise, I know, he would not wish me to concern myself. I have a brother's safety, too, to be anxious for.'

'You mean Major Falconer, your brother by the mother's side:—What can he possibly have to do with our present agreeable conversation?'

'You have had words together, Sir Philip,' said Lady Bothwell.

'Naturally; we are connexions,' replied Sir Philip, 'and as such have always had the usual intercourse.'

'That is an evasion of the subject,' answered the lady. 'By words, I mean angry words, on the subject of your usage of your wife.'

'If', replied Sir Philip Forester, 'you suppose Major Falconer simple enough to intrude his advice upon me, Lady Bothwell, in my domestic matters, you are indeed warranted in believing that I might possibly be so far displeased with the interference as to request him to reserve his advice till it was asked.'

'And, being on these terms, you are going to join the very army in which my brother Falconer is now serving?'

'No man knows the path of honour better than Major Falconer,' said Sir Philip. 'An aspirant after fame, like me, cannot choose a better guide than his footsteps.'

Lady Bothwell rose and went to the window, the tears gushing from her eyes.

'And this heartless raillery', she said, 'is all the consideration that is to be given to our apprehensions of a quarrel which may bring on the most terrible consequences? Good God! of what can men's hearts be made, who can thus dally with the agony of others?'

Sir Philip Forester was moved; he laid aside the mocking tone in which he had hitherto spoken.

'Dear Lady Bothwell,' he said, taking her reluctant hand, 'we are both wrong:—you are too deeply serious; I, perhaps, too little so. The dispute I had with Major Falconer was of no earthly consequence. Had anything occurred betwixt us that ought to have been settled *par voie du fait*, as we say in France, neither of us are persons that are likely to postpone such a meeting. Permit me to say that were it generally known that you or my Lady Forester are apprehensive of such a catastrophe, it might be the very means of bringing about what would not otherwise be likely to happen. I know your good sense, Lady Bothwell, and that you will understand me when I say that really my affairs require my absence for some months;—this Jemima cannot understand; it is a perpetual recurrence of questions, why can you not do this, or that, or the third thing; and when you have proved to her that her expedients are totally ineffectual, you have just to begin the whole round again. Now, do you tell her, dear Lady Bothwell, that *you* are satisfied. She is, you must confess, one of those persons with whom authority goes farther than reasoning. Do but repose a little confidence in me, and you shall see how amply I will repay it.'

Lady Bothwell shook her head, as one but half satisfied. 'How difficult it is to extend confidence, when the basis on which it ought to rest has been so much shaken! But I will do my best to make Jemima easy; and farther, I can only say that for keeping your present purpose, I hold you responsible both to God and man.'

'Do not fear that I will deceive you,' said Sir Philip; 'the safest conveyance to me will be through the general post-office, Helvoetsluys, where I will take care to leave orders for forwarding my letters. As for Falconer, our only encounter will be over a bottle of Burgundy! so make yourself perfectly easy on his score.'

Lady Bothwell could *not* make herself easy; yet she was sensible that her sister hurt her own cause by *taking on*, as the maid-servants call it, too vehemently; and by showing before every stranger, by manner and sometimes by words also, a dissatisfaction with her husband's journey, that was sure to come to his ears and equally certain to displease him. But there was no help for this domestic dissension, which ended only with the day of separation.

I am sorry I cannot tell, with precision, the year in which Sir Philip Forester went over to Flanders; but it was one of those in which the campaign opened with extraordinary fury; and many bloody, though indecisive, skirmishes were fought between the French on the one side, and the Allies on the other. In all our modern improvements, there are none, perhaps, greater than in the accuracy and speed with which intelligence is transmitted from any scene of action to those in this country whom it may concern. During Marlborough's campaigns, the sufferings of the many who had relations in, or along with, the army, were greatly augmented by the suspense in which they were detained for weeks, after they had heard of bloody battles in which, in all probability, those for whom their bosoms throbbed with anxiety had been personally engaged. Amongst those who were most agonized by this state of uncertainty, was the— I had almost said deserted—wife of the gay Sir Philip Forester. A single letter had informed her of his arrival on the Continent—no others were received. One notice occurred in the newspapers, in which Volunteer Sir Philip Forester was mentioned as having been entrusted with a dangerous reconnoissance, which he had executed with the greatest courage, dexterity, and intelligence, and received the thanks of the commanding officer. The sense of his having acquired distinction brought a momentary glow into the lady's pale cheek; but it was instantly lost in ashen whiteness at the recollection of his danger. After this, they had no news whatever, neither from Sir Philip, nor even from their brother Falconer. The case of Lady Forester was not indeed different from that of hundreds in the same situation; but a feeble mind is necessarily an irritable one, and the suspense which some bear with constitutional indifference or philosophical resignation, and some with a disposition to believe and hope the best, was intolerable to Lady Forester, at once solitary and sensitive, low-spirited, and devoid of strength of mind, whether natural or acquired.

CHAPTER II

As she received no further news of Sir Philip, whether directly or indirectly, his unfortunate lady began now to feel a sort of consolation, even in those careless habits which had so often given her pain. 'He is so thoughtless,' she repeated a hundred times a day to her sister, 'he never writes when things are going on smoothly; it is his way: had anything happened he would have informed us.'

Lady Bothwell listened to her sister without attempting to console her. Probably she might be of opinion that even the worst intelligence which could be received from Flanders might not be without some touch of consolation; and that the Dowager Lady Forester, if so she was doomed to be called, might have a source of happiness unknown to the wife of the gayest and finest gentleman in Scotland. This conviction became stronger as they learned from inquiries made at head-quarters, that Sir Philip was no longer with the army; though whether he had been taken or slain in some of those skirmishes which were perpetually occurring, and in which he loved to distinguish himself, or whether he had, for some unknown reason or capricious change of mind, voluntarily left the service, none of his countrymen in the camp of the Allies could form even a conjecture. Meantime his creditors at home became clamorous, entered into possession of his property, and threatened his person, should he be rash enough to return to Scotland. These additional disadvantages aggravated Lady Bothwell's displeasure against the fugitive husband; while her sister saw nothing in any of them, save what tended to increase her grief for the absence of him whom her imagination now represented,—as it had before marriage—gallant, gay, and affectionate.

About this period there appeared in Edinburgh a man of singular appearance and pretensions. He was commonly called the Paduan Doctor, from having received his education at that famous university. He was supposed to possess some rare receipts in medicine, with which, it was affirmed, he had wrought remarkable cures. But though, on the one hand, the physicians of Edinburgh termed him an empiric, there were many persons, and among them some of the clergy, who, while they admitted the truth of the cures and the force of his remedies, alleged that Doctor Baptista Damiotti made use of charms and unlawful arts in order to obtain success in his practice. The resorting to him was even solemnly preached against, as a seeking of health from idols, and a trusting to the help which was to come from Egypt.* But the protection which the Paduan doctor received from some friends of interest and consequence, enabled him to set these imputations at defiance, and to assume, even in the city

of Edinburgh, famed as it was for abhorrence of
witches and necromancers, the dangerous character of an expounder of futurity. It was at length
rumoured, that for a certain gratification, which,
of course, was not an inconsiderable one, Doctor
Baptista Damiotti could tell the fate of the absent,
and even show his visitors the personal form of
their absent friends, and the action in which they
were engaged at the moment. This rumour
came to the ears of Lady Forester, who had
reached that pitch of mental agony in which the
sufferer will do anything, or endure anything,
that suspense may be converted into certainty.

Gentle and timid in most cases, her state of
mind made her equally obstinate and reckless,
and it was with no small surprise and alarm that
her sister, Lady Bothwell, heard her express a
resolution to visit this man of art, and learn from
him the fate of her husband. Lady Bothwell
remonstrated on the improbability that such
pretensions as those of this foreigner could be
founded in anything but imposture.

'I care not', said the deserted wife, 'what
degree of ridicule I may incur; if there be any
one chance out of a hundred that I may obtain
some certainty of my husband's fate, I would not
miss that chance for whatever else the world can
offer me.'

Lady Bothwell next urged the unlawfulness
of resorting to such sources of forbidden knowledge.

'Sister,' replied the sufferer, 'he who is dying
of thirst cannot refrain from drinking even
poisoned water. She who suffers under suspense
must seek information, even were the powers

which offer it unhallowed and infernal. I go to
learn my fate alone; and this very evening will
I know it: the sun that rises to-morrow shall find
me, if not more happy, at least more resigned.'

'Sister,' said Lady Bothwell, 'if you are determined upon this wild step, you shall not go alone.
If this man be an impostor, you may be too much
agitated by your feelings to detect his villainy.
If, which I cannot believe, there be any truth in
what he pretends, you shall not be exposed alone
to a communication of so extraordinary a nature.
I will go with you, if indeed you determine to go.
But yet reconsider your project and renounce
inquiries which cannot be prosecuted without
guilt, and perhaps without danger.'

Lady Forester threw herself into her sister's
arms, and, clasping her to her bosom, thanked
her a hundred times for the offer of her company;
while she declined with a melancholy gesture the
friendly advice with which it was accompanied.

When the hour of twilight arrived,—which was
the period when the Paduan Doctor was understood to receive the visits of those who came to
consult with him,—the two ladies left their apartments in the Canongate of Edinburgh, having
their dress arranged like that of women of an
inferior description, and their plaids disposed
around their faces as they were worn by the same
class; for, in those days of aristocracy, the quality
of the wearer was generally indicated by the
manner in which her plaid was disposed, as well
as by the fineness of its texture. It was Lady
Bothwell who had suggested this species of dis-
guise, partly to avoid observation as they should
go to the conjurer's house, and partly in order to

make trial of his penetration, by appearing before him in a feigned character. Lady Forester's servant, of tried fidelity, had been employed by her to propitiate the doctor by a suitable fee, and a story intimating that a soldier's wife desired to know the fate of her husband; a subject upon which, in all probability, the sage was very frequently consulted.

To the last moment, when the palace clock struck eight, Lady Bothwell earnestly watched her sister, in hopes that she might retreat from her rash undertaking; but as mildness, and even timidity, is capable at times of vehement and fixed purposes, she found Lady Forester resolutely unmoved and determined when the moment of departure arrived. Ill satisfied with the expedition, but determined not to leave her sister at such a crisis, Lady Bothwell accompanied Lady Forester through more than one obscure street and lane, the servant walking before, and acting as their guide. At length he suddenly turned into a narrow court, and knocked at an arched door, which seemed to belong to a building of some antiquity. It opened, though no one appeared to act as porter; and the servant, stepping aside from the entrance, motioned the ladies to enter. They had no sooner done so, than it shut, and excluded their guide. The two ladies found themselves in a small vestibule, illuminated by a dim lamp, and having, when the door was closed, no communication with the external light or air. The door of an inner apartment, partly open, was at the further side of the vestibule.

'We must not hesitate now, Jemima,' said Lady Bothwell, and walked forwards into the inner room, where, surrounded by books, maps, philosophical utensils, and other implements of peculiar shape and appearance, they found the man of art.

There was nothing very peculiar in the Italian's appearance. He had the dark complexion and marked features of his country, seemed about fifty years old, and was handsomely, but plainly, dressed in a full suit of black clothes, which was then the universal costume of the medical profession. Large wax-lights, in silver sconces, illuminated the apartment, which was reasonably furnished. He rose as the ladies entered; and, notwithstanding the inferiority of their dress, received them with the marked respect due to their quality, and which foreigners are usually punctilious in rendering to those to whom such honours are due.

Lady Bothwell endeavoured to maintain her proposed incognito; and, as the doctor ushered them to the upper end of the room, made a motion declining his courtesy, as unfitted for their condition. 'We are poor people, sir,' she said; 'only my sister's distress has brought us to consult your worship whether——'

He smiled as he interrupted her—'I am aware, madam, of your sister's distress, and its cause; I am aware, also, that I am honoured with a visit from two ladies of the highest consideration— Lady Bothwell and Lady Forester. If I could not distinguish them from the class of society which their present dress would indicate, there would be small possibility of my being able to gratify them by giving the information which they come to seek.'

'I can easily understand,' said Lady Bothwell——

'Pardon my boldness to interrupt you, milady,'
cried the Italian; 'your ladyship was about to
say that you could easily understand that I had
got possession of your names by means of your
domestic. But in thinking so, you do injustice
to the fidelity of your servant, and, I may add, to
the skill of one who is also not less your humble
servant—Baptista Damiotti.'

'I have no intention to do either, sir,' said
Lady Bothwell, maintaining a tone of composure,
though somewhat surprised, 'but the situation is
something new to me. If you know who we are,
you also know, sir, what brought us here.'

'Curiosity to know the fate of a Scottish gentleman of rank, now, or lately upon the Continent,'
answered the seer; 'his name is Il Cavaliero*
Philippo Forester; a gentleman who has the
honour to be husband to this lady, and, with your
ladyship's permission for using plain language,
the misfortune not to value as it deserves that
inestimable advantage.'

Lady Forester sighed deeply, and Lady Bothwell replied—

'Since you know our object without our telling
it, the only question that remains is, whether you
have the power to relieve my sister's anxiety?'

'I have, madam,' answered the Paduan scholar;
'but there is still a previous inquiry. Have you
the courage to behold with your own eyes what
the Cavaliero Philippo Forester is now doing?
or will you take it on my report?'

'That question my sister must answer for herself,' said Lady Bothwell.

'With my own eyes will I endure to see whatever you have power to show me,' said Lady Forester, with the same determined spirit which had stimulated her since her resolution was taken upon this subject.

'There may be danger in it.'

'If gold can compensate the risk,' said Lady Forester, taking out her purse.

'I do not such things for the purpose of gain,' answered the foreigner. 'I dare not turn my art to such a purpose. If I take the gold of the wealthy, it is but to bestow it on the poor; nor do I ever accept more than the sum I have already received from your servant. Put up your purse, madam; an adept needs not your gold.'

Lady Bothwell considering this rejection of her sister's offer as a mere trick of an empiric, to induce her to press a larger sum upon him, and willing that the scene should be commenced and ended, offered some gold in turn, observing that it was only to enlarge the sphere of his charity.

'Let Lady Bothwell enlarge the sphere of her own charity,' said the Paduan, 'not merely in giving of alms, in which I know she is not deficient, but in judging the character of others; and let her oblige Baptista Damiotti by believing him honest, till she shall discover him to be a knave. Do not be surprised, madam, if I speak in answer to your thoughts rather than your expressions, and tell me once more whether you have courage to look on what I am prepared to show?'

'I own, sir,' said Lady Bothwell, 'that your words strike me with some sense of fear; but whatever my sister desires to witness, I will not shrink from witnessing along with her.'

'Nay, the danger only consists in the risk of your resolution failing you. The sight can only last for the space of seven minutes; and should you interrupt the vision by speaking a single word, not only would the charm be broken, but some danger might result to the spectators. But if you can remain steadily silent for the seven minutes, your curiosity will be gratified without the slightest risk; and for this I will engage my honour.'

Internally Lady Bothwell thought the security was but an indifferent one; but she suppressed the suspicion, as if she had believed that the adept, whose dark features wore a half-formed smile, could in reality read even her most secret reflections. A solemn pause then ensued, until Lady Forester gathered courage enough to reply to the physician, as he termed himself, that she would abide with firmness and silence the sight which he had promised to exhibit to them. Upon this, he made them a low obeisance, and saying he went to prepare matters to meet their wish, left the apartment. The two sisters, hand in hand, as if seeking by that close union to divert any danger which might threaten them, sat down on two seats in immediate contact with each other: Jemima seeking support in the manly and habitual courage of Lady Bothwell; and she, on the other hand, more agitated than she had expected, endeavouring to fortify herself by the desperate resolution which circumstances had forced her sister to assume. The one perhaps said to herself, that her sister never feared anything; and the other might reflect, that what so feeble a minded woman as Jemima did not fear, could not properly be a subject of apprehension to a person of firmness and resolution like her own.

In a few moments the thoughts of both were diverted from their own situation by a strain of music so singularly sweet and solemn, that, while it seemed calculated to avert or dispel any feeling unconnected with its harmony, increased, at the same time, the solemn excitation which the preceding interview was calculated to produce. The music was that of some instrument with which they were unacquainted; but circumstances afterwards led my ancestress to believe that it was that of the harmonica*, which she heard at a much later period in life.

When these heaven-born sounds had ceased, a door opened in the upper end of the apartment, and they saw Damiotti, standing at the head of two or three steps, sign to them to advance. His dress was so different from that which he had worn a few minutes before, that they could hardly recognize him; and the deadly paleness of his countenance, and a certain stern rigidity of muscles, like that of one whose mind is made up to some strange and daring action, had totally changed the somewhat sarcastic expression with which he had previously regarded them both, and particularly Lady Bothwell. He was bare-footed, excepting a species of sandals in the antique fashion; his legs were naked beneath the knees; above them he wore hose, and a doublet of dark crimson silk close to his body; and over that a flowing loose robe, something resembling a surplice, of snow-white linen; his throat and neck were uncovered, and his long, straight, black hair was carefully combed down at full length.

As the ladies approached at his bidding, he showed no gesture of that ceremonious courtesy of which he had been formerly lavish. On the contrary, he made the signal of advance with an air of command; and when, arm in arm, and with insecure steps, the sisters approached the spot where he stood, it was with a warning frown that he pressed his finger to his lips, as if reiterating his condition of absolute silence, while, stalking before them, he led the way into the next apartment.

This was a large room, hung with black, as if for a funeral. At the upper end was a table, or rather a species of altar, covered with the same lugubrious colour, on which lay divers objects resembling the usual implements of sorcery. These objects were not indeed visible as they advanced into the apartment; for the light which displayed them, being only that of two expiring lamps, was extremely faint. The master—to use the Italian phrase* for persons of this description —approached the upper end of the room with a genuflexion like that of a Catholic to the crucifix, and at the same time crossed himself. The ladies followed in silence, and arm in arm. Two or three low broad steps led to a platform in front of the altar, or what resembled such. Here the sage took his stand, and placed the ladies beside him, once more earnestly repeating by signs his injunctions of silence. The Italian then, extending his bare arm from under his linen vestment, pointed with his forefinger to five large flambeaux, or torches, placed on each side of the altar. They took fire successively at the approach of his hand, or rather of his finger, and spread

a strong light through the room. By this the
visitors could discern that, on the seeming altar,
were disposed two naked swords laid crosswise;
a large open book, which they conceived to be
a copy of the Holy Scriptures, but in a language
to them unknown; and beside this mysterious
volume was placed a human skull. But what
struck the sisters most was a very tall and broad
mirror, which occupied all the space behind the
altar, and, illumined by the lighted torches,
reflected the mysterious articles which were laid
upon it.

The master then placed himself between the
two ladies, and, pointing to the mirror, took each
by the hand, but without speaking a syllable.
They gazed intently on the polished and sable
space to which he had directed their attention.
Suddenly the surface assumed a new and singular
appearance. It no longer simply reflected the
objects placed before it, but, as if it had self-
contained scenery of its own, objects began to
appear within it, at first in a disorderly, indistinct, and miscellaneous manner, like form
arranging itself out of chaos; at length, in distinct
and defined shape and symmetry. It was thus
that, after some shifting of light and darkness
over the face of the wonderful glass, a long perspective of arches and columns began to arrange
itself on its sides, and a vaulted roof on the upper
part of it; till, after many oscillations, the whole
vision gained a fixed and stationary appearance,
representing the interior of a foreign church.
The pillars were stately, and hung with scutcheons;
the arches were lofty and magnificent; the floor
was lettered with funeral inscriptions. But there

were no separate shrines, no images, no display
of chalice or crucifix on the altar. It was, therefore, a Protestant church upon the Continent.
A clergyman, dressed in the Geneva gown and
band,* stood by the communion table, and, with
the Bible opened before him, and his clerk
awaiting in the background, seemed prepared to
perform some service of the church to which
he belonged.

At length there entered the middle aisle of the
building a numerous party, which appeared to
be a bridal one, as a lady and gentleman walked
first, hand in hand, followed by a large concourse
of persons of both sexes, gaily, nay richly, attired.
The bride, whose features they could distinctly
see, seemed not more than sixteen years old, and
extremely beautiful. The bridegroom, for some
seconds, moved rather with his shoulder towards
them, and his face averted; but his elegance of
form and step struck the sisters at once with the
same apprehension. As he turned his face suddenly, it was frightfully realized, and they saw,
in the gay bridegroom before them, Sir Philip
Forester. His wife uttered an imperfect exclamation, at the sound of which the whole scene stirred
and seemed to separate.

'I could compare it to nothing,' said Lady
Bothwell, while recounting the wonderful tale,
'but to the dispersion of the reflection offered by
a deep and calm pool, when a stone is suddenly
cast into it, and the shadows become dissipated
and broken.' The master pressed both the ladies'
hands severely, as if to remind them of their
promise, and of the danger which they incurred.
The exclamation died away on Lady Forester's

tongue, without attaining perfect utterance, and the scene in the glass, after the fluctuation of a minute, again resumed to the eye its former appearance of a real scene, existing within the mirror, as if represented in a picture, save that the figures were movable instead of being stationary.

The representation of Sir Philip Forester, now distinctly visible in form and feature, was seen to lead on towards the clergyman that beautiful girl, who advanced at once with diffidence, and with a species of affectionate pride. In the meantime, and just as the clergyman had arranged the bridal company before him, and seemed about to commence the service, another group of persons, of whom two or three were officers, entered the church. They moved, at first, forward, as though they came to witness the bridal ceremony, but suddenly one of the officers, whose back was towards the spectators, detached himself from his companions, and rushed hastily towards the marriage party, when the whole of them turned towards him, as if attracted by some exclamation which had accompanied his advance. Suddenly the intruder drew his sword; the bridegroom unsheathed his own, and made towards him; swords were also drawn by other individuals, both of the marriage party and of those who had last entered. They fell into a sort of confusion, the clergyman, and some elder and graver persons, labouring apparently to keep the peace, while the hotter spirits on both sides brandished their weapons. But now the period of the brief space during which the soothsayer, as he pretended, was permitted to exhibit his art, was arrived. The fumes again mixed together, and dissolved gradually from observation; the vaults and columns of the church rolled asunder and disappeared; and the front of the mirror reflected nothing save the blazing torches, and the melancholy apparatus placed on the altar or table before it.

The doctor led the ladies, who greatly required his support, into the apartment from whence they came; where wine, essences, and other means of restoring suspended animation, had been provided during his absence. He motioned them to chairs, which they occupied in silence; Lady Forester, in particular, wringing her hands, and casting her eyes up to heaven, but without speaking a word, as if the spell had been still before her eyes.

'And what we have seen is even now acting?' said Lady Bothwell, collecting herself with difficulty.

'That', answered Baptista Damiotti, 'I cannot justly, or with certainty, say. But it is either now acting, or has been acted, during a short space before this. It is the last remarkable transaction in which the Cavalier Forester has been engaged.'

Lady Bothwell then expressed anxiety concerning her sister, whose altered countenance, and apparent unconsciousness of what passed around her, excited her apprehensions how it might be possible to convey her home.

'I have prepared for that,' answered the adept; 'I have directed the servant to bring your equipage as near to this place as the narrowness of the street will permit. Fear not for your sister; but give her, when you return home, this composing draught, and she will be better to-morrow morn-

ing. Few', he added, in a melancholy tone,
'leave this house as well in health as they entered
it. Such being the consequence of seeking knowledge by mysterious means, I leave you to judge
the condition of those who have the power of
gratifying such irregular curiosity. Farewell, and
forget not the potion.'

'I will give her nothing that comes from you,'
said Lady Bothwell; 'I have seen enough of your
art already. Perhaps you would poison us both
to conceal your own necromancy. But we are
persons who want neither the means of making
our wrongs known, nor the assistance of friends
to right them.'

'You have had no wrongs from me, madam,'
said the adept. 'You sought one who is little
grateful for such honour. He seeks no one, and
only gives responses to those who invite and call
upon him. After all, you have but learned a little
sooner the evil which you must still be doomed
to endure. I hear your servant's step at the door,
and will detain your ladyship and Lady Forester
no longer. The next packet from the Continent
will explain what you have already partly witnessed. Let it not, if I may advise, pass too
suddenly into your sister's hands.'

So saying, he bid Lady Bothwell good-night.
She went, lighted by the adept, to the vestibule,
where he hastily threw a black cloak over his
singular dress, and opening the door entrusted
his visitors to the care of the servant. It was with
difficulty that Lady Bothwell sustained her sister
to the carriage, though it was only twenty steps
distant. When they arrived at home, Lady
Forester required medical assistance. The physi-

cian of the family attended, and shook his head on feeling her pulse.

'Here has been', he said, 'a violent and sudden shock on the nerves. I must know how it has happened.'

Lady Bothwell admitted they had visited the conjurer, and that Lady Forester had received some bad news respecting her husband, Sir Philip.

'That rascally quack would make my fortune were he to stay in Edinburgh,' said the graduate; 'this is the seventh nervous case I have heard of his making for me, and all by effect of terror.' He next examined the composing draught which Lady Bothwell had unconsciously brought in her hand, tasted it, and pronounced it very germane to the matter, and what would save an application to the apothecary. He then paused, and looking at Lady Bothwell very significantly, at length added, 'I suppose I must not ask your ladyship anything about this Italian warlock's proceedings?'

'Indeed, Doctor,' answered Lady Bothwell, 'I consider what passed as confidential; and though the man may be a rogue, yet, as we were fools enough to consult him, we should, I think, be honest enough to keep his counsel.'

'*May* be a knave—come,' said the doctor, 'I am glad to hear your ladyship allows such a possibility in anything that comes from Italy.'

'What comes from Italy may be as good as what comes from Hanover, Doctor. But you and I will remain good friends, and that it may be so, we will say nothing of Whig and Tory.'*

'Not I,' said the doctor, receiving his fee and taking his hat; 'a Carolus serves my purpose as

well as a Willielmus* But I should like to know
why old Lady Saint Ringan's, and all that set,
go about wasting their decayed lungs in puffing
this foreign fellow.'

'Ay—you had best set him down a Jesuit, as
Scrub says.'* On these terms they parted.

The poor patient—whose nerves, from an
extraordinary state of tension, had at length
become relaxed in as extraordinary a degree—
continued to struggle with a sort of imbecility,
the growth of superstitious terror, when the
shocking tidings were brought from Holland,
which fulfilled even her worst expectations.

They were sent by the celebrated Earl of Stair,*
and contained the melancholy event of a duel
betwixt Sir Philip Forester and his wife's half-
brother, Captain Falconer, of the Scotch-Dutch*,
as they were then called, in which the latter had
been killed. The cause of quarrel rendered the
incident still more shocking. It seemed that
Sir Philip had left the army suddenly, in consequence of being unable to pay a very considerable
sum which he had lost to another volunteer at
play. He had changed his name, and taken up
his residence at Rotterdam, where he had insinu-
ated himself into the good graces of an ancient
and rich burgomaster, and, by his handsome
person and graceful manners, captivated the
affections of his only child, a very young person,
of great beauty, and the heiress of much wealth.
Delighted with the specious attractions of his
proposed son-in-law, the wealthy merchant—
whose idea of the British character was too high
to admit of his taking any precaution to acquire
evidence of his condition and circumstances—

gave his consent to the marriage. It was about to be celebrated in the principal church of the city, when it was interrupted by a singular occurrence.

Captain Falconer having been detached to Rotterdam to bring up a part of the brigade of Scottish auxiliaries who were in quarters there, a person of consideration in the town, to whom he had been formerly known, proposed to him for amusement to go to the high church, to see a countryman of his own married to the daughter of a wealthy burgomaster. Captain Falconer went accordingly, accompanied by his Dutch acquaintance with a party of his friends, and two or three officers of the Scotch brigade. His astonishment may be conceived when he saw his own brother-in-law, a married man, on the point of leading to the altar the innocent and beautiful creature, upon whom he was about to practise a base and unmanly deceit. He proclaimed his villainy on the spot, and the marriage was interrupted of course. But against the opinion of more thinking men, who considered Sir Philip Forester as having thrown himself out of the rank of men of honour, Captain Falconer admitted him to the privilege of such, accepted a challenge from him, and in the rencounter received a mortal wound. Such are the ways of Heaven, mysterious in our eyes. Lady Forester never recovered the shock of this dismal intelligence.

'And did this tragedy,' said I, 'take place exactly at the time when the scene in the mirror was exhibited?'

'It is hard to be obliged to maim one's story,'

answered my aunt; 'but, to speak the truth, it happened some days sooner than the apparition was exhibited.'

'And so there remained a possibility', said I, 'that by some secret and speedy communication the artist might have received early intelligence of that incident.'

'The incredulous pretended so,' replied my aunt.

'What became of the adept?' demanded I.

'Why, a warrant came down shortly afterwards to arrest him for high treason, as an agent of the Chevalier St. George;* and Lady Bothwell, recollecting the hints which had escaped the doctor, an ardent friend of the Protestant succession,* did then call to remembrance, that this man was chiefly *prôné* among the ancient matrons of her own political persuasion. It certainly seemed probable that intelligence from the Continent, which could easily have been transmitted by an active and powerful agent, might have enabled him to prepare such a scene of phantasmagoria as she had herself witnessed. Yet there were so many difficulties in assigning a natural explanation that, to the day of her death, she remained in great doubt on the subject, and much disposed to cut the Gordian knot* by admitting the existence of supernatural agency.'

'But, my dear aunt,' said I, 'what became of the man of skill?'

'Oh, he was too good a fortune-teller not to be able to foresee that his own destiny would be tragical if he waited the arrival of the man with the silver greyhound* upon his sleeve. He made, as we say, a moonlight flitting, and was nowhere to be seen or heard of. Some noise there was about papers or letters found in the house, but it died away, and Doctor Baptista Damiotti was soon as little talked of as Galen or Hippocrates.'*

'And Sir Philip Forester,' said I, 'did he too vanish for ever from the public scene?'

'No,' replied my kind informer. 'He was heard of once more, and it was upon a remarkable occasion. It is said that we Scots, when there was such a nation in existence, have, among our full peck of virtues, one or two little barleycorns of vice. In particular, it is alleged that we rarely forgive, and never forget, any injuries received; that we used to make an idol of our resentment, as poor Lady Constance did of her grief,* and are addicted, as Burns says, to "nursing our wrath to keep it warm".* Lady Bothwell was not without this feeling; and, I believe, nothing whatever, scarce the restoration of the Stuart line, could have happened so delicious to her feelings as an opportunity of being revenged on Sir Philip Forester, for the deep and double injury which had deprived her of a sister and of a brother. But nothing of him was heard or known till many a year had passed away.

'At length—it was on a Fastern's E'en (Shrovetide) assembly, at which the whole fashion of Edinburgh attended, full and frequent, and when Lady Bothwell had a seat amongst the lady patronesses,* that one of the attendants on the company whispered into her ear that a gentleman wished to speak with her in private.

'In private? and in an assembly-room?—he must be mad—Tell him to call upon me to-morrow morning.'

'I said so, my lady,' answered the man; 'but he desired me to give you this paper.'

She undid the billet, which was curiously folded and sealed. It only bore the words, '*On business of life and death,*' written in a hand which she had never seen before. Suddenly it occurred to her that it might concern the safety of some of her political friends; she therefore followed the messenger to a small apartment where the refreshments were prepared, and from which the general company was excluded. She found an old man, who, at her approach, rose up and bowed profoundly. His appearance indicated a broken constitution; and his dress, though sedulously rendered conforming to the etiquette of a ballroom, was worn and tarnished, and hung in folds about his emaciated person. Lady Bothwell was about to feel for her purse, expecting to get rid of the supplicant at the expense of a little money, but some fear of a mistake arrested her purpose. She therefore gave the man leisure to explain himself.

'I have the honour to speak with the Lady Bothwell?'

'I am Lady Bothwell: allow me to say that this is no time or place for long explanations.—What are your commands with me?'

'Your ladyship', said the old man, 'had once a sister.'

'True; whom I loved as my own soul.'

'And a brother.'

'The bravest, the kindest, the most affectionate!' said Lady Bothwell.

'Both these beloved relatives you lost by the fault of an unfortunate man,' continued the stranger.

'By the crime of an unnatural, bloody-minded murderer,' said the lady.

'I am answered,' replied the old man, bowing, as if to withdraw.

'Stop, sir, I command you,' said Lady Bothwell.—'Who are you that, at such a place and time, come to recall these horrible recollections? I insist upon knowing.'

'I am one who intends Lady Bothwell no injury; but, on the contrary, to offer her the means of doing a deed of Christian charity which the world would wonder at, and which Heaven would reward; but I find her in no temper for such a sacrifice as I was prepared to ask.'

'Speak out, sir; what is your meaning?' said Lady Bothwell.

'The wretch that has wronged you so deeply', rejoined the stranger, 'is now on his death-bed. His days have been days of misery, his nights have been sleepless hours of anguish—yet he cannot die without your forgiveness. His life has been an unremitting penance—yet he dares not part from his burden while your curses load his soul.'

'Tell him', said Lady Bothwell sternly, 'to ask pardon of that Being whom he has so greatly offended; not of an erring mortal like himself. What could my forgiveness avail him?'

'Much,' answered the old man. 'It will be an earnest of that which he may then venture to ask from his Creator, lady, and from yours. Remember, Lady Bothwell, you too have a death-bed to look forward to; your soul may, all human souls must, feel the awe of facing the judgement-seat, with the wounds of an untented conscience, raw, and rankling—what thought would it be then that should whisper, "I have given no mercy, how then shall I ask it?"'

'Man, whosoever thou mayest be,' replied Lady Bothwell, 'urge me not so cruelly. It would be but blasphemous hypocrisy to utter with my lips the words which every throb of my heart protests against. They would open the earth and give to light the wasted form of my sister—the bloody form of my murdered brother—forgive him?—Never, never!'

'Great God!' cried the old man, holding up his hands, 'is it thus the worms which thou hast called out of dust obey the commands of their Maker? Farewell, proud and unforgiving woman. Exult that thou hast added to a death in want and pain the agonies of religious despair; but never again mock Heaven by petitioning for the pardon which thou hast refused to grant.'

He was turning from her.

'Stop,' she exclaimed; 'I will try; yes, I will try to pardon him.'

'Gracious lady,' said the old man, 'you will relieve the over-burdened soul, which dare not sever itself from its sinful companion of earth without being at peace with you. What do I know—your forgiveness may perhaps preserve for penitence the dregs of a wretched life.'

'Ha!' said the lady, as a sudden light broke on her, 'it is the villain himself!' And grasping Sir Philip Forester—for it was he, and no other—by the collar, she raised a cry of 'Murder, murder! Seize the murderer!'

At an exclamation so singular, in such a place,

the company thronged into the apartment, but Sir Philip Forester was no longer there. He had forcibly extricated himself from Lady Bothwell's hold, and had run out of the apartment which opened on the landing-place of the stair. There seemed no escape in that direction, for there were several persons coming up the steps, and others descending. But the unfortunate man was desperate. He threw himself over the balustrade, and alighted safely in the lobby, though a leap of fifteen feet at least, then dashed into the street and was lost in darkness. Some of the Bothwell family made pursuit, and, had they come up with the fugitive, they might have perhaps slain him; for in those days men's blood ran warm in their veins. But the police did not interfere; the matter most criminal having happened long since, and in a foreign land. Indeed, it was always thought that this extraordinary scene originated in a hypocritical experiment, by which Sir Philip desired to ascertain whether he might return to his native country in safety from the resentment of a family which he had injured so deeply. As the result fell out so contrary to his wishes, he is believed to have returned to the Continent, and there died in exile.

So closed the tale of the MYSTERIOUS MIRROR.

THE TAPESTRIED CHAMBER

OR

THE LADY IN THE SACQUE

THIS is another little story from the *Keepsake* of 1828. It was told to me many years ago, by the late Miss Anna Seward, who, among other accomplishments that rendered her an amusing inmate in a country house, had that of recounting narratives of this sort with very considerable effect; much greater, indeed, than any one would be apt to guess from the style of her written performances. There are hours and moods when most people are not displeased to listen to such things; and I have heard some of the greatest and wisest of my contemporaries take their share in telling them.

August, 1831.

THE following narrative is given from the pen, so far as memory permits, in the same character in which it was presented to the author's ear; nor has he claim to further praise, or to be more deeply censured, than in proportion to the good or bad judgement which he has employed in selecting his materials, as he has studiously avoided any attempt at ornament which might interfere with the simplicity of the tale.

At the same time, it must be admitted that the particular class of stories which turns on the marvellous, possesses a stronger influence when told than when committed to print. The volume taken up at noonday, though rehearsing the same incidents, conveys a much more feeble impression than is achieved by the voice of the speaker on a circle of fireside auditors, who hang upon the narrative as the narrator details the minute incidents which serve to give it authenticity, and lowers his voice with an affectation of mystery while he approaches the fearful and wonderful part. It was with such advantages that the present writer heard the following events related, more than twenty years since, by the celebrated Miss Seward, of Litchfield, who, to her numerous accomplishments, added, in a remarkable degree, the power of narrative in private conversation. In its present form, the tale must necessarily lose all the interest which was attached to it by the flexible voice and intelligent features of the gifted narrator. Yet still, read aloud, to an undoubting audience by the doubtful light of the closing evening, or in silence, by a decaying taper, and amidst the solitude of a half-lighted apartment, it may redeem its character as a good ghost story. Miss Seward always affirmed that she had derived her information from an authentic source, although she suppressed the names of the two persons chiefly concerned. I will not avail myself of any particulars I may have since received concerning the details of the locality, but suffer them to rest under the same general description in which they were first related to me; and, for the same reason, I will not add to or diminish the narrative by any circumstance, whether more or less material, but simply rehearse, as I heard it, a story of supernatural terror.

About the end of the American war, when the

officers of Lord Cornwallis's army which surrendered at York-town,* and others, who had
been made prisoners during the impolitic and
ill-fated controversy, were returning to their own
country, to relate their adventures and repose
themselves after their fatigues, there was amongst
them a general officer, to whom Miss S. gave the
name of Browne, but merely, as I understood, to
save the inconvenience of introducing a nameless
agent in the narrative. He was an officer of
merit, as well as a gentleman of high consideration for family and attainments.

Some business had carried General Browne
upon a tour through the western counties, when,
in the conclusion of a morning stage, he found
himself in the vicinity of a small country town,
which presented a scene of uncommon beauty
and of a character peculiarly English.

The little town, with its stately old church
whose tower bore testimony to the devotion of
ages long past, lay amidst pastures and cornfields
of small extent, but bounded and divided with
hedge-row timber of great age and size. There
were few marks of modern improvement. The
environs of the place intimated neither the solitude of decay, nor the bustle of novelty; the
houses were old, but in good repair; and the
beautiful little river murmured freely on its way
to the left of the town, neither restrained by a
dam, nor bordered by a towing-path.

Upon a gentle eminence, nearly a mile to the
southward of the town, were seen amongst many
venerable oaks and tangled thickets the turrets of
a castle, as old as the wars of York and Lancaster,*
but which seemed to have received important

alterations during the age of Elizabeth and her successor. It had not been a place of great size; but whatever accommodation it formerly afforded was, it must be supposed, still to be obtained within its walls; at least, such was the inference which General Browne drew from observing the smoke arise merrily from several of the ancient wreathed and carved chimney-stalks. The wall of the park ran alongside of the highway for two or three hundred yards; and through the different points by which the eye found glimpses into the woodland scenery, it seemed to be well stocked. Other points of view opened in succession; now a full one, of the front of the old castle, and now a side glimpse at its particular towers; the former rich in all the bizarrerie of the Elizabethan school, while the simple and solid strength of other parts of the building seemed to show that they had been raised more for defence than ostentation.

Delighted with the partial glimpses which he obtained of the castle through the woods and glades by which this ancient feudal fortress was surrounded, our military traveller was determined to inquire whether it might not deserve a nearer view, and whether it contained family pictures or other objects of curiosity worthy of a stranger's visit; when, leaving the vicinity of the park, he rolled through a clean and well-paved street, and stopped at the door of a well-frequented inn.

Before ordering horses to proceed on his journey, General Browne made inquiries concerning the proprietor of the chateau which had so attracted his admiration, and was equally surprised and pleased at hearing in reply a nobleman named whom we shall call Lord Woodville. How fortunate! Much of Browne's early recollections, both at school and at college, had been connected with young Woodville, whom, by a few questions, he now ascertained to be the same with the owner of this fair domain. He had been raised to the peerage by the decease of his father a few months before, and, as the general learned from the landlord, the term of mourning being ended, was now taking possession of his paternal estate in the jovial season of merry autumn, accompanied by a select party of friends to enjoy the sports of a country famous for game.

This was delightful news to our traveller. Frank Woodville had been Richard Browne's fag at Eton, and his chosen intimate at Christ Church;* their pleasures and their tasks had been the same; and the honest soldier's heart warmed to find his early friend in possession of so delightful a residence, and of an estate, as the landlord assured him with a nod and a wink, fully adequate to maintain and add to his dignity. Nothing was more natural than that the traveller should suspend a journey, which there was nothing to render hurried, to pay a visit to an old friend under such agreeable circumstances.

The fresh horses, therefore, had only the brief task of conveying the general's travelling carriage to Woodville Castle. A porter admitted them at a modern Gothic lodge, built in that style to correspond with the castle itself, and at the same time rang a bell to give warning of the approach of visitors. Apparently the sound of the bell had suspended the separation of the company, bent on the various amusements of the morning; for, on entering the court of the chateau, several young men were lounging about in their sporting dresses, looking at, and criticizing, the dogs which the keepers held in readiness to attend their pastime. As General Browne alighted, the young lord came to the gate of the hall, and for an instant gazed, as at a stranger, upon the countenance of his friend, on which war, with its fatigues and its wounds, had made a great alteration. But the uncertainty lasted no longer than till the visitor had spoken, and the hearty greeting which followed was such as can only be exchanged betwixt those who have passed together the merry days of careless boyhood or early youth.

'If I could have formed a wish, my dear Browne,' said Lord Woodville, 'it would have been to have you here, of all men, upon this occasion, which my friends are good enough to hold as a sort of holiday. Do not think you have been unwatched during the years you have been absent from us. I have traced you through your dangers, your triumphs, your misfortunes, and was delighted to see that, whether in victory or defeat, the name of my old friend was always distinguished with applause.'

The general made a suitable reply, and congratulated his friend on his new dignities, and the possession of a place and domain so beautiful.

'Nay, you have seen nothing of it as yet,' said Lord Woodville, 'and I trust you do not mean to leave us till you are better acquainted with it. It is true, I confess, that my present party is pretty large, and the old house, like other places of the kind, does not possess so much accommodation as the extent of the outward walls appears to promise. But we can give you a comfortable old-fashioned room; and I venture to suppose that your campaigns have taught you to be glad of worse quarters.'

The general shrugged his shoulders, and laughed. 'I presume', he said, 'the worst apartment in your chateau is considerably superior to the old tobacco-cask in which I was fain to take up my night's lodging when I was in the Bush, as the Virginians call it,* with the light corps. There I lay, like Diogenes* himself, so delighted with my covering from the elements, that I made a vain attempt to have it rolled on to my next quarters; but my commander for the time would give way to no such luxurious provision, and I took farewell of my beloved cask with tears in my eyes.'

'Well, then, since you do not fear your quarters,' said Lord Woodville, 'you will stay with me a week at least. Of guns, dogs, fishing-rods, flies, and means of sport by sea and land, we have enough and to spare: you cannot pitch on an amusement, but we will find the means of pursuing it. But if you prefer the gun and pointers, I will go with you myself, and see whether you have mended your shooting since you have been amongst the Indians of the back settlements.'

The general gladly accepted his friendly host's proposal in all its points. After a morning of manly exercise, the company met at dinner, where it was the delight of Lord Woodville to conduce to the display of the high properties of his recovered friend, so as to recommend him to his guests, most of whom were persons of distinction. He led General Browne to speak of the scenes he had witnessed; and as every word marked alike the brave officer and the sensible man, who retained possession of his cool judgement under the most imminent dangers, the company looked upon the soldier with general respect, as on one who had proved himself possessed of an uncommon portion of personal courage—that attribute, of all others, of which everybody desires to be thought possessed.

The day at Woodville Castle ended as usual in such mansions. The hospitality stopped within the limits of good order; music, in which the young lord was a proficient, succeeded to the circulation of the bottle: cards and billiards, for those who preferred such amusements, were in readiness: but the exercise of the morning required early hours, and not long after eleven o'clock the guests began to retire to their several apartments.

The young lord himself conducted his friend, General Browne, to the chamber destined for him, which answered the description he had given of it, being comfortable but old-fashioned. The bed was of the massive form used in the end of the seventeenth century, and the curtains of faded silk, heavily trimmed with tarnished gold. But then the sheets, pillows, and blankets looked delightful to the campaigner, when he thought of his mansion, the cask. There was an air of gloom in the tapestry hangings, which, with their worn-out graces, curtained the walls of the little chamber, and gently undulated as the autumnal breeze found its way through the ancient lattice-window, which pattered and whistled as the air gained entrance. The toilet too, with its mirror, turbaned, after the manner of the beginning of the century, with a coiffure of murrey-coloured silk, and its hundred strange-shaped boxes, providing for arrangements which had been obsolete for more than fifty years, had an antique, and in so far a melancholy, aspect. But nothing could blaze more brightly and cheerfully than the two large wax candles; or if aught could rival them, it was the flaming bickering faggots in the chimney, that sent at once their gleam and their warmth through the snug apartment; which, notwithstanding the general antiquity of its appearance, was not wanting in the least convenience that modern habits rendered either necessary or desirable.

'This is an old-fashioned sleeping apartment, General,' said the young lord; 'but I hope you will find nothing that makes you envy your old tobacco-cask.'

'I am not particular respecting my lodgings,' replied the general; 'yet were I to make any choice, I would prefer this chamber by many degrees to the gayer and more modern rooms of your family mansion. Believe me that when I unite its modern air of comfort with its venerable antiquity, and recollect that it is your lordship's property, I shall feel in better quarters here, than if I were in the best hotel London could afford.'

'I trust—I have no doubt—that you will find yourself as comfortable as I wish you, my dear General,' said the young nobleman; and once more bidding his guest good-night, he shook him by the hand and withdrew.

The general once more looked round him, and internally congratulating himself on his return to peaceful life, the comforts of which were endeared by the recollection of the hardships and dangers he had lately sustained, undressed himself, and prepared for a luxurious night's rest.

Here, contrary to the custom of this species of tale, we leave the general in possession of his apartment until the next morning.

The company assembled for breakfast at an early hour, but without the appearance of General Browne, who seemed the guest that Lord Woodville was desirous of honouring above all whom his hospitality had assembled around him. He more than once expressed surprise at the general's absence, and at length sent a servant to make inquiry after him. The man brought back information that General Browne had been walking abroad since an early hour of the morning, in defiance of the weather, which was misty and ungenial.

'The custom of a soldier,'—said the young nobleman to his friends; 'many of them acquire habitual vigilance, and cannot sleep after the early hour at which their duty usually commands them to be alert.'

Yet the explanation which Lord Woodville thus offered to the company seemed hardly satisfactory to his own mind, and it was in a fit of silence and abstraction that he awaited the return of the general. It took place near an hour after the breakfast-bell had rung. He looked fatigued and feverish. His hair, the powdering and arrangement of which was at this time one of the most important occupations of a man's whole day, and marked his fashion as much as, in the present time, the tying of a cravat or the want of one, was dishevelled, uncurled, void of powder, and dank with dew. His clothes were huddled on with a careless negligence, remarkable in a military man, whose real or supposed duties are usually held to include some attention to the toilet; and his looks were haggard and ghastly in a peculiar degree.

'So you have stolen a march upon us this morning, my dear General,' said Lord Woodville; 'or you have not found your bed so much to your mind as I had hoped and you seemed to expect. How did you rest last night?'

'Oh, excellently well! remarkably well! never better in my life,' said General Browne rapidly, and yet with an air of embarrassment which was obvious to his friend. He then hastily swallowed a cup of tea, and neglecting or refusing whatever else was offered, seemed to fall into a fit of abstraction.

'You will take the gun to-day, General,' said his friend and host, but had to repeat the question twice ere he received the abrupt answer, 'No, my lord; I am sorry I cannot have the honour of spending another day with your lordship; my post-horses are ordered, and will be here directly.'

All who were present showed surprise, and Lord Woodville immediately replied, 'Post-horses, my good friend! what can you possibly want with them, when you promised to stay with me quietly for at least a week?'

'I believe', said the general, obviously much

embarrassed, 'that I might, in the pleasure of my first meeting with your lordship, have said something about stopping here a few days; but I have since found it altogether impossible.'

'That is very extraordinary,' answered the young nobleman. 'You seemed quite disengaged yesterday, and you cannot have had a summons to-day; for our post has not come up from the town, and therefore you cannot have received any letters.'

General Browne, without giving any further explanation, muttered something of indispensable business, and insisted on the absolute necessity of his departure in a manner which silenced all opposition on the part of his host, who saw that his resolution was taken, and forbore all further importunity.

'At least, however,' he said, 'permit me, my dear Browne, since go you will or must, to show you the view from the terrace, which the mist that is now rising will soon display.'

He threw open a sash window, and stepped down upon the terrace as he spoke. The general followed him mechanically, but seemed little to attend to what his host was saying, as, looking across an extended and rich prospect, he pointed out the different objects worthy of observation. Thus they moved on till Lord Woodville had attained his purpose of drawing his guest entirely apart from the rest of the company, when, turning round upon him with an air of great solemnity, he addressed him thus:

'Richard Browne, my old and very dear friend, we are now alone. Let me conjure you to answer me upon the word of a friend, and the honour of a soldier. How did you in reality rest during last night?'

'Most wretchedly indeed, my lord,' answered the general, in the same tone of solemnity;—'so miserably, that I would not run the risk of such a second night, not only for all the lands belonging to this castle, but for all the country which I see from this elevated point of view.'

'This is most extraordinary,' said the young lord, as if speaking to himself; 'then there must be something in the reports concerning that apartment.' Again turning to the general, he said, 'For God's sake, my dear friend, be candid with me, and let me know the disagreeable particulars which have befallen you under a roof where, with consent of the owner, you should have met nothing save comfort.'

The general seemed distressed by this appeal, and paused a moment before he replied. 'My dear lord,' he at length said, 'what happened to me last night is of a nature so peculiar and so unpleasant, that I could hardly bring myself to detail it even to your lordship, were it not that, independent of my wish to gratify any request of yours, I think that sincerity on my part may lead to some explanation about a circumstance equally painful and mysterious. To others, the communication I am about to make might place me in the light of a weak-minded, superstitious fool who suffered his own imagination to delude and bewilder him; but you have known me in childhood and youth, and will not suspect me of having adopted in manhood the feelings and frailties from which my early years were free.' Here he paused, and his friend replied:

'Do not doubt my perfect confidence in the truth of your communication, however strange it may be,' replied Lord Woodville; 'I know your firmness of disposition too well, to suspect you could be made the object of imposition, and am aware that your honour and your friendship will equally deter you from exaggerating whatever you may have witnessed.'

'Well then,' said the general, 'I will proceed with my story as well as I can, relying upon your candour; and yet distinctly feeling that I would rather face a battery than recall to my mind the odious recollections of last night.'

He paused a second time, and then perceiving that Lord Woodville remained silent and in an attitude of attention, he commenced, though not without obvious reluctance, the history of his night adventures in the Tapestried Chamber.

'I undressed and went to bed, so soon as your lordship left me yesterday evening; but the wood in the chimney, which nearly fronted my bed, blazed brightly and cheerfully, and, aided by a hundred exciting recollections of my childhood and youth which had been recalled by the unexpected pleasure of meeting your lordship, prevented me from falling immediately asleep. I ought, however, to say, that these reflections were all of a pleasant and agreeable kind, grounded on a sense of having for a time exchanged the labour, fatigues, and dangers of my profession for the enjoyments of a peaceful life, and the reunion of those friendly and affectionate ties which I had torn asunder at the rude summons of war.

'While such pleasing reflections were stealing

over my mind, and gradually lulling me to slumber, I was suddenly aroused by a sound like that of the rustling of a silken gown, and the tapping of a pair of high-heeled shoes, as if a woman were walking in the apartment. Ere I could draw the curtain to see what the matter was, the figure of a little woman passed between the bed and the fire. The back of this form was turned to me, and I could observe, from the shoulders and neck, it was that of an old woman, whose dress was an old-fashioned gown which, I think, ladies call a sacque; that is, a sort of robe, completely loose in the body, but gathered into broad plaits upon the neck and shoulders, which fall down to the ground, and terminate in a species of train.

'I thought the intrusion singular enough, but never harboured for a moment the idea that what I saw was anything more than the mortal form of some old woman about the establishment, who had a fancy to dress like her grandmother, and who, having perhaps (as your lordship mentioned that you were rather straitened for room) been dislodged from her chamber for my accommodation, had forgotten the circumstance, and returned by twelve to her old haunt. Under this persuasion I moved myself in bed and coughed a little, to make the intruder sensible of my being in possession of the premises.—She turned slowly round, but gracious heaven! my lord, what a countenance did she display to me! There was no longer any question what she was, or any thought of her being a living being. Upon a face which wore the fixed features of a corpse, were imprinted the traces of the vilest and most hideous passions which had animated her while she lived. The body of some atrocious criminal seemed to have been given up from the grave, and the soul restored from the penal fire, in order to form, for a space, a union with the ancient accomplice of its guilt. I started up in bed and sat upright, supporting myself on my palms, as I gazed on this horrible spectre. The hag made, as it seemed, a single and swift stride to the bed where I lay, and squatted herself down upon it, in precisely the same attitude which I had assumed in the extremity of horror, advancing her diabolical countenance within half a yard of mine, with a grin which seemed to intimate the malice and the derision of an incarnate fiend.'

Here General Browne stopped, and wiped from his brow the cold perspiration with which the recollection of his horrible vision had covered it.

'My lord,' he said, 'I am no coward. I have been in all the mortal dangers incidental to my profession, and I may truly boast that no man ever knew Richard Browne dishonour the sword he wears; but in these horrible circumstances, under the eyes, and as it seemed, almost in the grasp of an incarnation of an evil spirit, all firmness forsook me, all manhood melted from me like wax in the furnace, and I felt my hair individually bristle. The current of my life-blood ceased to flow, and I sank back in a swoon, as very a victim to panic terror as ever was a village girl or a child of ten years old. How long I lay in this condition I cannot pretend to guess.

'But I was roused by the castle clock striking one, so loud that it seemed as if it were in the very room. It was some time before I dared open my eyes, lest they should again encounter the horrible spectacle. When, however, I summoned courage to look up, she was no longer visible. My first idea was to pull my bell, wake the servants, and remove to a garret or a hay-loft, to be ensured against a second visitation. Nay, I will confess the truth, that my resolution was altered, not by the shame of exposing myself, but by the fear that, as the bell-cord hung by the chimney, I might, in making my way to it, be again crossed by the fiendish hag, who, I figured to myself, might be still lurking about some corner of the apartment.

'I will not pretend to describe what hot and cold fever-fits tormented me for the rest of the night, through broken sleep, weary vigils, and that dubious state which forms the neutral ground between them. An hundred terrible objects appeared to haunt me; but there was the great difference betwixt the vision which I have described, and those which followed, that I knew the last to be deceptions of my own fancy and over-excited nerves.

'Day at last appeared, and I rose from my bed ill in health, and humiliated in mind. I was ashamed of myself as a man and a soldier, and still more so, at feeling my own extreme desire to escape from the haunted apartment, which, however, conquered all other considerations; so that, huddling on my clothes with the most careless haste, I made my escape from your lordship's mansion, to seek in the open air some relief to my nervous system, shaken as it was by this horrible rencounter with a visitant, for such I must believe her, from the other world. Your lordship has now heard the cause of my discomposure, and of my sudden desire to leave your hospitable castle. In other places I trust we may often meet; but God protect me from ever spending a second night under that roof!'

Strange as the general's tale was, he spoke with such a deep air of conviction that it cut short all the usual commentaries which are made on such stories. Lord Woodville never once asked him if he was sure he did not dream of the apparition, or suggested any of the possibilities by which it is fashionable to explain supernatural appearances, as wild vagaries of the fancy or deceptions of the optic nerves. On the contrary, he seemed deeply impressed with the truth and reality of what he had heard; and, after a considerable pause, regretted, with much appearance of sincerity, that his early friend should in his house have suffered so severely.

'I am the more sorry for your pain, my dear Browne,' he continued, 'that it is the unhappy, though most unexpected, result of an experiment of my own! You must know, that for my father and grandfather's time, at least, the apartment which was assigned to you last night had been shut on account of reports that it was disturbed by supernatural sights and noises. When I came, a few weeks since, into possession of the estate, I thought the accommodation which the castle afforded for my friends was not extensive enough to permit the inhabitants of the invisible world to retain possession of a comfortable sleeping apartment. I therefore caused the Tapestried Chamber, as we call it, to be opened; and without destroying its air of antiquity, I had such new articles of furniture placed in it as became the modern times. Yet as the opinion that the room was haunted very strongly prevailed among the domestics, and was also known in the neighbourhood and to many of my friends, I feared some prejudice might be entertained by the first occupant of the Tapestried Chamber, which might tend to revive the evil report which it had laboured under, and so disappoint my purpose of rendering it a useful part of the house. I must confess, my dear Browne, that your arrival yesterday, agreeable to me for a thousand reasons besides, seemed the most favourable opportunity of removing the unpleasant rumours which attached to the room, since your courage was indubitable and your mind free of any preoccupation on the subject. I could not, therefore, have chosen a more fitting subject for my experiment.'

'Upon my life,' said General Browne, somewhat hastily, 'I am infinitely obliged to your lordship—very particularly indebted indeed. I am likely to remember for some time the consequences of the experiment, as your lordship is pleased to call it.'

'Nay, now you are unjust, my dear friend,' said Lord Woodville. 'You have only to reflect for a single moment, in order to be convinced that I could not augur the possibility of the pain to which you have been so unhappily exposed. I was yesterday morning a complete sceptic on the subject of supernatural appearances. Nay, I am sure that had I told you what was said about that room, those very reports would have induced you, by your own choice, to select it for your accommodation. It was my misfortune, perhaps my error, but really cannot be termed my fault, that you have been afflicted so strangely.'

'Strangely indeed!' said the general, resuming his good temper; 'and I acknowledge that I have no right to be offended with your lordship for treating me like what I used to think myself— a man of some firmness and courage.—But I see my post-horses are arrived, and I must not detain your lordship from your amusement.'

'Nay, my old friend,' said Lord Woodville, 'since you cannot stay with us another day, which, indeed, I can no longer urge, give me at least half an hour more. You used to love pictures, and I have a gallery of portraits, some of them by Vandyke, representing ancestry to whom this property and castle formerly belonged. I think that several of them will strike you as possessing merit.'

General Browne accepted the invitation, though somewhat unwillingly. It was evident he was not to breathe freely or at ease till he left Woodville Castle far behind him. He could not refuse his friend's invitation, however; and the less so, that he was a little ashamed of the peevishness which he had displayed towards his well-meaning entertainer.

The general, therefore, followed Lord Woodville through several rooms, into a long gallery hung with pictures, which the latter pointed out to his guest, telling the names, and giving some account of the personages whose portraits presented themselves in progression. General Browne was but little interested in the details which these accounts conveyed to him. They were, indeed, of the kind which are usually

found in an old family gallery. Here was a
cavalier who had ruined the estate in the royal
cause; there a fine lady who had reinstated it by
contracting a match with a wealthy Roundhead.*
There hung a gallant who had been in danger
for corresponding with the exiled Court at St.
Germain's;* here one who had taken arms for
William at the Revolution;*and there a third that
had thrown his weight alternately into the scale
of Whig and Tory.

While Lord Woodville was cramming these
words into his guest's ear, 'against the stomach
of his sense,'*they gained the middle of the gallery,
when he beheld General Browne suddenly start,
and assume an attitude of the utmost surprise,
not unmixed with fear, as his eyes were caught
and suddenly riveted by a portrait of an old lady
in a sacque, the fashionable dress of the end of
the seventeenth century.

'There she is!' he exclaimed; 'there she is, in
form and features, though inferior in demoniac
expression to the accursed hag who visited me
last night!'

'If that be the case,' said the young nobleman,
'there can remain no longer any doubt of the
horrible reality of your apparition. That is
the picture of a wretched ancestress of mine, of
whose crimes a black and fearful catalogue is
recorded in a family history in my charter-chest.
The recital of them would be too horrible; it is
enough to say that in yon fatal apartment incest
and unnatural murder were committed. I will
restore it to the solitude to which the better
judgement of those who preceded me had con-
signed it; and never shall any one, so long as I

can prevent it, be exposed to a repetition of the supernatural horrors which could shake such courage as yours.'

Thus the friends, who had met with such glee, parted in a very different mood: Lord Woodville to command the Tapestried Chamber to be unmantled and the door built up; and General Browne to seek in some less beautiful country, and with some less dignified friend, forgetfulness of the painful night which he had passed in Woodville Castle.

DEATH OF THE LAIRD'S JOCK

[The manner in which this trifle was introduced at the time to Mr. F. M. Reynolds, editor of *The Keepsake* of 1828, leaves no occasion for a preface.]

August, 1831.

TO THE EDITOR OF 'THE KEEPSAKE'

YOU have asked me, sir, to point out a subject for the pencil, and I feel the difficulty of complying with your request; although I am not certainly unaccustomed to literary composition, or a total stranger to the stores of history and tradition, which afford the best copies for the painter's art. But although *sicut pictura poesis* is an ancient and undisputed axiom—although poetry and painting both address themselves to the same object of exciting the human imagination, by presenting to it pleasing or sublime images of ideal scenes; yet the one conveying itself through the ears to the understanding, and the other applying itself only to the eyes, the subjects which are best suited to the bard or tale-teller are often totally unfit for painting, where the artist must present in a single glance all that his art has power to tell us. The artist can neither recapitulate the past nor intimate the future. The single *now* is all which he can present; and hence, unquestionably, many subjects which delight us in poetry, or in narrative, whether real or fictitious, cannot with advantage be transferred to the canvas.

Being in some degree aware of these difficulties, though doubtless unacquainted both with their extent and the means by which they may be modified or surmounted, I have, nevertheless, ventured to draw up the following traditional narrative as a story in which, when the general details are known, the interest is so much concentrated in one strong moment of agonizing passion, that it can be understood, and sympathized with, at a single glance. I therefore presume that it may be acceptable as a hint to some one among the numerous artists who have of late years distinguished themselves as rearing up and supporting the British school.

Enough has been said and sung about

> The well-contested ground
> The warlike Border-land—*

to render the habits of the tribes who inhabited them before the union of England and Scotland familiar to most of your readers. The rougher and sterner features of their character were softened by their attachment to the fine arts, from which has arisen the saying that, on the frontiers, every dale had its battle, and every river its song. A rude species of chivalry was in constant use, and single combats were practised as the amusement of the few intervals of truce which suspended the exercise of war. The inveteracy of this custom may be inferred from the following incident:

Bernard Gilpin, the apostle of the north, the first who undertook to preach the Protestant doctrines to the Border dalesmen, was surprised on entering one of their churches, to see a

gauntlet, or mail-glove, hanging above the altar.
Upon inquiring the meaning of a symbol so
indecorous being displayed in that sacred place,
he was informed by the clerk that the glove was
that of a famous swordsman who hung it there
as an emblem of a general challenge and gage of
battle, to any who should dare to take the fatal
token down. 'Reach it to me,' said the reverend
churchman. The clerk and sexton equally declined the perilous office; and the good Bernard
Gilpin was obliged to remove the glove with his
own hands, desiring those who were present to
inform the champion that he, and no other,
had possessed himself of the gage of defiance.
But the champion was as much ashamed to face
Bernard Gilpin as the officials of the church had
been to displace his pledge of combat.

The date of the following story is about the
latter years of Queen Elizabeth's reign; and
the events took place in Liddesdale, a hilly and
pastoral district of Roxburghshire, which, on
a part of its boundary, is divided from England
only by a small river.

During the good old times of *rugging and riving*
(that is, tugging and tearing), under which term
the disorderly doings of the warlike age are
affectionately remembered, this valley was
principally cultivated by the sept or clan of the
Armstrongs. The chief of this warlike race was
the Laird of Mangerton. At the period of
which I speak, the estate of Mangerton, with
the power and dignity of chief, was possessed by
John Armstrong, a man of great size, strength,
and courage. While his father was alive, he was
distinguished from others of his clan who bore

the same name by the epithet of the *Laird's Jock*, that is to say, the Laird's son Jock, or Jack. This name he distinguished by so many bold and desperate achievements, that he retained it even after his father's death, and is mentioned under it both in authentic records and in tradition. Some of his feats are recorded in the Minstrelsy of the Scottish Border,* and others mentioned in contemporary chronicles.

At the species of singular combat which we have described, the Laird's Jock was unrivalled; and no champion of Cumberland, Westmoreland, or Northumberland, could endure the sway of the huge two-handed sword which he wielded, and which few others could even lift. This 'awful sword', as the common people term it, was as dear to him as Durindana or Fushberta* to their respective masters, and was nearly as formidable to his enemies as those renowned falchions proved to the foes of Christendom* The weapon had been bequeathed to him by a celebrated English outlaw named Hobbie Noble,* who, having committed some deed for which he was in danger from justice, fled to Liddesdale, and became a follower, or rather a brother-in-arms, to the renowned Laird's Jock; till, venturing into England with a small escort, a faithless guide, and with a light single-handed sword instead of his ponderous brand, Hobbie Noble, attacked by superior numbers, was made prisoner and executed.

With this weapon, and by means of his own strength and address, the Laird's Jock maintained the reputation of the best swordsman on the Border side, and defeated or slew many who ventured to dispute with him the formidable title.

But years pass on with the strong and the brave as with the feeble and the timid. In process of time, the Laird's Jock grew incapable of wielding his weapons, and finally of all active exertion, even of the most ordinary kind. The disabled champion became at length totally bed-ridden, and entirely dependent for his comfort on the pious duties of an only daughter, his perpetual attendant and companion.

Besides this dutiful child, the Laird's Jock had an only son, upon whom devolved the perilous task of leading the clan to battle, and maintaining the warlike renown of his native country, which was now disputed by the English upon many occasions. The young Armstrong was active, brave, and strong, and brought home from dangerous adventures many tokens of decided success. Still the ancient chief conceived, as it would seem, that his son was scarce yet entitled by age and experience to be entrusted with the two-handed sword, by the use of which he had himself been so dreadfully distinguished.

At length, an English champion, one of the name of Foster (if I rightly recollect) had the audacity to send a challenge to the best swordsman in Liddesdale; and young Armstrong, burning for chivalrous distinction, accepted the challenge.

The heart of the disabled old man swelled with joy when he heard that the challenge was passed and accepted, and the meeting fixed at a neutral spot, used as the place of rencontre upon such occasions, and which he himself had distinguished

by numerous victories. He exulted so much in
the conquest which he anticipated that, to nerve
his son to still bolder exertions, he conferred
upon him, as champion of his clan and province,
the celebrated weapon which he had hitherto
retained in his own custody.

This was not all. When the day of combat
arrived, the Laird's Jock, in spite of his daughter's
affectionate remonstrances, determined, though
he had not left his bed for two years, to be a personal witness of the duel. His will was still a law
to his people, who bore him on their shoulders,
wrapped in plaids and blankets, to the spot
where the combat was to take place, and seated
him on a fragment of rock which is still called
the Laird's Jock's stone. There he remained
with eyes fixed on the lists or barrier, within
which the champions were about to meet. His
daughter, having done all she could for his
accommodation, stood motionless beside him,
divided between anxiety for his health, and for
the event of the combat to her beloved brother.
Ere yet the fight began, the old men gazed on
their chief, now seen for the first time after several
years, and sadly compared his altered features
and wasted frame with the paragon of strength
and manly beauty which they once remembered.
The young men gazed on his large form and
powerful make, as upon some antediluvian giant
who had survived the destruction of the Flood.*

But the sound of the trumpets on both sides
recalled the attention of every one to the lists,
surrounded as they were by numbers of both
nations eager to witness the event of the day.
The combatants met. It is needless to describe

the struggle: the Scottish champion fell. Foster, placing his foot on his antagonist, seized on the redoubted sword, so precious in the eyes of its aged owner, and brandished it over his head as a trophy of his conquest. The English shouted in triumph. But the despairing cry of the aged champion, who saw his country dishonoured, and his sword, long the terror of their race, in possession of an Englishman, was heard high above the acclamations of victory. He seemed, for an instant, animated by all his wonted power; for he started from the rock on which he sat, and while the garments with which he had been invested fell from his wasted frame, and showed the ruins of his strength, he tossed his arms wildly to heaven, and uttered a cry of indignation, horror, and despair, which, tradition says, was heard to a preternatural distance, and resembled the cry of a dying lion more than a human sound.

His friends received him in their arms as he sank utterly exhausted by the effort, and bore him back to his castle in mute sorrow; while his daughter at once wept for her brother and endeavoured to mitigate and soothe the despair of her father. But this was impossible; the old man's only tie to life was rent rudely asunder, and his heart had broken with it. The death of his son had no part in his sorrow. If he thought of him at all, it was as the degenerate boy, through whom the honour of his country and clan had been lost; and he died in the course of three days, never even mentioning his name, but pouring out unintermitted lamentations for the loss of his noble sword.

I conceive that the moment when the disabled

chief was roused into a last exertion by the agony of the moment is favourable to the object of a painter. He might obtain the full advantage of contrasting the form of the rugged old man, in the extremity of furious despair, with the softness and beauty of the female form. The fatal field might be thrown into perspective, so as to give full effect to these two principal figures, and with the single explanation that the piece represented a soldier beholding his son slain, and the honour of his country lost, the picture would be sufficiently intelligible at the first glance. If it was thought necessary to show more clearly the nature of the conflict, it might be indicated by the pennon of St. George being displayed at one end of the lists, and that of St. Andrew at the other.

I remain, Sir,

Your obedient servant,

THE AUTHOR OF WAVERLEY.

EXPLANATORY NOTES

IN compiling these notes I have been particularly helped by the glossaries to the Dryburgh edition of the Waverley Novels and, for 'Wandering Willie's Tale', Kathryn Sutherland's notes to the recent World's Classics edition of *Redgauntlet*. Place-names are only included where some particular significance attaches to them (e.g. Cape Wrath). References to Scott's *Journal* and *Letters* and to Lockhart's biography of Scott (referred to as *Life*) are to the editions cited in the bibliography. Shakespeare references are based on the Oxford Standard Authors edition of his works. It should be noted that many of Scott's quotations are inaccurate; I have not pointed this out on each occasion. Notes in this section are by the editor unless preceded by the words 'Scott's Note'.

1 WANDERING WILLIE'S TALE: as Scott acknowledges in his note to p. 26, this story was originally told of Sir Robert Grierson of Lagg. Scott seems to have known it early in his life and a version of it was printed in his lifetime; see Joseph Train, *Strains of the Mountain Muse*, Edinburgh, 1814, pp. 191–5. The sources of the story are discussed in the articles by Parsons (1933) and Lascelles (1968) in the bibliography. For details about Grierson see Alexander Fergusson, *The Laird of Lagg*, Edinburgh, 1886, and W. S. Crockett, *The Scott Originals*, London, 1912, pp. 346–55. In *Redgauntlet*, the story is told by a blind fiddler, Wandering Willie, to Darsie Latimer, who later in the novel proves to be a descendant of the Redgauntlets who figure in the tale.

the Hielandmen in Montrose's time: James Graham, first Marquis of Montrose (1612–50), led an army of Highlanders and Irishmen on a highly successful campaign on behalf of Charles I in Scotland in 1644–5, but was defeated at the battle of Philiphaugh where, as Scott says, 'he lost the fruit of six splendid victories' (*Minstrelsy of the Scottish Border*, London, 1931, p. 246). Montrose figures in Scott's novel *A Legend of Montrose*.

wi' Glencairn in the saxteen-hundred and fifty-twa: William Cunningham, ninth Earl of Glencairn (?1610–64), led a royalist rising in Scotland against the forces of Cromwell. The rising began early in 1653, Glencairn took command of it in June or July and it reached its height late in that year and early in the next year.

when King Charles the Second came in: with the Restoration of the monarchy in 1660 after Cromwell's Commonwealth, Redgauntlet was in high favour, having demonstrated his fervent devotion to the royalist cause by joining the risings of Montrose and Glencairn.

the Laird of Redgauntlet: in Scotland the owner of a landed estate held directly from the crown was technically a *baron* but was normally called a *laird*.

a redhot prelatist: a supporter of an episcopal form of church government such as was re-introduced in the Church of Scotland by Charles II. *Prelatist* is an abusive term and reveals where Willie's sympathies lie.

commissions of lieutenancy . . . of lunacy: the former were commissions from the crown to raise forces to put down a rebellion, in this case the opposition of the Covenanters (see below) to the new system of church government; the latter were granted by the Lord Chancellor to allow someone to manage the affairs of a lunatic.

Whigs: after the 'Whiggamore Raid' of 1648, in which a group of insurgents from the south-west of Scotland marched on Edinburgh, those who were, like them, supporters of Presbyterianism were known as Whigs. From 1679 the term came to be applied to the Exclusioners who opposed the succession of James, Duke of York, a Roman Catholic, to the throne and subsequently to those who supported the Glorious Revolution and the Protestant succession (see notes to pp. 3, 271, 304).

Covenanters: a general name for those who supported the principles of the National Covenant of 1638 and the Solemn League and Covenant of 1643, both of which were aimed at the defence of Presbyterianism as the established church of Scotland. Here, it applies in particular to those who objected to the religious policies of Charles II and James II and VII. They were severely persecuted in both reigns.

Cavaliers: supporters of Charles I and II against Cromwell and the Parliament; here used loosely to mean supporters of the restored monarchy and its policies.

Claverhouse's or Tam Dalyell's: John Graham of Claverhouse, Viscount Dundee (1648–89), was one of the leading persecutors of the Covenanters. He figures in Scott's *Old Mortality* and, less favourably represented, in James Hogg's *The Brownie of Bodsbeck* (1818). According to Scott in a note to *Old Mortality* entitled 'John Grahame of Claverhouse' he 'united the seemingly inconsistent qualities of courage and cruelty, a disinterested and devoted loyalty to his prince, with a disregard of the rights of his fellow-subjects'. Sir Thomas Dalziell of the Binns (?1599–1685) commanded the army in Scotland from 1679 to 1685 and became renowned for his brutal treatment of the Covenanters.

dargle: this word is not found as a common noun

except here. It could possibly be a misreading for *dingle* but the more interesting possibility is that Scott had heard of the area called 'the Dargle' on the banks of the river of that name in Ireland and misunderstood it as a general name for a river valley.

hill-folk: the persecuted Covenanters met secretly in the hills to hold religious services and in many cases fled to the hills; they were known as *hill-men*, but Scott is the first recorded as using the variant term *hill-folk*.

tak the test . . . recusant: the Test Act of 1681 required the taking of an oath ('test') supporting the supremacy of the king in religious as well as civil matters. This was completely contrary to the principles of the Covenanters. The oath was legally required of any holder of public office but was in fact required of anyone suspect to the authorities. Anyone who refused to take the test was called a *recusant*.

2 *bullets happed aff . . . he had a mear*: bullets were said to 'hop' off Dalziell's boots; see Scott's note 'General Dalzell, usually Called Tom Dalzell' in *Old Mortality*. The story of the horse is taken from a story about Claverhouse; see Scott's note 'Claverhouse's Charger' in *Old Mortality*.

those killing times: the time of the worst persecution of the Covenanters is referred to as 'Killing Time' in the work of Patrick Walker (*Six Saints of the Covenant*, London, 1901, i. 71). He was one of the major contemporary chroniclers of the persecution and a favourite source of Scott here and in *Old Mortality* and *The Heart of Mid-Lothian*.

'Hoopers and Girders' . . . 'Jockie Lattin': both are names of tunes; 'Jockie Lattin' is recorded in James Johnson's collection *The Scots Musical Museum* (Edinburgh, 1787–1803, Vol. V, no. 430).

back-lilt: the reading in the first edition is *back-lill* which *The Scottish National Dictionary* defines as 'the thumb-hole in the back of the Lowland or Northumbrian small pipe chanter, the upper G note' (*s.v. lill*). The *SND* treats *back-lilt*, which only occurs here, as an error. But *lilt* occurs glossed as 'the hole of a wind instrument of music' in the glossary of David Herd's *Ancient and Modern Scottish Songs*, first published in 1776. The *SND* treats this too as an error, but it is possible that Scott took *lilt* from Herd and revised *back-lill* to *back-lilt*. The magnum reading has therefore been retained, especially as this would not be the only occasion on which Scott used an erroneous form of a word.

Tory: originally an Irish outlaw, later a royalist and then one of those who supported the accession of James II and VII to the throne (see note to *Whig*, p. 1). Here it means someone who supported the policies of Charles II and James II and VII.

Jacobites: a supporter of James II and VII and his descendants, the Stuart claimants of the throne, after the revolution of 1688. The name derives from *Jacobus*, the Latin for 'James'. Not all Tories were in fact Jacobites.

3 *hunting and hosting, watching and warding*: *hosting* was following one's feudal superior to war or on a raid, and *watching and warding* was keeping watch and guarding. The obligation of a tenant to fulfil these duties when called upon by his feudal superior was removed in 1717 but was still current at the time of which Wandering Willie is speaking.

the Revolution: that is the Glorious Revolution of 1688 when, after James II had left England, William III and Mary were made king and queen. The revolution led to the re-establishment of Presbyterianism in Scotland, and brought an end to the persecution of the Covenanters.

4 *fines of the nonconformists*: fines levied on those who would not conform with Charles II and James II and VII's establishment of episcopacy.

Whitsunday . . . Martinmas: two of the four days in the year on which in Scotland rents became due; Whitsunday was 15 May, and Martinmas 11 November.

5 *Major Weir*: Scott's vague reference in his note to 'other crimes' covers an extraordinary story. Thomas Weir (*c*.1600–70), an outwardly religious man, suddenly confessed to fornication, adultery, incest, and bestiality. He was tried and executed. Although later tradition saw him as a warlock, as does Willie here, he was in fact never accused of witchcraft. See Scott's *Letters on Demonology and Witchcraft*, London, 1830, pp. 329ff, Robert Chambers, *Traditions of Edinburgh*, London, 1869, pp. 42–6, and David Stevenson, 'Major Weir: A Justified Sinner?', *Scottish Studies*, 16 (1972), 161–73. Scott intended at one stage to use the story of Weir in fiction; see R. P. Gillies, *Recollections of Sir Walter Scott, Bart.*, London, 1837, pp. 108–9.

like a sheep's-head between a pair of tangs: this simile is proverbial: see, for example, Allan Ramsay *A Collection of Scots Proverbs*, Edinburgh, 1750, ch. 14, no. 18.

6 *the visible mark of a horseshoe in his forehead*: Scott took this detail from Major Weir's sister, Jean; it can be found in George Sinclair or Sinclar's *Satans Invisible World Discovered* (1685); see the reprint of Gainesville, 1969, p. 238. Scott quoted the relevant passage in his edition of the Somers Tracts a number of years before writing

Redgauntlet; see *A Collection of Scarce and Valuable Tracts*, 1809–13, viii. 550. In the novel the horseshoe frown is made part of the traditions of the Redgauntlet family and its origin is explained in a story in ch. 8.

7 *like a seething cauldron*: this detail is taken from Grierson of Lagg, the original of Sir Robert Redgauntlet; see Charles Kirkpatrick Sharpe, *Letters*, London, 1888, i. 142.

blood instead of burgundy: another detail from Grierson; see Scott's note in ch. 34 of *Old Mortality*.

sat in the last Scots Parliament . . . compensations: the last parliament of Scotland as an independent kingdom met on 6 May 1703. On 16 January 1707 it accepted a treaty of Union with England. The Union came into effect on 1 May; the two kingdoms were united as Great Britain with one Parliament at Westminster. Scotland retained its separate established church and legal system. Under the terms of the Union sums of money were made available to compensate people who suffered financial damage as a result of the various terms of the treaty. These sums were widely, and with some justification, seen as bribes. Scott's strong feelings against those who accepted the compensation money are revealed in *Tales of a Grandfather* (London, 1911, pp. 768–70).

9 *Davie Lindsay*: the poet, Sir David Lindsay of the Mount (1490–1555); his works remained popular for a long time and were available in cheap editions to people like Wandering Willie, which accounts for the familiarity of his reference to 'Davie' Lindsay. Scott draws a picture of him in *Marmion* (IV. vii).

10 *(In fact, Alan . . . . and bite him)*: Darsie Latimer is

relating Wandering Willie's tale to his friend, Alan Fairford, in a letter and he breaks in here to comment on Willie's skill as a narrator.

13 *the bailie and the baron-officer*: until heritable jurisdictions were abolished in 1747, lairds (see note to p. 1) had judicial powers in their baronies. These powers were exercised through the baron-bailie and baron-officer.

14 *they suld hae caa'd her Tibbie Faw*: *suld* is used like this in Scots in reporting another person's statement; here it means 'I am told that they called her'. *Faw* or *fa'* means, appropriately, 'fate'.

16 *my father would have thought*: Steenie is Wandering Willie's *gudesire* (i.e. grandfather) not his father. As Mary Lascelles has pointed out in 'Scott and the Art of Revision' (in *Imagined Worlds*, ed. Mack and Gregor, London, 1968, pp. 146, 151), Scott began by calling Steenie, Willie's father. Then, to improve the chronology in relation to the rest of the novel, he changed this to *gudesire* but failed to correct all occurrences of the word *father*. Ballantyne, his printer, picked up some more but some still survived in the magnum; see here and pp. 19 and 21. See also note to p. 25.

dancing and deray: *deray* means 'disorderly revelry' and is frequently used in this alliterative phrase derived from the fifteenth-century Scots poem 'Christis Kirk on the Grene'.

17–18 *Middleton . . . Rothes . . . Lauderdale . . . Dalyell . . . Earlshall . . . Cameron . . . Bonshaw . . . Cargill . . . Dumbarton Douglas . . . MacKenyie . . . Claverhouse*: Cameron and Cargill were Covenanters; the remainder were enemies and, in most cases, persecutors of the Covenanters. John Middleton, first Earl of Middleton (1619–74), changed from the Covenanting to the royalist side in 1648 and commanded with Glen-

cairn in 1653 (see note to p. 1). John Leslie, first
Duke of Rothes (1630–81), amongst other things
toured in 1665 with the king's guard to enforce
the persecution of the Covenanters. John
Maitland, first Duke of Lauderdale (1616–82),
was Charles II's Secretary of State for Scotland
from 1660 to 1680 and thus a major figure in im-
plementing the king's religious policies. Dalyell
(see note to p. 1), an ardent royalist, would not
shave his beard after the execution of Charles I;
see *Old Mortality*, ch. 30 and *Tales of a Grandfather*,
London, 1911, p. 592. Andrew Bruce of
Earlshall acted with Claverhouse in persecuting
the Covenanters in the south-west of Scotland. In
July 1680 he attacked a group of Covenanters on
Aird's Moss in Ayrshire, killing a number, including Richard Cameron who was one of the
main Covenanting leaders and held their views in
the most extreme form. In June 1680 Cameron
formally disowned the authority of the king in a
public declaration at Sanquhar. James Irvine of
Bonshaw captured Donald Cargill, another
leading Covenanter, in 1681. According to John
Howie's account of Cargill's life in his *Scots Worthies* (first published in 1775) Bonshaw, having set
Cargill on a horse bare-back, tied his feet cruelly
below the horse's belly. George Douglas, Earl of
Dumbarton (?1636–92) was commander-in-chief
of the Scottish army under James II and VII. I
am not sure why Scott calls him 'twice-turned
traitor' as he followed James into exile. Sir
George Mackenzie of Rosehaugh (1636–91) was
Lord Advocate in Scotland during the persecution of the Covenanters. He prosecuted them
with extreme severity, gaining the epithet of
'Bloody'. His 'worldly wit and wisdom' was
demonstrated in his book on Scots law and his
founding of the Advocates' Library, which later

became the National Library of Scotland. Claverhouse (see note to p. 1) was believed to be proof against lead bullets and to have been shot with a silver button (see Scott's note to *Old Mortality*, 'Proof against Shot given by Satan').

But, Lord take us . . . bullet had made: Scott's note:—

The personages here mentioned are most of them characters of historical fame; but those less known and remembered may be found in the tract entitled, "The Judgment and Justice of God Exemplified, or, a Brief Historical Account of some of the Wicked Lives and Miserable Deaths of some of the most remarkable Apostates and Bloody Persecutors, from the Reformation till after the Revolution." This constitutes a sort of postscript or appendix to John Howie of Lochgoin's "Account of the Lives of the most eminent Scots Worthies." The author has, with considerable ingenuity, reversed his reasoning upon the inference to be drawn from the prosperity or misfortunes which befall individuals in the world, either in the course of their lives or in the hour of death. In the account of the martyrs' sufferings, such inflictions are mentioned only as trials permitted by Providence, for the better and brighter display of their faith, and constancy of principle. But when similar afflictions befell the opposite party, they are imputed to the direct vengeance of Heaven upon their impiety. If, indeed, the life of any person obnoxious to the historian's censures happened to have passed in unusual prosperity, the mere fact of its being finally concluded by death, is assumed as an undeniable token of the judgment of Heaven, and, to render the conclusion inevitable, his last scene is generally garnished with some singular circumstances. Thus the Duke of Lauderdale is said, through old age but immense corpulence, to have become so sunk in spirits, "that his heart was not the bigness of a walnut."

18 *Lang Lad . . . Highland Amorites*: the 'Lang Lad' figures in the appendix mentioned by Scott in the previous note; see John Howie, *Biographia*

Scoticana, or . . . Scots Worthies, Edinburgh, 1796, App. 48. Archibald Campbell, ninth Earl of Argyll (1629–85), supported the Protestant James, Duke of Monmouth in 1685 in his bid to succeed to the throne in place of the Roman Catholic, James II and VII. He was captured and executed. The 'Deil's Rattle-bag' is David Mason, a Covenanter who became an informer; Scott's source was Patrick Walker; see *Six Saints of the Covenant*, London, 1901, i. 91. The 'wicked guardsmen' are Charles II's Life Guards of whom Claverhouse was colonel. The 'savage Highland Amorites' are a small army of Highlanders, the so-called 'Highland Host', which was employed in persecuting the Covenanters in 1678, especially in the south-west. The phrase 'Highland Amorites' is used in a Covenanting poem printed by Scott in a note to *Old Mortality* under the heading 'Royal Army at Bothwell Bridge'. For the Amorites see Deuteronomy 20.17 and Joshua 3.10.

19 *Donald of the Isles*: 'The principal possessors of the Hebrides were originally of the name of Macdonald, the whole being under the government of a succession of chiefs, who bore the name of Donald of the Isles . . . and were possessed of an authority almost independent of the Kings of Scotland' (*Tales of a Grandfather*, London, 1911, p. 410).

20 *the Earl of Douglas*: William, eighth Earl of Douglas. He killed Patrick Maclellan of Bombie in 1452 and was himself killed by the king later the same year; see *Tales of a Grandfather*, London, 1911, pp. 176–80.

Pitscottie's History of Scotland: see Robert Lindesay of Pitscottie, *The Historie and Cronicles of Scotland*, Edinburgh, 1898–99, i. 91.

22 *a tar-barrel and torch*: barrels of tar were used in making a fire for an execution by burning.

25 *my gudesire readily agreed*: in the first edition of *Redgauntlet* this read 'my father' but it was corrected in the magnum; see note to p. 16.

wi' a lang train . . . like a squib: another detail taken from the story of Major Weir; see George Sinclair, *Satans Invisible World Discovered* (1685), reprinted Gainesville, 1969, p. 228.

Dougal and my gudesire: earlier (see p. 9) Willie says it was Hutcheon rather than his grandfather, Steenie, who saw the 'foul fiend' on the laird's coffin; this sentence was inserted in Scott's final revision of the text for the first edition; for a discussion of the discrepancy see Mary Lascelles, 'Scott and the Art of Revision', in *Imagined Worlds*, ed. Mack and Gregor, London, 1968, pp. 152–3.

26 *charged for a warlock*: Scott's note:—

I have heard in my youth some such wild tale as that placed in the mouth of the blind fiddler, of which, I think, the hero was Sir Robert Grierson of Lagg, the famous persecutor. But the belief was general throughout Scotland, that the excessive lamentation over the loss of friends disturbed the repose of the dead, and broke even the rest of the grave. There are several instances of this in tradition, but one struck me particularly, as I heard it from the lips of one who professed receiving it from those of a ghost-seer. This was a Highland lady, named Mrs C—— of B——, who probably believed firmly in the truth of an apparition, which seems to have originated in the weakness of her nerves and strength of her imagination. She had been lately left a widow by her husband, with the office of guardian to their only child. The young man added to the difficulties of his charge by an extreme propensity for a military life, which his mother was unwilling to give way to, while she found it impossible to repress it.

About this time the Independent Companies, formed for the preservation of the peace of the Highlands, were in the course of being levied; and as a gentleman named Cameron, nearly connected with Mrs C——, commanded one of those companies, she was at length persuaded to compromise the matter with her son, by permitting him to enter this company in the capacity of a cadet; thus gratifying his love of a military life without the dangers of foreign service, to which no one then thought these troops were at all liable to be exposed, while even their active service at home was not likely to be attended with much danger. She readily obtained a promise from her relative that he would be particular in his attention to her son, and therefore concluded she had accommodated matters between her son's wishes and his safety in a way sufficiently attentive to both. She set off to Edinburgh to get what was awanting for his outfit, and shortly afterwards received melancholy news from the Highlands. The Independent Company into which her son was to enter had a skirmish with a party of catherans engaged in some act of spoil, and her friend the Captain being wounded, and out of the reach of medical assistance, died in consequence. This news was a thunderbolt to the poor mother, who was at once deprived of her kinsman's advice and assistance, and instructed by his fate of the unexpected danger to which her son's new calling exposed him. She remained also in great sorrow for her relative, whom she loved with sisterly affection. These conflicting causes of anxiety, together with her uncertainty whether to continue or change her son's destination, were terminated in the following manner:—

The house in which Mrs C—— resided in the old town of Edinburgh, was a flat or story of a land, accessible, as was then universal, by a common stair. The family who occupied the story beneath were her acquaintances, and she was in the habit of drinking tea with them every evening. It was accordingly about six o'clock, when, recovering herself from a deep fit of anxious reflection, she was about to leave the parlour in which she sat in order to attend this engagement. The door through which she was to pass opened, as was very common in

Edinburgh, into a dark passage. In this passage, and within a yard of her when she opened the door, stood the apparition of her kinsman, the deceased officer, in his full tartans, and wearing his bonnet. Terrified at what she saw, or thought she saw, she closed the door hastily, and, sinking on her knees by a chair, prayed to be delivered from the horrors of the vision. She remained in that posture till her friends below tapped on the floor to intimate that tea was ready. Recalled to herself by the signal, she arose, and, on opening the apartment door, again was confronted by the visionary Highlander, whose bloody brow bore token, on this second appearance, to the death he had died. Unable to endure this repetition of her terrors, Mrs C—— sunk on the floor in a swoon. Her friends below, startled with the noise, came up stairs, and, alarmed at the situation in which they found her, insisted on her going to bed and taking some medicine, in order to compose what they took for a nervous attack. They had no sooner left her in quiet, than the apparition of the soldier was once more visible in the apartment. This time she took courage and said, "In the name of God, Donald, why do you haunt one who respected and loved you when living?" To which he answered readily, in Gaelic, "Cousin, why did you not speak sooner? My rest is disturbed by your unnecessary lamentation—your tears scald me in my shroud. I come to tell you that my untimely death ought to make no difference in your views for your son; God will raise patrons to supply my place, and he will live to the fulness of years, and die honoured and at peace." The lady of course followed her kinsman's advice; and as she was accounted a person of strict veracity, we may conclude the first apparition an illusion of the fancy, the final one a lively dream suggested by the other two.

27 *'SIC ITUR . . . to heaven'*; from Virgil's *Aeneid*, ix. 641.

Canongate: the road (and the district around it) extending westwards from Holyroodhouse to the Netherbow, the eastern entrance to the old burgh of Edinburgh; the Canongate was a separate burgh until 1856. (An 1820 map of Edinburgh is conveniently reprinted in W. E. K. Anderson's edition of Scott's *Journal*.)

The gentle reader . . . Captain Bobadil's humour: although Bobadil in Jonson's *Every Man in his Humour* (1598) is a cowardly braggart, he constantly calls himself a gentleman and sees himself as fit for the company of gentlemen.

28 *the Forty-five*: 1745 was the year of a major rebellion of the Jacobites (see note to p. 2) led by Prince Charles Edward.

the Grand Climacteric: a climacteric is a critical stage in a person's life. It was believed that the years which were multiples of seven were climacteric; multiples of nine were also sometimes considered climacteric, hence the sixty-third year (seven multiplied by nine) was felt to be particularly critical and was known as the Grand Climacteric.

Parliament House: the building which housed the old Scots parliament before the Union of 1707 (see note to p. 7). Later used to house the Scottish law courts.

Bayle's, Fortune's, and Walker's: these were taverns in Edinburgh. Bayle's was in Shakespeare Square, which has now disappeared, but was near the present General Post Office. Fortune's and Walker's were in respectively Old Stamp Office Close and Writer's Court, both of which led off the High Street.

Covenant Close: an alley off the High Street in Edinburgh between St Giles and the Tron Kirk.

29 *Abbey of Holyrood*: Scott's note:—

HOLYROOD. The reader may be gratified with Hector Boece's narrative of the original foundation of the famous abbey of Holyrood, or the Holy Cross, as given in Bellenden's translation:

"Eftir death of Alexander the first, his brothir David come out of Ingland, and wes crownit at Scone, the yeir of God MCXXIV yeiris, and did gret justice, eftir his coronation, in all partis of his realme. He had na weris during the time of King Hary; and wes so pietuous, that he sat daylie in judgement, to caus his pure commonis to have justice; and causit the actionis of his noblis to be decidit be his othir jugis. He gart ilk juge redres the skaithis that come to the party be his wrang sentence; throw quhilk, he decorit his realm with mony nobil actis, and ejeckit the vennomus custome of riotus cheir, quhilk wes inducit afore be Inglismen, quhen thay com with Quene Margaret; for the samin wes noisum to al gud maneris, makand his pepil tender and effeminat.

"In the fourt yeir of his regne, this nobill prince come to visie the madin Castell of Edinburgh. At this time, all the boundis of Scotland were ful of woddis, lesouris, and medois; for the countre wes more gevin to store of bestiall, than ony productioun of cornis; and about this castell was ane gret forest, full of haris, hindis, toddis, and sicklike maner of beistis. Now was the Rude Day cumin, called the Exaltation of the Croce; and, becaus the samin wes ane hie solempne day, the king past to his contemplation. Eftir the messis wer done with maist solempnitie and reverence, comperit afore him mony young and insolent baronis of Scotland, richt desirus to haif sum plesur and solace, be chace of hundis in the said forest. At this time wes with the king ane man of singulare and devoit life, namit Alkwine, channon eftir the ordour of Sanct Augustine, quhilk wes lang time confessoure, afore, to King David in Ingland, the time that he wes Erle of Huntingtoun and Northumbirland. This religious man dissuadit the king, be mony reasonis, to pas to this huntis; and allegit the day wes so solempne, be reverence of the haly croce, that he suld gif him erar, for that day, to contemplation, than ony othir exersition. Nochtheles, his dissuasion is litill avalit; for the king was finallie so provokit, be inoportune solicitatioun of his baronis, that he past, nochtwithstanding the solempnite of this day, to his hountis. At last, quhen he wes cumin throw the vail that lyis to the gret eist fra the said castell, quhare now lyis the Canongait, the staik past throw the wod with sic noyis and din of rachis and bugillis, that all the bestis were rasit fra thair dennis. Now wes the king cumin to the fute of the crag, and all his nobilis severit, heir and thair, fra him, at thair game and solace; quhen suddenlie apperit to his sicht, the fairist hart that evir wes sene afore with levand creature. The noyis and din of this hart rinnand, as apperit, with awful and braid tindis, maid the kingis hors so effrayit, that na renzeis micht hald him; bot ran, perforce, ouir mire and mossis, away with the king. Nochtheles, the hart follwit so fast, that he dang baith the king and his hors to the ground. Than the king kest abak his handis betwix the tindis of this hart, to haif savit him fra the strak thairof; and the haly croce slaid, incontinent, in his handis. The hart fled away with gret violence, and evanist in the same place quhare now springis the Rude Well. The pepil richt affrayitly, returnit to him out of all partis of the wod, to comfort him efter his trubill; and fell on kneis, devotly adoring the haly croce; for it was not cumin but sum hevinly providence, as weill apperis; for thair is na man can schaw of quhat mater it is of, metal or tre. Sone eftir, the king returnit to his castell; and in the nicht following, he was admonist, be ane vision in his sleip, to big ane abbay of channonis regular in the same place quhare he gat the croce. Als sone as he was awalkinnit, he schew his visione to Alkwine, his confessoure; and he na thing suspended his gud mind, bot erar inflammit him with maist fervent devotion thairto. The king, incontinent, send his traist servandis in France and Flanderis, and brocht richt crafty masonis to big this abbay; syne dedicat it in the honour of this haly croce. The croce remanit continewally in the said abbay, to the time of King David Bruce; quhilk was unhappily tane with it at Durame, quhare it is haldin yit in gret veneration.''—BOECE, *book* 12, *ch.* 16.

It is by no means clear what Scottish prince first built a palace, properly so called, in the precincts of this renowned seat of sanctity. The abbey, endowed by successive sovereigns and many powerful nobles with munificent gifts of lands and tithes, came, in process of time, to be one of the most important of the ecclesiastical corporations of Scotland; and as early as the days of Robert Bruce, parliaments were held occasionally within its buildings. We have evidence that James IV. had a royal lodging adjoining to the cloister; but it is generally agreed that the first considerable edifice for the accommodation of the royal family erected here was that of James V., anno 1525, great part of which still remains, and forms the north-western side of the existing palace. The more modern buildings which complete the quadrangle were erected by King Charles II. The nave of the old conventual church was used as the parish church of the Canongate from the period of the Reformation, until James II. claimed it for his chapel royal, and had it fitted up accordingly in a style of splendour which grievously outraged the feelings of his Presbyterian subjects. The roof of this fragment of a once magnificent church fell in the year 1768, and it has remained ever since in a state of desolation.—For fuller particulars, see the *Provincial Antiquities of Scotland*, or the *History of Holyrood, by* MR CHARLES MACKIE.

The greater part of this ancient palace is now again occupied by his Majesty Charles the Tenth of France, and the rest of that illustrious family, which, in former ages so closely connected by marriage and alliance with the house of Stuart, seems to have been destined to run a similar career of misfortune. *Requiescant in pace!*

29 *John Doe and Richard Roe*: the fictitious names for the plaintiff and defendant in the obsolete English legal process, ejectment.

all pursuit for civil debt: in 1827 Scott was being pursued by a debtor and was worried that he might have to 'turn Chrystal Croftangry in good earnest and take Holyroodhouse' (*Letters*, x. 303).

29–30 *beginning at the northern gate . . . within the Sanctuary*: as is clear from the context, this defines an area surrounding the palace of Holyroodhouse. The Water Gate was the main entrance of the burgh of Canongate; the Tennis Court, originally attached

to the palace, was by this time a tennis court in
name only; a clack-mill is a rattle worked by the
wind to scare away birds.

30 *Maitland*: William Maitland (1693–1757) wrote a
History of Edinburgh (1753). That he reads 'same'
(p. 153) where the magnum reads 'sewer'
confirms the rather unclear manuscript reading.

31 *Kedron . . . Shimei*: see 1 Kings 2:37.

Elysium: in Greek mythology a pleasant place after
death for those especially favoured by the gods.

33 *Styx . . . Pluto . . . Limbo lake*: according to Greek
mythology the Styx was a river of the Underworld,
Hades, over which the dead must pass; Pluto was
god of this world. *Limbo Lake* seems to be used
loosely here for 'Hades'.

34 *Virgil's shepherd*: see his *Eclogues*, i. 27–30.

Rundell and Bridge: jewellers in Ludgate Hill,
London. Scott himself met Bridge; see his *Journal*,
8 May 1828.

35 *Brown's Square*: one of the first developments
outside the old Edinburgh. Built in the 1760s, it
was lost in the later nineteenth century when
Chambers Street was formed.

Mr Sommerville: Sommerville's illness as described in the following pages was based on
that of Scott's father; see Lockhart's *Life*,
i. 301.

38 *Mezentius*: see Virgil's *Aeneid*, vii. 481ff.

39 *omni . . . amici*: 'worse than any loss of control over
one's limbs is the failing mind which cannot
recognize the names of servants or the face of a
friend'; see Juvenal's *Satires*, x. 232–5.

42 *Many a lad . . . grown old*: from 'The Toper's
Apology' by Charles Morris (1745–1838).

Cicero: he wrote of old age in the work known as *De Senectute*, written in 45 or 44 BC.

42-3 *Beau Nash*: Richard Nash (1674–1762) presided over fashionable society in Bath in the earlier eighteenth century.

44 Epigraph: see p. 64.

45 *Croft-an-ri . . . the king his croft*: *righ* is the Gaelic word for 'king' and *croft* in Scotland and elsewhere meant 'a small piece of arable land adjacent to a house' (*OED*).

Croftangry: in the area near Holyrood Palace was 'a narrow lane leading into St Anne's Park, which bears the curious Gaelic title of *Croft-an-righ*, or the King's Field' (Daniel Wilson, *Memorials of Edinburgh in the Olden Time*, Edinburgh, 1886, p. 309). It led southward from the road called 'Abbey Hill'.

how prophets have been taken from the pleugh: see e.g. 1 Kings 19:19.

Cincinnatus: when messengers came about 458 BC to tell Cincinnatus that the Romans had chosen him as 'dictator' he was found ploughing his land.

46 *Virgilius . . . subduing the soil*: see Virgil, *Georgics*, I. 99.

flitting and faithless sands: Croftangry's grandfather's account is written by Scott in an imitation of earlier Scots: spellings like *sa*, *quha*, and *quhilk* and the use of *ane* as an indefinite article were obsolete by Scott's time.

lengthy, as our American friends say: before the nineteenth century the word was only used by American writers and it was still regarded in Britain as an Americanism in Scott's time; see also *Letters*, iii. 255.

Haec nos novimus esse nihil: 'we understood this to be nothing'.

47 *Vix ea nostra voco*: 'I scarcely call this ours'.

the wrong side of the blanket: i.e. illegitimately.

sub vexillo . . . . Floddenfield: 'under the king's standard, at the battle near Branxton, i.e. Flodden field'. James IV was defeated and killed here by Henry VIII of England in 1513.

Sir John Colville of the Dale: in Shakespeare's *Henry IV: Part I* Colevile, when accused of being a 'famous rebel', answers 'I am . . . but as my betters are / That led me hither' (IV. iii. 69, 71–2).

Langside: Mary, Queen of Scots, was defeated at this place, now a suburb of Glasgow, in 1568.

giving a martyr to the Calendar of the Covenant: that is, adding a name to the list of the 'saints' of the Covenanters; for the Covenanters see note to p. 1.

48 *such unnatural Neroes . . . devour the substance of their own house*: a reference to the extravagance of the Roman emperor Nero (37–68).

50 *natale solum . . . 'family estate'*: see Swift's poem, 'Whitshed's Motto on his Coach, *Libertas et natale Solum*, Liberty and my native Country':

> Libertas & natale Solum,
> Fine words; I wonder where you stole 'um.
> . . . But, let me now the words translate:
> *Natale Solum*: My Estate:
> My dear Estate, how well I love it (ll. 1–2, 5–7).

54 *two . . . freehold qualifications . . . two great families*: before the Reform Act of 1832 only those in Scotland who held land of a certain stipulated value qualified as 'freeholders' and were entitled to elect or be elected members of Parliament. The property of Glentanner is of sufficient extent to be divided into four and still qualify the holder of each section as a 'freeholder'. The reference to the coming parliamentary election is a hint that there might be profit to be made by dividing the property and selling the resultant votes.

55 Epigraph: from Act II of *The Stage-Coach* (1704) by George Farquhar (1678–1707).

56 *Mr Piper, best of contractors*: Scott met Edward Piper 'the Great Contractor for the Mail coaches' in 1830 to discuss the route for a road (*Journal*, 29 May 1830).

frampal jades: a favourite phrase of Scott's, borrowed from Middleton and Dekkers's *The Roaring Girl* (1611), III. i. 10; see also *Peveril of the Peak*, ch. 32.

Johnie Groat's House . . . Cornhill: Johnie Groat's House is the northernmost point of mainland Scotland while Ladykirk and Cornhill are villages on the Tweed and thus on the Scottish border with England.

57 *date . . . from the death of John Ostler*: compare the comment of a carrier in Shakespeare's *Henry IV: Part I*: 'this house is turned upside down since Robin Ostler died' (II. i. 11–12).

as Horace says, 'delight . . by your chariots': see Horace, *Epistles*, I. xvii. 6–8.

58 *Peri Bathous . . . make two lovers happy*: the *Peri Bathous* or, to give it its full title, *Martinus Scriblerus' ΠΕΡΙ ΒΑΘΟΥΣ, or the Art of Sinking in Poetry*, was a work by Pope, Swift, and others, published in 1727. In Chapter 11 the lines quoted here (the original source of which is unknown) are cited as an example of hyperbole and described as 'that modest request of two absent lovers'.

59 *There is . . . without them*: compare the epigram of Martial, *Nec tecum possum vivere nec sine te*, 'I cannot live with you or without you' (*Epigrammata* XII. xlvi).

60 *These were thy gods. O Israel!*: see Exodus 32:4,8.

61 *Corehouse Linn*: a waterfall on the Clyde.

62 *temples of Comus*: rather than the better known Comus of Milton's masque of that name who is a

god of lust and sensuality, Scott seems here to be thinking of the Comus in Ben Jonson's *Pleasure Reconciled to Virtue* (1619) who is described by one of the other figures in that masque as 'the god of *cheere*, or the *belly*'.

cages of some feudal Bastile: on the use of iron cages for the confining of prisoners of Louis XI of France see Scott's note to ch. 30 of *Quentin Durward*.

64 *Nunc ager . . . pectora rebus*: 'Now the field is under the name of Umbrenus, recently it was called by the name of Ofellus; it will be nobody's permanently; but it passes in use now to me now to another. Therefore live as brave men and set brave hearts against adversities' (Horace, *Satires*, II. ii. 133–6).

65 *Fairntosh*: whisky from Ferintosh in the Black Isle of Ross-shire.

67 *Horace and Prior*: the classical Latin poet and the English poet, Matthew Prior (1664–1721).

Which sloping hills . . . grows: I have not traced the source of these lines.

68 *Covenanter*: see note to p.1.

famous Covenanter . . . Captain Creichton: Scott's note:—

STEELE, A COVENANTER, SHOT BY CAPTAIN CREICHTON. The following extract from Swift's Life of Creichton gives the particulars of the bloody scene alluded to in the text:—

''Having drank hard one night, I (Creichton) dreamed that I had found Captain David Steele, a notorious rebel, in one of the five farmers' houses on a mountain in the shire of Clydesdale, and parish of Lismahago, within eight miles of Hamilton, a place that I was well acquainted with. This man was head of the rebels, since the affair of Airs-Moss; having succeeded to Hackston, who had been there taken, and afterward hanged, as the reader has already heard; for, as to Robert Hamilton, who was then Commander-in-chief at Bothwell Bridge, he appeared no more among them, but fled, as it was believed, to Holland.

"Steele, and his father before him, held a farm in the estate of Hamilton, within two or three miles of that town. When he betook himself to arms, the farm lay waste, and the Duke could find no other person who would venture to take it; whereupon his Grace sent several messages to Steele, to know the reason why he kept the farm waste. The Duke received no other answer, than that he would keep it waste, in spite of him and the king too; whereupon his Grace, at whose table I had always the honour to be a welcome guest, desired I would use my endeavours to destroy the rogue, and I would oblige him for ever.

"I return to my story. When I awaked out of my dream, as I had done before in the affair of Wilson, (and I desire the same apology I made in the introduction to these Memoirs may serve for both,) I presently rose, and ordered thirty-six dragoons to be at the place appointed by break of day. When we arrived thither, I sent a party to each of the five farmers' houses. This villain Steele had murdered above forty of the king's subjects in cold blood; and, as I was informed, had often laid snares to entrap me; but it happened, that although he usually kept a gang to attend him, yet at this time he had none, when he stood in the greatest need. One of the party found him in one of the farmers' houses, just as I happened to dream. The dragoons first searched all the rooms below without success, till two of them hearing somebody stirring over their heads, went up a pair of turnpike stairs. Steele had put on his clothes, while the search was making below; the chamber where he lay was called the Chamber of Deese,* which is the name given to a room where the laird lies, when he comes to a tenant's house. Steele suddenly opening the door, fired a blunderbuss down at the two dragoons, as they were coming up the stairs; but the bullets grazing against the side of the turnpike, only wounded, and did not kill them. Then Steel violently threw himself down the

---

*Or chamber of state; so called from the dais, *or canopy and elevation of floor, which distinguished the part of old halls which was occupied by those of high rank. Hence the phrase was obliquely used to signify state in general.*

stairs among them, and made towards the door to save his life, but lost it upon the spot; for the dragoons who guarded the house dispatched him with their broadswords. I was not with the party when he was killed, being at that time employed in searching at one of the other houses, but I soon found what had happened, by hearing the noise of the shot made with the blunderbuss; from whence I returned straight to Lanark, and immediately sent one of the dragoons express to General Drummond at Edinburgh."—*Swift's Works, Vol XII.* (*Memoirs of Captain John Creichton,*) pages 57–59, Edit, Edinb. 1824.

Wodrow gives a different account of this exploit—"In December this year, (1686,) David Steil, in the parish of Lismahagow, was surprised in the fields by Lieutenant Creichton, and after his surrender of himself on quarters, he was in a very little time most barbarously shot, and lies buried in the churchyard there."

70 Epigraph; from 'A true story of an Apparition' (ll. 57–8) by John Gay (1685–1732).

71 *Appian or Flaminian highways*: the Via Appia and Via Flaminia were important roads built by the Romans in Italy.

in a field diapré: i.e. on a background covered with a decorative design.

75 *a hundred pund sterling*: as opposed to £100 Scots. A Scots pound by this time was a money of account only and equalled 20 English pennies.

77 *For he did spend . . . auld gudeman*: these lines are from a poem which appeared in the second volume (published in 1725) of Allan Ramsay's *Tea-Table Miscellany*, under the title 'The Auld Goodman'. It was reprinted in Bishop Percy's *Reliques of Ancient English Poetry* (1765) and in David Herd's *Ancient and Modern Scottish Songs, Heroic Ballads &c* (1776).

Scott was well acquainted with all three of these collections.

80 *But with the morning cool reflection came*: cf. 'At length the morn and cold indifference came' from Nicholas Rowe's *The Fair Penitent* (1703), I. i. 162. Scott used the same words as here in a letter; see *Letters*, vi. 266.

81 *Norval . . . Glenalvon's*: characters in the tragedy *Douglas* (1756) by John Hume. The play was well known in the later eighteenth and early nineteenth centuries. The quotation 'although it sounded harshly' is from *Douglas*, IV. i. 371.

Epigraph: *As You Like It*, III. ii. 74–5.

82 *Cape Wrath*: the farthest point of mainland Scotland to the northwest.

Auld Reekie: Old Smoky, a traditional name for Edinburgh.

'And whare trew ye I gaed?' as Sir Pertinax says: Sir Pertinax MacSycophant in *The Man of the World* (1781) by Charles Macklin (1697–1797). Sir Pertinax asks this question in Act III.

82–3 *George's Square . . . Charlotte Square . . . old New Town . . . new New Town . . . Calton Hill . . . Canongate*: all of these were fashionable areas except the Canongate (for which see note to p. 27); George's Square (now called George Square) was built in 1763–4 to the south of the old medieval city of Edinburgh (the 'Old Town'); Charlotte Square was one of the original two squares in the first part of the New Town built to the north of the old city, beginning in 1767, referred to by Scott as the 'old New Town'; a new section of the New Town, usually referred to as the 'second New Town' (Scott's 'new New Town'), was begun in 1803 north of Queen Street Gardens; in 1812 the New Town began to expand towards the east around Calton Hill.

83 *rus in urbe*: 'the country in the midst of the town'; see Martial, *Epigrammata*, XII. lvii.

the trade of Pompey in Measure for Measure: Pompey was a bawd; of his trade he admits that 'it does stink in some sort' (III. ii. 29).

pah—an ounce of civet, good apothecary: see *King Lear*, IV. vi. 133–4.

84 *she is na a'body's Shanet*: for Janet's speech Scott uses a conventional and highly artificial representation of Highland speech; see Mairi Robinson, 'Modern Literary Scots: Fergusson and After', in *Lowland Scots*, ed. A. J. Aitken, Edinburgh, 1973, p. 39, and Graham Tulloch, *The Language of Walter Scott*, London, 1980, pp. 255–6. One feature of this pseudo-Highland speech is the use of *she* as a general purpose pronoun, especially to mean 'I'.

honi soit qui mal y pense: 'shame on him who thinks evil of it', the motto of the Order of the Garter.

86 *ped*: 'bed'; this use of *p* for *b*, found also in *pe, peast, pest, petter, pide*, etc, is an accurate reflection of the phonetic influence of Gaelic.

87 *gi'ed*: in the Lothian dialect *'t* can appear as *'d*; hence this phrase means 'give it'; *gi'ed* is the spelling in the magnum here, but a spelling *gie'd* would have been more consistent with the usual spelling of the magnum in which *gie* is preferred to *gi'e*.

88 *her nainsell*: 'I, myself', a common feature of pseudo-Highland speech.

90 *Bobadil says, 'I care . . . convenient'*: see Ben Jonson's *Every Man in his Humour* (Folio version), I. v. 36–7.

Portobello sands . . . when the cavalry have a drill: see the Preface for comments on Scott's personal connection with Portobello sands.

91 *theatre . . . Wil Murray*: William Murray

(1790–1852), actor and manager of the Theatre Royal built in 1768 and sited almost opposite the Register House in Edinburgh.

Bonassus: the Greek and Latin name for a bison and so used by Scott in a letter (*Letters*, x. 239). However, the French *bonasse*, which means 'simple-minded', would better suit the context here. Probably Scott confused the two words.

92 *What ails me . . . Caledonian wood*: from *Virgidemiarum*, VI. i. 217–24 by Bishop Joseph Hall (1574–1656). These lines are wrongly ascribed to Scott in the Oxford Standard Authors edition of his poems.

93 *the Spectator or the Guardian*: periodicals written by Addison, Steele, and others in 1711–13.

the Mirror or the Lounger: periodicals written by Mackenzie, Craig, Abercromby, and others in 1785–87.

Johnson . . . Ramblers: *The Rambler* was a periodical written by Dr Johnson in 1750–2.

94 *Comus*: the reference to the sacrifice of 'virtue itself' suggests that here Scott may well be thinking of Milton's Comus rather than Jonson's: see note to p. 62.

Mammon: the Aramaic word for 'riches', semi-personified in Matt. 6:24 and later seen as the name of of the devil of covetousness.

Zimmerman: Johann Georg Zimmerman (1728–95) was Swiss and the author of *Ueber die Einsamkeit* ('On Solitude') published in 1784 with an earlier version in 1756.

As the Spaniard, 'Viamos—Caracco!': in the *Letters* (vii. 278) Scott uses this phrase in the form 'Vamos Caracci' and again describes it as Spanish. *Vamos* is the Spanish for 'let us go' but the nearest

Spanish word to *caracco* or *caracci* is *carajo*, an
obscene exclamation.

95 *the Netherbow*: 'The Netherbow Port was the gate
which divided the city of Edinburgh from the
suburb called the Canongate. It had towers and
a spire, which formed a fine termination to the
view from the Cross. The gate was pulled down
[in 1764] in one of those fits of rage for in-
discriminate destruction with which the
magistrates of a corporation are sometimes
visited' (Scott, *Minstrelsy of the Scottish Border*, London, 1931, p. 480).

Prince's Street: the main street of the New Town of
Edinburgh, here seen as representing the more
fashionable districts.

under the name of a lion's head or an ass's: perhaps
meaning, I will neither claim to be a literary
celebrity ('lion') nor a fool ('ass') and will not ask
for contributions on either ground.

96 *Let every herring . . . hang by its own head*: glossed by
James Kelly in his *Complete Collection of Scotish Proverbs* (1721) as 'Every man must stand by his own
endeavour, industry and interest' (p. 240).

friendship . . . in the Scottish sense: in Scots *friend* can
mean 'relative'.

Mrs Bethune Baliol: the original for this character
was Mrs Anne Murray Keith (1736–1818); see
W.S. Crockett, *The Scott Originals*, London, 1912,
pp. 361–5, and Scott's magnum introduction to
Chronicles of the Canongate.

97 *Perhaps it may . . . sermon*: from Burns' 'Epistle to
a Young Friend', ll.7–8.

98 *Molière's recipe*: there is a story that Molière, the
French writer of comedies, read his plays to an
old woman and took great note of her criticisms.

Wilkie or Allan: Sir David Wilkie (1785–1841) and

Sir William Allan (1782–1850); both were Scottish painters and friends of Scott.

98–9 *the 'sweet word Mesopotamia'*: an allusion to a story of unknown origin that a woman told her minister that she 'had found great support in that heavenly word Mesopotamia'.

 99 *Timmerman*: Janet's mistake for *Zimmerman* (see p. 94). *Timmer* is the Scots form of *timber*, hence Janet's comment about the M'Intyres.

those Delilahs of the imagination, as Dryden calls them: Scott is misquoting Dryden's phrase 'those Dalilahs of the theatre', found in a letter to Lord Haughton, prefixed to *The Spanish Friar* (1681). Dryden used the phrase to refer to some passages in his own work which 'cry vengeance upon me for their extravagance' (*Of Dramatic Poesy and Other Critical Essays*, ed. George Watson, London, 1962, i. 276). Scott used the same misquotation in his autobiographical fragment (*Scott on Himself*, Edinburgh, 1981, p. 28) and in a letter (*Letters*, v. 60).

as much as Falstaff did paying back: see the character of Sir John Falstaff in Shakespeare's *Henry IV: Part I* and *Part II*, and *Henry V*.

applaud it done: cf. *Macbeth*, III. ii. 45–6: 'Be innocent of the knowledge, dearest chuck,/ Till thou applaud the deed'.

Almanzor: a character in Dryden's play *The Conquest of Granada* (1670). The quotation is from Part I, I. i. 206.

100 Epigraph: *Coriolanus*, II. i. 109–10.

101 *1745; Highland clans . . . in possession of the Scottish capital*: during the 1745 Jacobite rebellion Edinburgh was occupied by the army of Prince Charles which included a very large element of Scottish Highlanders.

103 *Garrick*: David Garrick (1717–79), the famous actor.

Lusignan: a character in *Zara* (1736), an adaptation of Voltaire's *Zaire* by Aaron Hill (1685–1750).

the King of Palestine: i.e. Lusignan; Guy de Lusignan was chosen King of Jerusalem in 1186 and the character in Hill's play is described as 'last of the blood of the Christian kings of Jerusalem'.

104 *an iron rasp*: Scott's note:—

IRON RASP. The ingenious Mr R. CHAMBERS'S *Traditions of Edinburgh* give the following account of the forgotten rasp or risp.

"This house had a *pin* or *risp* at the door, instead of the more modern convenience, a knocker. The pin, rendered interesting by the figure which it makes in Scottish song, was formed of a small rod of iron, twisted or notched, which was placed perpendicularly, starting out a little from the door, and bore a small ring of the same metal, which an applicant for admittance drew rapidly up and down the *nicks*, so as to produce a grating sound. Sometimes the rod was simply stretched across the *vizzying* hole, a convenient aperture through which the porter could take cognisance of the person applying; in which case it acted also as a stanchion. These were almost all disused about sixty years ago, when knockers were generally substituted as more genteel. But knockers at that time did not long remain in repute, though they have never been altogether superseded, even by bells, in the Old Town. The comparative merit of knockers and pins was for a long time a subject of doubt, and many knockers got their heads twisted off in the course of the dispute."

CHAMBERS'S *Traditions of Edinburgh*.

Beauffet: the name means 'sideboard'.

105 *He's sad . . . my fortunes*: *Twelfth Night*, III. iv. 5–6.

106 *Jameson*: George Jameson (1588–1644), a portrait painter, known as 'the Scottish Van Dyck'.

107 *Fontenoy*: a village in Belgium where the English,

Dutch, and Austrian allies were defeated by the French in 1745.

110 *Carthusian silence*: Carthusian monks follow a very strict rule which includes observing almost total silence.

112 *battle of Ramillies*: an important battle of 1706 in which the French were defeated by the allies led by Marlborough.

113 *during the last war . . . English nation*: during the Napoleonic wars (1803–15) Napoleon attempted to completely close the Continent of Europe to British commerce and British travellers were unable to visit Europe due to the state of war.

114 *Susannah, Countess of Eglinton*: Scott's note:—

—COUNTESS OF EGLINTON. Susannah Kennedy, daughter of Sir Archibald Kennedy of Cullean, Bart. by Elizabeth Lesly, daughter of David Lord Newark, third wife of Alexander 9th Earl of Eglinton, and mother of the 10th and 11th Earls. She survived her husband, who died 1729, no less than fifty-seven years, and died March 1780, in her 91st year. Allan Ramsay's Gentle Shepherd, published 1726, is dedicated to her, in verse, by Hamilton of Bangour.

The following account of this distinguished lady is taken from Boswell's Life of Johnson by Mr Croker.

"Lady Margaret Dalrymple, only daughter of John Earl of Stair, married in 1700, to Hugh, third Earl of Loudoun. She died in 1777, aged *one hundred*. Of this venerable lady, and of the Countess of Eglintoune, whom Johnson visited next day, he thus speaks in his *Journey*.—'Length of life is distributed impartially to very different modes of life, in very different climates; and the mountains have no greater examples of age than the Lowlands, where I was introduced to two ladies of high quality, one of whom (Lady Loudoun) in her ninety-fourth year, presided at her table with the full exercise of all her powers; and the other, (Lady Eglintoun,) had attained her eighty-fourth year, without any diminution of her vivacity, and little reason to accuse time of depredations on her beauty.' "

"Lady Eglintoune, though she was now in her eighty-fifth year, and had lived in the retirement of the country for almost half a century, was still a very agreeable woman. She was of the noble house of Kennedy, and had all the elevation which the consciousness of such birth inspires. Her figure was majestic, her manners high-bred, her reading extensive, and her conversation elegant. She had been the admiration of the gay circles of life, and the patroness of poets. Dr Johnson was delighted with his reception here. Her principles in church and state were congenial with his. She knew all his merit, and had heard much of him from her son, Earl Alexander, who loved to cultivate the acquaintance of men of talents in every department."

"In the course of our conversation this day, it came out that Lady Eglintoune was married the year before Dr Johnson was born; upon which she graciously said to him, that she might have been his mother, and that she now adopted him; and when we were going away, she embraced him, saying, 'My dear son, farewell!' My friend was much pleased with this day's entertainment, and owned that I had done well to force him out."

"At Sir Alexander Dick's, from that absence of mind to which every man is at times subject, I told, in a blundering manner, Lady Eglintoune's complimentary adoption of Dr Johnson as her son; for I unfortunately stated that her ladyship adopted him as her son, in consequence of her having been married the year *after* he was born. Dr Johnson instantly corrected me. 'Sir, don't you perceive that you are defaming the Countess? For, supposing me to be her son, and that she was not married till the year after my birth, I must have been her *natural* son.' A young lady of quality who was present, very handsomely said, 'Might not the son have justified the fault?' My friend was much flattered by this compliment, which he never forgot. When in more than ordinary spirits, and talking of his journey in Scotland, he has called to me, 'Boswell, what was it that the young lady of quality said of me at Sir Alexander Dick's?' Nobody will doubt that I was happy in repeating it."

Allan Ramsay: Ramsay (1686–1758) played an important part in the eighteenth-century revival of Scots poetry.

the Hon. Mrs. Colonel Ogilvy: young ladies, including Scott's mother, were sent to live with this lady (who died in 1753) to be 'finished off'. She was 'supposed to be the *best-bred* woman of her time in Scotland' (Robert Chambers, *Traditions of Edinburgh*, London, 1869, p. 253).

St James's . . . Billingsgate: St James's is the English royal court, while Billingsgate was a fish market in London renowned for its colourfully abusive language, so much so, that foul language came to be called 'billingsgate'. For a discussion of Scott's references to speech like that of Mrs Bethune Baliol see Graham Tulloch, *The Language of Walter Scott*, London, 1980, pp. 172–3.

116 *Fletcher of Salton*: Andrew Fletcher of Saltoun (1655–1716) was an ardent opponent of the 1707 parliamentary Union of England and Scotland.

Graham of Claverhouse: see note to p. 18.

Duchess of Lauderdale: Elizabeth Murray (d. 1697), an important figure in the reign of Charles II and second wife of John Maitland, Duke of Lauderdale.

117 *Elfland*: Mrs Bethune Baliol is either referring to the supposed longevity of fairies or to legends of humans who were carried off to Fairyland and returned to human life many years, even centuries, later.

the Empress Queen, or Frederick of Prussia: Maria Theresa (1717–80) was Holy Roman Empress and Queen of Hungary and Bohemia, and Frederick II (1712–86), called 'the Great', was King of Prussia.

the riding of the last Scottish Parliament: the Scots parliament was opened with a cavalcade of dignitaries and members; see also note to p. 7.

Lord Moray's Lodging in the Canongate: built about 1628 by the Dowager Countess of Home and still standing.

the wandering Jew: a legendary figure, supposedly condemned to wander the world until Christ's second coming because, as Christ carried His cross to Calvary, the Jew reproached Him and told Him to go faster.

118 *battle of Flodden*: see note to p. 47.

Bruce and Wallace: King Robert Bruce (1274–1329) successfully asserted Scotland's independence from England and William Wallace (?1272–1305) was a Scottish national hero of the same period.

wake my Baliol blood: an allusion to the fact that Robert Bruce and John Baliol were rival claimants to the Scottish throne in 1290.

the accession of James the Sixth: James VI of Scotland became James I of England in 1603.

It was an ill omen . . . cousin: Scott's note:—

EARL OF WINTON. The incident here alluded to is thus narrated in Nichols' Progresses of James I., Vol. III. p. 306.

"The family" (of Winton) "owed its first elevation to the union of Sir Christopher Seton with a sister of King Robert Bruce. With King James VI. they acquired great favour, who, having created his brother Earl of Dunfermline in 1599, made Robert, seventh Lord Seton, Earl of Winton in 1600. Before the King's accession to the English throne, his Majesty and the Queen were frequently at Seton, where the Earl kept a very hospitable table, at which all foreigners of quality were entertained on their visits to Scotland. His Lordship died in 1603, and was buried on the 5th of April, on the very day the King left Edinburgh for England. His Majesty, we are told, was pleased to rest himself at the south-west round of the orchard of Seton, on the high-way, till the funeral was over, that he might

not withdraw the noble company; and he said that he had lost a good, faithful, and loyal subject.''
NICHOLS' *Progresses of K. James I. Vol. III. p.*306.

119 *Jacobite*: see note to p. 2.

the Cross: the Cross, 'a handsome octagonal building in the High Street' (Robert Chambers, *Traditions of Edinburgh*, London, 1869, p. 191), was a place for promenading and doing business; see Chambers (p. 14) for a description of the activity there. Scott strongly condemned its demolition in 1756; see his note to *Marmion*, V. xxv.

Assembly Rooms: from 1720 'assemblies' (that is dances) were held in Assembly Close, off the High Street, in the Old Town of Edinburgh; in 1785 new Assembly Rooms were opened in Buccleuch Place, off George Square; in 1787 other new Assembly Rooms were opened in George Street in the New Town; eventually, as fashionable society moved to the New Town, the rooms there became the accepted venue.

120 *Dean of Saint Patrick's*: i.e. Swift, who held this position.

Birrel: Robert Birrel (1567–1605) kept a diary of current events; the passage alluded to is quoted in Scott's note.

Maccallan Mhor: i.e. Mac Cailean Mor, son of Colin the Great, a name borne by the earls and dukes of Argyll as descendants of Colin Campbell of Lochow who died in 1294. Scott's spelling of this patronymic is very varied.

Berwick: Berwick-upon-Tweed, on the Border between Scotland and England.

121 *other side of the Tweed*: that is, over the border in England.

a Highlandman's promise: Scott's note:—

—MACGREGOR OF GLENSTRAE. The 2 of Octr:
(1603) Allaster MacGregor of Glenstrae tane be the
laird Arkynles, bot escapit againe; bot after taken be
the Earle of Argyll the 4 of Januarii, and brought to
Edr: the 9 of Januar: 1604, wt: 18 mae of hes friendes
MacGregors. He was convoyit to Berwick by the
gaird, conform to the Earle's promes; for he promesit
to put him out of Scottis grund: Sua he keipit an
Hielandman's promes, in respect he sent the gaird to
convoy him out of Scottis grund; bot yai wer not direc-
tit to pairt wt: him, bot to fetche him bak againe. The
18 of Januar, he came at evin againe to Edinburghe;
and upone the 20 day, he was hangit at the crosse, and
ij of his freindes and name, upon ane gallows: himself
being chieff, he was hangit his awin hight above the
rest of hes freindis.—BIRRELL's *Diary, (in* DALZELL's
Fragments of Scottish History,) p. 60–1.

122 *sennachie*: in the Highlands, a professional teller
and student of traditional tales of family history
and legend.

Harley: Edward Harley, second Earl of Oxford
(1689–1741), patron of Prior and Pope.

Prior: see note to p. 67; the quotation is from
Prior's 'Erle Robert's Mice', ll. 60–1.

124 *THE HIGHLAND WIDOW*: Scott learnt this
story from Mrs Murray Keith, as he
acknowledged in his magnum introduction to
Chronicles of the Canongate: see also his *Journal*, 27
May 1826.

Epigraph: from Coleridge's 'Christabel' (ll.
39–42). The magnum text reads *wound* in the first
line, but this is a misreading of Scott's unclear
manuscript *moand* since Coleridge's poem reads
moaned and in Scott's handwriting *u* and *a, w* and *m*
are virtually indistinguishable. Moreover *moaned*
suits the context better. This seems to be a mistake
in transcribing Scott's hand, not one of his
misquotations.

military roads: see note to p. 130.

125 *Greatheart*: the escort of Christiana and her children in Part II of *Pilgrim's Progress* (1678) by John Bunyan.

126 *they would 'be killing' lamb*: the use of *will* (here appearing as *would*) with continuous forms of the verb instead of the present tense is often found 'as a literary device to indicate a Highland speaker' (*Scottish National Dictionary, will* v¹ B3).

the Land of Cakes: a popular name for Scotland arising from the importance of oatcakes in the Scottish diet.

127 *Gil Blas or Don Quixote*: the former is a picaresque romance (1715–35) by Alain René Le Sage and the latter a satirical romance (1605, 1615) by Miguel de Cervantes.

Falkirk or Preston: Falkirk was the scene of a victory by the Jacobite forces in 1746 while Preston, more often known as Prestonpans, was where the Jacobites defeated General Cope in 1745; Scott describes the latter battle in ch. 47 of *Waverley*.

128 *Gideon's fleece*: see Judges 6: 36–40.

129 *stern chiefs of Loch Awe . . . and the other lords . . . of Kilchurn*: Sir Colin Campbell of Lochow (an alternative spelling of Loch Awe) built Kilchurn castle at the western end of the loch in 1440. His descendants were lords of Glenorquhy and earls of Breadalbane. In the introduction to *Rob Roy* Scott wrote of 'A Sir Duncan Campbell of Lochow, known in the Highlands by the name of *Donacha Dhu nan Churraichd*, that is, Black Duncan with the Cowl'. This seems to be the same person as 'Duncan with the thrum bonnet'. He died in 1631. A thrum bonnet is one made with waste thread ('thrums').

Scott's note:—

—LOCH AWE. "Loch Awe, upon the banks of which the scene of action took place, is thirty-four miles in length. The north side is bounded by wide muirs and inconsiderable hills, which occupy an extent of country from twelve to twenty miles in breadth, and the whole of this space is enclosed as by circumvallation. Upon the north it is barred by Loch Eitive, on the south by Loch Awe, and on the east by the dreadful pass of Brandir, through which an arm of the latter lake opens, at about four miles from its eastern extremity, and discharges the river Awe into the former. The pass is about three miles in length; its east side is bounded by the almost inaccessible steeps which form the base of the vast and rugged mountain of Cruachan. The crags rise in some places almost perpendicularly from the water, and for their chief extent show no space nor level at their feet, but a rough and narrow edge of stony beach. Upon the whole of these cliffs grows a thick and interwoven wood of all kinds of trees, both timber, dwarf, and coppice; no track existed through the wilderness, but a winding path, which sometimes crept along the precipitous height, and sometimes descended in a straight pass along the margin of the water. Near the extremity of the defile, a narrow level opened between the water and the crag; but a great part of this, as well as of the preceding steeps, was formerly enveloped in a thicket, which showed little facility to the feet of any but the martins and wild cats. Along the west side of the pass lies a wall of sheer and barren crags. From behind they rise in rough, uneven, and heathy declivities, out of the wide muir before mentioned, between Loch Eitive and Loch Awe; but in front they terminate abruptly in the most frightful precipices, which form the whole side of the pass, and descend at one fall into the water which fills its trough. At the north end of the barrier, and the termination of the pass, lies that part of the cliff which is called Craiganuni; at its foot the arm of the lake gradually contracts its water to a very narrow space, and at length terminates at two rocks (called the Rocks of Brandir), which form a strait channel, something resembling the lock of a canal. From this outlet there is a continual descent towards Loch Eitive, and from hence the river Awe pours out its current in a furious stream, foaming over a bed broken with holes, and cumbered with masses of granite and whinstone.

"If ever there was a bridge near Craiganuni in ancient times, it must have been at the Rocks of Brandir. From the days of Wallace to those of General Wade, there were never passages of this kind but in places of great necessity, too narrow for a boat, and too wide for a leap; even then they were but an unsafe footway formed of the trunks of trees placed transversely from rock to rock, unstripped of their bark, and destitute of either plank or rail. For such a structure, there is no place in the neighbourhood of Craiganuni, but at the rocks above mentioned. In the lake and on the river, the water is far too wide; but at the strait, the space is not greater than might be crossed by a tall mountain pine, and the rocks on either side are formed by nature like a pier. That this point was always a place of passage, is rendered probable by its facility, and the use of recent times. It is not long since it was the common gate of the country on either side the river and the pass: the mode of crossing is yet in the memory of people living, and was performed by a little currach moored on either side the water and a stout cable fixed across the stream from bank to bank, by which the passengers drew themselves across in the manner still practised in places of the same nature. It is no argument against the existence of a bridge in former times, that the above method only existed in ours, rather than a passage of that kind, which would seem the more improved expedient. The contradiction is sufficiently accounted for by the decay of timber in the neighbourhood. Of old, both oaks and firs of an immense size abounded within a very inconsiderable distance; but it is now many years since the destruction of the forests of Glen Eitive and Glen Urcha has deprived the country of all the trees of sufficient size to cross the strait of Brandir; and it is probable, that the currach was not introduced till the want of timber had disenabled the inhabitants of the country from maintaining a bridge. It only further remains to be noticed, that at some distance below the Rocks of Brandir, there was formerly a ford, which was used for cattle in the memory of people living; from the narrowness of the passage, the force of the stream, and the broken bed of the river, it was, however, a dangerous pass, and could only be attempted with safety at leisure and by experience.''—*Notes to the Bridal of Caolchairn*.

Wellington: Arthur Wellesley, Duke of Wellington (1769–1852). The leading British general during the Napoleonic wars and victor at the Battle of Waterloo, he was greatly admired by Scott.

130 *Bonaparte*: the French Emperor, Napoleon Bonaparte (1769–1821). Scott wrote a nine-volume life of him, published in 1827.

Robert Bruce, even a Baliol: see note to p. 118.

defence and protection: Scott's note:—

—BATTLE BETWIXT THE ARMIES OF THE BRUCE AND MACDOUGAL OF LORN. "But the King, whose dear-bought experience in war had taught him extreme caution, remained in the Braes of Balquhidder till he had acquired by his spies and outskirries a perfect knowledge of the disposition of the army of Lorn, and the intention of its leader. He then divided his force into two columns, intrusting the command of the first, in which he placed his archers and the lightest armed troops, to Sir James Douglas whilst he himself took the leading of the other, which consisted principally of his knights and barons. On approaching the defile, Bruce dispatched Sir James Douglas by a pathway which the enemy had neglected to occupy, with directions to advance silently, and gain the heights above and in front of the hilly ground where the men of Lorn were concealed; and, having ascertained that this movement had been executed with success, he put himself at the head of his own division, and fearlessly led his men into the defile. Here, prepared as he was for what was to take place, it was difficult to prevent a temporary panic, when the yell which, to this day, invariably precedes the assault of the mountaineer, burst from the rugged bosom of Ben Cruachan; and the woods which, the moment before, had waved in silence and solitude, gave forth their birth of steel-clad warriors, and, in an instant, became instinct with the dreadful vitality of war. But although appalled and checked for a brief space by the suddenness of the assault, and the masses of rock which the enemy rolled down from the precipices, Bruce, at the head of his division, pressed up the side of the mountain. Whilst this party assaulted the men of Lorn with the utmost fury, Sir James Douglas and his party shouted suddenly upon the heights in their front, showering down their arrows upon them; and, when these missiles were exhausted, attacking them with their swords and battle-axes. The consequence of such an attack, both in front and rear, was the total discomfiture of the army of Lorn; and the circumstances to which this chief had so confidently looked forward, as rendering the destruction of Bruce almost inevitable, were now turned with fatal effect against himself. His great superiority of numbers cumbered and impeded his movements. Thrust, by the double assault, and by the peculiar nature of the ground, into such narrow room as the pass afforded, and driven to fury by finding themselves cut to pieces in detail, without power of resistance, the men of Lorn fled towards Loch Eitive, where a bridge thrown over the Awe, and supported upon two immense rocks, known by the name of the Rocks of Brandir, formed the solitary communication between the side of the river where the battle took place, and the country of Lorn. Their object was to gain the bridge, which was composed entirely of wood, and, having availed themselves of it in their retreat, to destroy it, and thus throw the impassable torrent of the Awe between them and their enemies. But their intention was instantly detected by Douglas, who, rushing down from the high grounds at the head of his archers and light-armed foresters, attacked the body of the mountaineers, which had occupied the bridge, and drove them from it with great slaughter, so that Bruce and his division, on coming up, passed it without molestation; and, this last resource being taken from them, the army of Lorn were, in a few hours, literally cut to pieces, whilst their chief, who occupied Loch Eitive with his fleet, saw, from his ships, the discomfiture of his men, and found it impossible to give them the least assistance.''—TYTLER'S *Life of Bruce*.

General Wade's military road: beginning in 1726, George Wade (1673–1748) laid out a number of roads in the Highlands as an aid to military control of the area after the uprising of 1715.

pathetic ballad . . . been printed: Edgeworthstown was the home in Ireland of the novelist Maria Edgeworth (1767–1849) whom Scott visited in 1825. Scott quoted the line given here more than once in his letters (see *Letters*, x. 320, xi. 296) and also quoted further lines in another letter (viii. 90). According to Dr Corson's note on the extra verses (in his *Notes and Index* to *Letters*) the song is to be found with the music in Mrs Hope-Scott's MS music book at Abbotsford.

131 *Had you but . . . Wade*: according to a footnote in the fifth edition of Edward Burt's *Letters from a Gentleman in the North of Scotland* (London, 1818, ii. 219) which quotes these lines, 'To perpetuate the memory of the Marshal's [i.e. Wade's] chief exploit, in making the road from Inverness to Inveraray, an obelisk is erected near Fort-William, on which the traveller is reminded of his merits by the following *naive* couplet.' Scott contributed material to this edition of Burt and had used Burt earlier as a source for information on the Highlanders when writing *Waverley*.

Simplon: a road over the Alps between France and Italy begun in 1800 under the direction of Napoleon Bonaparte.

136 *the Furies*: or Eumenides; seen by the Greeks as the avengers of crime.

Orestes and Oedipus: Orestes killed his mother after she had murdered his father, Agamemnon. Oedipus unknowingly killed his father and committed incest with his mother.

138 *My beautiful—my brave*: the words of Lady Randolph from *Douglas* (see note to p. 81), V. i. 734.

Lady Randolph's grief is 'ideal' in the sense that it is from a work of fiction rather than described from real life like that of the Highland Widow.

Epigraph: from 'The Highland Widow's Lament', a Jacobite song which appeared in James Johnson's *Scots Musical Museum* in 1796. No author's name was given, hence Scott calls it an 'Old Song', but it was probably written by Burns who, according to his editor James Kinsley, 'seldom signed his Jacobite songs'. (See his note to this song in Burns' *Poems and Songs*, Oxford, 1968, iii. 1515.) The title of the poem may have suggested Scott's title for his story.

139 *MacTavish Mhor*: Gaelic *mór* means 'great'; aspiration, represented in the spelling by adding *h* after the initial letter of a word, is a feature of Gaelic but would not normally be expected with *mór* here. MacTavish's exploits after the failure of the Forty-Five rising (see p. 140) recall those of similar outlaws in the Highlands of that period of whom Scott writes in *Tales of a Grandfather* (London, 1911, pp. 1186–7). One of these was a Sergeant Mor Cameron whose nickname, *Mor*, may have suggested to Scott the use of the same nickname for Hamish MacTavish.

140 *old Cretan warrior . . . all that cowards have is mine*: this is the second verse of a classical Greek poem by Hybrias the Cretan as translated by John Leyden (1775–1811) under the title 'The Cretan Warrior'. Scott quoted the whole poem in a note to his Introduction to his *Minstrelsy of the Scottish Border* (London, 1931, pp. 60–1). The original Greek poem can be found in *Lyra Graeca* (ed. by J. M. Edmonds, Cambridge, Mass., 1952, iii. 573).

the expedition of Prince Charles Edward: the Jacobite rebellion of 1745.

142 *called in Gaelic song, 'the stormy sons of the sword'*: for
an interesting discussion of Scott's knowledge of
Gaelic see Arthur Melville Clark, *Sir Walter Scott:
The Formative Years*, Edinburgh, 1969, pp.
214–20. His knowledge of the language was
somewhat limited, but how limited it is hard to
say. From early in his life he was interested in the
work of James Macpherson (1736–96) who
claimed to have discovered early Gaelic epic
poems and to have translated them into English.
He published his translations in the 1760s. While
Macpherson had some Gaelic material to work
from, it is clear that he also invented a great deal.
He presented his poems as the work of Ossian,
the son of the hero Fingal. The phrase Scott uses
here has a parallel in Macpherson's 'stormy son
of war' (*Fingal*, Book IV).

Bean: Gaelic *bàn* 'fair'.

144 *the long-skirted Lowland coat . . . at his side*: after the
Jacobite rising of 1745 the Highland dress was
prohibited; the prohibition was not lifted until
1782. The belted plaid was a long piece of tartan
cloth wound round the body and held by a belt;
it was an early form of the kilt.

147 *the calf of her heart*: the Gaelic *laogh* meaning 'calf'
is used in a number of phrases as a term of
endearment.

Taymouth Castle: the seat of the Earl of
Breadalbane near the north end of Loch Tay.

148 *tacksman*: a chief tenant who leased land from the
landowner and sublet it to lesser tenants.

149 *Fear them not . . . the thrush's song*: passages like this
have led various writers to describe Elspat's
language as Ossianic (see note to p. 142). In fact,
while it has some similarities to Macpherson's
style in his poems of Ossian, it is not a very close
copy of the Ossianic style and is really Scott's

own creation to suit his purposes in the story.

150 *a book sealed and a fountain closed*: cf. Song of Solomon 4.12

the battle of Culloden: on 16 April 1746 the forces of Prince Charles Edward were defeated by the army of the Duke of Cumberland. This brought to an end the major Jacobite rebellion of 1745–6. It was followed by savage repression in the Highlands which helped earn the duke the name of 'Butcher Cumberland'.

152 *she arose . . . and was refreshed*: see 2 Samuel 12:20.

153 *decorated with boughs . . . Feast of the Tabernacles*: see Leviticus 23:34–43, especially v. 40.

the cloud-berry, a scarlet fruit: in fact a cloud-berry is orange-red in colour.

155 *Hope deferred . . . maketh the heart sick*: see Proverbs 13:12.

156 *Fort Augustus*: a military station at the west end of Loch Ness.

158 *the new regiments . . . against the French in America*: the Highland regiments (see note to p. 175) were active in the fighting against the French in Canada which ended in 1760. This is perhaps rather early for the supposed date of the story's setting.

159 *MacAllan Mhor*: see note to p. 120.

Glengary, Lochiel, Perth, Lord Lewis: the last three, Donald Cameron of Lochiel (?1695–1748), James Drummond, Duke of Perth (1713–46), and Lord Lewis Gordon (d. 1754), were leaders of the 1745 rebellion. John Macdonell of Glengarry did not join the rebellion in person (although he was held in prison after the rebellion until 1749) and the clan regiment, which was an important element in Prince Charles' army, was led by his son. Scott was perhaps thinking of the younger Glengarry here or possibly of the earlier Alexander MacDonell of Glengarry (d. 1724) who figured prominently in the 1715 rising.

Caberfae . . . high Chief of Seaforth: the crest of the Mackenzies, Earls of Seaforth, was a deer's antlers (Gaelic *cabair féidh*).

160 *Drummossie-muir*: that is the battle of Culloden (see note to p. 150). The battle was fought on the moor which is adjacent to Culloden and about five miles from Inverness.

Barcaldine's son: Barcaldine is a territorial designation; his surname is Campbell (see p. 202).

161 *Hanover's yoke . . . the royal Stuart*: Elspat is ironically urging Hamish to accept the reigning house of Hanover and to reject his family's Jacobite sympathies.

the race of Dermid: the Campbells.

162 *Glencoe*: Scott's note:—

—MASSACRE OF GLENCOE. The following succinct account of this too celebrated event, may be sufficient for this place:—

"In the beginning of the year 1692, an action of unexampled barbarity disgraced the government of King William III. in Scotland. In the August preceding, a proclamation had been issued, offering an indemnity to such insurgents as should take the oaths to the King and Queen, on or before the last day of December; and the chiefs of such tribes, as had been in arms for James, soon after took advantage of the proclamation. But Macdonald of Glencoe was prevented by accident, rather than design, from tendering his submission within the limited time. In the end of December he went to Colonel Hill, who commanded the garrison in Fort William, to take the oaths of allegiance to the government; and the latter having furnished him with a letter to Sir Colin Campbell, Sheriff of the county of

Argyll, directed him to repair immediately to Inverary, to make his submission in a legal manner before that magistrate. But the way to Inverary lay through almost impassable mountains, the season was extremely rigorous, and the whole country was covered with a deep snow. So eager, however, was Macdonald to take the oaths before the limited time should expire, that, though the road lay within half a mile of his own house, he stopped not to visit his family, and after various obstructions, arrived at Inverary. The time had elapsed, and the sheriff hesitated to receive his submission; but Macdonald prevailed by his importunities, and even tears, in inducing that functionary to administer to him the oath of allegiance, and to certify the cause of his delay. At this time Sir John Dalrymple, afterwards Earl of Stair, being in attendance upon William as Secretary of State for Scotland, took advantage of Macdonald's neglecting to take the oath within the time prescribed, and procured from the King a warrant of military execution against that chief and his whole clan. This was done at the instigation of the Earl of Breadalbane, whose lands the Glencoe men had plundered, and whose treachery to government in negotiating with the Highland clans, Macdonald himself had exposed. The King was accordingly persuaded that Glencoe was the main obstacle to the pacification of the Highlands; and the fact of the unfortunate chief's submission having been concealed, the sanguinary orders for proceeding to military execution against his clan were in consequence obtained. The warrant was both signed and countersigned by the King's own hand, and the Secretary urged the officers who commanded in the Highlands to execute their orders with the utmost rigour. Campbell of Glenlyon, a captain in Argyll's regiment, and two subalterns, were ordered to repair to Glencoe on the first of February with a hundred and twenty men. Campbell being uncle to young Macdonald's wife, was received by the father with all manner of friendship and hospitality. The men were lodged at free quarters in the houses of his tenants, and received the kindest entertainment. Till the 13th of the month the troops lived in the utmost harmony and familiarity with the people; and on the very night of the massacre, the officers passed the evening at cards in Macdonald's house. In the night Lieutenant Lindsay, with a party of soldiers, called in a friendly manner at his door, and was instantly admitted. Macdonald, while in the act of rising to receive his guest, was shot dead through the back with two bullets. His wife had already dressed; but she was stripped naked by the soldiers, who tore the rings off her fingers with their teeth. The slaughter now became general, and neither age nor infirmity was spared. Some women, in defending their children, were killed; boys, imploring mercy, were shot dead by officers on whose knees they hung. In one place nine persons, as they sat enjoying themselves at table, were butchered by the soldiers. In Inverriggon, Campbell's own quarters, nine men were first bound by the soldiers, and then shot at intervals one by one. Nearly forty persons were massacred by the troops; and several who fled to the mountains perished by famine and the inclemency of the season. Those who escaped owed their lives to a tempestuous night. Lieutenant-Colonel Hamilton, who had received the charge of the execution from Dalrymple, was on his march with four hundred men, to guard all the passes from the valley of Glencoe; but he was obliged to stop by the severity of the weather, which proved the safety of the unfortunate clan. Next day he entered the valley, laid the houses in ashes, and carried away the cattle and spoil, which were divided among the officers and soldiers.''—*Article* ''BRITAIN;'' *Encyc. Britannica—New edition.*

house of Glenlyon: as Scott's note reveals, the soldiers at Glencoe were led by Captain Campbell, of Glenlyon.

167 *seannachies*: see note to *sennachie*, p. 122.

Green Colin: i.e. Barcaldine; for his fictional character Scott has borrowed the name of a historical figure, a Campbell, 'the laird of Dunstaffnage, called Cailen Uaine, or Green Colin, from the green colour which predominated in his tartan' (*Tales of a Grandfather*, London, 1911,

p. 420). Barcaldine's son also bears this nickname (see p. 202).

169 Epigraph: *Coriolanus*, V. iii. 187–9.

170 *a white cockade*: the badge of the Jacobites.

175 *Earl of Chatham*: William Pitt, first Earl of Chatham (1708–78). Under his direction a number of regiments were raised for the British army from Highland clans of both Jacobite and Hanoverian sympathies.

176 *the German wars*: the War of the Austrian Succession (1741–8) and possibly also the Seven Years War (1756–63).

177 *the General's power*: Scott's note:—

—FIDELITY OF THE HIGHLANDERS. Of the strong, undeviating attachment of the Highlanders to the person, and their deference to the will or commands of their chiefs and superiors—their rigid adherence to duty and principle—and their chivalrous acts of self-devotion to these in the face of danger and death, there are many instances recorded in General Stewart of Garth's interesting Sketches of the Highlanders and Highland Regiments, which might not inaptly supply parallels to the deeds of the Romans themselves, at the era when Rome was in her glory. The following instances of such are worthy of being here quoted:—

"In the year 1795, a serious disturbance broke out in Glasgow, among the Breadalbane Fencibles. Several men having been confined and threatened with corporal punishment, considerable discontent and irritation were excited among their comrades, which increased to such violence, that, when some men were confined in the guard-house, a great proportion of the regiment rushed out and forcibly released the prisoners. This violation of military discipline was not to be passed over, and accordingly measures were immediately taken to secure the ringleaders. But so many were equally concerned, that it was difficult, if not impossible, to fix the crime on any, as being more prominently guilty. And here was shown a trait of character worthy of a better cause, and which originated from a feeling alive to the disgrace of a degrading punishment. The soldiers being made sensible of the nature of their misconduct, and the consequent necessity of public example, *several men voluntarily offered themselves to stand trial*, and suffer the sentence of the law as an atonement for the whole. These men were accordingly marched to Edinburgh Castle, tried, and four condemned to be shot. Three of them were afterwards reprieved, and the fourth, Alexander Sutherland, was shot on Musselburgh Sands.

"The following demi-official account of this unfortunate misunderstanding was published at the time:—

" 'During the afternoon of Monday, when a private of the light company of the Breadalbane Fencibles, who had been confined for a *military* offence, was released by that company, and some other companies who had assembled in a tumultuous manner before the guard-house, no person whatever was hurt, and no violence offered; and however unjustifiable the proceedings, it originated not from any disrespect or ill-will to their officers, but from a mistaken point of honour, in a particular set of men in the battalion, who thought themselves disgraced by the impending punishment of one of their number. The men have, in every respect, since that period conducted themselves with the greatest regularity, and strict subordination. The whole of the battalion seemed extremely sensible of the improper conduct of such as were concerned, whatever regret they might feel for the fate of the few individuals who had so readily given themselves up as prisoners, to be tried for their own and others' misconduct.'

"On the march to Edinburgh, a circumstance occurred, the more worthy of notice, as it shows a strong principle of honour and fidelity to his word and to his officer in a common Highland soldier. One of the men stated to the officer commanding the party, that he knew what his fate would be, but that he had left business of the utmost importance to a friend in Glasgow, which he wished to transact before his death; that, as to himself, he was fully prepared to meet his fate; but with regard to his friend, he could not die in peace unless the business was settled, and that, if the officer would suffer him to return to Glasgow, a few hours there would be sufficient, and he would join him before he reached Edinburgh, and march as a prisoner with the party. The soldier added, 'You have known me since I was a child; you know my country and kindred, and you may believe I shall never bring you to any blame by a breach of the promise I now make, to be with you in full time to be delivered up in the Castle.' This was a startling proposal to the officer, who was a judicious, humane man, and knew perfectly his risk and responsibility in yielding to such an extraordinary application. However, his confidence was such, that he complied with the request of the prisoner, who returned to Glasgow at night, settled his business, and left the town before daylight to redeem his pledge. He took a long circuit to avoid being seen, apprehended as a deserter, and sent back to Glasgow, as probably his account of his officer's indulgence would not have been credited. In consequence of this caution, and the lengthened march through woods and over the hills by an unfrequented route, there was no appearance of him at the hour appointed. The perplexity of the officer when he reached the neighbourhood of Edinburgh may be easily imagined. He moved forward slowly indeed, but no soldier appeared; and unable to delay any longer, he marched up to the Castle, and as he was delivering over the prisoners, but before any report was given in, Macmartin, the absent soldier, rushed in among his fellow prisoners, all pale with anxiety and fatigue, and breathless with apprehension of the consequences in which his delay might have involved his benefactor.

"In whatever light the conduct of the officer (my respectable friend, Major Colin Campbell) may be considered, either by military men or others, in this memorable exemplification of the characteristic principle of his countrymen, fidelity to their word, it cannot but be wished that the soldier's magnanimous self-devotion had been taken as an atonement for his own misconduct and that of the whole, who also had made a high sacrifice, in the voluntary offer of their lives for the conduct of their brother soldiers. Are these a people to be treated as malefactors, without regard to their feelings and principles? and might not a discipline, somewhat different from the usual mode, be, with advantage, applied to them?''—Vol. II. p. 413–15. 3d Edit.

''A soldier of this regiment, (The Argyllshire Highlanders,) deserted, and emigrated to America, where he settled. Several years after his desertion, a letter was received from him, with a sum of money, for the purpose of procuring one or two men to supply his place in the regiment, as the only recompense he could make for 'breaking his oath to his God and his allegiance to his King, which preyed on his conscience in such a manner, that he had no rest night nor day.'

''This man had had good principles early instilled into his mind, and the disgrace which he had been originally taught to believe would attach to a breach of faith now operated with full effect. The soldier who deserted from the 42d Regiment at Gibraltar, in 1797, exhibited the same remorse of conscience after he had violated his allegiance. In countries where such principles prevail, and regulate the character of a people, the mass of the population may, on occasions of trial, be reckoned on as sound and trustworthy.''—Vol. II. p. 218. 3d Edit.

''The late James Menzies of Culdares, having engaged in the rebellion of 1715, and been taken at Preston, in Lancashire, was carried to London, where he was tried and condemned, but afterwards reprieved. Grateful for this clemency, he remained at home in 1745, but, retaining a predilection for the old cause, he sent a handsome charger as a present to Prince Charles, when advancing through England. The servant who led and delivered the horse was taken prisoner, and carried to Carlisle, where he was tried and condemned. To extort a discovery of the person who sent the horse, threats of immediate execution in case of refusal, and offers of pardon on his giving information, were held out ineffectually to the faithful messenger. He knew, he said, what the consequence of a disclosure would be to his master, and his own life was nothing in the comparison;

when brought out for execution, he was again pressed to inform on his master. He asked if they were serious in supposing him such a villain. If he did what they desired, and forgot his master and his trust, he could not return to his native country, for Glenlyon would be no home or country for him, as he would be despised and hunted out of the Glen. Accordingly he kept steady to his trust, and was executed. This trusty servant's name was John Macnaughton, from Glenlyon, in Perthshire; he deserves to be mentioned, both on account of his incorruptible fidelity, and of his testimony to the honourable principles of the people, and to their detestation of a breach of trust to a kind and honourable master, however great might be the risk, or however fatal the consequences, to the individual himself.''— Vol. I. pp. 52, 53. 3d Edit.

180 *the seed fell among the brambles and thorns*: see Mark 4:3–20 and Luke 8:5–15.

182 *Corri dhu (black precipice)*: Gaelic *coire dubh*; in Gaelic a *coire* is 'a circular hollow surrounded by hills'.

Dun of the double-crest: Dumbarton Castle stands on a rock which is divided and has two summits.

183 *the children of Kenneth*: the Mackenzies.

Skooroora: a phonetic spelling of the Gaelic mountain name, Sgurr Fhuaran.

190 *Fion*: the hero of Irish legend whom Macpherson (see note to p. 142) made into the Scot Fingal in his poems of Ossian.

197 *MacDhonuil Dhu*: the patronymic of the Camerons, meaning 'descendant of Black Donald'.

add a stone to your cairn: cairns were piles of loose stones and were often raised as a memorial over a grave or a place where someone had died. Passers-by were expected to add a stone, hence the Gaelic saying *cuiridh mi clach 'nad chàrn*, that is 'I will add a stone to your cairn', meaning 'I will honour you when you are dead'.

205 *the civil wars*: the Jacobite rebellion of 1745.

207 *Cloght-dearg*: cf. Gaelic *cleoc* 'cloak', *dearg* 'crimson'; this figure seems to be Scott's own invention.

211 *the Black Abbot of Inchaffray*: Elspat is recalling pre-Reformation times when Inchaffray, eight miles west of Perth, was the site of an important monastery founded in 1200. The Abbot of Inchaffray celebrated mass in front of the Scottish army at Bannockburn, an incident described in Scott's *Lord of the Isles* (VI. xxi; see also Scott's note on this scene). For an abbot of the forcefulness ascribed by Elspat to the Abbot of Inchaffray see an earlier scene in the same poem (II. xxi–xxxii).

218 Epigraph: from Milton's 'Lycidas' (1637), ll. 25–7.

that Otium . . . sea or land: an allusion to the opening lines of a poem by Horace (*Odes*, II. xvi).

219 *Gillie-whitefoot*: the term *gillie-wet-foot* is a literal translation of the Gaelic *gille-cas-fliuch*, the name given to a chieftain's attendant who carried him over streams. It sometimes appeared in Scots in forms such as *gilliewitfitt*, and the middle element was mistaken for *whit* 'white' as Scott does here.

an imp of the devil: the errand boy in a printing-house is called the printer's devil.

rudas queen: this is the spelling in the magnum and is found elsewhere in Scottish literature; however a more common spelling for this word is *quean* which avoids confusion with the word meaning 'female monarch, consort of a king'; the meaning here is 'evil woman'.

220 *when the MacRaas broke out*: in 1778 the 42nd Regiment, made up mostly of Macraes, mutinied in Leith. They camped on Arthur's Seat for several days but were finally persuaded to return to duty.

that woful day beside Leith Pier: in April 1779 a group of Highland recruits refused to embark for America due to a rumour that they would be attached to two Lowland regiments rather than Highland regiments as they had been promised. Troops from Edinburgh Castle were ordered to arrest them and, when the Highlanders resisted, a number of them were killed.

Justice Shallow . . . goodnights: see *Henry IV: Part I*, III. ii. 344–6.

Caledonian ball: a ball where the participants wear Highland dress.

Mrs. Grant of Laggan: Anne Grant (1755–1838) was the widow of the minister of Laggan and wrote several books on the Highlands which are named in the footnote by Scott.

221 *add a stone to the cairn*: cf. note to p. 197.

a tale of Two Drovers: Scott heard the story from George Constable of Wallace-Craigie (1719–1803), an Edinburgh lawyer, as he acknowledged in his magnum introduction to *Chronicles of the Canongate*. He notes that Constable 'had been present, I think, at the trial at Carlisle, and seldom mentioned the venerable judge's charge to the jury without shedding tears'.

An oyster . . . Tilburina: Tilburina is a love-struck maiden in *The Critic* (1779) by Sheridan; the quotation is from Act III.

222 *Doune Fair*: held each year in early November at Doune, near Stirling.

the drove-roads: see A. R. B. Haldane, *The Drove Roads of Scotland*, Edinburgh, 1952.

223 *Donald*: a generic name for a Highlander, due to the commonness of the name in the Highlands.

224 *Glunamie*: a Lowland name for a Highlander. Scott discusses its origin in his note 'Glune-Amie' in *The Fair Maid of Perth*.

John Highlandman: for the use of this name see Burns' song 'A Highland lad my Love was born' in 'Love and Liberty—A Cantata'.

225 *Rob Roy*: Rob Roy MacGregor (1671–1734), a famous outlaw and an important character in Scott's *Rob Roy*.

'*Of such ancestry . . . be proud*': see Boswell, *Life of Johnson, together with Boswell's Journal of a Tour to the Hebrides* . . ., Oxford, 1934–64, v. 25n.

226 *the Carse of Stirling*: a strip of fertile alluvial land lying on both sides of the Forth in the old county of Stirlingshire.

St. Mungo's knot: St Kentigern (*c*.514–*c*.601), otherwise known as St Mungo, founded a monastery in Glasgow which later became the site of the cathedral. According to legend he was guided to Glasgow by two untamed bulls, hence his association with cattle in popular superstition.

Dimayet: a hill near Stirling.

227 *Muhme*: Gaelic *muime* 'nurse, step-mother, god-mother'.

228 *Stirling Brig*: a bridge across the Forth near Stirling and an important point of access to the Highlands.

229 *the Manly Morrisons*: a traditional epithet; see Robert Chambers, *Popular Rhymes of Scotland*, London, 1870, p. 313.

you cannot have . . . grumph: cf. 'But what can be expected of a *Sow* but a *grumph*?' (*Journal*, 10 April 1827). *Grumph* means 'grunt'.

230 *Falkirk*: the scene of a very important fair or 'tryst' for sale of cattle, sheep, and horses, held three times a year.

keep the rounds at Smithfield: to be be successful at a boxing match at Smithfield in London, where there was a major cattle market.

231 *the shibboleth Llhu, which is the Gaelic for a calf*: the Gaelic word for 'calf' is *laogh*; as Dwelly in his introductory essay on 'The Gaelic Language' in his *Illustrated Gaelic-English Dictionary* notes, 'l, before a broad vowel [i.e. *a, o* or *u*] has no sound in English exactly like it'. A shibboleth is a particular word or feature of pronunciation in a language which people who do not speak that language have difficulty in pronouncing; for the origin of the term see Judges 12:4–6.

232 Epigraph: a 'good part' of the poem 'Duke Upon Duke' was ascribed by Joseph Spence to Pope; see his *Anecdotes, Observations, and Characters, of Books and Men*, London, 1820, p. 285. However, we cannot be absolutely certain of the correctness of this attribution. Scott knew the poem from his edition of Swift's *Works* (Edinburgh, 1814) where it is included as forming part of *Miscellanies in Verse by Mr Pope, Dr Arbuthnot, Mr Gay &c Collected by Dr Swift and Mr Pope* (1727); see Scott's Swift, xiii. 333–8. The verses quoted here are wrongly ascribed to Scott in the Oxford Standard Authors edition of his poetry.

234 *The drove can pe gang . . . if she was*: Robin is given pseudo-Highland speech including the use of *she* for *I* (see note to p. 84); the otiose use of the verb *to be* in this way is another common feature of this conventional literary language but is not found in real Highland speech.

Sawney: or *Sandie*, short for *Alexander*, and used in the eighteenth and nineteenth centuries as a nickname for a Scotsman.

235 *Goshen*: figuratively, a place of plenty: see Genesis 45:10.

239 *Christenbury Crag*: a hill in the east of Cumberland.

242 *the fords of Frew*: on the river Forth near Kippen in the former county of Stirlingshire.

Whitson Tryste, Wooler Fair, Carlisle Sands, or Stagshaw Bank: these are fairs; Whitsun Tryste was held at Whitsuntide at Wooler in Northumberland; it is thus the same as Wooler Fair. Stagshaw Bank is near Hexham. Scott in his autobiographical fragment tells a story of his grandfather, who later became a drover, at Whitsun Tryste; see *Scott on Himself*, Edinburgh, 1981, p. 4.

243 *Corby Castle*: four miles from Carlisle; Scott visited it in 1815 (*Letters*, iv. 101).

A hundred curses on the swine-eaters: the Highlanders, great breeders of cattle, did not like eating pork.

245 *the curse of Cromwell . . . as the man says in the play*: according to Carlyle the phrase 'the curse of Cromwell' is an expression used by the 'common Irish people'; see *Cromwell's Letters and Speeches* in Carlyle's *Works*, London, 1897–9, vii. 165. However I can find no earlier example of the phrase than another use by Scott in *The Heart of Mid-Lothian*, ch. 8. 'As the man says in the play' seems to be merely a meaningless catch-phrase here.

246 *betwixt Esk and Eden*: two rivers: the Esk is near Edinburgh and Carlisle stands on the Eden.

248 *the Scots dyke*: an earthwork built along part of the Scottish-English border in the latter half of the sixteenth century; in Scots, *dyke* means 'a boundary wall of turf or stones'.

the Eskdale callants . . . Lustruther: for Fighting Charlie and the Dandies of Lustruther see Scott's notes 'Mump's Ha' and 'Clan Surnames' in *Guy Mannering*.

the Black Watch: see note to p. 107.

249 *the braes of Balquidder*: in the south-west of the former county of Perthshire; *braes* in this context means a mountainous district.

what though my name . . . cart—: these lines are from

a poem in the fourth volume (published in 1732) of Allan Ramsay's *Tea-Table Miscellany* under the title 'Hodge of the Mill and buxome Nell'.

250 *to have his cauld kail het again*: to have his re-heated broth, that is, figuratively, to have another 'serve' of boxing from Harry Wakefield.

256 *Moderamen inculpatae tutelae*: mitigating circumstances of blameless defence, i.e. a plea of self-defence.

the benefit of clergy: a privilege, allowed to the clergy and later to anyone who could read, of claiming exemption from the jurisdiction of a secular court or, later, from the execution of its sentence. Before the privilege was abolished in 1827 many people had, through it, escaped punishment for serious crimes.

258 *Cherokees or Mohawks*: two North American Indian tribes.

Revenge . . . as described by Bacon: see the essay 'Revenge' in *Essays or Counsels Civil and Moral* (1625) by Francis Bacon.

259 *'Vengeance is mine'*: see Romans 12:19.

I give a life for the life I took: see Exodus 21:23.

what can I do more?: Scott's note:—

—ROBERT DONN'S POEMS. I cannot dismiss this story without resting attention for a moment on the light which has been thrown on the character of the Highland Drover since the time of its first appearance, by the account of a drover poet, by name Robert Mackay, or, as he was commonly called, Rob Donn, *i.e.* brown Robert, and certain specimens of his talents, published in the 90th Number of the Quarterly Review. The picture which that paper gives of the habits and feelings of a class of persons with which the general reader would be apt to associate no ideas but those of wild superstition and rude manners, is in the highest degree interesting; and I cannot resist the temptation of quoting two of the

songs of this hitherto unheard of poet of humble life.
They are thus introduced by the reviewer:—

"Upon one occasion, it seems, Rob's attendance
upon his master's cattle business detained him a whole
year from home, and at his return he found that a fair
maiden, to whom his troth had been plighted of yore,
had lost sight of her vows, and was on the eve of being
married to a rival, (a carpenter by trade,) who had pro-
fited by the young Drover's absence. The following
song was composed during a sleepless night, in the
neighbourhood of Creiff, in Perthshire, and the home
sickness which it expresses appears to be almost as much
that of the deer-hunter as of the loving swain.

'Easy is my bed, it is easy,
  But it is not to sleep that I incline;
The wind whistles northwards, northwards,
  And my thoughts move with it.
More pleasant were it to be with thee
  In the little glen of calves,
Than to be counting of droves
  In the enclosures of Creiff.
          Easy is my bed, &c.

'Great is my esteem of the maiden,
  Towards whose dwelling the north wind blows;
She is ever cheerful, sportive, kindly,
  Without folly, without vanity, without pride.
True is her heart—were I under hiding,
  And fifty men in pursuit of my footsteps,
I should find protection, when they surrounded me most
    closely,
  In the secret recess of that shieling.
          Easy is my bed, &c.

'Oh for the day for turning my face homeward,
  That I may see the maiden of beauty:—
Joyful will it be to me to be with thee,—
  Fair girl with the long heavy locks!
Choice of all places for deer-hunting
  Are the brindled rock and the ridge!
How sweet at evening to be dragging the slain deer
  Downwards along the piper's cairn!
          Easy is my bed, &c.

'Great is my esteem for the maiden
  Who parted from me by the west side of the enclosed field;

Late yet again will she linger in that fold,
  Long after the kine are assembled.
It is I myself who have taken no dislike to thee,
  Though far away from thee am I now.
It is for the thought of thee that sleep flies from me;
  Great is the profit to me of thy parting kiss!
          Easy is my bed, &c.

'Dear to me are the boundaries of the forest;
  Far from Creiff is my heart;
My remembrance is of the hillocks of sheep,
  And the heath of many knolls.
Oh for the red-streaked fissures of the rock,
  Where in spring time, the fawns leap;
Oh for the crags towards which the wind is blowing—
  Cheap would be my bed to be there!
          Easy is my bed, &c.

"The following describes Rob's feelings on the first discovery of his damsel's infidelity. The airs of both these pieces are his own, and, the Highland ladies say, very beautiful.

'Heavy to me is the shieling, and the hum that is in it,
Since the ear that was wont to listen is now no more on the watch.
Where is Isabel, the courteous, the conversable, a sister in kindness?
Where is Anne, the slender-browed, the turret-breasted, whose glossy hair pleased me when yet a boy?
Heich! what an hour was my returning!
Pain such as that sunset brought, what availeth me to tell it?

'I traversed the fold, and upward among the trees—
Each place, far and near, wherein I was wont to salute my love.
When I looked down from the crag, and beheld the fair-haired stranger dallying with his bride,
I wished that I had never revisited the glen of my dreams.
Such things came into my heart as that sun was going down,
A pain of which I shall never be rid, what availeth me to tell it?

'Since it hath been heard that the carpenter had persuaded thee,
My sleep is disturbed—busy is foolishness within me at midnight.
The kindness that has been between us,—I cannot shake off that memory in visions;
Thou callest me not to thy side; but love is to me for a messenger.

There is strife within me, and I toss to be at liberty;
And ever the closer it clings, and the delusion is growing to me as a tree.

'Anne yellow-haired daughter of Donald,' surely thou
  knowest not how it is with me—
That it is old love, unrepaid, which has worn down from me
  my strength;
That when far from thee, beyond many mountains, the
  wound in my heart was throbbing,
Stirring, and searching for ever, as when I sat beside thee on
  the turf.
Now, then, hear me this once, if for ever I am to be without thee,
My spirit is broken—give me one kiss ere I leave this land!

'Haughtily and scornfully the maid looked upon me;
Never will it be work for thy fingers to unloose the band from
  my curls;
Thou hast been absent a twelvemonth, and six were seeking
  me diligently;
Was thy superiority so high, that there should be no end of
  abiding for thee?
Ha! ha! ha!—hast thou at last become sick?
Is it love that is to give death to thee? surely the enemy has been in no
  haste.

'But how shall I hate thee, even though towards me thou hast
  become cold?
When my discourse is most angry concerning thy name in
  thine absence,
Of a sudden thine image, with its old dearness, comes visibly
  into my mind;
And a secret voice whispers that love will yet prevail!
And I become surety for it anew, darling,
And it springs up at that hour lofty as a tower.'

"Rude and bald as these things appear in a verbal
translation, and rough as they might possibly appear,
even were the originals intelligible, we confess we are
disposed to think they would of themselves justify Dr
Mackay (their Editor) in placing this herdsman-lover
among the true sons of song."—*Quarterly Review, No.*
XC. July 1831.

260 *Mr. Ackermann*: Rudolph Ackermann (d. 1834)
    introduced annuals into Britain.

   The Keepsake: see Note on the Text.

261 *lady of* . . . *the* . . . *house of Swinton*: Margaret Swinton

(d. 1780) was the sister of Scott's maternal grand-mother, Jean, wife of Dr John Rutherford. The story of her death is related in Lockhart's *Life* (Edinburgh, 1837–8, i. 105). As well as the story of 'My Aunt Margaret's Mirror', she told Scott the story of his drama *Halidon Hill*; see *Letters*, vii. 62.

262 *the story of the Magic Mirror*: 'The tale is a good one and is said actually to have happened to Lady Primrose, my great grand-mother having attend-ed her sister on the occasion' (*Journal*, 13 April 1828). Lady Primrose later became Countess of Stair (see note to p. 302). This story is also related in Robert Chambers' *Traditions of Edinburgh* (London, 1869, pp. 76–82).

I tell the tale as it was told to me: cf. 'I tell the tale as it is told' (Byron, *Don Juan*, XIII. xiii. 1) and 'I say the tale as it was said to me' (*The Lay of the Last Minstrel*, I. xxii).

263 *There are times . . . realities of life*: these lines are pro-bably by Scott: he often composed chapter mottoes and ascribed them to various sources when unable to think of a suitable quotation, as he explained in his original introduction to *Chronicles of the Canongate*.

265 *sold for an old song*: an allusion to a phrase used by Lord Seafield as he signed the Act of Union of Scotland and England: 'there's the end of an auld song'. Scott often alludes to it; see *Waverley*, ch. 65 and his *Journal*, 9 June 1826.

The horrid plough . . . summer shade: from *A Tale*, ll. 309–12, by John Logan (1744–88), a Scottish poet. Scott quoted these lines in his *Journal* (4 April 1826), applying them to his feelings about Ashetiel, his former home.

266 *the stile . . . shout and bound*: this may well be a recollection from Scott's own childhood, since he was lame as a child.

die under Nelson's banner: that is to die in the Napoleonic Wars while serving in the British Navy under Horatio, Lord Nelson (1758–1805).

267 *some fifty-six years*: Scott was born in 1771 and wrote this story in 1827 (see Note on the Text). He thus has made his narrator the same age himself.

270 *his old Mumpsimus to the modern Sumpsimus*: the story is told in Richard Pace's *De Fructu Doctrinae* (1517, p. 80), that an old priest who had fallen into the habit of misreading *Mumpsimus* for *Sumpsimus* in his Latin breviary refused to change to the 'new-fashioned' way when the error was pointed out to him.

They fought . . . hearts unsubdued: I have not traced the origin of these lines.

271 *the Stuart right . . . Succession in his favour*: in 1807 the last legitimate descendant of the Stuart King James II and VII died: many people felt that the right of birth then passed to the ruling Hanoverian kings although there were other descendants of Charles I who, by strict primogeniture, had a stronger claim than the Hanoverians. By the Act of Succession of 1701 (officially called the Act of Settlement) the Protestant George I and his descendants had become kings of Great Britain. The crown passed to them in 1714 after the deaths of William III and Queen Anne without surviving issue.

jure divino: 'by divine right'. Aunt Margaret is declaring that the succession should be determined by the 'will of the nation' (as had been the case with the Glorious Revolution of 1688 when William III and Mary were offered the throne by the Convention Parliament) rather than by reference to divinely ordained rights of kings.

Whimsicals: a section of the Tories in the reign of Queen Anne.

272 *the Gaelic song . . . waken me*: Scott's spelling of the Gaelic words here is, as is his frequent practice, more or less phonetic. It appears to represent a line such as *Cadal, mo chadal, na duisgibh mi*, 'Sleep, my sleep, do not waken me', or, closer in sound but further from his translation, *Cha til mo chadal . . .* 'My sleep will not return . . .'. The words *Tha mi am chadal 's na dùisgibh mi*, 'I am asleep and do not waken me', form the refrain to a song by Silis Nighean Mhic Raonaill (Cicely or Julian M'Donald) who lived in the later seventeenth and earlier eighteenth centuries. See John Mackenzie ed., *Sar-Obain nam Gaelach: The Beauties of Gaelic Poetry and Lives of the Highland Poets*, Edinburgh, 1907, p. 66.

what . . . Wordsworth calls 'moods of my own mind': 'Moods of My Own Mind' is the title of a section of volume II of Wordsworth's *Poems in Two Volumes* (London, 1807).

273 *the translator of Tasso . . . which he sung*: these lines are from the poem known as 'Ode on the Popular Superstitions of the Highlands of Scotland', written 1749–50 by William Collins. Collins is actually referring to Tasso, not, as Scott's words would suggest, to his English translator Edward Fairfax. Collins does, however, refer to Fairfax in the line preceding the two quoted by Scott.

your ears . . . Theodore . . . spectral huntsman: see ll. 90–5 of Dryden's 'Theodore and Honoria' in his *Fables* (1699).

274 *the spells of Hallowe'en . . . learned in childhood*: in a note to stanza xiii of his poem 'Hallowe'en', Burns describes various actions to be carried out in order to see one's future spouse in a mirror 'as if peeping over your shoulder'.

275 *the Sir Charles Easy and the Lovelace of his day*: Sir Charles is a character in *The Careless Husband*

(1705) by Colley Cibber, and Lovelace figures in Samuel Richardson's *Clarissa Harlowe* (1747–8).

'if laws were made for every degree': from *The Beggar's Opera* (1728) by John Gay; see III. xiii. 22.

Sillermills: a small village north Edinburgh, now part of the city.

Lord Advocate: the chief law officer of the crown in Scotland.

276 *the Duke of A—:* probably an allusion to John Campbell, second Duke of Argyle (1678–1743), a major figure in Scotland at the time of this story's setting.

277 *the termagant Falconbridge*: a reference to the character of the Bastard Faulconbridge in Shakespeare's *King John*.

279 *from Leith to Helvoet*: Leith is the port for Edinburgh and Hellevoetsluis is a port in the south of Holland about 17 miles from Rotterdam.

280 *the Gazette*: either the official journal for publishing government notices or, possibly, a newspaper.

284 *Flanders . . . French . . . Allies . . . Marlborough's campaigns*: this refers to the war of the Spanish Succession (1700–13) in which Britain, Holland, Germany, and Austria were allies against France. Much of the most crucial fighting was in Flanders where the British forces were commanded by John Churchill, first Duke of Marlborough (1650–1722).

286 *a seeking of health . . . Egypt*: cf. Isaiah 19:3, 31:1.

290 *philosophical utensils*: *philosophical* is here used in the now obsolete sense of 'scientific'.

291 *Il Cavaliero*: 'the knight'; presumably Damiotti is to be seen as using an Italian phrase; however, the Italian form of the word is actually *cavaliere*; Scott's form here is a variation on the Spanish form and is

found in Shakespeare and other writers of that period.

294 *The music . . . of the harmonica*: Scott's description of the sound suggests he is referring to an instrument invented about 1762 by Benjamin Franklin 'consisting of a row of hemispherical glasses fitted on an axis turned by a treadle and dipping into a trough of water, played by the application of a finger' (*Oxford English Dictionary*). The sound it made was often described as having a very powerful effect on its hearers. If it is this instrument Scott is referring to, it would appear to be an anachronism since the story is set early in the eighteenth century.

295 *The master—to use the Italian phrase*: the Italian word *maestro* is used for someone who has become an expert in some art, and was formerly also used of a doctor. Either sense would be appropriate here.

297 *Geneva gown and band*: a black gown with a collar or neckband extending into two hanging strips of square-ended material; the dress of the Calvinist clergy of Geneva and later extended to other Protestant churches.

301 *Italy . . . Hanover . . . Whig . . . Tory*: the Jacobites (see note to p. 2) were strongly supported by the Pope, and after the early eighteenth century the Stuart claimants to the throne mostly resided in Rome; in 1714 the elector of Hanover became king of Great Britain as George I, thus continuing the displacement of the Stuarts; the Whigs (see note to p. 1) supported the Hanoverian succession, while many Tories (see note to p. 2) were sympathetic to the Jacobite cause. The Jacobite sympathies of Lady Bothwell in this story are reflected in Lady Primrose, the real-life original of her sister, at whose house the Stuart Prince Charles Edward, on a secret visit to London in 1750, met Dr William King, at the time a keen Jacobite; see Scott's

introduction to *Redgauntlet*, where he quotes King's account of this meeting.

301–2 *a Carolus . . . a Willielmus*: i.e. I am as happy to be paid by Jacobites as by supporters of William III; however, there was no coin officially known as a *Willielmus* and the current Jacobite claimant was James 'III and VIII' (1688–1766). His heir was called Charles but was not born until 1720, after the events of this story.

you had best . . . as Scrub says: see *The Beaux' Stratagem* (1707) by George Farquhar, I. i.

Earl of Stair: John Dalrymple, second Earl of Stair (1673–1747), fought under Marlborough in Flanders from 1703 to 1711. He later married Lady Primrose, the real life heroine of this story (see note to p. 262).

the Scotch-Dutch: the Scots Brigade, made up of Scottish soldiers, was in the service of the government of the Netherlands.

304 *Chevalier St. George*: a name for James 'III and VIII'.

the Protestant succession: the succession of William III and Mary, Anne, and George I rather than the Roman Catholic descendants of James II and VII.

to cut the Gordian knot: there was a prophecy that whoever should undo an intricate knot tied by Gordius, a king in Phrygia, would rule Asia. Alexander the Great cut through it with his sword.

the silver greyhound: the badge of the King's Messengers who were charged with arresting prisoners of state.

305 *Galen or Hippocrates*: both were celebrated physicians of ancient Greece.

idol of our resentment . . . her grief: see Shakespeare's *King John*, III. iv. 90ff.

nursing our wrath to keep it warm: from Burns' 'Tam o' Shanter', l. 12.

305 *Lady Bothwell had a seat amongst the lady patronesses*: on the organization of Edinburgh 'assemblies', or dances, see Robert Chambers, *Traditions of Edinburgh*, London, 1869, pp. 288–91.

310 *Miss Anna Seward*: Anna Seward (1747–1809), 'the Swan of Lichfield', was a correspondent of Scott's from 1802 and bequeathed him her poems which he published in 1810 with a memoir. Scott visited her in Lichfield in 1807, which is presumably when she told him this story since on the next page he states that he heard it from her 'more than twenty years since'.

311 *details of the locality*: the manuscript, the original *Keepsake* text, and the magnum all read *localities of the detail* but this makes little sense and is clearly a slip in the manuscript for the reading adopted here.

the American war: the American War of Independence (1775–83).

312 *Lord Cornwallis's army . . . York-town*: in October 1781 the British army at Yorktown in Virginia, commanded by Charles, Earl (later Marquis) Cornwallis (1738–1805), surrendered to the combined American and French forces. This event was decisive in bringing about an end to the American War of Independence.

the wars of York and Lancaster: the Wars of the Roses (1455–85), when the rival families of York and Lancaster laid claim to the English throne.

314 *Christ Church*: the college of that name at Oxford.

316 *the Bush, as the Virginians call it*: the phrase *the bush* is now particularly associated with Australia, but

it is first recorded in English in the United States and is probably directly borrowed from the Dutch *bosch, busch*.

Diogenes: a Greek Cynic philosopher born about 412 BC who adopted an extremely austere lifestyle and, according to tradition, lived in a tub or large earthenware jar.

329 *Vandyke*: Sir Anthony Van Dyck (1599–1641), one of the greatest of portrait painters.

330 *cavalier . . . Roundhead*: the Cavaliers supported the king and the Roundheads supported Parliament in the English civil wars of the seventeenth century.

court at St. Germains: after he left England in 1688 James II was given residence at the château of St Germain near Paris by Louis XIV of France who continued to recognize him as king. James, and later his son, James 'III and VIII', held court there until obliged to leave France by the treaty of Utrecht (1713).

taken arms for William at the Revolution: see note to p. 271.

'against the stomach of his sense': see *The Tempest*, II. i. 113–4.

332 *Mr. F.M. Reynolds*: Frederic Mansell Reynolds (d. 1850), editor of *The Keepsake* 1828–35, 1838–9. Scott's relations with him were not cordial and he referred to him in his *Journal*, as 'that impudent lad Reynolds' (12 April 1829).

sicut pictura poesis: 'as with a painting, so with poetry'; see Horace's *Ars Poetica*, l. 361.

333 *The well-contested . . . Border-land—*: I have not been able to trace the source of this quotation.

Bernard Gilpin: rector of Houghton-le-Spring, County Durham; he lived from 1517 to 1583.

334 *the Armstrongs*: for Scott's account of this clan see

his introduction to 'Johnie Armstrang' in *The Minstrelsy of the Scottish Border*. In the introduction to 'Hobbie Noble' in the same work he describes the remaining vestiges of the castle of Mangertown.

335 *his feats . . . recorded . . . in the Minstrelsy of the Scottish Border*: see the ballads 'Dick o' the Cow' and 'Jock o' the Side' with their introductions and notes in Scott's *Minstrelsy of the Scottish Border*.

Durindana or Fushberta: the names of the swords respectively of Orlando and Rinaldo in *Orlando Furioso* (1516) by Ludovico Ariosto.

the foes of Christendom: the Saracens, against whom Orlando and his cousin Rinaldo fought.

Hobbie Noble: see the ballads 'Jock o' the Side' and 'Hobbie Noble' in Scott's *Minstrelsy of the Scottish Border*.

337 *antediluvian giant who had survived . . . the Flood*: see Genesis, chs 6–8, especially 6:4.

339 *the pennon of St. George . . . and that of St. Andrew*: the flags of England and Scotland, the two saints being their respective patrons.

APPENDIX I

An Earlier Version of 'The Tapestried Chamber'

This version of the story of 'The Tapestried Chamber' seems to be by Scott despite its appearance under the initials A.B.; see Coleman Oscar Parsons, 'Scott's Prior Version of "The Tapestried Chamber" ', *Notes and Queries*, 207 (1962), 417–20. It appeared in *Blackwood's Edinburgh Magazine* in September, 1818 (pp. 705–7).

STORY OF AN APPARITION.

MR EDITOR,

OBSERVING that you have frequently introduced into your Miscellany popular fables collected from various quarters, I send you the following, which I solemnly protest is no invention of mine, but a ghost-story of natural growth, which I heard in conversation. If you can find room for it, it will probably afford more amusement than the Welsh superstitions you published some time ago, which were rather heavy. I am, yours, &c.   A.B.

About the fall of the leaf, in the year 1737, Colonel D. went to visit his friend Mr N. at his country seat in the north of England. As this country seat was the scene of a very singular adventure, it may be proper to mention its antiquity and solemnity, which were fitted to keep in countenance the most sombre events. The following circumstances were well known in the family, and are said to have been related by one of its members to a lady much celebrated in the literary world, but now deceased.

Upon arriving at the house of his friend, Colonel D. found there many guests, who had already got possession of almost all the apartments. The chillness of an

October evening, and the somewhat mournful aspect of nature, at that season, collected them, at an early hour, round the blazing hearth, where they thought no better amusement could be found than the ancient and well approved one of story-telling, for which all mankind seem to have a relish. I do not mean the practice of circulating abominable slanders against one's friends, but the harmless, drowsy, and good-natured recreation of retailing wonderful narratives, in which, if any ill is spoken, it is generally against such as are well able to bear it, namely, the enemy of mankind, and persons who, having committed atrocious crimes, are supposed, after death, to haunt the same spots to which their deeds have attached dismal recollections.

While these tales went round, the evening darkened apace, and the windows ceased any longer to contrast the small glimmerings of external twilight with the bright blaze of the hearth. The rustling of withered leaves, casually stirred by the wind, is always a melancholy sound, and, on this occasion, lent its aid to the superstitious impressions which were gaining force by each successive recital of prodigies. One member of the family began to relate a certain tradition, but he was suddenly stopped by their host, who exhibited signs of displeasure, and whispered something to him, at the same time turning his eyes upon Colonel D. The story was accordingly broken off, and the company went to supper with their hair standing on end; but so transitory are human impressions, that in a few minutes they had all recovered their gayety, except the Colonel, who was unable to comprehend why any tradition should be concealed from him in particular.

When they separated to go to sleep, he was led by Mr N. (as the reader will probably anticipate), to a chamber at a great distance from the other bed-rooms, and which bore evident marks of having been newly opened up, after remaining long unoccupied.

In order to dissipate the confined air of the place, a large wooden fire had been lighted, and the gloomy bed-curtains were tucked stiffly up in festoons. I have not heard whether there was tapestry in the room or not; but one thing is certain, that the room looked as dreary as any tapestry could have made it, even if it had been worked on purpose by Mrs Ann Radcliffe herself. Romance writers generally decorate their imaginary walls with all the wisdom of Solomon; but, as I am unable to vouch for the truth of every particular mentioned in this story, I mean to relate the circumstances faithfully as they were told me, without calling in so wise a man to lend his countenance to them.

Mr N. made apologies to Colonel D. for putting him into an apartment which was somewhat uncomfortable, and which was now opened only because all the rest were already filled. With these excuses, and other suitable compliments, he bade his guest good night, and went away with a good deal of seriousness in his countenance, leaving the door a-jar behind him.

Colonel D——, observing that the apartment was large and cold, and that but a small part of the floor was covered with carpet, endeavoured to shut the door, but found he could only close it half way. Some obstacle in the hinges, or the weight of the door pressing upon the floor, opposed his efforts. Nevertheless, being seized with some absurd fancies, he took the candle, and looked out. When he saw nothing, except the long passage and the vacant apartments beyond, he went to bed, leaving the remains of the fire still flickering upon the broad hearth, and gleaming now and then upon the door as it stood half open.

After the Colonel had lain for a long while, ruminating half asleep, and when the ashes were now nearly extinguished, he saw the figure of a woman glide in. No noise accompanied her steps. She advanced to the fire-place, and stood between him and the light, with her back towards him, so that he could not see her features. Upon observing her dress, he found that it exactly corresponded in appearance with the ancient silk robes represented in the pictures of English ladies of rank, painted three centuries ago. This circumstance filled him with a degree of terror which he had never experienced before. The stately garniture of times long past had a frightful meaning, when appearing, as it now did, not upon a canvass, but upon a moving shape, at midnight. Still endeavouring to shake off those impressions which benumbed him, he raised himself upon his arm, and faintly asked "who was there?" The phantom turned round—approached the bed—and fixed her eyes upon him; so that he now beheld a countenance where some of the worst passions of the living were blended with the cadaverous appearance of the dead. In the midst of traits which indicated noble birth and station, was seen a look of cruelty and perfidy, accompanied with a certain smile which betrayed even baser feelings. The approach of such a face near his own, was more than Colonel D—— could support; and when he rose next morning from a feverish and troubled sleep, he could not recollect how or when the accursed spectre had departed. When summoned to breakfast, he was asked how he had spent the night, and he endeavoured to conceal his agitation by a general answer, but took the first opportunity to inform his friend Mr N——, that, having recollected a certain piece of business which waited him at London, he found it impossible to protract his visit a single night. Mr N—— seemed surprised, and anxiously sought to discover whether any thing occurred to render him displeased with his reception; but finding that his guest was impenetrable, and that his remonstrances against his departure were in vain, he insisted upon shewing Colonel D—— the beauties of his country residence, after which he would reluctantly bid him farewell. In walking round the mansion, Colonel D—— was shewn the outside of the tower where he had slept, and vowed, mentally, never to enter it again. He was next led to a gallery of pictures, where Mr N—— took much delight in displaying a complete series of family portraits, reaching back to a very remote era. Among the oldest, there was one of a lady. Colonel D—— had no sooner got a glimpse of it, than he cried out, "May I never leave this spot, if that is not she." Mr N——asked whom he meant? "The detestable phantom that stared me out of my senses last night;" and he related every particular that had occurred.

Mr N——, overwhelmed with astonishment, confessed that, to the room where his guest had slept, there was attached a certain tradition, pointing it out as having been, at a remote period, the scene of murder and incest. It had long obtained the repute of being haunted by the spirit of the lady, whose picture was before him; but there were some circumstances in her history so atrocious, that her name was seldom mentioned in his family, and his ancestors had always endeavoured as much as possible to draw a veil over her memory.

APPENDIX II

'A Highland Anecdote'

Like 'The Death of the Laird's Jock' this piece was sent to the editor of *The Keepsake* to provide the subject for an illustration; see Note on the Text. It appeared in *The Keepsake* for 1832 (pp. 283–6).

A HIGHLAND ANECDOTE.

BY SIR WALTER SCOTT, BART.

TO THE EDITOR OF THE KEEPSAKE.

THE same course of reflection which led me to transmit to you the account of the death of an ancient borderer,* induces me to add the particulars of a singular incident, affording a point which seems highly qualified to be illustrated by the pencil. It was suggested by the spirited engraving of the Gored Huntsman, which adorned the first number of your work, and perhaps bears too close a resemblance to the character of that print to admit of your choosing it as a subject for another. Of this you are the only competent judge.

The story is an old but not an ancient one: the actor and sufferer was not a very aged man, when I heard the anecdote in my early youth. Duncan, for so I shall call him, had been engaged in the affair of 1746, with others of his clan; and was supposed by many to have been an accomplice, if not the principal actor in a certain tragic affair, which made much noise a good many years after the rebellion. I am content with indicating this, in order to give some idea of the man's character, which was bold, fierce, and enterprising. Traces of this natural disposition still remained on

---

* "The Death of the Laird's Jock," published in the "Keepsake" for 1829.—ED

Duncan's very good features, and in his keen grey eye. But the limbs, like those of the aged borderer in my former tale, had become unable to serve the purposes and obey the dictates of his inclination. On the one side of his body he retained the proportions and firmness of an active mountaineer; on the other, he was a disabled cripple, scarce able to limp along the streets. The cause which reduced him to this state of infirmity was singular.

Twenty years or more before I knew Duncan, he assisted his brothers in farming a large grazing* in the Highlands, comprehending an extensive range of mountain and forest land, morass, lake, and precipice. It chanced that a sheep or goat was missed from the flock, and Duncan, not satisfied with despatching his shepherds in one direction, went himself in quest of the fugitive in another.

In the course of his researches, he was induced to ascend a small and narrow path, leading to the top of a high precipice. Dangerous as it was at first, the road became doubly so as he advanced. It was not much more than two feet broad, so rugged and difficult, and, at the same time, so terrible, that it would have been impracticable to any but the light step and steady brain of a Highlander. The precipice on the right, rose like a wall, and on the left, sunk to a depth which it was giddy to look down upon, but Duncan passed cheerfully on, now whistling the Gathering of his Clan, now taking heed to his footsteps, when the difficulties of the path peculiarly required caution.

In this manner, he had more than half ascended the precipice, when in midway, and it might almost be said, in middle air, he encountered a buck of the red-deer species coming down the cliff by the same path in an opposite direction. If Duncan had had a gun no rencontre could have been more agreeable, but as he had not this advantage over the denizen of the wilder-

---

* A pastoral farm.

ness, the meeting was in the highest degree unwelcome. Neither party had the power of retreating, for the stag had not room to turn himself in the narrow path, and if Duncan had turned his back to go down, he knew enough of the creature's habits to be certain that he would rush upon him while engaged in the difficulties of the retreat. They stood therefore perfectly still, and looked at each other in mutual embarrassment for some space.

At length the deer, which was of the largest size, began to lower his formidable antlers, as they do when they are brought to bay, and are preparing to rush upon hound and huntsman. Duncan saw the danger of a conflict in which he must probably come by the worst, and as a last resource, stretched himself on the little ledge of rock, which he occupied, and thus awaited the resolution which the deer should take, not making the least motion for fear of alarming the wild and suspicious animal. They remained in this posture for three or four hours, in the midst of a rock which would have suited the pencil of Salvator, and which afforded barely room enough for the man and the stag, opposed to each other in this extraordinary manner.

At length the buck seemed to take the resolution of passing over the obstacle which lay in his path, and with this purpose approached towards Duncan very slowly, and with excessive caution. When he came close to the Highlander he stooped his head down as if to examine him more closely, when the devil, or the untameable love of sport, peculiar to his country, began to overcome Duncan's fears. Seeing the animal proceed so gently, he totally forgot not only the dangers of his position, but the implicit compact which certainly might have been inferred from the circumstances of the situation. With one hand Duncan seized the deer's horn, whilst with the other he drew his dirk. But in the same instant the buck bounded

over the precipice, carrying the Highlander along
with him. They went thus down upwards of a hundred feet, and were found the next morning on the
spot where they fell. Fortune, who does not always
regard retributive justice in her dispensations,
ordered that the deer should fall undermost and be
killed on the spot, while Duncan escaped with life, but
with the fracture of a leg, an arm, and three ribs. In
this state he was found lying on the carcass of the deer,
and the injuries which he had received rendered him
for the remainder of his life the cripple I have described. I never could approve of Duncan's conduct
towards the deer in a moral point of view (although,
as the man in the play said, he was my friend), but the
temptation of a hart of grease, offering, as it were, his
throat to the knife, would have subdued the virtue of
almost any deer-stalker. Whether the anecdote is
worth recording, or deserving of illustration, remains
for your consideration. I have given you the story exactly as I recollect it.

GLOSSARY

THIS glossary includes Scots words, legal terms, unusual English words or meanings of words, and foreign words and phrases. Only meanings used in these stories are included, and words explained in context are omitted. Pronunciations only found in the English or Scots speech of Gaelic-speaking Highlanders (see note to p. 84) are marked '(H.)'. For further information readers should consult *The Scottish National Dictionary*, *The Concise Scots Dictionary* and *The Oxford English Dictionary*.

a', all
aboon, above
ae, one
aff, off
ain, own
ainsell, your, you (emphatic)
alane, alone
amang, among
Amatus and Amata, male and female beloved
ance, once
ane, one, a
aneath, beneath
anent, concerning
anes and aye, forever from that moment
aneugh, enough
Argyleshires, a breed of cattle
arles, token payment on engagement of services
a'thegether, altogether
auld, old
auld-world, old-fashioned
awfu', awful, terrible
awmous, alms
awn, own
ay, yes
aye, always
axing, asking

back-ganging, behind hand with rent
bairns, children
baith, both
banes, bones
banged, dashed
bannocks, round flat cakes made with oat-, barley- or pease-meal
bar-keeper, keeper of the barriers in court
barns-breaking, mischievous action
barony, estate of a feudal baron, held direct from the crown
bartizan, battlemented parapet
basket-hilt, a basket-like hilt to protect a swordsman's hand
bastile, fortress prison
bating, except
bauld, bold
beau cousin, good cousin
beau garçon, handsome fellow, man of fashion
Beelzebub, the Devil
behind the hand, overdue
belang, belong

betimes, early

bickering, with quick-moving flames

bien, well-off

biggit, built

bink, dresser, plate-rack

birling, long-oared boat

birling, pouring out

bit, bit of a, small

bit, small piece of ground

Black Tree of the Law, the, the gallows

blaud, bit, piece

blear a man's eye, hoodwink, deceive

blink, short time

blude, blood

board-head, head of the table

bodach, spectre, bugbear

bodies, persons, people

bodle, coin of two pence Scots, one-sixth of an English penny

bogle, ghost

bogle-wark, ghost-work

bohea, fine quality tea

bonbonnière, sweet-box

bond, mortgage

bondtenant, a tenant required to perform feudal services ('bondage')

bonnet, soft, flat cap without a brim

borrel, unlearned

bothy, rough hut used for temporary accommodation

box, cover with boards

brae, hillside

braid, broad

brash, gust, short storm (used figuratively)

braw, fine, splendid

brocket, cow or bull with white streak down its face

broil, turmoil

buckler, shield

buff-coat, stout coat of buff leather

busked, fastened, arranged

bytime, at a, occasionally

ca', call

caa'd, called

call, whistle

caller, fresh

cam, came

cambric, fine white linen

cankered, ill-natured

canna, cannot

canny, lucky

cantrips, spells

carles, fellows

carlin, old woman (a term of disparagement)

carmen, cart-drivers

carried, carried away, elated

carritch, catechism

castor, beaver hat

cateran, Highland marauder

cauld, cold

chaffer, bargain, haggle

chamber of dais, best room

change-house, small inn

chanter, the pipe part of a bagpipe, with finger holes

chap, customer, buyer

chape, metal mounting on a scabbard

chasse café, brandy or liqueur taken after coffee

chaude mêlée: sharp conflict

chère exquise, exquisite fare

chiel, chield, fellow

circumduce the term, declare the time for producing evidence to have elapsed

claymore, a large sword

clear, certain, confident

clock-house, part of the house with a public clock set in it

clothyard shafts, long-bow arrows

communing, meeting for discussion

condescendence, specification

conditions, behaviour

conducteur, guide

conformable, agreeable

cood, good (H.)

coodman, goodman, i.e. husband (H.)

coronach, lament for the dead

Cot, God (H.)

cottar body, tenant of a cottage

couldna, could not

coverit, covered

cowped, tumbled

cracks, stories

crawing, crowing

craze, graze (H.)

creagh, cattle raid

creat, great (H.)

croft-rig, piece of land on a small-holding

cropped, with clipped ears

cue, a long roll or plait of hair worn hanging down at the back of a wig

curch, kerchief

daddles, fists

dang, knock

danger, power to harm

daured, dared

dear years, years of dearth

deevil, devil

deil, devil

deil speed the liars, a dispute

delate, denounce, accuse

didna, did not

dinna, do not

dirdum, blame

dirk, short dagger

dirking, stabbing

doch-an-dorroch, parting drink

doddy, hornless cow or bull

doer, agent

doesna, does not

dollars, five-shilling pieces

door-cheek, doorway

douce, quiet, sensible

doun, down

dour, hard, stern, unyielding, stubborn

drap, drop of

Dunlap cheese, Dunlop, a kind of cheese

Dunniè-wassel, Highland gentleman

durst na, dared not

duties, money paid to a feudal superior

dyvour, bankrupt, rogue

een, eyes

e'en, just, simply

empiric, quack

en bagatelle, as a trifle

Enemy, Auld; Man's, the Devil

enow, enough

Epicurishnesse, voluptuousness, sensuality

evened him, made him out

evidents, legal documents establishing a claim

ex capite lecti, from the head of the deathbed

factor, manager of property

Faculty, the, the medical profession

falchions, swords

fancies, musical improvisations

Fancy, the, boxing

fand, found

fasherie, troublesome behaviour

fashing, bothering

faulding, folding

fause, false

faut, fault

feared, afraid

fee, a servant's wages

feeders, trainers

fey, doomed, especially when this is shown by unusually elated behaviour

fleech, flatter

flees, flies

flit, move house

flitting, shifting

foretauld, foretold

forfeited, subjected to forfeiture of one's estates

forthink, regret

fou, full

frae, from

frampal, mettlesome

freats, superstitions, omens

freend, friend

Frith, firth, arm of the sea

fule, foolish

gae, gave

gae, go; *gaed*, went; *gaen*, *gane*, gone

Gael, Gaelic-speaking Highlander

Galashiels grey, a coarse woollen cloth made at Galashiels

gang, go

ganging back in the world, going down in the world

gar, cause to; *garr'd*, caused to

gash, pale, dismal

gate, way

gauger, exciseman

gaun, going

gear, possessions

gentlemans, gentleman (H.)

ghaist, ghost

gie, give; *gied*, gave (also *gae*); *gien*, given

gillie, lad, young man

gin, if

girdle cakes, cakes baked on a girdle (an iron plate)

girned, grimaced

girth, asylum

goodman, tenant

goodnights, goodnight songs

goodwife, female head of a house, used as polite form of address

graned, groaned

grat, wept

gravel, a urinary disease, pain in passing urine

gree'd, agreed

grit, great; *grit oath*, solemn oath

grue, creep

grund, estate

grund-officer, manager of an estate

gude, good

gude-e'en, good evening

gudeman, landlord

gudesire, grandfather

gudewife, landlady

gyrecarlin, ogress

gyves, shackles

ha', have

ha' door, main door

hae, have

ha'en, having

haill, whole

halberds, brought to the, flogged

halding, holding

hale, whole

hame, home

happed, hopped

hauld, house and, house and home

heartsome, hearty, merry

hersell, herself

hesp, length of yarn

himsell, himself

hirdy-girdie, topsy-turvy

hoddled, waddled

hogged, with mane cut short

hooly and fairly, slowly and gently, cautiously

hornworks, outworks in fortification

hotels, town mansions

Hout, exclamation expressing remonstrance

howlets, owls

humdudgeons, sulks

humorsome, humorous

Ilk, of that, of the same; e.g. *Redgauntlet of that Ilk* means 'Redgauntlet of Redgauntlet'

ilka, each

ill, hard

ill-deedie, mischievous, unruly

ill-faured, ill-favoured, ugly

in pari casu, in equal circumstances

infare, coming into a new situation

Inquisitio post mortem, post-mortem examination

intercommuned, prohibited from communication with others, outlawed

in terrorem, as a fright

ipsa corpora, the very pieces

ither, other

jackanape(s), monkey

jades, horses

John Barleycorn, malt liquor

jointure-house, a house set aside to be used by a widow after her husband's death

kail-pots, pots for making broth in

kain, rent paid in kind, especially poultry

keepit, kept

ken, know; *kenned*, knew

kennel, street-gutter

kenning, sight, view

kirk, church

kirkyard, churchyard
kiven, given (H.)
kyloes, Highland cattle

labels, mouldings over doors
laird, landed proprietor (see note to p. 1)
lairdship, the estate of a laird
lang, long
lang day, take a, give a long period of credit
langsyne, auld, long ago
lap, leapt
latchets, shoelaces
lawing, tavern bill
leal, honest
leasing-making, lie, seditious slander
leesome lane, his, completely alone
leg, make a, bow, bending one leg
lifted, collected
like, likely
livery-men, servants
lofted, with a second storey
looten, let
Lords of Council and Session, the judges of the Court of Session, the highest Scottish court
loup, leap
Luckie, a familiar form of address to an elderly and lowerclass woman
lum, chimney

ma belle cousine, my beautiful cousin
mails, rent
main, cockfight

mains, the home farm of an estate
mair, more
maist, almost
maister, master
mak, make
malice prepense, premeditated evil
malison, curse
maun, must
mayhap, perhaps
mear, mare
Mechlin lace, lace produced at Mechelen in Belgium
megrim, migraine
memento mori, reminder of death
menstruum, solvent
menus plaisirs, little pleasures
merk, mark, i.e. 13s 4d Scots; a pound Scots equalled one twelfth of a pound sterling
messengers, men who executed summonses for debt
messuage, site for houses
mettle, mettlesome
mezzo-termini, half measures
mill, fist-fight
mind, remember
miscaa'd, slandered
misguider, waster, spendthrift
mither, mother
mizzles, measles
mon beau cousin, my good cousin
monotrochs, one-wheeled vehicles, wheelbarrows
mony, many

morbus sonticus, serious disease affording a valid excuse for absence

morn, the, tomorrow

morning, morning drink of liquor

morn's morning, the, the day after tomorrow

moulds, grave

mountain dew, whisky

muckle, much

muils, slippers

murrey-coloured, purple-red

mutchkin, one quarter of a Scots pint, equal to three quarters of an English pint

mysell, myself

nae, no

naebody, nobody

nailer, tip him the, give him the finishing blow

nane, none, not one

needcessity, necessity

neer-do-weel, good-for-nothing

neist, next

no, not

noblesse, nobility

o', of

Och, exclamation of sorrow, exasperation etc.

Odd's mercy, God's mercy

Ohellany, exclamation of sorrow

Ohonari, exclamation of sorrow

ony, any

ordinar, by, unusual

or molu, an alloy with the colour of gold

orra, odd, occasional

ostler-wife, woman inn-keeper

o't, of it

over-scutched, worn out

ower, over, too

owsen, oxen

Pace, Easter

pactions, bargains

panel, the accused

par voie du fait, by an act of violence

park, field

parochine, parish

parsonage, the part of the teinds due to the parson

passenger, passer-by

pe, by (H.)

peace officer, constable

pendicle, outlying part of estate

pen-fold, an enclosure for penning animals

pibroch, bagpipe music

pickthank, toady

pit, put

plaid, length of grey or tartan woollen cloth worn as an outer garment

pleugh, plough

pochays, postchaises

pock, bag

polish, police

polypus, reproducing by budding like the hydra, more commonly spelt *polypous*

porte cochère, gate for carriages

pratty, pretty

preceese, precise

Presbytery, a church court, above the kirk-session and below the synod

pretty, fine, gallant

prix juste, fair price

professor, someone professing unusual sanctity

prôné, extolled, cracked up

propale, make a fuss

proper, depicted in its natural colours

Prutt trutt, exclamation of scorn

puir, poor

pund, punds, pounds

purpy, water, the plant brooklime

pursuer, plaintiff

quaigh, shallow drinking bowl

quean, girl, young woman

quha, who

quhilk, which

quhom, whom

quotha, said he; used contemptuously

raff, worthless fellow

raid, rode

rambling, dissipated

ranting, uproarious

ratten, rat

rattling, lively

receipts, formulae for medicines

reduction, annulment

reiving, thieving

rencontre, encounter, contest

rental, rent-roll

resetting, giving shelter to (a proscribed person)

revêche, crabbed

riding days, times of Border raiding between Scotland and England

riding-wand, a riding switch

rigging-tree, the ridge-beam of a roof

rin, run

riped, searched

round, circular tower or turret

rudas, hag-like, coarse

rug, a good share, a 'haul'

runts, small Highland cattle

sa, so

sack-doudling, bagpipe-playing

sacque, a kind of loose gown

sae, so

saftest, softest

sain, bless

sair, hard, bad

sang, song

Sassenach, the, the English and the Lowland Scots

saul, soul

saunt, saint

sconces, candlesticks fixed to the wall

scowp wi', Deil, the Devil take

scratch, bring to the, lead someone to beginning a boxing match

sculduddry, obscenity; used adjectivally, obscene, obscenity

scutcheon, coat of arms on a shield

selt, sold

sept, a sub-division of a clan

serve him out, punish him

shairman, chairman, someone who carried a sedan-chair (H.)

shentleman(s), gentleman (H.)

sheriff-officers, officials who carry out the warrants of a sheriff, including executing summonses for debt

shieling, hut

shoon, shoes

shudge, judge (H.)

sic, such

sicklike, *siclike*, such, such things

siller, money

sindry, sundry

skelloch, screech

skirling, creaking

sleekit, smooth, unctuous

sneeshing, snuff

snuff-mulls, snuff-boxes

sough, breath

soumons, summons

Southrons, the, the English

spaewife, female fortune-teller

speerings, information

spellit, spelt

spontoon, sort of half-pike

sprack, lively

spule-blade, shoulder-blade

spunk, spark, life

stamoch, stomach

stend, rear on its hind legs

stirk, young bullock

stocking, livestock and implements on a farm

stots, young castrated oxes

strath, valley

suddenty, of a, all of a sudden

summat, something

supple, cudgel, stick

surtout, man's overcoat

sweepit, swept

tabatière, snuff-box

ta'en, taken

ta'en on, enlisted

tak, take

taking-on, making a great fuss

talis qualis, of some kind or other, not necessarily such as is legally required

tangs, tongs

tartans, full Highland dress

tass, goblet, cup

tauld, told

teedling, humming

teinds, tithes

tenement, house

thae, those

thegither, together

themsells, themselves

threap, assert

ticketed, carrying a licence (a 'ticket')

tippenny, twopenny ale

tod, fox

toilet, table on which items for dressing oneself are displayed; the act of dressing

toom, empty

topsmen, head drovers

toustie, testy

trances, passages

troth, indeed
tryste, market, fair
turnpike stairs, a spiral staircase
turnpikes, toll-roads
turn-up, fist-fight
Tush, exclamation of impatience
twa, two
twopenny, twopenny ale
tyned, wasted

unco, remarkable
upset price, publicly announced minimum acceptable price at an auction
usquebaugh, whisky

valet-de-place, courier
valziant, valiant
vermint, vermin
vicarage, teinds other than grain, originally due to the vicar
vins extraordinaires, unusual and rare wines
vis major, a stronger force

wa' stane, stone for walls
wad, would
waes me, woe is me, alas
waiter, gate watchman
wake, keep vigil over a corpse
walth o', plenty of
walthier, wealthier
wame, belly; *the worst word in his wame*, the worst words he could find
wanchancie, -y, unluckly
wared, spent, wasted
wark, work

warld, world
warlock, male witch
warst, worst
wasna, was not
waur, worse
wee, a, a little bit
weans, children
weel-freended, well provided with friends
weel, well
weel-a-day, alas
weepers, a sign of mourning, a strip of white material stitched to the cuff of a man's sleeve
werena, were not
westlandman, man from west of Scotland
wha, who
wheen, few
whilk, which
white feather, show, show cowardice
wi', with
winna, will not
winterers, cattle kept and fed on a particular place through the winter
wot, I, indeed
wraith, ghost
wrang, wrong
wunna, will not
wuss, wish

yauds, (worn out) horses
yelloch, yell, shriek
yetts, gates
yon, that . . . over there
yoursell, yourself
yowling, howling, wailing

Zounds, God's wounds, an oath

THE WORLD'S CLASSICS

A Select List

Robinson Crusoe
Edited by J. Donald Crowley

Roxana
Edited by Jane Jack

SIR WALTER SCOTT: The Heart of Midlothian
Edited by Claire Lamont

Redgauntlet
Edited by Kathryn Sutherland

Waverley
Edited by Claire Lamont

MARY SHELLEY: Frankenstein
Edited by M. K. Joseph

PERCY BYSSHE SHELLEY: Zastrozzi & St. Irvyne
Edited by Stephen Behrendt

SIDNEY SMITH: Selected Letters
Edited by Nowell C. Smith
With an introduction by Auberon Waugh

LAURENCE STERNE: A Sentimental Journey
Edited by Ian Jack

Tristram Shandy
Edited by Ian Campbell Ross